Beau

The Walkers of Coyote Ridge, 5

Dead Heat Ranch
Boots Optional
Betting on Grace
Overnight Love

Devil's Bend
Chasing Dreams
Vanishing Dreams

Misplaced Halos
Protected in Darkness
Salvation in Darkness
Bound in Darkness

Office Intrigue
Office Intrigue
Intrigued Out of the Office
Their Rebellious Submissive
Their Famous Dominant
Their Ruthless Sadist
Their Naughty Student
Their Fairy Princess

Pier 70
Reckless
Fearless
Speechless
Harmless
Clueless

Sniper 1 Security
Wait for Morning
Never Say Never
Tomorrow's Too Late

Southern Boy Mafia/Devil's Playground
Beautifully Brutal
Without Regret
Beautifully Loyal
Without Restraint

Beau

The Walkers of Coyote Ridge, 5

NICOLE EDWARDS

Published by Nicole Edwards Limited
PO Box 1086, Pflugerville, Texas 78691

Beau
The Walkers of Coyote Ridge, 5
Nicole Edwards

This is a work of fiction. Names, characters, businesses, places, events and incidents either are the products of the author's imagination or used in a fictitious manner. Any resemblance to actual persons, living or dead, business establishments, events, or locals is entirely coincidental.

COVER DETAILS:
Image: © Wander Aguiar | WanderBookClub.com
Model: Randy & Eisman
Image: © Vitaly Korovin (picture frame - 14901223) | 123rf.com
Image: © picsfive (background - 14359053) | 123rf.com
Design: © Nicole Edwards Limited

INTERIOR DETAILS:
Formatting: Nicole Edwards Limited
Editing: Blue Otter Editing | BlueOtterEditing.com

ISBN:
Ebook 9781644180006 | Paperback 9781644180013

SUBJECTS:
BISAC: FICTION / Romance / Gay
BISAC: FICTION / Romance / General

Dedication

To the doctors and nurses at St. David's Hospital in Round Rock and Austin, who took care of my little one from the moment he came into this world until the day I got to bring him home from the NICU.

Although that was back in 2003, I still remember it like it was yesterday. He weighed eight pounds, four ounces and he was five weeks premature, unable to breathe on his own. I didn't get to hold him for the first three days of his life, but you were there, taking care of him, ensuring he was growing stronger. I am forever grateful for the love, compassion, and kindness you showed my baby and all the babies in your care. Not to mention your strength and your patience.

Dear reader,

Before you start reading, it's important to know BEAU is the sequel to ETHAN (Alluring Indulgence, 5). If you have not read ETHAN, I suggest you do, so that you understand the hardships they've suffered and all that they've overcome to get to where they are now.

When I first started writing Ethan's books back in 2013, I knew they were going to have an amazing, if not heartbreaking, story to tell. Little did I know the range of emotions that book would span and the sort of response it would receive.

Because I've thought about them every day since I finished writing their book, I knew their story wasn't over yet. Beau's book picks up in current day. You get a firsthand glimpse at how the Walker family has grown over the years, as well as walk alongside them for a year and a half as they undergo one of the hardest periods of their lives.

This book tore at my heartstrings, but in a completely different way than ETHAN did. I love every minute I get to spend with the Walker family and I hope you do, too.

Love,
Nicole

Chapter One

"SO, I WAS THINKIN'…"

Ah, hell.

Perched on the arm of the couch, Ethan Walker glanced over at the stairs willing his husband to stop while he was ahead. Ethan knew what was coming before Beau even finished that statement and now was not the time for—

"Maybe we could skip dinner," Beau continued, the deep cadence of his voice echoing off the walls as he made his way down the stairs. "And I could just lay you out on the kitchen table and feast on you tonight."

Every inch of skin from Ethan's chest to the tips of his ears flamed hot.

Well, technically, his entire body turned into a giant inferno before Beau rounded the landing and started down the second set of steps because, as was the way his life went, Ethan wasn't the only one to have heard his husband's sexy proposition.

Not by a long shot.

While Ethan's life was a twelve on a scale of one to ten these days, it did seem that karma or fate or whatever the hell you wanted to call it was hell-bent on ensuring he suffered as much embarrassment as physically possible. As though life couldn't be copacetic without a routine dose of mortification.

Today's dose was a little more humiliating than others.

Ethan swallowed hard and stared at Beau, silently wishing the floor would open up and suck him down. The man Ethan loved more than life was sans shirt, shoes, and socks, wearing only a pair of well-worn blue jeans and a sexy smile.

It could've been worse. Maybe. At least Beau was wearing *something*.

The chuckle that sounded from Ethan's sister-in-law said their guests were still there *and* they'd gotten more than an earful.

"Oh, shit." Beau's dark brown eyes widened as he came to a stop on the last step, his shocked gaze bouncing from one face to another.

"Hey, babe," Ethan said tersely, trying to shrug off the embarrassment of having his husband proposition him while their company witnessed it firsthand. "Guess who's here?" As though Beau couldn't see with his own eyes, Ethan announced, "Travis, Kylie, Gage, and V."

"And Zane," Ethan's youngest brother declared as he stepped out from the hallway. "I heard it, too."

Fucking *yeah*.

Beau didn't move, his gaze still darting from one person to the next. "Good to see you guys."

Good wasn't quite the word Ethan was thinking.

Figuring what the hell, Ethan risked a glance at their guests. Just as he thought, Travis was smirking, Kylie's cheeks had turned a rosy pink, Gage was smiling, V was pretending she wasn't there, and Zane was grinning like a loon.

The fucker.

"We were gonna suggest y'all join us at the diner," Gage said after clearing his throat, his grin far too wide.

Zane—ever helpful—added, "But it sounds to me like you've already got plans. You know, with the table and all."

Ethan coughed to cover a strained laugh. He wasn't sure why he was laughing. Probably because he was seconds away from Forrest Gump-ing it out of the house. Once he made it past the porch, he'd be home free. Maybe if he ran long enough, one day they'd all forget this ever happened.

He peered up at Travis, then shot a look in Zane's direction.

Nope. He couldn't get that lucky. Ethan knew his brothers would never forget—ever, ever, ever—so he might as well save the time and energy.

"Lorrie and Curtis offered to watch the babies tonight," Kylie explained. "So we thought we'd get outta the house for a bit. We stopped by to see if y'all wanted to join us."

"Clearly, you two were thinkin' about stayin' in," Travis offered, his deep voice ringing with mirth.

Ethan locked his eyes on Beau, refusing to look at his oldest brother again. He did not want to see any more amusement on the man's face.

"Well, I think that's our cue to go," V said sweetly, grabbing Zane's hand. "Come on, babe."

Zane glanced at Ethan and smirked.

Fuck.

"Oh, but Ethan," Gage stated, grinning as he turned toward the door, "you might wanna reinforce that table before … you know."

Ethan discreetly flipped his brother-in-law off by rubbing the bridge of his nose with his middle finger.

Gage laughed.

"Come on, y'all," Travis said, pushing off the wall and taking his wife's hand. "Maybe we'll see if Sawyer and Kennedy wanna grab a bite."

"We'll go," Beau added, his tone reluctant. He clearly didn't want to go.

"Oh, no," Gage said dramatically. "I suggest you stay here and do exactly what you were plannin'."

Zane's head appeared in the doorway. "*Far* more interesting than a burger and fries."

Ethan's gaze shot to his husband's, noticing the cocky grin that formed on Beau's mouth.

"Don't have to tell me twice."

Ethan blushed.

Again.

His husband liked to do that to him. In fact, Ethan wouldn't put it past Beau to have known that Travis and Zane, as well as their significant others, were here before he made that raunchy request.

"Talk to ya later," Travis added on his way out the door. "And reinforce that table, E. Gage is right. Safety's key."

Ethan's brother offered a backhanded wave over his head as he shifted his other hand behind Kylie's back and urged her out of the house and down the porch steps.

Ethan didn't hesitate before shutting the door.

Fucking hell.

As soon as they were alone, Ethan spun around to face Beau. "Did you do that on purpose?"

"Who me?" Beau was a picture of innocence, which made Ethan laugh. There wasn't a damn thing virtuous about his barely dressed husband.

"Asshole," Ethan grumbled, but he couldn't stop the grin from pulling at the corners of his mouth.

Beau approached him, wrapping his big arms around Ethan and jerking him closer. "But you love me. Asshole and all."

Ethan choked on a laugh. "Literally," he agreed.

"I know what'll make you love me more," Beau whispered, leaning in and brushing his lips along Ethan's jaw. "You know when I do that thing ... with my tongue?"

Ethan moaned, tilting his head and offering Beau better access as his lips caressed Ethan's neck. He stumbled a couple of steps until his back was against the wood door. The man's mouth alone made his fucking knees weak.

"Yeah. You know what I'm talkin' about," Beau mumbled against his skin.

They might've been married for four and a half years now, but Ethan had to admit, the honeymoon still wasn't over for them. In fact, if he had his way, the honeymoon would *never* be over.

The ridiculously attractive man who was his husband reached down and unbuttoned Ethan's jeans, then slowly lowered the zipper as he kissed and licked Ethan's neck.

Ethan placed his hand on Beau's, halting his movements. "What do you think you're doin'?"

Beau's smile could be felt against his neck. "Makin' it up to you."

"Making *what* up?"

"My little blunder." Beau's breath fanned his neck. "I'm thinkin' I can make you forget all about it by using my wicked oral skills on your cock as a distraction."

Well, hell. Who could say no to that?

"Right now. Right here." Beau's words rasped against Ethan's ear as Beau worked his T-shirt up his torso, then over his head. "My mouth wrapped around your cock."

"That's a good start." A groan escaped as Beau stroked his dick slowly, leisurely.

"Is that what you need?"

"Oh, yeah." Ethan would never turn down a blow job from Beau. "Put your mouth on me."

Beau pushed Ethan's jeans down his hips, freeing his cock. When his big hand fisted Ethan's shaft again, it was difficult not to get lost in the sensation. The man knew every single one of Ethan's buttons. He even knew just how hard to press them to make Ethan's head spin.

"You know I could do this all day, every day." Beau's dark eyes were full of heat as he lowered himself to his knees.

Ethan planted his palms against the door behind him, his gaze dropping to Beau's face as warmth enveloped his cock. He shuddered as the pleasure radiated through him. It didn't matter where they were, whenever Beau turned his full attention on Ethan, he knew he was a goner. Resistance was futile.

Not that he had any intention of resisting. That desire had died a long time ago, back when Ethan had given in to Beau's persistence in the beginning. Back when the man currently on his knees before him had insisted Ethan give in and take what was being offered.

Sliding one hand into Beau's thick blond hair, Ethan tugged him closer, then pushed him back. He repeated the motion, getting lost in the glorious suction of his husband's mouth.

"Love your mouth," Ethan moaned. "So fucking much."

"Well, you're in luck." Beau pulled back and licked Ethan from root to tip. "Because my mouth loves your cock."

"Your mouth loves all of me," Ethan said on a groan.

"True. Every delicious inch."

His husband knew that saying shit like that would send Ethan racing to the edge. It always worked.

"Suck me." Ethan tightened his grip on Beau's hair. "All of me."

Beau opened his mouth wide and Ethan took the offer that was given to him. He pushed his hips forward, driving his rock-hard cock deep into Beau's throat before retreating slowly, watching as his shaft slid over Beau's lips. The man had perfect lips. Hell, the man had perfect *everything*.

Ethan reached down and cupped Beau's head with both hands, then began fucking his mouth hard and deep. The wet rasp of Beau's tongue caused a tremor to shoot down his spine. Pumping his hips forward and back, Ethan rode the waves of pleasure that crashed into him.

Beau gripped Ethan's thighs and took every punishing thrust until Ethan's orgasm was barreling down on him, making him gasp and moan.

"I'm gonna come down your throat," Ethan warned.

Beau's only response was a growl of encouragement.

"Fuck, baby." Ethan inhaled sharply, succumbing to the pleasure as his cock pulsed in Beau's mouth. "Fuck, yes. Beau … baby … I'm comin'."

Beau sucked hard and Ethan melted back against the door as his knees threatened to give out, his climax slamming into him, stealing his strength.

Ethan shuddered, weak from the all-consuming pleasure. "I don't know how you do that." He attempted to draw air into his lungs. "Every fuckin' time."

"The secret…" Beau got to his feet and successfully crushed Ethan between his big body and the door, "is in the fact that I love doing it."

"What? Embarrassing me?"

Beau's grin was wicked and contrite at the same time, but his eyes glowed with the love Ethan was so familiar with. "No. Sucking your cock."

Ethan jerked Beau's head down and fused their lips together, holding him tightly as he plundered his mouth.

"I would return the favor"—Ethan nipped Beau's bottom lip—"but I think you deserve to suffer for a little while."

Beau leaned his forehead against Ethan's and grinned. "You know I love when you make me wait."

That he did. While Ethan was all about instant gratification, Beau did enjoy when Ethan tortured him, giving him something to look forward to.

"I love you, E," Beau said, his lips brushing Ethan's.

"Love you, too." Ethan chuckled. "Even if you do insist on embarrassing me in front of my brothers."

"Me?" Beau pulled back, his dark brown eyes twinkling. "Not me."

Uh-huh.

Four years or forty, Ethan knew without a doubt that he would never get enough of this man.

Never.

BEAU WALKER SMILED TO HIMSELF AS HE climbed behind the wheel of his Chevrolet Silverado while Ethan walked around to the passenger side.

Shortly after going upstairs to clean up, Ethan had come back down and suggested they join Travis and the others for dinner. Since Beau couldn't find any reason to object, he had hurried upstairs to get dressed. He definitely didn't mind spending a couple of hours in town. A burger and a beer sounded just about perfect. Plus, he had no problem hanging out with Ethan's family, who happened to also be their closest friends.

Turning to peer over his shoulder, Beau backed the truck out to the dirt road that would lead out of the Walker ranch. "You sure you wanna do this?"

Ethan clicked his seat belt into place. "Yeah. Why not? Travis'll make fun of me whether we join 'em for dinner or not."

"True. But I'm sure he'll be surprised to see you." The last thing Travis would expect was for Ethan to show up after that.

"Doesn't mean he won't be prepared to give me shit." Ethan shot him a smile, his eyes dragging over Beau's face. "Seriously? Did you know they were there?"

"Nope." Beau smirked. "Not that it would've changed anything if I had."

Granted, if he'd known Zane was there, he would've thought twice. Zane was still Beau's best friend, which meant he had to deal with that man's over-the-top antics on any given day. Beau preferred *not* to be the center of Zane's attention if at all possible.

Sure, Beau liked ribbing Ethan whenever the opportunity presented itself, but he didn't make a point of embarrassing him in front of others. And he'd seen the amused gleam in Travis's eyes for himself. The man was going to give Ethan shit, there was no doubt about that.

"Zane already texted to give me shit that we weren't comin'," Ethan said. "I figure it'll be worse if I hide out."

It had taken some time, but Ethan had come out of his shell where his family was concerned. The Walker brothers had grown up knowing something tragic had happened to Ethan when he was a teenager, and because Beau had been Zane's best friend growing up, he'd known it, too. However, until five years ago, they hadn't realized exactly *what* had caused the man to keep everyone at arm's length. The fact that Ethan's teenage love had taken his own life because he was gay had been a shock, even if it had cleared up so many unanswered questions.

Worse than that, Ethan had spent most of his teenage years and part of his early twenties being bullied by the man's brother. In a word, Ethan's life had been hell. Rather than reach out to those who cared about him, Ethan had suffered in silence, keeping his family at a distance in order to protect them.

Thankfully, Ethan had opted to come out of the closet to his family, and since then, he'd opened up in so many ways. He was still hesitant to show his affection in public, but that was something Beau understood. In fact, Beau was so fucking proud of his husband. Ethan truly was the strongest man Beau knew.

"So, what'll you say when Sawyer confronts you? 'Cause you know it's comin'." Beau cut his gaze to Ethan as he pulled out of the Walker ranch and onto the main road to town.

"To fuck off," Ethan said, still grinning.

Beau laughed because he'd heard it a million times over the years. Ethan gave back as good as he got.

They drove in silence for a couple of minutes and Beau thought back to the impromptu blow job he'd given Ethan. While his own cock still ached with need, he knew Ethan would take care of him later. Having to wait only heightened his need and his anticipation, something Ethan knew he enjoyed.

"You get any updates today?"

Beau's good mood instantly soured as he processed Ethan's question. He stared out the window, his eyes locked on the road as he turned the truck onto the main drag that ran through what used to be a one-horse town. "No. Nothing."

For the past year, they'd been working toward starting a family. After agreeing they were both ready, they'd actively started pursuing a gestational surrogate—a woman who would carry their child but not use her own eggs for insemination. They'd learned it was more expensive this way—using donor eggs added an additional cost—however, it was the route they wanted to take.

As one could imagine, an announcement like that caused quite the fuss in the Walker family. In the beginning, it seemed every single person had something to contribute. Suggestions, ideas. It didn't take long before it became overwhelming. It got to the point Beau and Ethan decided it would be best if they did it on their own. There were too many variables to begin with. Adding others' input into the mix would've complicated an already complicated process.

Unfortunately, complicated was an understatement. The only part that had been easy was their initial decisions.

Surrogate or adoption? Since they both wanted a child who was biologically theirs, they had decided on a surrogate.

Surrogate's egg or donor egg? They'd been told that there was always a risk that the woman could change her mind when the baby was born, and they were hoping to eliminate some of that by keeping it as clinical as possible for her. Not that any of it was clinical. Not in Beau's mind. His emotions were firmly tethered to the thought of their baby growing inside a stranger. But it was something he knew had to happen.

Who would be the father? Although Beau would've been content knowing Ethan was their child's father, Ethan had decided they would use both of their sperm and they wouldn't predetermine paternity.

So, after those decisions had been made, they spent months learning the ins and outs along with the risks of in vitro fertilization via a surrogate. Once Beau assured Ethan he was comfortable, they had finally started the process.

While they had already selected the donor eggs—a process that allowed them to choose from donor's hair color, eye color, and ethnicity—they still had to find a willing surrogate. Preferably someone who would not try to interfere after the baby was born. Someone who would allow Beau and Ethan to become the parents they wanted to be.

Now they were simply waiting for an update regarding whether or not a surrogate had been located. Aside from a viable uterus, they had everything else. The fertility clinic they were working with had handled its part of things seamlessly. The donated eggs had been retrieved and were now frozen, waiting to be inseminated by their sperm so the embryos could be implanted into their surrogate's uterus. They simply had to make a sperm donation once they found a willing woman to carry their baby to term.

So far, they'd had no luck.

The woman at the agency responsible for locating a surrogate had told them their chances were good for finding someone quickly, but Beau was beginning to question what her idea of quick actually was. When they'd surpassed the six-month point, he'd started to lose faith.

To be fair, the agency had identified one woman very early on. When Beau had gotten the call, he'd been over the moon. That elation had died a quick and horrifying death when they met her in person. It had been going well, right up until the woman mentioned she preferred to go the natural route, rather than artificial insemination. Considering neither of them was willing to have sex with someone else, that was *not* going to happen.

Needless to say, Ethan had lost his shit. The meeting hadn't ended well at all.

In the months since they'd started this, Beau had learned one very important lesson: having a baby wasn't easy for a gay couple.

He was trying to hide his disappointment from Ethan because he wanted to shield the man from the pain of rejection. And it wasn't that Beau wasn't content with their marriage or their life in general. Beau had never been happier. He was married to the greatest man in the world and they had a good life. The last thing he wanted was to appear ungrateful, but with every day they didn't hear anything, his heart broke a little more.

Ethan reached over and squeezed Beau's thigh. "Soon, baby. It's gonna happen soon."

"I know." The words came out of Beau's mouth, but he didn't feel them. Not anymore.

Something was wrong, he just didn't know what. For the past month, he'd been reaching out to the woman who was helping them, but he wasn't getting much response. When he called, he got her voicemail. She would respond a day or two later with an email, telling him these things took time, that it was proving more difficult than she'd thought to find a woman who was willing to carry a child for a gay couple. According to her, not everyone was as open-minded as they were.

Funny, because the ad for the clinic had said they were same-sex-couple friendly. He was starting to question that along with everything else.

It sucked, but Beau knew there wasn't much he could do. They had to be patient, and he was doing his best to shield Ethan from the worst of it, but there was no denying it was starting to wear him down.

"You okay?" Ethan asked, his eyes boring into Beau's face.

Forcing a smile, Beau nodded. "Of course. Just hungry."

"You're always hungry."

It was true. He was.

A few minutes later, they were pulling into the diner. There were several familiar trucks parked throughout the lot, all belonging to one member of the Walker clan or another. Travis, Sawyer, Zane, Braydon, Brendon, and Kaleb. They were all there.

Beau parked in an empty spot and climbed out, waiting at the front of the truck for Ethan to join him.

When they walked in the door, the hostess greeted them both with a smile. "They actually have a bet going on whether or not you'd show up," she teased. "They're in the back."

"Perfect." Beau motioned for Ethan to precede him before following.

A few Coyote Ridge residents nodded or waved as they weaved their way through the crowded diner. Being that it was such a small town, it wasn't unusual to see people they knew out and about. Certainly not on a Friday night.

"Well, I'll be damned," Zane said when they approached the table, a mischievous grin splitting his face as he threw his arm over his wife's shoulder. "Told you they'd show up, babe."

Beau did a quick head count when he noticed several more bodies crowded around the tables that had been pushed together. Ethan's cousins—Wolfe and Lynx Caine—had obviously driven in from Embers Ridge to join them. Wolfe's significant others—Amy and Rhys—were sitting on either side of him while Lynx and Reagan were a little farther down.

"You did," V replied, smiling up at them before peering over at Zane. "That means Travis owes you ten bucks."

For a man now out ten dollars, Travis didn't look at all disappointed. His grin was devilish.

Beau grabbed a chair from an empty table and passed it over to Ethan before taking one for himself. Zoey and Kaleb shifted down so they could fit.

"So…" Gage pointed his beer bottle their direction. "That table need reinforcement?"

Ethan smiled deviously. "As a matter of fact, it didn't."

Beau nearly choked as their waitress appeared. "We'll … uh… Two Coors Lights, please. And two burger baskets, well done."

"Sure thing." She shot him a wink before turning and heading toward the kitchen.

"Your parents have *all* the babies tonight?" Beau asked Zane, hoping to keep the subject from reverting back to their kitchen table. "As in every single one?"

Zane smirked. "Yep. We offered to split them up, but Mom refused. Said she loves when they're all there."

"Please tell me someone's there to help them with all those kids." Beau couldn't imagine. And it had nothing to do with the fact that Lorrie and Curtis were in their seventies, either.

"Jared and Hope are there," V told him.

Great. But that would mean there were even more babies since Jared and Hope had two of their own.

"Kylie's dad and stepmom are there, too," Travis added.

"Plus Bristol," Kylie inserted. "She stopped by to check on Lorrie and Curtis."

Bristol Newton was everyone's favorite person these days. She owned the daycare center in town. The feisty blonde was a natural drill instructor when it came to keeping all those kiddos in line. And somehow she always did it with a smile.

"Well, seven adults are certainly better than two," Ethan said, taking one of the beers from their waitress.

Seven was better than two, but Beau wasn't sure that was even enough. There was an overwhelming number of kids in that house, which meant all hands on deck when they got together. Beau had volunteered to babysit on many different occasions and he found he could only handle roughly three at a time, max. Definitely not fifteen.

Yep, Curtis and Lorrie now had fifteen grandbabies, all under the age of five, and there were currently three more on the way, all of which were due before the end of the year.

The Walker family had expanded by leaps and bounds in recent years. A lot of babies and even more to come. And every single time Beau had the pleasure of being around one or more of them, it cemented his desire for him and Ethan to have a baby of their own. So much so, it was all he could think about these days.

Unfortunately, unlike the rest of the Walker clan, they didn't have a uterus available, so it required a different sort of effort on their part.

Beau only hoped that in the very near future, things would fall into place and they would be that much closer to becoming parents. Until then, Beau would enjoy every second he got to spend with all his nieces and nephews.

Although, he wouldn't be spending any time with all fifteen of them at once. He was a lot of things, but he certainly wasn't crazy.

CURTIS WALKER PEERED UP AT HIS NEPHEW when Jared joined him in the living room. Jared had a huge grin on his face and his eleven-month-old daughter, Kassidy, on his hip as he surveyed the ruckus taking place before them.

Out of all of Curtis's nieces and nephew, Jared was the one who came around the most. Truth be told, Curtis enjoyed having the boy there. Especially now that Jared had a genuine smile on his face most days. After the hell Jared's ex-wife had put him through, it was good that things were finally on track for Jared and his family.

"This remind you of anything?" Jared asked, continuing to peer down at the kids sprawled across the floor.

Curtis scanned the room, taking it all in. "A zoo?"

Jared laughed as he darted to the side, avoiding a Hot Wheels car being launched at high speed from the small race track they'd set up a few minutes ago. Kassidy thought it was a game and giggled fiercely.

"Hey, now." Curtis purposely pitched his voice low enough to get all the kids' attention. "Keep 'em on the floor."

"Sorry, Grandpa." Mason's expression was sheepish, but not for long. He shot a glare at his brother, Kellan, obviously shifting the blame.

Curtis grinned, leaning back in his recliner and observing all the little ones. There were several walking, more crawling, and a handful sitting or being held. It was chaotic and wonderful at the same time.

Sometimes it was hard to believe his family had expanded so rapidly.

Not that he was disappointed. In fact, as far as Curtis was concerned, his sons could continue having babies, and Curtis would continue to love each and every one of them.

Granted, if the numbers grew much more, they'd have to figure out a way to handle all of them at once. At fifteen and counting, these nights they came to visit with Grandma and Grandpa were getting harder with every passing year.

Travis, Kylie, and Gage had four little ones running rampant at home, two boys—Kade, who was almost two, and Haden, who was only two weeks old—and two girls—Kate, who would be four in November, and Avery, who would be one in just a few weeks.

Sawyer and Kennedy had one—Matthew, turning two in October—with another due any day now.

Kaleb and Zoey had four—Mason, now four, Kellan, almost three, Barrett, turning two in September, and Gabriel, who would be one next week. According to Zoey that was it for them.

Braydon and Jessie had two—Rhett, turning two at the beginning of September, and Zach, who would be one in about a month—and Jessie was currently pregnant with their third, due at the end of November.

Brendon and Cheyenne had one—Remington, aka Remy, who had turned one in March—and their second child was due at the end of October.

And, of course, Zane and V had three boys—Reid, now three, Asher, who was one and a half, and Theo, who was four months. And just yesterday, Zane had assured them they were working hard on the next one. His youngest boy had no shame whatsoever.

Needless to say, Curtis was grateful that Kylie's parents were there to help out, along with Bristol, the girl who'd become an honorary member of his family in recent months. Considering Bristol spent almost as much time with Curtis's grandkids as their own parents, he felt it important to ensure she was taken care of. Without a family of her own, Bristol needed to feel needed and Curtis's lovely wife had ensured that she did.

Curtis's gaze strayed to Lorrie, who was sitting at the kitchen table with Haden, their youngest grandchild, in her arms. Her beautiful face was lit up the way it always was when she got to spend time with her grandbabies.

They were about to celebrate fifty-five years of wedded bliss and Curtis was almost positive his wife had never been more stunning than she was in this very moment. Although her hair had grayed over the years and there were a few more lines around her eyes, Lorrie was just as radiant, just as full of life and love as she'd always been.

And when she peered over at him and smiled…

After all this time, Curtis still melted when he saw her smile. In fact, he lived every single day to see that beautiful smile.

"What prompted you to volunteer to watch all these heathens?" Jared teased.

Curtis chuckled, glancing down at the heathens Jared was referring to. "Glutton for punishment," he said with a smile, while he was thinking, *Because it makes my wife smile.*

And God knew, Curtis would do anything to make Lorrie smile.

Anything.

Chapter Two

Tuesday, July 24, 2018
(Four days later)

"HAPPY BIRTHDAY, DEAR *GABRIEL*…HAPPY BIRTHDAY TO *you*."

Ethan had to admit, his family was good at a lot of things, but singing wasn't their strong suit.

They could demolish damn near anything in record time, turn a small-town hotel into one of the most prestigious fetish resorts in the country, cut a few bullies off at the knees, stop crazed stalkers, take down conniving ex-wives and hold a family reunion at the same time … all while keeping the family ranch running.

But they couldn't for the life of them carry a tune.

Fortunately for them, they had the one and only Cheyenne Montgomery, a.k.a. the West Texas princess—one of country music's brightest stars, who happened to be Brendon's wife—in their midst. Perhaps they should consider leaving the singing to her in the future.

On the other hand, Ethan had to give them credit for trying.

He smiled to himself, keeping his position at the back of his mother's dining room while the bigger kids, including Zane, crowded around Kaleb's youngest, who was poking at the blue icing on the cupcake Zoey had placed in front of him. In a few minutes, that cupcake would be decorating at least one kid, maybe more, and probably the legs of every chair in the room.

Despite the fact that it was a Tuesday, everyone had gathered at Curtis and Lorrie's for the birthday party ritual they'd been partaking in ever since Mason's first birthday. And by everyone, he meant half the fucking town of Coyote Ridge. Granted, Ethan was related to almost every single person in the house, which meant the town was comprised of mostly Walkers.

Granted, that wasn't really true, but some days it sure felt like it.

It was now Gabriel's turn to celebrate the big oh-one, and everyone had shown up, canceling any other plans they might've had. While Sundays had always been reserved for the family dinner, small birthday parties had become the norm as well. Even if there was a bigger party planned, this was tradition for the Walkers, and Ethan hadn't missed a single one yet.

After the scare a couple of years ago, when his mother had ended up in the hospital with a life-threatening illness, Ethan didn't take much of anything for granted anymore. Nothing in his life had prepared him for almost losing his mother. Thankfully, Lorrie had pulled through and she was a picture of health these days.

Beau glanced over and smiled. "Will there ever be a time when they're all over a year old?" He nodded toward Haden, the youngest Walker in the room, who was currently cradled in Gage's arms.

"Nope." Ethan pressed his shoulder against Beau's and pointed at Theo, Zane's four-month-old son, who was being rocked by V. "Doesn't look like the under-one group's gonna slow down anytime soon."

Certainly not the case since Ethan's sisters-in-law continued to pop out nine-pound miniatures of their fathers, one right after the other. In fact, there had been at least one of them pregnant for the past three years straight. There for a while, he was almost positive Braydon and Brendon were in a race to see who could have the most kids first. For the record, Braydon was currently winning, two-to-one, but both Cheyenne and Jessie were pregnant. Brendon was gonna have to work harder if he expected to best his twin.

And with so many kids now, it seemed there were always streamers to be strung up, candles to be blown out, a cake to be devoured, and ice cream to turn into a gooey mess on the floor. Every day was a party, it seemed.

Ethan enjoyed being around the little ones as much as everyone else, but if he was being honest, he attended these family functions to watch Beau's face light up. Because that was exactly what happened when the big guy laid eyes on one of those kids.

When it came to those munchkins, Beau was by far their favorite uncle. Every single one who was old enough to move on their own made a beeline for Beau anytime he appeared. Ethan was pretty sure Beau wanted it that way, too. In fact, there was a bucket full of toys that Beau kept with him at all times, and a car seat always strapped into Beau's truck just in case they were asked to babysit. The man lived to spend time with these kiddos.

No one in the world would deny that Beau would be the best dad. He certainly deserved to have a child of his own.

And that was what kept Ethan up at night. He would do just about anything to give Beau a baby, but unfortunately, his hands were tied. They had to depend on someone else to contribute in order to make that happen. It had sounded simple in the beginning. Find some eggs, fertilize with their sperm, implant them in a willing uterus, and boom. They'd be dads.

Yeah. Not that easy.

Beau

Ethan had realized his optimism was wasted when he met the woman who flat-out told them she would only carry their baby if she could have sex with one of them and go the traditional route for conception. Ethan had been honest with her when he told her he'd never slept with a woman and damn sure wasn't about to start now. Nor was he going to allow his husband to do it, either.

He shouldn't have been surprised. Ethan had read up on it, knew horror stories of surrogates who extorted the very people they were carrying a child for. Turned out, while the majority probably were, not all the women who were willing to help were on the up and up. That one encounter had been a huge disappointment to say the least.

If it were up to Ethan, he would've given Beau a baby yesterday. He would do whatever it took to keep the light in Beau's eyes. A few times in recent weeks, he'd actually seen that light dim and it scared the shit out of him. Every time Beau opened his email, expecting to find something that would say a surrogate had been located, only to be left wanting, he would lose a little of his eagerness. It killed Ethan to see Beau's pain, but other than wait right along with him, he didn't know what else he could do.

"Oh, boy." Kennedy's clipped tone drew everyone's attention her way.

"What's wrong?" Sawyer asked, a frown marring his forehead as his wife eased into a chair at the table, her hand curling protectively over her rounded belly.

"Nothing," she said, her expression reassuring as she peered up at Sawyer even as she grimaced. "Just a little out of breath."

Yeah, she wasn't out of breath. That woman was in labor. Ethan had seen it enough times at this point to know.

It didn't take long for the light to click on in Sawyer's head, too. At that point, Ethan understood why Kennedy had tried to downplay the event.

"Hospital," Sawyer barked, his voice loud in the crowded room. "We've gotta go. Who's parked behind me? I need you to move, whoever you are. I've gotta get her to the hospital." His harried gaze shot over at Kennedy. "It's all right, baby. I'll get you there in no time. You just relax and breathe." His wild eyes shot through the crowd, briefly stopping on each of the adults. "Who's parked behind me?"

Travis chuckled and stepped up to Sawyer's side, placing a firm hand on his shoulder. "No one's parked behind you. It's all good."

Ethan couldn't help but chuckle. Travis had been through this four times and not once had he been as calm as he was now. In fact, when Kylie had gone into labor with Haden last month, they'd had to cover the babies' ears because Travis's mouth had gotten away from him. Travis could out-curse a sailor, and unfortunately, all those little ones now had a few new words in their vocabulary. Some of the adults, too.

"We gotta go," Sawyer insisted. "Let's go."

He started for the door and several people laughed, Ethan included, as he glanced over to see Kennedy still sitting in the chair, her husband evidently leaving without her.

"Probably oughta take the momma bear, don't you think?" Zane suggested.

"Shit." Sawyer's eyes rounded. "I mean shoot. Where's Matt?" Sawyer glanced at Travis, then to the munchkins standing around. "Matthew! Where are you, little man?"

Ethan pointed to the spot directly in front of Sawyer where Matt was currently eyeing his father as though the man was crazy.

"Hey, little guy." Sawyer swung him up into his arms and kissed his cheek before his gaze shot over to Travis again. "Can you watch him?"

"We've got him," Beau assured Sawyer. "I'll keep an eye on him and bring him to the hospital when you're ready for him to meet his brother."

"Okay, good." Sawyer sighed, deposited Matt on the floor, and started for the door again.

Travis was the one to clear his throat this time. "Your wife, bro."

Sawyer spun back around and it was obvious he was flustered. He held out his hand and helped Kennedy to her feet. Her back was bowed as she cradled her huge belly, waddling toward the door.

Sawyer took her hand and helped her along, but not before yelling out one more time that whoever was parked behind him needed to move.

"I think we should go with him," Zane told V.

"And I'll help out," Bristol said. "I'll take your kiddos back to your house. When you want us to join you, just call."

"That'd be great," Zane told her.

Travis snapped his fingers and pointed at Zane. "I'll follow you." He turned to Gage. "I'll call when they're close if you wanna come up there."

Gage nodded.

Travis turned to their parents. "Momma, Pop, I'll call you when I've got news. Everyone else, keep your phones on."

"Will do," a few people chimed in.

Yep. Just like the last fifteen times they'd been down this road … it was going to be fun.

Chaotic, too. But fun, nonetheless.

BEAU SLIPPED INTO ETHAN'S OLD BEDROOM AT Curtis and Lorrie's house, closing the door softly behind him.

"Matt's finally asleep." Beau turned to find Ethan reclining on the bed, looking far too comfortable with his hands behind his head, ankles crossed. "Any word from Sawyer or Travis?"

"Nope." Ethan shook his head as his eyes did a slow perusal over Beau. "Not yet."

Ethan's childhood bedroom looked pretty much the same as it had when Ethan was a kid. Same full-sized mattress on a metal frame, no headboard. The nightstand beside it was worn and nicked. The dresser didn't match and the navy-blue comforter was thin from age. The walls were bare because Ethan had long ago taken down whatever had been up there; however, there were a few yellowed spots from where the posters of heavy equipment had once hung.

"You think it'll be a while?" Beau moved to stand in front of the dresser, leaning back against it, pretending to be unaffected by Ethan's heated stare.

"How long was she in labor last time?" Ethan asked.

Beau shrugged. "Ten hours, I think."

"I'm sure it'll be at least that long then."

Beau grinned. He knew Ethan had no idea how long it would take, and based on the gleam in his eyes, that certainly wasn't what was on his mind now. Beau had heard that the second labor was generally shorter than the first, but he wasn't about to mention it.

"You wanna take a shower?" Beau asked.

Ethan shook his head.

"You want me to go down and grab you a cupcake?"

"Nope."

"You need somethin' to drink?"

Ethan shook his head again.

"You want me to strip naked so you can ravish me?"

Ethan's dark eyebrow slowly lifted. "Bingo."

"Even with your parents in the house?"

The smirk on Ethan's face was one Beau recognized well. His man liked to walk on the wild side.

"What if we wake them up?" Beau taunted.

"I suggest you be quiet," Ethan countered.

"*Me?*"

When Ethan got to his feet, Beau's insides tightened, his cock hardening as his sexy man sauntered toward him. "Yes, you."

"What if I can't?" Beau asked, his voice lowered to a whisper as Ethan pressed up against him.

"Then I guess it'll be an awkward conversation over breakfast, now won't it?"

The thought of having Curtis confront him made Beau's face heat. He wasn't usually the one who got embarrassed, but there would be no way to avoid it if his father-in-law even said the word *sex*.

"I can be quiet," he assured Ethan.

"Is that a promise? Or a dare?"

Beau narrowed his eyes. "You wouldn't."

Ethan leaned in and kissed Beau right below his ear. "Baby, you know I love to hear you scream."

Yeah. That gruff whisper did it for him in so many ways.

Ethan's mouth fused to Beau's neck and all thought fled. He moaned softly, trying to remember he had to be quiet since Lorrie and Curtis were right downstairs. Because his in-laws' house was set up to handle the kids staying over, Beau had figured it would be easier to keep an eye on Matthew here, rather than take him to their house. Of course, Ethan told him *after* Beau had talked to Curtis and Lorrie that they could've easily gone to Sawyer's for the night.

That would've been less awkward, sure.

Too late to worry about it now, though.

Warm hands slid beneath his T-shirt, forcing the cotton higher up his chest. Beau helped Ethan remove it, swallowing a groan when Ethan's mouth slid lower, seeking Beau's nipple. He wrapped his hand behind Ethan's head and held him there, heat slamming into him when Ethan nipped him. His eyes rolled back; his cock twitched and thickened.

"Ethan…" He wasn't sure how much of this he could take. Every time Ethan touched him, Beau's body went up in flames. It had been like that since the very first time.

"Are you beggin' already?" Ethan slipped his fingers into the waistband of Beau's jeans and tugged him away from the dresser. "'Cause I fuckin' love to hear you beg."

Oh, he'd be begging, all right. And he wasn't ashamed of it, either. Quietly, of course. Because, you know, in-laws and all.

Ethan tugged him toward the bed. When Beau's calves hit the mattress edge, Ethan put his hands on Beau's chest and shoved. He fell back willingly, staring up at the most gorgeous man in the world and taking every inch of him in. From his dark hair to those beautiful blue-gray eyes, that stubborn chin, all those sleek muscles and tanned skin covering his six-foot-five-inch frame… Lord have mercy, Ethan had the ability to make Beau drool.

"Boots off," Ethan ordered.

While Beau toed off his boots, Ethan stripped off his own shirt. It was hard to focus on what he should've been doing when Ethan started undressing. The man's body was a work of art and Beau's tongue and fingers itched to explore as Beau recalled the pleasure of outlining all those glorious muscles.

"You're still dressed, baby," Ethan taunted.

"Not for long." Beau worked his jeans open, then shoved them down to his knees along with his boxer briefs. He discarded them quickly before reaching for his cock, fisting it while he watched Ethan.

Beau loved the way Ethan's eyes heated when he watched his movements. The way Ethan's breathing increased as Beau slid his fist up and down his shaft.

"What're you gonna do to me now?" Beau asked, squeezing the swollen head of his cock, inviting Ethan to explore.

Ethan's attention shifted to Beau's face. He grinned as he stepped over to the nightstand and opened the drawer. "What do you *want* me to do?"

Beau tracked his movements, shivering as Ethan retrieved a bottle of lube he'd obviously stashed there at some point. God, he hoped Lorrie hadn't seen that. Talk about awkward.

Forcing his thoughts to the naked man standing before him, Beau grinned. "I want you to fuck me."

"Hmm." Ethan pumped the lubricant into his hands, then stroked himself, slicking his cock.

Beau's ass clenched at the thought of having Ethan inside him.

"I was thinkin' I'd make love to you." The gleam in Ethan's eyes was so fucking hot.

"Yeah?" His voice cracked like it had when he'd hit puberty.

Ethan smirked as he moved toward him. When he reached the side of the bed, Beau shifted so that his head was resting on the pillow. Granted, his feet hung off the end of the mattress, but in a few minutes, his position would rectify that issue.

He held out his arms and welcomed Ethan.

"Fuck, I love you," Ethan whispered as he crawled over him, his knees resting between Beau's spread thighs.

"I love you, too, baby." Ethan was the only person Beau had ever been in love with. And he would love him until the day he died.

Ethan's eyes raked over his face, and it was clear he was waiting for Beau to make a move. Unable to resist, he pulled Ethan's head down so he could reach his mouth.

That was all she wrote. As soon as their lips met, Beau got lost in Ethan's warmth. This was the one place he felt like he belonged. Right here with this man. When he had Ethan in his arms, nothing else mattered.

"I wanna be inside you," Ethan muttered against his mouth.

Beau shifted, giving Ethan the access he needed.

"I'm gonna go slow."

Beau knew that wasn't possible. Ethan would start out slow, sure. But just like every time, they were combustible when they came together. Sex with Ethan was explosive.

When Ethan's cock pressed against his anus, Beau pulled Ethan's head down again. He worked his tongue into Ethan's mouth, teasing slowly, savoring the sweet, minty taste of him. He fucking loved kissing Ethan. It was unlike anything else he'd ever experienced. He could've spent days just like this.

"God, you feel good," Ethan groaned, sliding one arm beneath Beau's neck and bringing them closer together as his thick cock inched deep into Beau's ass. "So fucking good."

Beau kissed him, taking his time, exploring Ethan's mouth while Ethan fucked him so sweetly. He knew this wouldn't last long. It was merely the calm before the storm.

Ethan broke the kiss, pressing his face into Beau's neck and breathing deeply. Beau knew what was coming. Ethan's patience was never as fortified as he pretended and he had clearly reached his breaking point.

Honestly, it was so fucking hot to watch the man he loved come apart like this.

"Beau..." Ethan moaned against his neck. "You feel too good."

Ethan's hips shifted forward, back, his cock filling Beau, brushing against that spot that made his eyes cross.

Wrapping his arms around Ethan, Beau held on. "Love me, E. I just need you to love me."

"Forever and always." Ethan growled as he fucked into him roughly, his control slipping even further.

Beau's heart expanded the way it always did when Ethan was vulnerable. This was a side of the man people rarely saw. But Beau did because Ethan had opened his heart and allowed him in.

Ethan's hips continued to thrust and retreat, his cock pushing in deep while Beau allowed the sensations to overwhelm him.

"Fuck, Beau. Baby..." Ethan nipped his ear, his voice lowering even more. "I need to fuck you. Hard."

Beau's entire body shuddered with need, and when Ethan pushed up on his hands, staring down at him, he watched him as he always did, with so much fucking love in his heart he could hardly stand it.

Ethan began pumping his hips faster, driving in deeper, filling Beau to capacity. He knew they had to be quiet, but it wasn't easy.

Placing his hands over his head, Beau pressed his palms against the wall to hold himself in place as Ethan's control shattered. Ethan slammed into him harder, faster, deeper. The cheap metal bed frame creaked from their combined weight. Beau prayed Ethan's parents couldn't hear it.

Within minutes, Beau was biting his lip, grunting as the intensity filled him. He was close. So ... fucking ... close.

Ethan fucked him hard, his eyes never leaving Beau's face. They were the only two people in the world. Nothing and no one intruded on this moment between them.

As though he couldn't take it anymore, Ethan fell on top of him, pressing his face in Beau's neck again and groaning. "I'm gonna come, Beau. Fuck, baby. Gonna come."

Wrapping his arms around Ethan once more, he held him there, allowing Ethan's shallow thrusts to send him over the edge. "Come for me, E. Come for me right now."

They both came, their breaths racing, bodies covered in sweat.

And just like always, it was so fucking perfect Beau never wanted to move again.

This was his heaven.

Right here with Ethan.

Chapter Three

As WITH PRETTY MUCH ANYTHING IN ETHAN'S family, a Walker birth was quite the spectacle. More so than even the birthday parties. While there weren't streamers or cupcakes, it was still a celebration.

The text from Travis came in at the ass crack of dawn. Four thirty to be exact. Ethan was dragged from a peaceful, dreamless sleep, which he could thank Beau for. Whenever he indulged in Beau's delicious body, he always slept better.

It took a moment to process where he was as his hand fumbled in air to find his phone, his tired brain ready to shut off the alarm that wasn't really an alarm. When his knuckles hit the nightstand that was definitely not in the right place, his brain was instantly awake.

After nudging Beau, Ethan headed downstairs to ensure his parents were up. While they got ready and Beau took a quick shower, Ethan went in to wake Matthew. Of course, anyone who had an almost-two-year-old knew what a feat that actually was. He'd managed to get the kid dressed before he ever even opened his eyes, but the instant Ethan told him they were going to see Matthew's new baby brother, the little boy's energy switch had been flipped.

Thankfully for Ethan, Beau was a pro at handling hyperactive kids. He had gotten Matt strapped into the car seat in his truck while Ethan had ensured his mom and dad got settled in their own. Once his parents pulled out of the driveway, Ethan was riding shotgun as Beau followed, carrying on an animated conversation with their nephew. Apparently, the little boy was so excited—they knew this because he nodded frequently in response to their questions—to have someone to play with. Ethan admired his enthusiasm, but he wasn't sure the little boy understood how it all worked just yet.

He would. Eventually.

As they drove and the sun began peeking over the horizon, Ethan allowed himself to pretend they were heading to the hospital for the birth of their child. Boy, girl, it didn't matter. What he really wanted was a kid with big brown eyes like Beau. A little girl, perhaps. Some estrogen to balance out all the testosterone. Ethan knew the Walkers hadn't had girls in ... well, technically, none of his brothers had produced girls. Yet. Travis, Kylie, and Gage had two daughters, but the little fairy princesses looked just like Gage while their boys were perfect miniatures of Travis.

Truth was, Ethan didn't care either way but it was a fantasy he only allowed himself to have from time to time. When he spent too much time dwelling on it, his heart hurt because it wasn't as easy for them to have a baby as it was for his brothers.

One day. He had faith it would happen. Beau was meant to be a father; therefore, he would be.

Once they were at the hospital, they joined the others in the waiting room. His eyes shot to the coffeemaker in the corner, and he realized caffeine would have to wait because the empty carafe was currently burning on the warmer. It had evidently been drained by those patiently anticipating the happy moment when Sawyer's little bundle of joy would be born.

It was a packed house. Reese Tavoularis, the guy running point at Walker Demolition, Jaxson Briggs, one of their many cousins, Zane and V, Brendon and Cheyenne, Braydon and Jessie, Kaleb and Zoey, Kylie and Gage, Jared and Hope, plus Jared's brothers—more cousins—Kaden and Keegan, as well as Bristol and Sheriff Endsley, Kennedy's father, were all milling about, chatting softly. Even the youngest Walkers were in attendance, though there were quite a few asleep in car seats scattered around the room on the floor.

Although it wasn't exactly the best idea in the world, his brothers had started bringing the kids along with them years ago so everyone could experience the joyous occasion together. Good thing there weren't many other expectant families in the room. There wasn't much seating left.

Ethan located his mother and father, then sauntered over. "Where's Travis?"

Curtis nodded toward the doors to the Labor and Delivery sign. "Stalking them from the hallway."

Sounded like Travis, all right.

Despite the fact that birds were hardly even awake yet, it didn't seem to matter to the four-and-under crowd. Those who weren't still snoozing—roughly ten of them—were wired for sound and the only person who could keep them under control was Beau. Not even Bristol had the power Beau did. She was good, but Beau was better. He was their saving grace.

While Ethan took a seat by his father, the man he loved herded the kids into a small area and produced his magic bucket of toys appropriate for all ages. You would've thought it was Christmas.

"He's good with them," Curtis said, his deep voice soft.

"He is." Ethan tried to ignore the pang in his chest at the thought of not finding a surrogate soon. He wanted to give Beau a baby.

And yes, Ethan continued to tell himself that it was because he wanted to see that beautiful light in Beau's eyes, but he knew it was more than that. Deep down, Ethan still fought his demons. No matter how irrational his fears were, his brain seemed set to worst-case scenario much of the time. His biggest fear? That he would one day not be enough for Beau, and without a baby, he risked losing the man he loved.

Irrational? Sure. Beau had never given him any reason to believe otherwise. However, Ethan's depression didn't always allow him to see things logically. Of course, this train of thought was something he did his best not to think about because the mere idea of life without Beau in it was unbearable.

"He's gonna make a great dad," Lorrie said, leaning around Curtis.

Ethan smiled because she was right.

Granted, Beau had his own reservations and they all stemmed from the shitty parents he'd grown up with. Ben and Arlene Bennett were horrific people. Ethan would never say that aloud, but he didn't feel bad for thinking it. It was a wonder Beau had turned out to be such an amazing man considering the fucking bigots who'd raised him.

"Wipe the scowl off, boy," Curtis commanded.

Glancing over at his dad, Ethan schooled his features. "Sorry, Pop."

"It's gonna work out."

Ethan knew his dad was referring to them having a baby. He'd seen the sympathy in everyone's eyes when they had to tell them that, no, a surrogate still hadn't been found. While all of his brothers were popping out kids left and right, Ethan and Beau were left wanting.

Beau's head lifted and his eyes searched until they landed on him. Ethan didn't have to force a smile when Beau grinned. That man was his life and he smiled without meaning to simply because he loved him so damn much.

The door that led back to the L and D rooms opened and all heads turned. Ethan broke eye contact with Beau to see who it was.

"We've got a boy," Travis announced, a huge grin on his face. "Brody Aaron Walker is a screamer."

As though they'd all had a hand in the conception, everyone got to their feet and congratulated everyone else. It was a little strange and a lot amusing, but they were so close that it felt as though they'd all just had a baby.

Ethan pushed to his feet and headed over to Beau. He hugged him, something he rarely did in public. For whatever reason, he couldn't help himself.

"I love you," Beau whispered, causing Ethan to pull back and stare at him.

Ethan smiled. "I love you, too."

"It'll be a while before we can go in and see them," Travis explained. He'd obviously been waiting in the hall outside the birthing room for the news for this very reason. "Figured we'd go down to the cafeteria. Grab some coffee and food."

Yes. Coffee.

"Daddy, I want donut holes!" Kate announced.

That, of course, led to the rest of the munchkins agreeing. The under-four set who could vocalize, anyway.

"Okay, here's what we're gonna do," Beau said, addressing the shortest folks in the room. "We're gonna get in a line and play a game. Who wants to play a game?"

A chorus of cheers sounded from the kiddos who could understand what was going on.

Within a minute, they were all in a line, following Beau as he led the way to the donut holes. Ethan knew the donut holes were going to be in the form of fruit, but whatever. It wouldn't matter once they got there, because those kids thought Beau hung the moon.

Then again, Ethan thought so, too.

BRISTOL NEWTON COULDN'T KEEP FROM SMILING AS she sat in the hospital cafeteria and watched the craziness around her. Toddlers snacking on pretzels and grapes—more than a few being launched into the air when the little ones thought no one was looking—husbands, wives, moms, and dads chatting and laughing, babies sleeping in car seats or on their fathers' shoulders, grandparents congratulating one another, ticking off on their fingers how many grandbabies they now had.

Needless to say, the Walker family was a powerhouse all their own and their very presence could be felt, even when there weren't a couple dozen of them in one room.

For the past year or so, Bristol had found herself inside their inner sanctum, a place she never would've imagined was quite so … normal.

Okay, fine. Normal might be a stretch. But overall, they were the typical small-town family with small-town values, more than enough love to go around, and patience of steel. All of which she found herself admiring.

While she wasn't a stranger to the Walkers, nor them to her, these days she was looking at them in a different light. Her entire life had been spent in Coyote Ridge, so she was all too familiar with every single one of the boys, having heard millions of stories about them over the years, a few she knew to be true. Mostly those involving Zane, the youngest of the seven brothers. In fact, Bristol had been in the same grade as Zane and for quite a few years she'd shared the same classes with him.

But this … the family vibe, the sense of belonging to something bigger than herself… *That* was what she admired most about these people and she was more than grateful that she'd somehow ended up in their purview.

And truth be told, while always an adventure, it was sometimes a little overwhelming. Especially for a girl who'd been raised by a single father whose entire world revolved around his work. Because of that, Bristol had spent the majority of her youth alone. Since Larry Newton had passed his time working at the small mechanic shop he'd owned, Bristol had been left to fend for herself. She'd had the run of her house from the time she was six, when her mother left them for greener pastures outside of Coyote Ridge.

With her mother in the wind and her father in Heaven looking down upon her, Bristol was now alone. Well, except for this wonderful family who'd seemingly adopted her, changing her world for the better.

Her eyes scanned the faces of all the kids. Every single one of them was registered at her daycare center. While most of them only came two or three days a week, she still owed her recent success to this family alone. Not only because the Walker kids were enrolled there, either. Turned out, the Walker name went a long way with a lot of people. She'd had more than a handful of new clients who had signed up simply because the Walkers trusted her.

Because of them, Bristol was now a successful entrepreneur and she'd made a lot of friends to go along with the steady income.

Bristol's eyes shot to the doorway, her gaze zeroing in on the two cowboys who had just walked in. Strolled really. Maybe sauntered. Their loose-hipped gaits drew her attention even as she scolded herself.

Mysteries wrapped in enigmas drizzled with sex appeal.

Yep. That was the best description of Kaden and Keegan Walker. Identical twin brothers. Cousins to the Walker brothers.

Bristol knew their father, Gerald, was Curtis's brother, but other than that, she really didn't know much about them. Aside from the fact that they were thirty-five years old, their birthday in April, and they were approved to pick up any of the Walker kids from the daycare, of course.

Those were the facts she'd acquired over time. Then there was the obvious.

Mirror images of one another, Kaden and Keegan had dark brown hair, steel-blue eyes, quick smiles, and smoldering stares. They fit in nicely with the six-feet plus group they were related to.

She did her best not to stare as Keegan waltzed over to Mason and gave him a high five. Of the twin brothers, Keegan was the more outgoing one, very much like Zane and Sawyer. Lighthearted, fun. She'd only spoken to him once, and that was the one time he'd stopped in to pick up Remy for Brendon and Cheyenne. The conversation had consisted of pleasantries mostly, but Bristol still remembered the shockingly deep cadence of his voice and the sexy smirk he'd gifted her with.

Her gaze swung to Kaden, who was talking to Curtis. As though he felt her looking at him, Kaden's eyes slid over to her. His dark eyebrows disappeared into the shadow cast by the straw Stetson on his head but she felt the heat of his stare all the same.

Their eyes met, held. It was as though she'd been sucked into a vortex that transcended time and space and any erotic encounter she'd ever experienced. In her defense, the latter was embarrassingly small.

Kaden offered a slight nod, letting her know he saw her watching him. Bristol fought the urge to nod back. The last thing she needed was to encourage something that could never happen.

It was bad enough she found herself attracted to the two of them. There was something about them, something that intrigued her in a way she'd never felt before.

Not that it mattered. Kaden and Keegan weren't from Coyote Ridge. And though she knew they were here more and more these days, it was pointless to give in to her fantasies. That stupid one that had somehow superimposed her in the middle of a hot twin sandwich.

And, boy, was that fantasy a doozie. It, along with her battery-operated-boyfriend, had gotten her through several lonely nights.

Bristol was out of her mind, there was no doubt about it. For one, her divorce papers had only been dry for nine months. The last thing she wanted was to deal with another man trying to run roughshod over her. And for another thing, Bristol had heard the rumors about the twins. They shared their women between them. Always. And casual was how they preferred their hookups.

Bristol was anything but casual when it came to sex. There would be no wham-bam-thank-you-ma'ams in her future. Not ever.

A small smirk formed on Kaden's full lips, sending a flash of heat racing through her veins. Bristol tore her gaze away, focusing on the kids. Her breath raced in and out of her lungs as though she'd just finished one of her CrossFit sessions.

Her eyes bounced from one kid to another until she paused on Kate, who was currently talking ninety miles a minute to Keegan. Bristol couldn't hear what she was talking about, but she couldn't help but smile at the little girl's animated expressions.

Before she could look away, Keegan's eyes shifted to her.

Bristol sucked in a breath from the flash of heat she saw when he met her gaze.

Damn it.

Now she'd been busted.

By both of them.

KADEN WALKER EXCUSED HIMSELF, THEN HEADED OVER to join Keegan, who appeared to be having an argument with Travis's older daughter.

"Uncle Kaden!" she yelled when he appeared.

Kaden wasn't sure why all the kids called him and Keegan uncle considering they were merely cousins, but ever since Kate had said it the first time, it had stuck. Now he figured it would only cause confusion if he tried to explain.

"Hey, shorty," he said, mussing her hair. "What's shakin'?"

She giggled, and in the true spirit of a three-year-old, she turned and ran away.

"That's becomin' a trend," Keegan said, turning toward him.

"What's that?"

"You runnin' off all the girls."

Kaden grinned, scanning the room until his eyes landed on the cute little daycare owner sitting at a table alone. He suspected his brother's statement would ring true if he tried to approach her, so he fought the urge. Granted, it was one he was fighting harder and harder these days for some reason.

"Ahh, so the cute one's snagged your attention, too?" Keegan asked, stepping close to him.

Cute wasn't the right word. No, Bristol Newton was hotter than a bonfire in July. Her tight little body and all those curves had captured his eye a long damn time ago.

"We should ask her out," Keegan suggested.

Without taking his eyes off Bristol, Kaden shook his head. "Ain't gonna happen, bro."

Keegan grunted his displeasure. "How'd I know you were gonna say that?"

Because Kaden had a sixth sense about these things. Whenever they set their sights on a woman, Kaden always followed his gut. He could easily tell the ones who would take them up on their offer of a one-night romp and the ones who would think they'd lost their minds. It had only taken a few slaps to the face for him to figure out which to approach and which to steer clear of.

Bristol wasn't the sort who would do bodily harm, but she would be offended enough to shoot daggers from her beautiful blue eyes.

That woman might fantasize about what they could offer her, but he suspected she was far too pure to allow that fantasy to turn into reality. It was one thing to think about all the things they could do to her when they got her naked between them, but something else to give in to the urge.

Plus, Kaden knew she wasn't the sort of woman to entertain some casual encounters with a couple of cowboys. On top of that, she was close to Curtis's family. The last thing Kaden wanted was to cause problems on that front. There were too many warm, willing women who would welcome their advances and not bat an eyelash when they never called them again to risk causing a stir in the family.

As he stood there, Bristol's gaze slid over to them once more. Kaden met her stare and held it. Her eyes were the brilliant blue of a cloudless summer sky, her hair honey-gold silk. Even from this distance, he could see how smooth and soft her skin was.

An image of her laid out beneath them, her blond hair spilling over her shoulders, those pretty blue eyes burning with lust, flashed in his mind. For a moment, he was positive he could hear her soft gasps and urgent cries as they rode her through her orgasm.

It was so real his breath locked in his chest.

It took effort, but Kaden managed to look away. Whatever had transpired between them just now…

"You okay?" Keegan asked, breaking into his thoughts.

Kaden nodded, but the voice in his head was saying, *No. Not even remotely okay.*

Chapter Four

Saturday, August 25, 2018
(Four weeks later)

HIS BED WAS COZY, HIS HUSBAND WARM beside him, yet Beau forced himself to crawl out of bed on Saturday morning while Ethan snored softly.

Generally, they were working on Saturdays, but with the ridiculous heat, they'd decided to take the day off. Beau wanted nothing more than to remain curled up with his man, but he had things to do. And he knew Ethan needed some uninterrupted sleep. The past few weeks had been chaotic to say the least.

With two new babies in the family, everyone was pitching in to help out with the bigger little ones, allowing for bonding time as well as those extra minutes of sleep the parents were eager to get. Travis and crew were busy with Haden, now just shy of two months old. Sawyer and Kennedy had their hands full with Brody. Apparently, the little boy was a very healthy eater and getting him to sleep for longer than two hours at a time was a stretch.

On top of that, there had been three more birthday celebrations. Kellan—Kaleb and Zoey's second child—had turned three. Avery—Travis, Kylie, and Gage's third child—as well as Zach—Braydon and Jessie's second child—had both turned one.

Needless to say, with so many events and so many people needing them to pitch in, the pressure was taking its toll on him and Ethan. Between the overload of work at Walker Demolition, the heat that made working ridiculously painful, family needing them at every turn, and the emotional stress that came along with trying to have a baby through unconventional methods, they had a lot on their plates.

Beau was hoping they could have a day to themselves. Perhaps go out to lunch, catch a movie. Something that would allow them a little time to decompress.

After heading to the guest bathroom to relieve himself, Beau washed his hands, then made his way to the kitchen to start a pot of coffee. While the java brewed, Beau grabbed his laptop and placed it on the kitchen table. As was his ritual, he squeezed his eyes shut, sent up a silent prayer that there was good news waiting for him, then leaned over and pulled up his email. He hurriedly skimmed his inbox without sitting down.

He warned himself not to be disappointed as he sought one specific email, the one that would change their lives forever. But as had been the case for the past seven months, Beau's heart sank when the only thing he saw was a couple of advertisements. Good news was, Bass Pro Shop and Cabela's were both having a sale. Bad news was, there was no news on a surrogate.

Pushing away from the table with a heavy sigh, Beau went to pour the coffee. It had been hard enough going through the process of getting the donor eggs. First approval, then selection. After they'd been assured the eggs were ready and waiting for them, Beau had breathed a huge sigh of relief, only to be let down when they'd been told there wasn't a surrogate at the time.

Which meant having a baby wasn't going to happen for them yet.

According to Ethan, the key word there was _yet_. They would have a baby when the time was right. Beau was ready to have a baby with Ethan _now_. In fact, he'd already mentally designed the baby's room. And it took everything in him not to make a trip to the hardware store to buy paint.

As he took a sip of coffee and stared out the window over the kitchen sink, he frowned.

It looked as though today was not going to be the day they got to start planning the rest of their lives, either.

Two hours later, Beau was sitting on the couch, flipping through the cartoon channels, when he heard Ethan stomping down the stairs. The man wasn't silent when he woke up in the morning. In fact, Ethan was rarely silent in anything he did. Not these days, anyway.

"Mornin'," Beau greeted, admiring his husband's shirtless torso as he paused to glance his way.

"Why didn't you wake me up?" Ethan scrubbed his hand over the stubble on his cheeks as he looked between Beau and the television.

"You needed to sleep."

Beau continued to watch Ethan as the man debated on whether he was going to the kitchen or the living room. His abs flexed as he started for the kitchen, then paused. That perfect V was defined, dipping down into his pajama pants, which were sitting ridiculously low on his hips as though teasing Beau with what lay just a bit south of the drawstring.

Before he could crook a finger to invite his husband for some early-morning sexual fun, Ethan turned toward the kitchen, clearly giving in to his need for coffee.

A minute later, Ethan returned, setting his steaming mug on the table before plopping down on the couch beside him. "What're we doin' today?"

"I was thinkin' we could go——" Before he could get the sentence out, Beau's cell phone rang.

He leaned toward the coffee table to see who it was. The name that appeared on the screen had him picking up his phone.

"Who is it?" Ethan asked, clearly sensing Beau's panic.

"My mother." Arlene Bennett. The woman who had given birth to him. The same woman who had written him off when Beau had come out, admitting he was in love with a man.

Beau stared at the phone, his brain attempting to process why she might be calling him.

He hadn't heard from Arlene in three years. And the last time she'd texted him, it had been to ask him to come over so they could talk. Beau had shot a single word back—*no*—because he knew what she wanted to talk about.

From the moment he'd come out, his parents tried to convince him that he was not gay, he was simply confused. But they assured him that was all right because they knew of a place that could help him get better. Like being gay was an illness. They claimed it was some faith-based, church-run bullshit with a ninety-nine percent success rate of helping confused people realize they weren't gay. According to Ben and Arlene, this place fully believed the demons needed to be exorcised and replaced with God in order for people to be allowed to live a normal, happy, *straight* life.

Faith-based, his ass. Fucked up was what it was.

In a word, Beau's parents were crazy.

"Well, answer it," Ethan urged, shifting to face him. "If she's callin' after all this time, it has to be important."

"I have nothin' to say to her."

Before he could put the phone down, Ethan stabbed a finger toward him. "Answer the phone."

With a resigned sigh, Beau hit the button to answer the call, then put the phone to his ear as though it was a snake that would strike at any second.

Not looking away from Ethan, Beau found his voice. "Hello?"

"Beau?"

"Yeah."

"It's ... your mother."

"What's wrong?" He could hear the urgency in her tone and instantly knew this wasn't a social call. Then again, why would it be?

"It's... Oh, God. It's your father."

Beau sat up straight. He hadn't talked to his parents since he walked out of their house the day he told them he was gay. Although they lived relatively close and he saw them at church almost every Sunday, they hadn't said two words to him. His father didn't approve of his choices and his mother stood by the man's side, regardless of whether she shared his beliefs or not.

"Tell me what's goin' on, Mom." He tried to hold down his fear, but he knew it could be heard in his voice.

Ethan placed his hand on Beau's arm, squeezing gently. Beau dropped his gaze to the floor, listening to his mother.

"He's in the hospital. The doctors said he had a stroke. He's... Sometimes he's awake, but he's sleeping too much and they've got him hooked up to all these wires." Arlene Bennett sobbed, her voice cracking as she relayed the details. "I didn't know who else to call."

Well, hell. She could've hit him upside the head with a cast iron skillet and it wouldn't have hurt as bad. From her tone, he got the feeling she hadn't wanted to call him at all.

"What's wrong?" Ethan asked, urging Beau to look at him.

Beau cut his gaze to Ethan's face. As soon as their eyes met, he wanted to drown in the blue-gray depths, to let the man soothe his soul the way only Ethan could.

"My father had a stroke." Beau tried to keep the emotion from his voice. "He's in the hospital."

"Shit." Ethan pushed to his feet. "Tell her we'll be up there as soon as we can."

Beau relayed the information to his mother.

"Beau?"

"Hmm?" He stood, surprised his legs were steady enough to keep him upright.

"I'd prefer you didn't bring ... *him*. Your father wouldn't want him here."

Beau choked on a laugh, but there was absolutely no humor in it. "Are you kidding me? You want me to come up there *without* my husband?"

"I really wish you wouldn't call him that." Her tone was soft.

"*Why?*" he barked the single word. "That's who he is. Ethan's my husband."

"Not in the eyes of the Lord," she argued.

Seriously? She was going to do this now? His father had had a stroke and could be a few breaths away from death's door for all Beau knew and the woman wanted to tell him God didn't approve?

"Fine," he countered hotly. "If you don't want him up there, then I'm not comin' either. Tell Dad… You know what? Don't tell him anything. Pretend you didn't call."

"Beau!" Ethan chastised.

His mother's voice sounded in his ear, softer this time. "The prognosis isn't good, Beau. I just thought … I thought maybe you'd want to apologize in case you never got the opportunity again."

Holy shit. Was the woman smoking crack?

"Apologize? What do I have to apologize for?"

Beau already knew what was coming, but he waited anyway.

"For making such a mess of your life, Beau. You've thrown all our hard work away with this nonsense. We've only ever wanted you to be happy, but—"

He cut her off. "Really? Because Mom, here's a thought. I *am* happy." Happier than he'd been in all the years he'd spent before he fell in love with Ethan.

And Beau knew that if it came down to it, he would spend the rest of his life happy.

Just as long as he had Ethan.

KNOWING THE CONVERSATION WAS GOING TO HELL quickly, Ethan got Beau's attention. "Tell her you'll be there soon."

Beau narrowed his eyes but did as Ethan instructed before disconnecting the call.

Ethan put his hand on Beau's arm. "Now let's go upstairs, get dressed, then we'll go to the hospital."

Although having to deal with those two people was the absolute last thing Ethan wanted to do, he would put aside his hatred for them because they were Beau's parents.

Having spent years dealing with people who thought he was an abomination all because of who he loved, he had no tolerance for them anymore. Coyote Ridge, being such a small town, was chock full of homophobic assholes like Ben and Arlene Bennett who had no problem looking down their nose at him. Some acted as though being gay was an illness and, by getting too close, they risked some of his gayness rubbing off on them.

He was often given a wide berth from those who looked down on him because no matter how much people were preaching for tolerance, there were still those who were ready to cast him into hell. They were the very reason Ethan had put so much distance between himself and his family when he was younger. He'd been protecting them. Or at least he'd thought he had been.

The good news was, while there were those who would never approve, there were a lot who were tolerant.

Fortunately, Ethan didn't have to hide anymore because he had a loving, supportive family who didn't make him feel like an outcast. They were there for him in all the ways that counted. Not once since his brothers had confronted the fucker who had spent years making Ethan's life pure hell had anyone in his hometown tried to fuck with him. It had been so effective most people kept their thoughts to themselves these days.

The key word there was *most*.

But Ethan had learned to deal. He'd found a way to push them out of his head, to remind himself he was in a position to defend himself and his husband when necessary. The bullies no longer had any control over him. His family was there for them both and that was all that mattered.

Unfortunately, Beau didn't have the same support structure when it came to his biological parents. However, Beau did have Ethan's family, so at least there was that.

Despite the falling-out Beau had had with his folks, Ethan knew that the news of his father's stroke wasn't easy for him. The big guy was pretending as though it didn't matter, but it did. Beau had spent his entire life trying to live up to the ridiculously high standards Ben Bennett had for him.

"I don't want to go," Beau pleaded, his heavy footsteps sounding behind Ethan as they climbed the stairs and moved through the bedroom.

Stopping just short of the adjoining bathroom, Ethan turned to face his husband. "Yes, you do, Beau. He's your father."

Beau shook his head, his gaze somewhere on the floor between them.

Sighing, Ethan moved forward. How he'd become a man who could feel as much as he did for one person, he didn't know. Having spent his whole life pushing away everyone who tried to get close, Ethan now found it difficult to do so.

That was what Beau had done for him. The man had forced his way right into Ethan's world and taken up residence. He'd shown Ethan that there was more to life than the demons that had consumed him for so long. He'd shown Ethan love and respect, and because of that, Ethan had learned to love and trust those in his inner circle.

Which was why Ethan knew he had to be the one to push back when necessary.

It was now necessary.

"My mother wants me to apologize." Beau's wide shoulders slumped forward in defeat.

"Do you *want* to apologize?" Ethan already knew the answer, but he was trying to make a point.

Beau frowned. "Of course not. I have nothin' to apologize for."

"Then who says you have to?"

Ethan held back a laugh when Beau glared at him as though he'd just dropped onto earth and had no clue what was going on.

"I told you, my mother wants—"

Ethan placed his hands on Beau's hips and grinned. "I know what you said. But what I'm tellin' you is that what she wants doesn't matter. You're thirty years old and happily married. You don't owe them anything."

Beau's dark eyes shot up to his face. "Are you sayin' I'm old?"

"No." Ethan smirked. "You said it."

Beau narrowed his eyes and a small smile tugged at his lips. "But you'll always be older."

Ethan grinned. "True." He sobered as he held Beau's gaze. "Do you want to see your father?"

"Yes and no." Beau breathed out heavily. "If he dies, I'll regret not goin' to see him. On the other hand, I know it'll cause more harm than good."

Ethan cocked his head to the side, studying the man he loved. "Do you want me to stay home?"

"Fuck no."

Ethan wasn't sure he could sit back and let Beau go to the hospital alone. He wanted to be by his side, to have his back and shield him should it be necessary. Not that Beau couldn't hold his own. The man could and he would.

"Good. Because I want to be with you. But I'll do whatever you need me to do."

Beau stepped away and took a seat on the edge of the mattress. "Does it make me a bad person if I say I don't care what happens to him?"

Although Beau said the words, the way his voice cracked told Ethan otherwise. Enough that Ethan's heart broke a little more for him.

Going to his knees in front of Beau, Ethan placed his hands on the man's thighs, then looked him directly in the eye. "If you were any other person, I might believe you mean that. And honestly, it wouldn't make you a bad person. Your father is a cruel man, and believe me, I've wanted to kick his ass at least a dozen times."

"Only a dozen?" Beau forced a smile.

"It wouldn't've taken more than that," Ethan quipped. He squeezed Beau's thigh. "But I know you love him because he's your father. And I think goin' to the hospital is what's best."

Beau swallowed hard, then covered Ethan's hands with his own. "I'll only go if you're there."

"I don't wanna be anywhere else."

An hour and a half later, Ethan was sitting in the intensive care unit waiting room beside Beau. They had informed the nurses' station that they were there to see Ben Bennett, plus Beau had texted his mother, but no one had come out to get them, so they waited.

"She's doin' this on purpose," Beau grumbled.

Maybe so. But Ethan refused to let that woman get to him. Beau wanted to see his father, therefore, Beau would see his father. Ethan would make damn sure of it.

Twenty minutes passed before Arlene appeared. Her eyes scanned the few people there before coming to land on Beau. Ethan noticed the instant she saw her son because her eyes lit up. They dimmed just as quickly when she glanced over at Ethan.

"Your mother's up there," he whispered.

Beau lifted his head, then groaned low in his throat. Obviously he noticed her expression as well.

"I'll wait right here. If you need me, shoot me a text and I'll come back there."

It was obvious Beau didn't want him to stay back, but Ethan knew better than to cause a scene. That was the last damn thing he wanted. Sure, over the years he'd managed to get used to being with Beau in public and not caring who knew were together. It had taken a long time to get to that place. On the flip side, it was still something he was cognizant of. He'd never been one who wanted to draw attention to himself and that was something he couldn't seem to change.

Beau stood, then straightened his shirt before making his way over to his mother. At six feet six inches, Beau towered over her. Then again, the man towered over most people. Well, except for Ethan and his brothers. In fact, Beau fit in rather well with all of them.

When Beau and his mother disappeared down the hall, Ethan retrieved his cell phone from his pocket. He pulled up his father's number and shot him a text to let him know what had happened.

His father was quick to respond.

Pop: *You need us to come up there?*

Ethan: *No. Good for now. Just wanted you to know.*

Pop: *Let me now if you or Beau need me, boy. I'll be there in a heartbeat.*

Ethan's chest constricted at his father's response. There had never been a doubt in his mind that his parents loved him. And even now that he was grown and married, Curtis and Lorrie ensured he knew. They were the same with Beau because he was as much family as the rest of them.

He took a deep breath and tried to fight down the panic that threatened. He hadn't bothered to mention his intense distaste for hospitals to anyone. While he tolerated the labor and delivery wings, he'd always hated the sterility of it all, knowing there were sick people all around him, but when his mother had nearly died, Ethan had faced a fear he'd prayed he would never have to face.

And sitting here brought it all back.

"I THOUGHT I TOLD YOU IT WOULD be best not to bring him here," Arlene said as soon as they slipped out of the waiting room and into the wide hallway lined with rooms.

Beau wasn't sure what to say to that. His first instinct was to go on the defensive, but that would only cause a scene. Considering they were in a hospital, now wasn't the time and this certainly wasn't the place, so he held his tongue.

"At least have the decency to remove that ... thing on your finger."

Beau glanced down at his hand, then stopped mid-stride and held up his ring finger. "It's a tattoo, Mom. It's permanent." He and Ethan had gone the tattoo route because there was too much risk of wearing a ring with the work they did. The chance of losing a finger or damaging the ring was far too great. Beau was grateful the tattoo was permanent.

His mother glared at him. "That's ridiculous."

Beau sighed. "I think it'd be better if you ... kept your opinions to yourself."

Arlene's eyes widened and she jerked back as though he'd slapped her. "How dare you speak to me that way."

Not moving, Beau crossed his arms over his chest, his thumb rubbing circles over his ring finger. It was a nervous tic he found himself doing quite frequently. While he couldn't feel the ink on his skin, he knew it was there.

Despite his desire to keep this meeting civil, Beau refused to back down from this woman. Growing up, Beau had never stood up to his mother or his father. He'd been the good kid, living the life his father wanted for him even though he'd detested the path he'd been going down. It wasn't until his senior year of high school, when an injury had kept him from his father's football dream, that Beau had understood he was merely a pawn in his father's chess game of life. Their relationship had started to deteriorate soon after.

However, Beau had learned a thing or two being a part of the Walker family. He didn't have to sit back and let people walk all over him. Yeah, his mother and father had brought him into the world, but he owed them nothing. Not anymore. He'd been the dutiful son, but he wasn't a child. He was a grown man who was proud of who he'd become. And he was damn proud to call Ethan his husband.

Not even his mother could take that from him.

"Maybe it'd be best if I come back when you're not here," he said, keeping his voice low.

"And if he dies in the meantime?" she snapped.

Beau knew his mother was hanging on by a thread. Despite her nasty remarks, he could see the fear in her eyes. She was likely terrified that his father would die and she'd be left all alone. Ben Bennett had made sure to alienate his wife from everyone. And because of her determination to indulge his every whim as well as his ignorance when it came to others, Arlene didn't have anyone who supported her.

After taking a deep breath in through his nose, Beau slowly exhaled through his mouth, reining in his patience. "Let's go in and see him. Then I'll be out of your hair."

That seemed to appease her. Somewhat.

"I'd appreciate if you don't mention anything about your … friend."

"My husband," Beau corrected.

Her eyes narrowed. "Just don't mention him. The last thing we need is for you to cause another stroke. If he dies while you're here, it'll be all on you. You'll live the rest of your life knowing you disappointed him and he died because of it."

Oh, for fuck's sake. She was completely out of control.

He merely needed to go into the room, see his father, then be on his way. And if Ben Bennett died...

Well, that wasn't something Beau wanted to contemplate. He might not care much for the man, but he still loved the old bastard. He was his father, after all.

Squaring his shoulders, Beau followed Arlene into the room. His father was in the bed, hooked up to various machines. He was pale and much smaller than Beau remembered him being.

"Ben? Beau's here," Arlene said softly, gently touching his hand. "Your son's here."

"I don't have a son," Ben mumbled, his eyes still closed.

Beau ignored the pain in his chest. His father had disowned him a long time ago, but he thought for sure...

"What does he want?" Ben asked. "Why is he here?"

Well, it didn't appear the stroke had affected his attitude much.

"He wants to apologize," Arlene said.

Beau glared at his mother. He was not going to do anything of the sort.

"It's about time." Ben's eyes fluttered, then opened. "Apologize then."

Beau shook his head. "I'm not here to apologize. I came 'cause Mom called me. I wanted to see how you're doin'."

Ben stared at him, the same disappointment he'd always seen glittering in his eyes making the dark brown irises almost black.

"I'm none of your concern anymore," Ben said, his tone weak but still ringing with the same fury and indignation Beau was used to.

Seconds felt like hours as they stood there and stared at one another. Beau could see the hatred in his father's face, knew the man found him to be lacking in every way. It hadn't mattered how many times Beau had tried to be who Ben wanted him to be, he'd never succeeded. And he never would, either. And *that* had absolutely nothing to do with his sexual preference.

"Beau, it's time you stop this nonsense," Arlene said, drawing Beau's attention to her. "Your father ... is sick. It's time this charade came to an end because he needs you."

Beau inhaled and exhaled slowly. He wasn't going to rise to the bait. He had nothing to prove to these people anymore.

"You shacking up with that ... *devil man*... That's why your father can't look at you. You've embarrassed him ... *us*," Arlene continued.

Hmm. Was that a blunder on her part? Did she really buy into his father's filthy ideals? Or was she merely supporting him because she was the dutiful wife?

This were questions Beau couldn't ponder right now. Based on the way Arlene was glaring at him, Beau knew she was gearing up for another round.

"I love Ethan," he stated firmly, his gaze darting between the two of them. "That's not a charade. We're married and..."

Ben's dark eyebrow lifted as though urging him to continue.

For the longest time, Beau had secretly wished he could make amends with his parents. Fantasized that he would see them and they'd welcome him and Ethan with open arms. And for some absurd reason, he wanted so badly for his parents to be part of his child's life...

"We're gonna have a baby."

Ben's eyes widened in horror. "The hell you are," he snapped. "No son of mine is gonna bring a child into this world like that."

"But I'm *not* your son, remember?"

Arlene touched Ben's arm. "It's okay, Ben. It's not true. They can't have a baby together. God doesn't allow it."

Beau's attention jerked to her. He didn't like the way she said that. "There are ways."

"What?" she asked, sounding nothing like the meek woman who had raised him. "That adoption place? The one you're hoping will find you a surrogate?" Her lips thinned. "I know all about it, Beau. They called me." She patted Ben's hand as though comforting him. "I assured them you were in no position to have a child. That by allowing it, they were casting that child into hell."

Beau's eyes widened and his chest constricted. His voice was eerily calm when he spoke. "*What* did you say?"

"Did you think we were going to allow that?" Arlene asked, her eyes harder than he'd ever seen them. "I informed the kind woman who called that you did not have a family who supported this decision and that any woman who agreed to carry a child for you would be condemned as well. I told them how the Walkers had brainwashed you."

Was that true? Had she really told them that? Beau didn't want to believe it, but it made sense. Too much sense. At first, the woman at the agency had been eager to help them. Now she seemed...

"We will never support such a ridiculous act, and it's time you realize it. If you want a baby, settle down with a *woman*. One who will take care of you the way she's supposed to. *That's* the way God intended."

Beau didn't understand how his mother could support a sexist asshole like his father. But he'd long ago stopped trying to figure her out.

"I don't care what you support," Beau hissed. "It's not your place."

"But it is," Arlene said. "And I'm glad to see those places care about the children they bring into this world. They said it's procedure to call family members and make house visits to determine if there would be any risk to the children. I assured them a visit wasn't necessary because I confirmed there was a risk. I also informed them of … that man's problems."

Beau was shaking where he stood, his hands balled into fists at his side. "His *problems?*"

"Yes," Ben said, his voice weak but firm. "How he killed his high school friend, Beau. It's public knowledge. That young man took his own life because he was tormented by the devil. And now the devil's got his clutches on you."

Beau couldn't breathe. The room was closing in on him. He wanted nothing more than to wrap his hands around his father's throat and strangle him.

"You bastard!" Beau yelled.

Ben jerked as though Beau had struck him. The monitor he was hooked up to started beeping faster. Good. Beau hoped he was struck down for what he'd done.

The door opened and a nurse appeared. "Is everything all right in here?"

Beau ignored her. "It wasn't enough that you made my life hell? Now you can't mind your own damn business?"

"You *are* our business," Arlene said, here tone syrupy sweet. Obviously a front for their audience. "You're our child, Beau, and we love you. As your parents, we only want what's best. And we think you need psychiatric help."

"No, *Arlene*," Beau snapped, using her name because he knew it would hurt her. "I'm no longer your child. I'm a grown man, and I can make my own decisions."

She shook her head as though she pitied him. "If only you could make the *right* decisions."

"I think it's best you leave," the nurse said. "Or I'll have to call security."

Beau's gaze shot to his father. "I knew I shouldn't have come."

He pivoted to go but paused with his hand on the edge of the door when his mother called his name.

"We won't allow you to bring a child into this world, Beau. Not with that man. I'll do whatever it takes to ensure that never happens."

Beau turned to face his mother. "I pray for you every Sunday. Both of you." He nodded toward his father. "I only hope you find peace before it's too late."

Beau shoved the door, letting it hit the wall with a thud.

"You're going to hell, Beau!" his mother yelled. "You and that … *devil man*."

"Mrs. Bennett," the nurse scolded. "This is not good for your husband."

As he walked out of the room, Beau knew he would never see his parents again after this. Not willingly, anyway.

Still, he managed to put one foot in front of the other, even as he wondered how in the hell he was going to tell his husband that it was his fault they couldn't have a child. That it was his fault they would never have that opportunity.

Why is it so hard to breathe?

Chapter Five

THE INSTANT BEAU APPEARED IN THE WAITING room, Ethan knew something bad had happened. He could only assume the shouting he'd heard had been a confrontation between Beau and his parents.

Not that he was surprised. Beau's parents were poisonous.

Still, he had hoped like hell this visit would be different for Beau. He hated the idea of anyone hurting the man he loved. If Ethan could've kept them from Beau, he would have. Unfortunately, in this case, that wasn't an option, because Ethan would do whatever it took to make Beau happy, to ensure he didn't have any regrets. If his father died, Ethan knew Beau would never be able to live with himself knowing he hadn't spoken to him one last time.

However, based on the way Beau looked as he made a beeline for the hallway, Ethan was questioning that decision. Perhaps regrets weren't shit in the grand scheme of things.

Son of a bitch. What the fuck had they said to him?

Shooting to his feet, Ethan took off after Beau. He would've had to jog to catch up, so in an effort not to draw attention to himself, he maintained a quick pace but fought the urge to run. He followed Beau through the corridors, past the gift shop, and then out the doors into the courtyard that led to the parking lot.

When he stepped out into the bright August sunshine, Ethan paused. Beau wasn't heading toward the truck. No, he'd started to pace the sidewalk. Back and forth, again and again, his chest heaving as though he was trying to hold his anger in.

He moved closer. "Beau?"

Beau shook his head. "I need a minute, E."

Considering all the times he'd needed a minute, Ethan understood. However, he had to take one from Beau's book. When Ethan needed space, Beau didn't give it to him. Sometimes it irritated him, but he understood it. They were there for each other when it mattered, thick or thin, good and bad.

And it was his turn to step up to the plate and be the man Beau needed.

"Talk to me," Ethan urged, taking another step, then another, watching the way Beau's shoulders tensed. "How's your dad?"

"He's ... he's..." Beau snarled. "That man is *not* my father. Not anymore."

Shit. "What happened?"

Beau came to an abrupt halt, then spun to face him.

Ethan held his breath when he saw the pain in Beau's eyes. The light that usually made Beau's brown eyes sparkle was gone completely.

"You wanna know why we haven't found a surrogate yet?" Beau asked, his words hot, fueled by the barely repressed rage Ethan could feel coming off him in waves.

Ethan frowned, adjusting his ball cap on his head, confused as to how that had anything to do with this.

"My parents interfered, E. They fucking told the agency we weren't fit to be parents." His forehead creased. "They said they would ensure we never have a kid of our own."

"How did they do that?"

"The agency called them," Beau growled. "I put down their names because the form asked, but I never thought they would call them."

Ethan sighed. That made perfect sense. The information they'd had to divulge just to be considered was all-inclusive. The agency they were working with was privy to so much of their personal information, including their family members.

Why he hadn't figured that out before now, Ethan wasn't sure. He'd known the agency had called everyone in his family. His brothers, even his parents had told Ethan about how they'd received calls asking about the two of them. However, Ethan had put them down specifically as references, not merely family members.

Ethan hadn't considered they would've weighed their decision on two homophobic assholes, but he should've known. That was the way things went for him. There was always someone there to take him down a peg or two.

"I'm sorry, E."

Ethan's head snapped up, his eyes locking on Beau's face. "For what?"

"It's all my fault. We're never gonna have a family."

Without thinking, Ethan closed the distance between them. He stepped right up to the big guy and cupped Beau's face. "We're already a family."

There were tears in Beau's eyes and Ethan's insides squeezed. He could feel Beau's pain, knew deep down that Beau wanted a baby more than anything. "I know, but … I'm so sorry, E."

"Don't you dare apologize for this. This is *not* your fault," Ethan assured Beau. "I will find a way to give you a baby."

"I just don't understand," Beau whispered, his voice full of torment. "How can they do this? I couldn't imagine hurting my own flesh and blood this way."

Ethan couldn't, either. He'd never been perfect, but even so, his own parents had loved him and his brothers unconditionally.

In his peripheral vision, Ethan saw people walking past them, watching. His first instinct was to pull away, to put distance between him and Beau. Only he didn't want to. Beau was the only person who mattered out here. Not the onlookers who were curious as to why they were standing so close.

"I love you, Beau," Ethan said, keeping his tone firm, probably loud enough the people around them could hear. Fuck them. It wasn't their business. "I love you more than anything. We'll get through this, I swear it."

As though he felt Ethan's tension, Beau started to pull away, but Ethan snaked his hand behind Beau's neck and held him there. "Don't walk away from me."

"Never," Beau said softly. His eyes darted to the strangers moving around them. "I just don't want to embarrass you."

Ethan sucked in air because it was suddenly scarce. *"Embarrass me?* You could *never* embarrass me, Beau. You're my husband, and I love you."

"I know how hard it is for you."

"It's not hard anymore. I have you. That makes it easy. You're the only thing that matters." To prove it, Ethan leaned in and kissed him. "The *only* thing."

"I'm ready to go home," Beau stated, his tone defeated.

"Okay." Ethan dropped his hands. "We can go home. But I need to go back inside for a minute."

Beau nodded. "I'll wait here."

Ethan was shocked that Beau hadn't asked him why, but he didn't offer up the information, either. Instead, he turned and headed back into the hospital, going straight for the ICU. Rather than barge into Ben's room, Ethan went to the nurses' station and requested they ask Arlene to come out.

The nurse eyed him cautiously, but finally nodded before slipping down the hall.

Surprisingly, Arlene appeared a few minutes later. The hatred in her eyes was familiar, but he ignored it. Knowing she wouldn't follow him to somewhere private, he merely paired off with her right there in the hallway.

"What do you want?"

Ensuring he kept his back straight, Ethan stared down at the woman who shouldn't have the honor of calling herself Beau's mother.

"I have vowed to love, cherish, and take care of Beau until the day I die," he informed her. "I think it's fair you know I fully intend to do that. He told me what you said. About how we shouldn't be allowed to have kids... If you could see that man with his nieces and nephews, you'd want that for him, too." Ethan pointed toward the room she'd come out of. "Unfortunately, you've allowed that man to poison your mind with his venom. Otherwise, I wouldn't have to tell you this. You'd've already seen it for yourself."

"No one has poisoned my mind," Arlene argued, although Ethan could see the doubt in her death glare. "My opinions are my own."

"I hope so," he told her. "Because you pay for your own sins. No one else pays for yours."

Her eyes narrowed, but she didn't respond.

"I have every intention of expanding our family with a child, regardless of what you want. I will ensure Beau becomes a father. You might've interfered up to this point, but you won't stop it from happening."

"I wouldn't bet on that, Mr. Walker. God has a plan, and it's my duty to ensure it's followed to the letter."

Ethan smirked, ensuring she saw the ferocity he felt when it came to protecting the man he loved. "I've dealt with the likes of you my entire life, Mrs. Bennett. People who think they're warriors for the cause because they don't agree with who I am. I failed to stand up for myself, but I assure you, I will stand up for Beau, no matter the cost."

"You're going to hell," she hissed. "And you're gonna take my son with you. That's on you, Mr. Walker. You're the one who'll pay for that. Not me. *My* God does not approve of you."

Ethan exhaled in relief. "Well, it's a good thing your god isn't my God. Because *my* God doesn't approve of me passing judgment and making those decisions for Him. I feel sorry for you, Mrs. Bennett. I really do. It must be hell living with so much hate in your heart."

She gasped, her mouth opening, then closing.

"I'm not here to seek your permission or your approval." He kept his voice low, calm. "I've never needed that to love Beau. His opinion is the only one that matters to me." Ethan ensured she held his gaze. "I'm not one to make threats, Mrs. Bennett, but I suggest you don't call Beau or interfere with his life again. Because if you do and you break his heart the way you did today, you won't like the man I become."

Without waiting for her to respond, Ethan turned and walked away. He hadn't come here intending to confront that hateful woman, but it was high time he stood up for what was important to him. Beau meant everything to him, and Ethan didn't give a shit who Arlene and Ben Bennett thought they were. They certainly wouldn't come between the two of them and happiness.

Ethan would make damn sure of that.

BEAU CONTINUED TO PACE THE PARKING LOT for several minutes. He appreciated the fact that Ethan had given him some time to cool off. The rage that had burned in his veins had settled from a boil to a simmer, and he could finally breathe.

He saw the door to the building open and he peered over to look. Ethan was sauntering toward him, his expression calm.

"Where'd you go?"

"I'm driving." Ethan held out his hand for the keys when he approached.

Not wanting to argue, Beau passed them over. "Where'd you go?" he repeated.

"I had a few things to say to your mother." Ethan walked around to the driver's side, his words just as cool as his expression.

Beau stopped suddenly, staring at Ethan over the hood of the truck. "You did *what?*"

Ethan didn't respond as he opened the driver's door and climbed inside. Beau had no choice but to get in the truck, so he did.

His eyes shot to the hospital, then back to Ethan. He couldn't help wondering what had been said. He hated the idea of Arlene hurting him in any way, even with words.

Ethan backed out of the parking space and headed toward the exit.

Beau wanted to apologize again, but he held his tongue. The last thing he wanted was to upset Ethan more than he already was. Having learned that Beau's parents had hindered—perhaps indefinitely—their ability to have children was hard enough to deal with. Knowing that it was his own fault made it worse.

He should've never come here today. If he hadn't, Beau wouldn't have known the true depth of his parents' hatred for him. Although he hadn't talked to them in years, it still hurt that they would so cold-heartedly stab him in the back like that. They hadn't parted on good terms, but there was no denying he'd hoped they could make up one day. He'd even imagined his mother holding his son or daughter.

Evidently that was never going to happen.

"What did you say to her?" Beau asked when they'd driven in silence for almost twenty minutes.

"I told her she wouldn't interfere going forward."

He said it so matter-of-factly. As though there hadn't been some sort of argument.

Beau knew his mother. She might play the meek card, but the woman could be vicious when she wanted to be. He'd seen it plenty. She lived her life to support her husband, but she had a backbone underneath the layers of weakness she'd shrouded herself in. Unfortunately, the only time she allowed others to see it was when she was defending her husband.

"I'm sorry," Beau whispered, peering over at Ethan.

Surprisingly, Ethan took his hand, linking their fingers. "Don't apologize for them. It's not worth the breath."

For the rest of the drive, they remained silent. Beau didn't know what to say, but he took comfort in the fact that Ethan was holding his hand. He had no idea whether or not he could fix this, but at least he still had Ethan.

A short time later, Ethan was pulling into the driveway that led toward their house at the back of the Walker ranch. Instead of following the winding dirt road, Ethan pulled over in front of Curtis and Lorrie's.

Beau looked around, surprised by the detour. "What're we doin'?"

"We're gonna have a chat with my folks," Ethan said, as though there was no discussion to be had.

Once again, Beau found himself following Ethan's lead.

He hopped out of the truck and forced his legs to carry him up the porch steps that led to the kitchen door. He stepped inside, his eyes taking a moment to adjust to the dim light. When he was able to focus, he noticed Curtis and Lorrie sitting at their kitchen table, two coffee mugs and a large vase of flowers between them.

"How's your father?" Curtis asked, his gaze locked on Beau.

Not having a real answer for that, he offered a shrug. "Never really got that far."

Curtis nodded, then pointed to the chair across from him. "Sit."

Lorrie smiled, then peered over at Curtis. "I'm gonna finish up the laundry."

Curtis gave his wife a quick smile but didn't argue.

Beau knew she was offering them a few minutes of privacy because it was clear Curtis had something on his mind. Only after Lorrie exited the room did Beau realize Ethan wasn't standing in the kitchen.

"Tell me what happened," Curtis urged.

Resigned to having this conversation, Beau pulled out one of the chairs and dropped into it. He explained the phone call from his mother, his reluctance to go, Ethan's insistence that he see his father.

"As expected, my mother asked that I not bring Ethan to the hospital with me. When she saw him, she was angry." He shrugged again. "Ended up takin' it out on me."

"What did she say?" Curtis glanced toward the living room when Ethan's voice rose, several curse words falling from his lips.

Beau had to assume Ethan was on the phone, because he could hear him pacing the floor in the living room.

When Curtis turned back to Beau, his eyebrows were raised as he nodded toward Ethan. "Somethin' obviously happened to trigger his temper."

Yeah. Beau's parents had happened.

"From what they told me," Beau explained, "they interfered with our attempt to find a surrogate." Beau felt the coldness seep into his chest when he thought about what his parents had done.

"How?"

"When the agency called to talk to them, they told them any child they helped us have would be condemned to hell because God didn't approve of us having children."

Curtis leaned back, his wrist resting on the table, fingers curled around his coffee mug handle. He appeared calm and collected, the complete opposite of how Beau was feeling.

"Honestly," Beau admitted, "I never put two and two together. Not once did I think my parents were behind this."

"Why would you?"

Beau was pretty sure that was a rhetorical question.

"You heard me, Travis," Ethan snarled from the other side of the wall. "I want it dealt with. People like that don't get to sit on their fucking high horse and control the world around them."

Curtis appeared unfazed by Ethan's outburst, but Beau's eyes widened. Was he talking about Beau's parents?

"All right. Yeah. Thanks." Ethan appeared a second later.

"What was that about?" Beau asked, his curiosity getting the best of him.

Ethan took a seat in one of the empty chairs. "That service helping to find a surrogate is at fault for this." His eyes lifted from the table, darting between Beau and Curtis. "Travis vouched for that agency and they've failed us. Since they had the audacity to send that woman who propositioned us and then they decided they couldn't help us, I'm gonna make sure they feel some of the heat for this."

"Not gonna change the outcome," Curtis said, his gaze on his son.

"Maybe not. But I'll feel better about it."

Beau took a deep breath and stared at Ethan. "I'm sorry."

"Don't you apologize," both Walker men said at the same time.

Feeling appropriately chastised, Beau nodded. "It's just—"

Curtis cut him off. "Life isn't always easy, boy. We take the good with the bad and we learn to deal. There are times we can't control the situation, nor can we help when things seem to be out of control. However, we can stick together. Your parents have their own beliefs, Beau. It's their prerogative."

"It's not fair that they can affect our happiness," Beau argued.

"No, it's not." Curtis sat up straight, his other arm coming to rest on the table as he faced Beau. "It's times like these that I remind myself of one thing."

Beau waited, eager for Curtis to bestow his wisdom upon him.

Curtis smirked. "Karma's a bitch."

Ethan chuckled, then leaned back in his chair. "And what karma doesn't take care of, my brother will."

Okay, when they put it that way, maybe Beau had no choice but to let nature take its course. Because Ethan was right. Travis Walker was a force to be reckoned with.

Beau wasn't even sure karma would go up against that guy.

TRAVIS WALKER DID HIS BEST TO PRETEND his head wasn't about to explode off his body.

After hearing Ethan relay the details of what those fucking assholes did to Beau—his own fucking *parents*—he was ready to kill someone.

Not that he would. Travis was a lot of things, but taking a life wasn't something he would seriously contemplate. However … if he were, Arlene and Ben Bennett would be first on his list of lives to eliminate.

Once safely seated in his truck, he gripped the steering wheel with both hands and squeezed it so tightly his knuckles turned white.

"Relax," he ordered himself as he unwound one hand so he could put the key in the ignition.

He started the truck and turned down the radio. As he was pulling out of the gas station parking lot, he hit the button to call Gage.

"Hey," his husband greeted. "Thought you were comin' into the office this mornin'."

"I am. Had to stop for gas, then got a call from Ethan."

Gage's tone went serious. "Somethin' wrong?"

"You could say that." Travis took a deep breath. "Ben Bennett had a stroke. The bastard's too ornery to keel over, so I'm sure he'll be fine, but Arlene took the opportunity to invite Beau to the hospital so she could belittle him."

"Doesn't surprise me," Gage said. "They're homophobic assholes."

"Yeah. Well. That's not all."

"Shit," Gage grumbled. "What'd they do?"

"Arlene informed Beau that she talked to the agency they've been working with. She's the reason they can't find a surrogate. She told them that they were unstable and any child they brought into the world would be cast into hell."

"For fuck's sake."

Exactly.

Travis was all about the sticks-and-stones bullshit. He'd heard plenty of shit in his life and he honestly couldn't care less what people said about him. But his tolerance disappeared when it came to standing in the way of someone's happiness.

For those people to interfere with Beau and Ethan's desire to have a baby, to expand their family… They had no fucking right.

It irked the shit out of him that there was nothing anyone could do to move things along for his brother. While Travis couldn't exactly relate to Ethan's pain, he understood it. He was lucky in the sense that he had a wife who could bear their children, but he could put himself in Ethan's shoes, too. Travis was bisexual and he was lucky enough to have both Kylie and Gage. He loved them equally. But if Kylie hadn't been in their lives, Travis would still spend the rest of his days with Gage, and if they had decided to pursue a family the unconventional way, he would've moved heaven and earth to ensure no one interfered with that plan.

His brother deserved the same.

"When did this happen?" Gage's rough voice came through the phone.

"The incident happened today. At the hospital."

"Son of a bitch."

"My thoughts exactly." Travis sighed. "Look, I'm headin' in now. I wanna talk about this some more. I want to know who they were workin' with at the surrogate service. Whoever they are, they no longer have a job as far as I'm concerned. I don't care how high I have to go."

"Understood. I'll do some digging."

"Thanks. Love you."

"Love you, too. See you when you get here."

The call disconnected and Travis focused on the road while a million thoughts raced through his head.

How the fuck could parents turn on their kids like that? He would protect his children with his life if it came to it. Without batting an eyelash. And people like Arlene and Ben Bennett did their best to hurt their own child in ways that Travis couldn't even fathom.

He punched another button on his phone to make another call.

"Tavoularis."

"Hey, Reese. Need your help."

"What's up, Trav?"

Travis relayed the details of what had happened with Beau's parents. He was met with the same disbelief from a man who'd become close to the Walkers in recent years. A man Travis personally knew he could trust to handle the things that he needed to keep his hands clean of.

"That fuckin' sucks," Reese told him. "I can't imagine what I'd do if my brother was up against some shit like that."

Reese's brother, Z, was married to a man. While Travis didn't know whether RT and Z intended to have a family one day, if they did, it was highly likely they could end up in the same boat, depending on a service that got to pick and choose who was worthy and who was not.

Travis would handle the service, but he needed someone to keep an eye out for Ethan and Beau.

"I want you to watch Ben and Arlene," Travis stated.

"Like follow them around?"

"Not necessarily. But you need to have eyes on them at all times." Travis would let Reese figure out how to make that happen.

"Sure thing. He still in the hospital?"

"Yeah. Not sure how long he'll be there. I'll have Gage get you the details when he has them. But once he's released, I need to know whenever they leave the house and where they go. I don't care what you have to do, but you ensure they don't get close to Ethan or Beau again."

"And if I end up in jail?" Reese asked with a chuckle.

"I know a good lawyer."

"Great."

"Anytime. I just need you to keep an eye on 'em."

"Got it."

"Keep me updated, Reese."

"Will do."

Travis pulled into the resort parking lot as he replayed his conversation with Ethan in his head.

"I need your help, Trav."

"What's up?"

"It doesn't look like we're gettin' a surrogate after all."

"What? Why?"

That was when Ethan had gone through the details of what Arlene had told Beau. Travis had done his best to keep his cool. Somehow he'd managed.

"What do you need from me?"

Ethan's voice held more emotion than Travis had ever heard. *"I know I asked you to stay out of it before, but…" Ethan sighed. "I fully intend to give Beau a baby. I won't let them interfere again. And if they come near Beau—"*

"Say no more. I got it. Do you know who they talked to at the agency?"

"No. And I don't know the name of the woman Beau's been talkin' to, either."

The only thing Travis had been able to do was agree that he would help Ethan in any way he needed. Since Travis had given them the name of the service thanks to a friend of a friend vouching for them, he felt somewhat responsible.

At the very least, Travis would ensure those who had interrupted his brother's attempt to have a family wouldn't have the ability to do so for a little while. They would be unemployed by the end of today. That he could guarantee.

He shut off the truck and climbed out. Maybe if he brainstormed with Gage, they could come up with an idea on what else they could do to help out. Unfortunately, he knew finding someone who would carry Beau and Ethan's child and not cause more damage was going to be difficult. It wasn't like he could simply put an ad in the paper.

On the other hand, Travis had never backed down from a challenge before. And if it was within his power to help his brother, he would.

No matter what it took.

Chapter Six

Friday, August 31, 2018
(Six days later)

BEAU WAS FINISHING UP BENEATH THE TRUCK he'd been working on when he heard a familiar voice echo off the metal walls of the shop.

"Ethan? Where're you at?" Travis called out.

"In the office," Ethan hollered back.

While it wasn't unusual for Travis to stop by unexpected, it hadn't happened in quite some time. And certainly not at the shop on a Friday. Perhaps that was the reason Beau was curious as to what had prompted this Friday afternoon drop-in.

Beau heard the office door click shut and his curiosity intensified. He couldn't remember the last time that office door had been closed unless Beau and Ethan were getting down and dirty inside the small office.

Rolling himself out from under the truck, Beau grabbed a nearby grease rag and wiped his hands before pushing to his feet. He stared at the closed office door for a minute, wondering what the hell Ethan and Travis were talking about. He knew it could've been anything.

Perhaps something to do with Walker Demolition, although he doubted it. Travis had long ago shifted his focus to Alluring Indulgence Resort. Years ago, when he implemented his dream of a world-famous fetish resort, Travis had passed on the day-to-day business of the demolition company. Initially, the lead-the-charge baton had been handed off to Ethan's cousin Jared. Since that time, the lead spot had been transferred from Jared to Reese Tavoularis when Jared got hitched to Hope and started helping out at Dead Heat Ranch. Regardless of who was at the helm these days, things had been running smoothly. Beau and Ethan didn't see much of Reese because he trusted them to take care of their shit, which they did.

So he doubted it was related to the demolition company.

Maybe a family issue?

Nah. Probably not. Beau would've been included.

Perhaps it was—

Beau didn't get a chance to speculate further or debate on whether he should interrupt or not because the door opened and Travis sauntered out.

"Hey," Travis greeted with a wave on his way out the door.

Well, he didn't look guilty. Then again, Travis probably hid his guilt well.

"Hey back." Beau watched Travis leave as quickly as he'd arrived.

Ethan stepped out of the office behind him and Beau turned his attention toward the sexy man with his ball cap on backward. Admittedly, Beau fucking fell completely in lust all over again when Ethan did that. He wasn't sure what it was about him, but there was something that lit Beau up from the inside out.

"What was that about?" he asked Ethan, unable to quell his curiosity.

Ethan's gaze shot over to him as though he hadn't expected him to be standing there. "Nothin'. Just had to ask him a question."

"About?" Beau tossed the grease rag onto the truck.

"Nothin' important."

Now why did that sound like a lie?

For the past week, ever since Beau had visited his father in the hospital, Ethan had been acting ... different. Not upset, necessarily, but certainly not happy. Beau had pretended it had nothing to do with him, but he suspected it did. While Beau was the one who'd been pushing for them to have a baby, he knew Ethan was open to the idea. In fact, he'd go so far as to say he was looking forward to it.

Unfortunately, that was no longer an option for them. After his mother revealed what she'd done, Beau had immediately contacted the woman who'd been helping them. Surprisingly, she had come clean, informing him that their agency would not be able to assist. She said it was important that a child be brought up in a family full of love and that it was obvious theirs wasn't stable. She had apologized and informed him that she would no longer be seeking a surrogate for them.

Yesterday afternoon, unable to resist, Beau had called to try to reason with her. That was when he had learned that the woman who'd been running the agency was no longer employed there. He had no idea what had happened but he suspected Travis had something to do with it.

Regardless of whether she'd been punished or not, the fact that they wouldn't be having a baby had broken his fucking heart. For the first time in a long time, Beau had broken down and cried. Ethan had been there. He'd even held Beau for the longest time, but Ethan had masked his emotion. He'd locked it down deep, and for the past six days, it had been festering inside him. He was upset and his indifference to the situation bothered Beau.

"Talk to me, E," he urged, ignoring the concern churning in his gut.

Ethan smiled, but it was forced. He lifted his ball cap, slid his hand over his hair, then put it back on. That simple move made Beau's blood heat.

Ethan glanced out the door, then back to Beau. "About what?"

"Why did Travis come by?"

Ethan frowned. "Do you have a problem with my brother stopping by the shop?"

"No. Of course not." Beau recognized Ethan's tactic. The man went on the defensive whenever he didn't want to talk. It was a situation Beau had found himself in plenty of times over the years.

Oddly enough, Ethan's evasive attitude spurred the fear and anger Beau had buried deep since his encounter with his parents. He stalked Ethan until his husband was backed up against the wall.

"Is somethin' goin' on?" Beau probed, his voice low, his concern palpable.

"No." Ethan put his hands on Beau's chest and pushed. "I've got shit to do, Beau."

Yep. Defensive.

Before Ethan could walk by him, Beau grabbed his shirt and jerked him back.

Ethan stumbled. "What the fuck?"

Beau crowded him against the wall, their eyes locked. Beau did his best to read Ethan's mind, to figure out what the hell was going on.

When Ethan tried to move past him once more, Beau held him there by placing his hand on Ethan's neck. He didn't press down, simply kept him from getting away.

"I don't have time for this, Beau." The gleam in his eyes belied his words.

"You've always got time for this," Beau countered.

The instant the words were out, Ethan's eyes flashed with heat. Yeah. That was what Beau thought. Ethan was looking for a fight. Something was bothering him, but he wasn't going to talk. Which meant Beau would have to push him, and as was usually the case, they would fight it out with some rough, raunchy sex.

Like he'd said, this wasn't new.

Beau leaned in until his mouth was only a fraction of an inch away from Ethan's. "Why was your brother here?"

Ethan glared at him but didn't speak.

So Beau did what he knew would work. He slammed his lips against Ethan's, kissing him roughly.

In an instant, Ethan's hands were fisted in Beau's shirt, jerking him closer. This was the distraction Ethan always needed. He thought it would keep Beau from asking questions, but it wasn't going to work this time.

Before he could get lost in Ethan's kiss, he pulled back, then forcefully spun Ethan around so that he was face-first against the wall.

"What the fuck?" Ethan bellowed, trying to push back against him.

Beau pressed his chest to Ethan's back, eliminating his ability to escape. "Either you talk or I torture you."

Ethan's head turned and he smirked. "Do your worst, baby."

Beau leaned in and nipped Ethan's neck. "Oh, I plan to."

And now was as good a time as any.

It would've been easy to tell Beau why Travis had stopped by, but personally, Ethan preferred this method of interrogation. While he didn't have anything to hide, he sure did have a fond appreciation for Beau's need to force his hand.

"You gonna stand there all day or what?" Ethan taunted.

Ethan couldn't count how many times they'd had sex in the office, but it never got old.

Beau's arm slid around Ethan's neck as he tugged him backward. Ethan grinned, knowing Beau couldn't see his smile. When Beau urged him toward the small office, Ethan pretended to fight him.

"Scared someone might walk in on us?"

Beau stopped suddenly, shoving Ethan against the wall once again, his mouth sliding against Ethan's ear.

It amused Ethan how rough Beau was. It was just enough to exert dominance, but he always ensured he didn't hurt Ethan. It was a game, something to keep the embers burning between them. And sure, Ethan could admit he enjoyed the hell out of provoking the beast.

"You want that?" Beau growled roughly, his breath fanning Ethan's cheek. "You want me to fuck you right here? Out in the open?"

"Fuck, yes," he moaned, unable to hide his need.

The warehouse was hot, but it didn't matter to him. He'd take Beau any way he could get him. Especially when he was like this. Beau's dominant side was a force of nature that had the power to blow Ethan's mind.

And yes, he knew just how to push Beau's buttons, too. It was what kept things between them interesting.

"Tough shit," Beau said. "You're not in charge this time."

Ethan chuckled as Beau yanked him backward again before guiding him in the direction of the office. Once inside, Beau released him, shoving him toward the desk.

"Pants down," Beau commanded. "And bend over the fucking desk."

Hell yeah. This was what he needed. What Beau needed, too. There was no denying things had been tense these past few days. Ever since Beau broke down, Ethan had been fighting his own demons. However, he'd decided he wouldn't succumb to them this time.

No, Ethan wasn't going to be a victim of hatred the way he'd spent his entire life. It was time he took matters into his own hands. And with Travis's help, Ethan knew he would succeed in giving Beau everything he'd ever wanted.

Ethan unbuttoned and unzipped, then shoved his jeans down to his ankles. Without an ounce of shame, he bent over the desk while Beau rummaged through it. Somewhere in that mess of shit was lube, which he knew was what Beau was looking for.

Beau must've found it because he slammed the drawer shut and stood tall. Rather than lube himself up, he set the bottle on the desk beside Ethan, then moved behind him. Big hands palmed his ass, squeezing and kneading, ratcheting up his desire tenfold.

Ethan held his breath, waiting for Beau to do what he intended to do, but it never came. Beau was tormenting him, all right.

"Fuck me," Ethan growled. "Stop fuckin' playin'."

"Where's the fun in that?"

Ethan groaned when Beau shoved his shirt up, his lips landing in the center of his back, trailing down his spine. The cool air from the vents overhead made his skin prickle with awareness, but it was nothing compared to the way Beau's mouth inched lower.

Without a word, Beau spread Ethan's ass cheeks wide, his tongue diving between, making him hiss and moan. Raw pleasure slammed into him.

"Hell, yes," Ethan groaned. "Your fucking tongue … oh, damn, it feels so good."

Beau moaned, but he didn't stop, rimming Ethan's asshole ruthlessly. The only time he paused was to thrust his tongue inside Ethan's ass. When Ethan tried to grind back against him, Beau smacked his ass.

He chuckled to himself but gripped the desk firmly, holding on while Beau assaulted him in the most exquisite way.

That wicked tongue never faltered, but Ethan felt Beau's hand when it reached for the lube. It appeared his husband wasn't nearly as patient as he pretended to be. He needed this as much as Ethan did.

"You want my dick?" Beau finally asked as he stood.

"Yes."

Beau pressed the head of his cock against Ethan's asshole. "Hard and fast? Or slow and easy?"

Ethan knew not to tell him. Whatever he said, Beau would do the opposite. "Either way works for me."

Beau chuckled. "Of course it does. You just want my cock."

Yep. Beau knew him better than anyone else.

Ethan groaned when Beau finally pushed inside him. Those strong hands gripped Ethan's hips, holding him still as Beau's cock stretched his ass, filling him.

Damn. He loved these moments … when the two of them came together like this. It didn't matter if it was sweet and indulgent or fast and dirty, with Beau it was always an adventure. The world was brighter, sounds sharper when he was one with the man.

And yes, he knew how all that shit sounded, but he didn't care. Beau had opened his eyes to a world he'd never known. Thanks to Beau, Ethan knew love on a level that transcended everything.

"I love watching my dick slide inside you," Beau said roughly. "It blows my fucking mind every time."

Beau was going to torture him. He always did. While Ethan tried to do the same, it never worked. His need for Beau won out every single time and he ended up fucking him hard, claiming him in the most brutally magnificent ways. Beau, on the other hand, could last far longer than Ethan.

And he did.

Minutes passed as Beau pushed in, then retreated. He continued the slow, torturous pace until Ethan was sweating, his body trembling. He needed more, but he didn't dare ask for it.

"You gonna tell me what your brother wanted?"

"No." The last thing he wanted to do was talk about Travis.

"Then I guess you're not gonna come."

Oh, he would come one way or the other. Beau had no control over that. As it was, he could easily come like this. Simply having Beau moving inside him was enough to push him over the edge.

Beau suddenly stopped, his cock lodged to the hilt inside Ethan. "I won't move until you tell me."

Damn it.

Ethan tried to buck against him, but Beau's legs kept him trapped in place.

"Fuck me, damn you," Ethan growled after a few painful moments. He couldn't take this. He was on edge. He needed Beau to send him over.

"Can't do it," Beau said, his cock pulsing inside Ethan's ass.

Okay, fine. He'd underestimated Beau. The man had figured out just how to bring him to his knees.

"Fine," Ethan snapped. "Fuck me, and I'll tell you."

"Doesn't work that way, baby. Start talkin'."

"I asked Travis to stop by," he admitted.

As a reward, Beau pulled out and pushed back in, but he stopped instantly.

Ethan hissed. "Fuck me."

"Talk."

"I wanted to ask him a question."

Again, Beau pulled out and pushed back in but he stopped.

Fuck.

Maybe if he pleaded, Beau would give in. "You're killin' me, Beau."

"You can endure."

No, actually, he couldn't. Once more, Ethan tried to impale himself on Beau's cock, but he was held firmly in place.

"I need you," Ethan whispered.

He felt Beau's hands loosen, but they quickly tightened. He wasn't falling for Ethan's usual tactics.

Son of a bitch.

"Spill it," Beau commanded.

"Fine. I asked Travis for a favor."

Beau pulled out, pushed in, stopped.

Ethan waited for long seconds. While he didn't have anything to hide, he wasn't sure how Beau would react to what Ethan was asking Travis to do.

"Tell me," Beau insisted. "And I'll make you come."

Aw, fuck.

"Okay," Ethan said, gripping the desk. "But you have to promise not to get mad."

Beau shifted, leaning over him. When he did, his cock pushed in deeper, brushing that blessed spot inside him, making his eyes roll back.

"I wanna give you a baby," Ethan admitted. "I'm askin' Travis to help. To find someone who'll carry our baby. I told him, at this point, I don't even care how he does it."

Beau's sharp inhale had Ethan's body tightening and not in a good way.

"Are you mad?"

"No." Beau's voice cracked on the single word.

Before Ethan could explain further, Beau pulled out and pushed in. He didn't rush, his hands sliding over Ethan's back as he fucked him. Slow, easy.

"Oh, fuck," Ethan moaned, allowing the desk to take his weight as Beau's hands curled over his shoulders, holding him in place. "Beau ... baby ... that feels good."

"E ... I'm gonna come. I can't..." Beau grunted and groaned.

"Come for me," Ethan commanded.

A few seconds, a few thrusts and then Beau cried out, his release triggering Ethan's. His head spun as his cock exploded. Thank fuck the desk was there, otherwise, Ethan would've been on the fucking floor.

He didn't give a shit that he was coming all over the side of the desk, either.

It could be cleaned.

Just as soon as he caught his breath.

BEAU DIDN'T WAIT FOR ETHAN TO CLEAN up before he tore out of the small office and headed to the bathroom. He fought the emotions overwhelming him.

Ethan had gone to Travis. He'd sought his brother's help because all other avenues had failed for them.

Beau wasn't sure how he felt about that.

He understood it, of course. Everyone in the Walker family had tried to help in the beginning, but they had respected their request to stay out of it. Several times Beau had wondered if things would've been different had they asked for help sooner.

He wasn't mad. Not by a long shot. However, there was a part of him that hurt because he couldn't do this for them. They would have to rely on Travis, something they'd all done a time or two. Travis came through for everyone again and again.

Which meant, if history repeated itself, then they were that much closer to having a baby.

Had Ethan done it because he felt they'd run out of options? He had said he told Travis he didn't care how it happened. Beau cared. He didn't want just any stranger carrying their baby. The pregnancy was extremely important. But maybe Travis knew someone who was willing to help.

A sob caught in his chest as hope built once more.

Leaning down, Beau splashed water on his face, then proceeded to clean himself up. Once he was finished, he was a little more in control.

That lasted until Ethan knocked on the door.

Swallowing hard, Beau pulled it open and stared back at the man he loved with all his heart. The worried look on Ethan's face nearly shattered him.

"I'm sorry," Ethan said. "I only went to Trav because I knew we needed his help. As much as I expect the system to work, it never does. Following rules has never worked in my favor."

Beau reached for Ethan, pulling him close and burying his face in Ethan's neck. "I love you, E."

"I love you, too. I know you wanted us to do this on our own, Beau, but——"

Beau shook his head, his nose pressing against Ethan's neck. "I don't care how it happens. I just want——"

"A baby. I know. I'll do anything to make you happy."

There was something in Ethan's tone that made Beau pull back. He stared into those beautiful blue-gray eyes. "I am happy, Ethan. *You* make me happy."

Ethan smiled, but it was sad. "But I know this means everything to you."

The tone of Ethan's voice said something entirely different than his words. Beau got the impression Ethan honestly believed this was the only thing that would keep them together. It wasn't true, but Beau knew Ethan's insecurities often overwhelmed him. He started believing that he wasn't worthy.

Beau shook his head and took a step back. "No. That's not true. Nothing's more important to me than you, Ethan."

He didn't appear convinced, and for a second, Beau saw the ghosts of Ethan's demons reflected in his eyes.

Holy shit.

Ethan honestly believed this was the only way Beau would be happy.

That tore something inside him wide open. Had he given Ethan that impression? He knew he'd been focused on this for a long time, but had he done it at Ethan's expense?

Oh, God.

Beau cupped Ethan's face, forcing him to look at him. "You mean more to me than anything in this world, E. Anything."

"I know how much you want a baby."

"You don't?"

"Of course I do. Because I want to make you happy."

Fucking hell. That sounded far too much like Ethan was only doing this because it was what Beau wanted.

"But I want a baby with you, E."

Ethan nodded. "Whatever I have to do to keep you, I will."

And there it was.

Beau's heart cracked at the pain he heard in Ethan's voice. They'd been going strong for so long, sometimes Beau forgot how fragile Ethan could be.

"You have me, Ethan. Now and always. Nothing will ever change that."

Ethan nodded again, as though he agreed, but Beau could see his skepticism. The last thing Beau wanted was for Ethan to agree only for Beau's benefit. They had to be in this together.

Maybe now wasn't the time.

"I'll call Travis," Beau said on a rush of air. "Let's tell him to hold off for now. I think this is a sign. Maybe we're not ready to be parents."

Ethan shook his head, his eyes hardening. "You're more than ready. And I'm tired of this shit. I'm not gonna let the hate that fills your parents win this time. You deserve to be happy. I'm gonna make that happen."

"Only if it's what you want, too," he said, unable to hide the plea in his tone.

Ethan's face sobered. "Of course it is. Don't doubt that for a second. I want a baby with you, Beau."

When Ethan started to pull away, Beau wrapped his arms around him and pulled him close. It felt as though something was cracking. A fissure that threatened to turn into a crater between them. Beau couldn't deal with that. He'd never been happier in his life than he was with Ethan.

"I love you," Beau whispered.

Ethan responded in kind, his body relaxing in Beau's hold.

Knowing that they could keep this up all day, Beau settled for kissing Ethan quickly, then releasing him. Despite their afternoon rendezvous, there was still work to be done. And Beau knew that once Ethan had his mind made up, he wouldn't budge. He was as hardheaded as they came.

Something must've clicked in Ethan's head because his eyes cleared as he stared back at Beau.

"I'm gonna call Reese," Ethan said. "Told him I'd let him know when he could bring some equipment in." He scanned the area. "If you're almost done with the truck, you can shift your focus to the dozer."

Beau nodded. "Ready when you are."

Ethan turned to go, but Beau reached for him once more.

"I mean it, E. You're it for me. Nothing is more important."

This time when Ethan smiled, it *almost* reached his eyes. "I know, baby. We're good."

"Swear it?"

"Swear."

Beau would have to settle for that. He would keep an eye on Ethan for a while, ensure he reinforced his words with actions so Ethan had no doubts. Once the man retreated, it became damn near impossible to pull him back.

"Let me know when you're done with that." Ethan nodded toward the truck. "Then I'll get the next one pulled in."

"Will do."

And with that, Beau turned his attention to work.

Granted, his focus was for shit, but for now, it was the best he had to offer.

Chapter Seven

Sunday, September 16, 2018
(Two weeks later)

"HOW'RE YOU FEELIN'?" BEAU ASKED CHEYENNE WHEN he came over and joined Ethan on the couch.

Ethan had been sitting there watching the houseful of people while Cheyenne sat quietly beside him, doing the same. They'd all shared dinner, just as they did every Sunday, but no one seemed in a hurry to leave. Usually, at least someone was out the door shortly after because they had something to do.

Didn't appear to be the case today.

"Better now that it's not quite so hot," Cheyenne told him, her hand coming to rest on her rounded belly. "Only a few more weeks and it can't get here soon enough."

Ethan looked away from his sister-in-law. He couldn't bear to listen to one more of them talk about how they were ready for their next child to be born. Earlier, he'd endured Jessie talking about how she could no longer see her feet while Ethan had done his best to smile. It wasn't that he held it against them, he was just struggling to listen to their hardships when he would give anything for him and Beau to experience it for themselves.

Sure, he'd tried his best not to let the disappointment flood him, but with every passing day, it was getting more and more difficult.

Beau leaned in closer. "You doin' all right?"

"Peachy," he lied.

"Babe—" Before Beau could question what was bothering him—which undoubtedly he would do—someone cleared their throat.

"Hey, everyone." Travis's voice broke through the various conversations taking place. "Would you mind comin' into the living room?"

Ethan glanced up from his spot on the couch, watching as the room filled. Pop moved into his recliner and Mason and Kate battled for the spot on his lap. Of course, Curtis didn't pick, he simply pulled them both up, seating them on his legs.

Zane quickly gave up his seat to their mother, smiling when she thanked him. Sawyer squeezed his way against the wall, cradling Brody to him. Several of the kids continued to play on the floor, not caring one bit that Travis had called a family meeting.

Travis's gaze came to rest on Ethan's face and suddenly his nerves rioted. Making eye contact, Ethan did his best to read his oldest brother's thoughts. Before he could contemplate what this could possibly be about, Ethan started shaking his head, urging Travis to abort whatever he was planning.

Of course, Travis's gaze swung elsewhere.

"I know this is gonna put someone on the spot, and I'll likely have to do some groveling later." Travis's eyes slid from one person to another. "But you know me. I tend to skip the asking permission part and move right into asking for forgiveness because it's already done."

A round of chuckles sounded but Ethan didn't so much as crack a smile. In fact, he felt like he was going to be sick.

"A few weeks ago, I was made aware of a situation. One that … let's just say, it didn't sit right with me. So, I've been doing some research, talking to people." Travis's gaze landed on Ethan again. "While I was able to right one of the wrongs, unfortunately, I couldn't make any headway on another front."

"Cryptic much?" Zane asked, grinning.

A swarm of disappointment flooded Ethan, but he fought to keep his expression masked. This wasn't the time or place for Travis to drop this bomb. Not if it meant hurting Beau in the process. While Ethan couldn't deny that he'd leaned on Travis more than once to get things taken care of, he hadn't considered the fact that his brother might not be able to make it happen.

"*However*," Travis continued, "there comes a time when someone throws you a curveball. One that surprises the shit out of you, but not because you're necessarily surprised."

Someone cleared their throat. "Language."

Travis's gaze shot to Kylie. "Sorry, baby."

She smiled back at him.

"That makes no sense," Zane offered. "Surprises you but doesn't?"

Travis rolled his eyes and held up his hand to silence Zane. "Anyway. I'm not here to put anyone on the spot, but I felt it was extremely important for everyone to hear this. Because, like I said, I was floored by the suggestion, but not at all surprised."

"Get on with it, Trav," Ethan stated, his tone reflecting the churning in his gut.

Travis cleared his throat but he didn't continue. In fact, he moved over to sit on the arm of the couch beside his wife.

"Ethan? Beau?"

Ethan's head snapped over when Zoey got to her feet. She squeezed Kaleb's hand, then moved toward them.

There was no way to hide the confusion on his face. Whatever was going on here, he couldn't figure it out. Had Travis talked to Zoey about their situation? Did she possibly know someone? Anyone who could find them a surrogate?

Suddenly, Zoey went to her knees in front of them, her small hands reaching for theirs. Ethan allowed his fingers to go slack, not sure what the hell she was doing.

"I heard what happened," Zoey started, her eyes darting between him and Beau. "With your parents."

Ethan held his breath, wishing like hell she wouldn't bring this up.

"And I'm going to preface this by saying that no one came to me directly. I actually overheard a conversation I wasn't meant to hear, and yes, I've been called nosy on more than one occasion." She smirked over at V. "But in this case, I consider that a good trait to have."

Ethan frowned. He wanted her to get to the point. For one, he hated that every eye in the room was on him.

Zoey smiled sweetly, squeezing his hand. "First of all, you should know that you're not alone in this. It might not seem like it, but we've all been rooting for the two of you. Every single person in this room, in fact. And when you hurt, we hurt." Her eyes paused on Beau's face. "I heard what your parents said to you, Beau. And I might be small, but as soon as I heard, I wanted to kick their butts for you. Know that we've got your back, now and always. "

Oh, hell. This was not the direction Ethan wanted this to go.

"But that's beside the point," she added, glancing at Ethan again. "I have a proposition for you both. And know that you don't have to accept what I'm offering. If it makes you uncomfortable, I won't be offended."

Ethan swallowed hard. He wanted to snap at her, to tell her to spit it out, but he held his tongue.

"Ethan, Beau..." Zoey swallowed hard and tears suddenly sprang to her eyes. "I'd like to be your surrogate."

Beau's sharp inhale was the only sound in the room other than the blood suddenly rushing in Ethan's ears. Even the babies were quiet.

He cut his eyes to Kaleb, a silent question lingering between them. *Is she for real?* Kaleb's response was a head nod and a smile, which translated to: *She is.*

"When I heard Travis talking," Zoey continued with tears lining her eyelashes, "it hit me instantly. So, I went to Kaleb." She smiled over at her husband. "He thought it was a great idea."

"Zoey..." Beau's voice cracked.

Suddenly, the tears Zoey was trying to hold back started to flow down her cheeks and Ethan had to look away for fear he would cry. That was the last damn thing he needed to do in a room full of people. His gaze found Kaleb's again and his brother nodded once more.

Could this really be happening?

"I've already gone to my doctor," Zoey stated. "Since I've had four babies already, I wanted to ensure he thought it was safe before I talked to you about it. I didn't want to offer false hope." She smiled. "I'm happy to say, my doctor said he didn't foresee anything except for a healthy pregnancy."

Beau was breathing hard, his eyes wide and glassy.

"That is, if you want me to carry your baby. I thought maybe if you could do it this way, you'd be able to enjoy all the aspects of becoming parents. Believe it or not, the pregnancy is a very important time, too."

Fuck.

Ethan took a breath, but it sounded strangled. That was when he realized the tears he was fighting were falling. He tried to force them back but he couldn't. His hands were shaking and he could feel himself falling apart.

Beau must've realized because instantly his husband's arms surrounded him. Ethan shoved his face in Beau's neck and breathed. He heard people moving, but he couldn't bring himself to care. He knew his brothers would likely make fun of him for breaking down, but in that moment, he wasn't worried about that, either.

Several minutes passed as Ethan let Beau hold him. He felt his husband's shuddered breaths, knew he was fighting to keep it together.

This was exactly what he'd been praying for.

Yet he still couldn't wrap his head around it.

BEAU HELD ETHAN CLOSE, SHIELDING HIM FROM the others. He knew how Ethan felt about showing too much of what he was feeling in front of an audience, and Beau wanted to protect him. Granted, he knew everyone understood Ethan's emotional overload, but that didn't stop Beau from wanting to protect him.

While almost everyone slipped out of the room, Zoey, Kaleb, Lorrie, and Curtis remained. Beau didn't try to hide the tears tracking down his cheeks as he stared at his sister-in-law.

"We would never ask you to do this," Beau whispered, his voice strained from the emotion choking him.

"I know," she said, still kneeling before them, her hands holding theirs. "That's why I'm offering."

Beau glanced over at Kaleb to see the man smiling. His support, although not voiced, was evident.

"I've told you," Zoey continued, "Kaleb and I aren't planning to have any more babies. That was a decision we came to after Gabriel was born. It's the reason Kaleb got fixed."

Beau's gaze shot over to Kaleb once more. He hadn't known that.

"It's true," he admitted sheepishly.

Zoey squeezed his hand and Beau turned back to her.

"But I did love being pregnant. And honestly, this would be as much for me as it would be for you. Knowing that I could do this for you..." Tears fell from her eyes. "I love you both with all my heart. I've known you my entire life, and this feels right to me. I've witnessed the love you have for each other and I see with my own eyes just how much you love all these babies. You and Ethan deserve to be daddies. You'll be amazing fathers."

Beau swallowed past the lump in his throat. He shifted when Ethan sat up and wiped his face with the backs of his hands.

When their eyes met, Beau saw the hope there. The hope that had faded over the past year as they hit one road bump after another.

"Please let me do this for you, Ethan," Zoey said softly, drawing Ethan's attention to her. "I've done some research on the insemination process. It sounds relatively straightforward. I know you're using donor eggs. And once the two of you make a deposit, they'll do what they need to do. And I'm ready as soon as they are."

Beau waited for Ethan to look at him again, and when he did, Beau held his breath. His husband nodded and offered the sweetest smile he'd ever seen.

"Okay." Ethan's voice was barely a whisper. "If Beau's okay with it, I am, too."

Zoey peered up at him with big eyes as though he might possibly say anything other than yes.

"Thank you," Beau told her, then glanced over at Kaleb. "And you, too. You don't know what this means to us."

"Actually, we do." She squeezed their hands before pushing to her feet. "And you have my permission to beat up Travis. It was his idea to make this a big deal."

"It *is* a big deal," Curtis said, perched on the arm of the couch, his arm wrapped around Lorrie's shoulder as he held her.

"A very big deal," Lorrie agreed.

Beau laughed to keep himself from crying.

As though summoned, Travis appeared before them. "I'm tellin' you, it wasn't me. She came up with this all on her own."

Beau believed that. Zoey was one of those women who would do anything for her family. She'd proven it time and again. But this… He wondered if she even realized she was an answer to their prayers.

"Would you mind givin' us a minute?" Ethan asked, his gaze stopping on everyone else in the room.

"Of course," Lorrie said, getting to her feet. She stopped in front of them and squeezed Ethan's hand and then Beau's. "You boys deserve all the happiness in the world. You're going to be amazing daddies."

Beau couldn't find words, but he managed a nod.

Ethan continued to wipe his eyes as the footsteps faded. Beau shifted so he could face Ethan.

"You okay?"

"Are you?"

Beau shrugged. "If it's what you want." He leaned in closer, lowering his voice. "I just need you to know that I only want this if you do. Otherwise, I'll spend the rest of my life growing old with you. You're my heart, Ethan. A baby would be a blessing, but without you in my life, I wouldn't be complete."

"I'm here for as long as you'll have me."

Well, if that was the case, then forever it was.

Beau's chest swelled. "So, we're havin' a baby?"

Ethan nodded, then hugged him, holding him tight. Once again, Ethan started to shake and Beau cradled the back of his head, holding him there as he whispered into his ear. "I love you with all my heart, E."

"I love you, too."

A few minutes passed before Ethan drew back from him. This time his eyes were dry but still full of emotion. Beau knew how he felt. Zoey's offer was more than he could've ever imagined. She would carry their baby, keep him or her safe until it was time to come into the world. They would be able to check on Zoey, make sure she was okay. And yes, maybe they could even spoil her, because that was what Beau wanted. The woman who brought their child into this world deserved to be cherished more so than she already was.

"I need to talk to Kaleb," Ethan said, inching closer to the edge of the cushion.

Beau nodded. "I'll tell him you're lookin' for him."

"Thanks." Ethan motioned to the front door. "I'll be on the porch."

When Ethan left, Beau sat there for a minute, staring after Ethan and letting it all sink in. A smile formed on his face because he couldn't hide the joy he felt.

Taking a deep breath, Beau pushed to his feet and headed into the kitchen. He found Kaleb leaning against the counter talking to Curtis. Beau interrupted and informed Kaleb that Ethan was waiting for him.

"You okay, boy?" Curtis asked when Kaleb excused himself.

"Yes, sir. I am."

Curtis shifted, placing one hand on the counter behind him. "Some people might say kids are the most precious thing in the world." Curtis put his other hand on Beau's shoulder. "I'm a firm believer, the most precious thing is love. With it, you've got an instant family. Without it, you've got nothin'."

Beau stared at his father-in-law, not sure what to say.

"I think things are gonna get rough for Ethan for a bit. He's selfish when it comes to you and no one can blame him. It's your job to show him there's more than enough of you to go around."

Beau nodded. "Yes, sir."

"You're a good man, Beau." Curtis squeezed his shoulder.

Damn it. He did not want to cry again.

"And it's a true honor to call you son."

Yep. That did it.

Fuck.

ETHAN LEANED ON THE PORCH RAILING, ONE boot hooked over the bottom rung as he stared out at his father's land quickly being swallowed by the night.

He remembered the first time he kissed Beau on this porch. It had been on Christmas, back before he ever believed he could have something real, something good. Some days it felt like a lifetime ago, others like it was yesterday.

He heard the door open then close, followed by the sound of footsteps on the wooden porch planks. Kaleb appeared around the side of the house a moment later.

"What's up?" his brother asked, coming to stand beside him and taking up the same position against the railing. "Beau said you wanted to talk."

Ethan peered over at Kaleb. "You sure you're okay with this?"

Kaleb frowned back at him. "Why wouldn't I be? My wife wants to help my brother. How the hell could I *not* be okay with that?"

"It's a huge commitment. Not only for her, but you ... your kids."

"Yes, it is. And it's something we've talked about at length, E. Don't think this was a half-assed plan. Zoey's already read up on the process. At this point, I would bet she knows more than you do."

Ethan smiled. "That's a given. But I guarantee she doesn't know as much as Beau."

Kaleb chuckled. "No, probably not. But it'll give them plenty to talk about."

Ethan stared out at the darkness for a minute as he let his brain process everything that had happened in such a short amount of time.

"It's extremely generous," he noted.

"Yeah, well. My wife's one of a kind. Plus, Zoey loves you, E. We all do."

Ethan stared out at the pastures in the distance. "I was startin' to think this would never happen for us."

Kaleb didn't respond.

"I'd do anything to make Beau happy, Kaleb. That includes takin' Zoey up on her offer to carry our baby. I need to know you're not gonna regret it later."

"No regrets, little brother." Kaleb turned around, his ass resting against the railing as he crossed his arms over his chest. "I remember the day I found out she was pregnant with Mason. No matter how old or senile I get, that's a day I'll never forget."

Ethan could only imagine.

"You're gonna be a great dad," Kaleb added.

Ethan shook his head. "No. Beau's gonna be a great dad. Our kid … they'll be lucky as hell to have that man for a father. I'm just glad I'll be along for the ride."

"Do you not want a baby, E?"

Standing up tall, he shook his head. "That's not what I'm sayin'."

Kaleb's hands came up in a defensive gesture. "I'm not sayin' it is. But it sounds to me like you're worried."

"I am. Just because Zoey's volunteered her uterus doesn't mean it'll be easy. The embryos have to take and all that shit. I don't know how it works the way Beau does, but I seriously doubt the rough road's just gonna smooth out."

Kaleb's expression sobered. "You've suffered more than your fair share. There's no denying that. But you do deserve to be happy. Don't cast doubts because you're scared. We've all been there. Having kids … it's amazing. But it's also the scariest thing I've ever done. I remember the first time we gave Mason Cheerios." Kaleb laughed. "I stood there, terrified. I remember wondering if I could even perform the Heimlich if I needed to.

"Even now, I go to bed every night praying that God will keep them safe so I can spend another minute, another day with them. As a parent, your fears grow tenfold, but so does your love. It doesn't get any easier, but you have to learn to enjoy the path you're on. Otherwise, what the hell do you have?"

Ethan knew Kaleb was right. But Ethan had always been a glass-half-empty kind of guy.

"Zoey's excited," Kaleb said. "More than I expected. She's eager to start the process."

"They've gotta do the harvesting or whatever it is they do," Ethan told him.

Kaleb laughed, a full blown laugh this time. "They've already got the eggs, so no harvesting necessary."

Ethan narrowed his eyes. "I told you I don't know what the process is."

"I know. But you will because you'll be right there for the entire journey."

That he would.

"From my understanding, they'll thaw the eggs, you'll go down, shoot into a cup, and they'll be ready to fertilize. And then what? Like four or five days before they're ready to implant?"

Ethan shrugged. "No clue."

"Well, it's time you read up on it." Kaleb stood tall. "We're all in this together. Not just you and Beau and Zoey. The rest of us are in your corner, cheerin' you on. So, how about we start lookin' on the bright side of things, huh?"

Ethan met his brother's gaze. "Easier said than done sometimes."

"But not impossible."

"No. Not impossible."

They stared at one another for a moment, the silence lingering until finally Kaleb spoke.

"Well, I'm gonna go find my wife and my kids and I'm gonna take them home, put them to bed. And before my head hits the pillow, I'll send up a prayer that it all works out. Like I said, you and Beau deserve to be happy."

Ethan nodded.

"Just do me a favor, will ya?"

"What's that?"

"Love that man in there and make sure he knows how important he is to you. You've got doubts, which means he does, too. The last thing either of you need is to add to them unnecessarily."

Ethan nodded again. "I'll do my best."

Kaleb patted his shoulder before heading back toward the front door. "Oh, and E?"

"Yeah?"

"You might wanna wait until Zane leaves before you come back in. He's gonna give you shit for bein' a crybaby."

Ethan choked on a laugh but found himself smiling. "Had to get that one in, did ya?"

"Damn straight, bubba. I take 'em where I can."

Even when Kaleb slipped into the house, Ethan continued to smile. He felt as though his insides were lit up. Although he was terrified for reasons he couldn't explain, he was happy.

He was going to be a dad. He and Beau.

The door opened and someone stepped outside. Ethan figured it was Zane coming to give him shit. But Zane wasn't the one who turned the corner.

No, this was far better.

Beau's expression was solemn, as though he didn't know what to expect. Ethan knew that was his fault. Due to his depression, it was always a gamble for Beau. Ethan wished he could change that. Maybe one day he would.

Unable to resist, Ethan moved toward him, not stopping until he was in Beau's arms.

"I love you," he told Beau. "Never doubt that for a minute."

"I won't. But you have to promise the same."

Pulling back, he stared into the warmest brown eyes he'd ever seen. "I'll do my best. But remember who you're dealin' with. I'm still learnin' how to be a good husband."

"Baby, you don't need lessons for that. You've got it down."

Ethan leaned in and kissed Beau. "What do you say we go home? Get some sleep. Somethin' tells me it's gonna be a very long week."

Beau smiled, then took his hand. "Sounds like a plan. Well, except for the sleepin' part. I had somethin' else in mind."

"Did you now?" Ethan followed Beau toward the door.

"Oh, yeah. And trust me, sleep' s the last thing you'll be thinkin' about in a little while."

On that note, Ethan followed Beau in the house. He was walking on a cloud, so high Zane couldn't even bring him down.

Didn't mean his little brother didn't give it his best shot.

The fucker.

Chapter Eight

Wednesday, October 24, 2018
(Five weeks later)

BEAU GLANCED AT HIS CELL PHONE FOR the hundredth time since he'd woken up. As was their usual routine, they came to the shop, started coffee, then planned out their day.

And while he was stalking his cell phone, willing the damn thing to ring, Beau tried his best to remember he had a job to do. Unfortunately, that wasn't easy considering he was waiting for Zoey to call with ... news.

The past five weeks had been a whirlwind of activity. The first thing they had done after Zoey offered to be their surrogate was call the fertility clinic, and surprisingly, things had gotten underway quickly.

Honestly, Beau hadn't expected such a rush, but that was how it had felt.

The clinic had scheduled an appointment for the four of them—Kaleb included—to come in and discuss how it would all go down. They had snatched up the first appointment available, and a week later, they'd learned every detail of what could be expected as well as been able to ask all the questions they'd had. Beau hadn't been shy, either. He'd asked a dozen questions, along with Zoey, while Kaleb and Ethan sat by patiently.

Before they left the clinic that day, they had determined the best date for implantation based on Zoey's cycle. More appointments went onto the calendar, including Ethan and Beau going in to give their sperm deposit. Contrary to what Beau had thought, that hadn't been nearly as easy as he would've expected. Apparently, his sperm were rather shy when it came to forced ejaculation.

Once that was done, the next step was fertilization and embryo culture, which was done in a lab, followed by the embryo evaluation to determine the number to transfer, which was a big decision because of the risk of multiples.

The next thing Beau knew, they were taking Zoey in for the implantation. While she had assured them it was no big deal, Beau had his doubts. Just the mention of a catheter had him cringing.

The insertion had taken place on October twelfth. While Ethan and Beau sat in the waiting room, Zoey had undergone the procedure with Kaleb at her side. She had offered for them to be in the room with them, but Beau and Ethan had graciously declined. He wasn't sure they were ready for something like that.

And now, thirteen days later, they were waiting for the results of the blood test she'd had done yesterday to find out if Zoey was pregnant.

Beau was trying his best not to get his hopes up, but it was far more difficult than he expected. Part of him had started to believe they would never make it this far, so his hope was taking on a life of its own.

When he heard the crunch of tires on gravel, Beau looked up to see who was coming their way. Curtis's truck had come to a stop in the grass beside Beau's truck. The older man climbed out and sauntered toward them.

"Mornin'," Curtis greeted. "Thought I'd stop in, grab a cup of coffee."

Curtis's smile said that wasn't entirely true, but Beau offered him some coffee anyway. They trekked through the warehouse building to the small office. As they neared, Ethan stepped out, his eyes widening when he saw his father.

"Just came for coffee," Curtis assured him.

Beau knew Ethan was wondering the same thing he was. Did Curtis have news about Zoey?

Fortunately, Ethan was far less patient and he voiced his question to his father immediately. "You hear anything?"

"Nope. You?"

Beau released the breath he'd been holding. There was no reason to be disappointed. No news was still good news at this point.

Ethan poured his father some coffee. "Nope."

"Well, then there's nothin' to fret about yet, is there?"

Beau smiled. That was far easier said than done. Hell, Beau had been fretting since the day they brought Zoey home from the appointment. In fact, he'd hovered over her that day until she'd had to shoo him out of her house. With a smile, of course.

That hadn't stopped Beau from calling and texting her every day to see how she was doing. He was trying his best not to overwhelm her, but it wasn't easy.

Curtis took a sip from his mug, his gaze darting between him and Ethan.

"What's on your mind, Pop?"

Curtis's face sobered. "I did need to mention somethin'."

Beau's chest instantly constricted as it prepared for bad news. He should've expected it. After all, things had been going far too well lately.

"Nothin' about the baby," Curtis said. "However, Zoey and Kaleb had to go down and get a protective order last Tuesday."

Fucking hell. "Against who?" Beau blurted.

"Beau's parents?" Ethan questioned.

Curtis nodded, then peered over at Beau. "Your mother."

Why the hell couldn't she leave well enough alone?

"Bein' that this is a small town," Curtis continued, "word travels fast. Obviously, your parents got wind of what's goin' on. Your mother came by their house, tried to talk. Kaleb kindly ordered her to leave. She refused."

Damn it.

"Kaleb called the sheriff's department. They came and escorted her off the property. Told 'em it'd be wise to get a protective order to keep her from harassing them any further. They only want to keep her off their property and away from their children."

Beau knew a protective order would only help in theory. It wouldn't matter if Arlene was ordered to remain five hundred feet away at all times; there was no doubt she would violate it at some point. Especially if Zoey saw her in town.

"I need to talk to Arlene," Beau said, even as the idea made his stomach churn.

"No, boy, you don't," Curtis countered. "We're not gonna let them intrude on this. They have a right to their opinions, but they have to learn we're not interested in hearin' them."

"What if they confront Zoey somewhere else?" Ethan asked, his eyes narrowed.

"I'll make sure that doesn't happen."

Beau stared at his father-in-law wondering what that meant. He knew Curtis wielded a lot of power in this town, considering the town had belonged to the Walkers in the beginning. Curtis had sold off pieces of his family's land, and ultimately, Coyote Ridge had been created. In fact, Beau knew that Lorrie had been the one to name the town.

"Why the fuck can't they just leave us alone?" Ethan snarled, turning and heading out the open bay door, evidently not expecting an answer.

"How're you holdin' up?" Curtis asked as Beau watched his husband flee.

"Nervous," Beau admitted. "Anxious." He took a deep breath and met Curtis's stare. "Scared."

"All normal, boy." He smiled, but it seemed almost sad. "I remember when Lorrie first got pregnant. I was terrified. Not only did I have to take care of her, but I had a baby on the way. I was over the moon, but still scared shitless."

Beau didn't move. He'd actually heard this story, knew that Lorrie and Curtis's first pregnancy had resulted in a miscarriage. The thought alone made him sick to his stomach, fear clutching his intestines and twisting.

"Nothin' can prepare you for the emotions you go through, Beau," Curtis said, his eyes locked on Beau's face. "You pray day and night, make promises to God that you fully intend to keep. In the end, you learn that it's not your path to pave. What happens is in God's hands."

Beau wasn't sure where Curtis was going with this.

Curtis's warm hand curled over his shoulder. "Your parents don't have a say. No matter what they think. When it comes to the people who care about you, they can't sway us. You need to remember that."

"Maybe if I talk to them—"

Curtis shook his head, his hand falling to his side. "I can't tell you not to, boy, but I can ask that you don't. Leave it to me. If you haven't learned already, I protect what's mine. And my family comes before anyone else. They won't hurt any of you. I'll make sure of that."

Beau nodded. He'd seen Curtis stand up for his own. The man had turned seventy-three a few days ago, yet if you didn't know him, you wouldn't know it. Age was definitely just a number.

"Promise me, boy."

Beau considered it for a moment. If he confronted his parents, it would only make things worse. He remembered what had happened at the hospital. No. Definitely wouldn't help. Curtis was right, they had their opinions on the matter and he seriously doubted they would ever change.

Finally, he nodded at Curtis. "I promise. I'll stay clear."

"Good." Curtis's gaze strayed out to the parking lot. "Now, I'll go talk to the boy and get outta your hair." He glanced back to Beau. "You let us know when you hear somethin'."

"Will do."

Beau took Curtis's empty mug and watched as the man walked out into the early-morning sunshine.

He had no idea what Curtis was going to say to Ethan, but whatever it was, he hoped like hell it settled Ethan, because with every passing day, Beau watched as his husband slipped a little further away. Beau had no idea how to pull him back, but he knew he had to do something.

And he prayed that Zoey called with good news.

"WHAT DO YOU WANT, POP?" ETHAN KICKED a rock across the winding driveway that led back to their shop. "'Cause I'm not in the mood for a lecture."

He'd come out here to be alone. He didn't need his father trying to fix things he had no control over. As it was, Ethan was hanging by a thread.

"Watch your mouth, boy."

Ethan spun around to face his father and voiced the question that had been plaguing him. "What if they're right?"

Curtis's forehead creased, his eyes narrowing. "Who?"

"Beau's asshole parents. What if they're right? What if I'm not supposed to have a kid?"

"Bullshit, Ethan." Curtis closed the distance between them in an instant, his hand wrapping around Ethan's head, holding him still as their eyes locked. "Those people are ignorant. They don't get to make those decisions. And they damn sure don't make decisions for this family."

Ethan's chest tightened painfully as his eyes locked with his father's. The turmoil churning inside him caused his words to come out in a broken whisper. "I wanna give him a baby."

As soon as the words were out of his mouth, the dam broke. Ethan sobbed roughly.

His father jerked him to him, holding him in his strong embrace. Ethan gave in, letting himself fall apart. He was trying to be strong for Beau, not wanting the man to have anything else to worry about, but it wasn't easy. Every night when he crawled into bed, he prayed that he wouldn't fail Beau. So far, his prayers had gone unanswered and it was killing him slowly.

"It's normal to be scared," Curtis said, his voice low.

"I'm not scared." Ethan pulled back and met his father's concerned gaze. "I'm fuckin' terrified. What if I can't give Beau what he needs? What then, Pop? How long till he gets tired of dealin' with my shit?"

Curtis's eyebrows shot downward. "That man loves you, boy. Don't doubt that for a second. He's in it for the long haul."

"How do you know?" Ethan screamed, his lungs feeling as though they were filled with glass. Every breath hurt. The thought of Beau leaving him because he couldn't make him happy…

"Because I know." Curtis's adamant tone matched the fierceness in his eyes. "Because I've seen the way he looks at you, Ethan. He's not goin' anywhere."

Ethan wanted to believe it, but in the past few weeks, his walls had deteriorated. All the ones he'd built up, trying to protect himself from the demons that had suffocated him his entire life. They were crumbling, and for the first time in years, Ethan felt vulnerable. As though a strong breeze had the ability to take him out at the knees.

"Quit lookin' for the worst, boy. And stop tryin' to give Beau things because you think that's the only way to keep him." Curtis's voice softened. "Open your eyes and see what's right in front of you." Curtis pointed toward the building. "That man's the same man who married you. He's the same man who said *for better or worse*. He knew what he was gettin' into by takin' you as his husband. Give him the credit he deserves. He's strong enough to handle every part of you."

"But he deserves something from me," he argued.

"Yes, he does. He deserves for you to love him unconditionally."

"I do."

"That's all he needs, boy."

Ethan scrubbed his eyes with the heels of his hands. He hated that he couldn't keep his shit together.

As he was trying to breathe through the pain in his chest, he heard the sound of tires on gravel. He looked up to see Kaleb's truck bouncing down the dirt road.

His heart leapt into his throat as he waited for his brother to park and get out. Those few seconds felt like an eternity. His hands trembled, his heart so fucking hopeful but suffocated by fear.

Kaleb was on the phone when he climbed out, but he quickly ended the call and tucked his phone in his pocket.

The instant Ethan met Kaleb's eyes from across the driveway, he knew.

They weren't pregnant.

"I'm sorry, E," Kaleb said softly. "Zoey's at home. She's devastated."

Swallowing was damn near impossible. The lump in his throat was so thick it was difficult to breathe.

"I'm gonna go talk to Beau," Kaleb said, his eyes filled with sympathy.

Ethan nodded. He knew he should be the one to share the news with Beau, but he wasn't sure he could watch his husband's heart break all over again.

Digging his keys from his pocket, Ethan started for his truck.

"Where're you goin', boy?" Curtis shouted.

Ethan shrugged, but he didn't turn around.

CURTIS'S HEART ACHED AS HE WATCHED HIS son walk away. Pain for Ethan and Beau swelled up, hot and fierce. It was a father's right to hurt for his children and Curtis did. Anytime his boys hurt, he did, too.

This time was no different.

Didn't matter which of his boys was having a hard time, Curtis always felt their pain. Perhaps doubly so with Ethan. He knew his boy was tormented by his past, and though he put on a strong front, deep down, Ethan was still dealing with the depression he'd suffered for years. Despite the fact that Ethan was now married to Beau, and he had so much to look forward to, it seemed those demons were still there, still haunting him.

"Pop?" Kaleb called out, his eyes watching Ethan's truck as it kicked up dirt. "Do I need to go after him?"

"No." Ethan needed his space for now. And if anyone needed to go after him, it was Beau.

"You sure?"

Curtis turned to face Kaleb. "I'm sure." He waved toward the building. "Come on. Let's go talk to Beau."

This was a conversation Curtis had hoped he would never have to have. Relaying information that would hurt any of his kids, Beau included, wasn't something he wanted to do. Ever.

But he knew it had to be done.

When they stepped into the warehouse, Beau appeared from behind one of the trucks. He was carrying a grease rag, his eyes darting between them and then past them, as though he expected Ethan to appear.

From the look on Beau's face, it was obvious he knew what Kaleb was there to say, but he didn't speak, his full attention turning to Kaleb.

"Zoey asked me to come by," Kaleb began. "The doctor called a little while ago with the results from the blood test. She's not pregnant, Beau."

Tears formed in Beau's eyes, but the man fought them back. Curtis watched as he squared his shoulders, ready to take the weight of the world on them.

"Does Ethan know?"

Kaleb glanced over at him.

Curtis nodded. "Yeah."

"Where is he?"

"He took off."

Beau's face fell as though that had been his worst fear.

"He'll be back," Curtis assured his son-in-law. "Give him a little time."

Beau instantly shook his head, tossing the rag onto a nearby tool chest. "Can't do that. Ethan doesn't need to be alone. He needs me."

Curtis wasn't going to argue with him because he happened to believe that to be true. "Go on. We'll lock up here."

Without another word, Beau headed out of the building, leaving Curtis standing there with Kaleb.

Curtis took a deep breath and exhaled slowly. He wished he could do something to change the outcome for them. Unfortunately, it was out of their control.

"This fuckin' sucks," Kaleb mumbled.

That it did.

"You want me to call Travis? Let him know what's goin' on?" Kaleb offered. "Tell him to keep an eye out for Ethan?"

"Nope. Beau's got this."

"We knew this might happen," Kaleb said, his tone tormented.

"This isn't about Zoey not bein' pregnant." It was about something much deeper than that, something Beau eased inside Ethan. Curtis had seen it coming for a while. Ethan's fears had never abated. He didn't believe he deserved to be loved although he accepted that Beau did love him.

"She already scheduled another appointment," Kaleb added. "November seventh."

Curtis turned to his son. "That's good. There's no reason to give up."

"Trust me..." Kaleb chuckled softly. "My wife'll never give up on this. She's in it for the long haul."

That's what Ethan needed. For every one of them to have his back.

While Curtis knew they did, he had a feeling it wasn't going to be quite as easy to convince Ethan.

But if anyone could, it was Beau.

Chapter Nine

BEAU KNEW WHERE ETHAN WAS WITHOUT EVEN checking his phone. He'd long ago ensured Ethan was set up on his Find My Friends app in the event something like this happened. After all, this certainly wasn't the first time Ethan had stormed off.

Thankfully, Beau had never needed to use it to find his husband's location.

In the beginning, right after they were married, Ethan had seemed a different man. He'd gone to counseling, talked through his issues, opened up, smiled more. When Ethan asked, Beau went with him to see his therapist so he could learn how to support the man he loved.

While the gray clouds had all but disappeared from Ethan's eyes, Beau had been warned not to believe the storms were gone for good. Depression was a disease and it had to be managed. Although medicine and professional counseling helped, Beau had learned that there would still be times Ethan would have to battle to get back to him.

About a year in, Ethan had gone through what Beau called an episode. He'd fallen into a dark depression—similar to those he'd had before they were married—and rather than force him to open up, Beau had given him space. That had backfired in his fucking face. Ethan had gone off the rails, insisting Beau didn't love him.

He'd realized something very important about the man he loved at that point. Ethan didn't *want* to succumb to the darkness. He wanted someone there to help him through it.

Lesson learned, although it hadn't helped in that particular situation.

Thankfully, Beau had managed to rein Ethan in, assuring him that he loved him more than anything. That episode had taught Beau that Ethan wanted to be loved, and when he acted out like that, he wasn't necessarily in control, but he was seeking reinforcement.

Fortunately, Ethan didn't have these episodes often. In fact, it had been nearly two years since anything like this had happened. The last time, Ethan had disappeared for hours, claiming he had needed time to think. And while Beau had gone searching for him, he hadn't found him.

However, Beau knew Ethan had gone home this time. He'd sensed it. This was one of those times when Ethan needed his love and support. Beau fully intended to give that to him.

When he pulled up to the house, Beau parked beside Ethan's truck, then climbed out. While his heart was aching from the news Kaleb had delivered, Beau realized he had to push that aside for the time being. He could deal with the pain later. Right now, he needed to tend to Ethan.

Beau walked inside, set his keys on the table, and closed the door behind him. All the lights in the house were off. There were no sounds coming from the kitchen, which meant Ethan wasn't trying to cook away his frustrations.

He paused in the living room, listening for something to tell him which direction Ethan had gone. Was he upstairs or down? It took a second, but he finally heard it.

Guest room.

He'd had a feeling that was where Ethan would go. It was the room they would eventually fix up for their son or daughter. And yes, he was still thinking that they would have a child. Beau wasn't going to let this get him down. When the time was right, they would have a baby. And if they couldn't get pregnant with Zoey as their surrogate, they would adopt. There were plenty of children who needed good homes.

Pushing open the door to the guest room, Beau found Ethan sitting on the floor, his back to the wall. There were at least two dozen paper airplanes strewn across the floor, the bed, the dresser. Evidently that was how Ethan had opted to pass the time.

When Beau stepped into the room, Ethan didn't look up at him, but he hadn't expected it. Although to an outsider, it might appear that Ethan was acting out in an effort to get attention, he wasn't. He was merely coping and Beau had learned those demons that haunted Ethan pulled no punches. Ethan had admitted he wasn't proud of his reactions, but he had a hard time fighting them.

Rather than ask if he was all right, Beau took a seat on the floor beside Ethan. He raised his knees and rested his arm on them.

"I'm sorry I ran," Ethan said softly.

They'd had this discussion numerous times, and the few times Ethan had bolted, Beau had asked him not to do it again. While Ethan always promised he wouldn't, they both knew that he would.

However, he'd come home, which was a damn good start.

"As I was drivin' away, I realized what an asshole I'm bein'."

Beau sighed. "You're not bein' an asshole."

"No?" Ethan cast a sideways glance his way. "Then explain why I stormed off."

"Because you're human, E. Because you're dealin' with this in the only way you know how."

Ethan was quiet for a few minutes, but when he spoke again, Beau's entire body went eerily still.

"I'm scared, Beau," Ethan whispered. "I'm scared I'm not gonna be enough for you."

"E—"

"Hear me out," Ethan stated firmly.

Beau nodded.

"You've spent all this time helping me heal. Taking care of me when I can't take care of myself. And yet I'm still broken. I'm not as strong as I need to be to take care of you, Beau, and it fucking kills me to admit that."

Beau didn't say a word even if he wanted to argue that point. No matter how many times he told Ethan he was far stronger than he gave himself credit for, Ethan didn't listen.

"Thinkin' about bringin' a baby into it all scares the shit outta me. Do I want a baby with you? Hell yeah. Do I think I won't fuck a kid up with all the shit in my head? I'm not so sure. Even worse than that is thinkin' that if I can't give you a baby, you'll eventually realize I'm too fucked up. Everyone tells me my fears are irrational." Ethan turned his head to look at him. "But they damn sure don't feel irrational to me. They feel heartbreakingly real, Beau. To the point I can't breathe sometimes."

"I know, E." Beau reached over and grabbed Ethan's hand, twining their fingers and bringing Ethan's hand back to his knee. "I know it's not easy for you, but you have to know that I'll never give up. I love you. Not just with my heart, either. My entire soul belongs to you. And it always will."

Ethan squeezed his hand.

"Anytime you need me to tell you that, all you have to do is ask," Beau told him. "And the rest of the time, I'll continue to show you."

Ethan shifted so that his head rested on Beau's shoulder. "Kaleb tell you?"

"Yeah."

For the longest time, they remained like that, side by side, Ethan's head resting on his shoulder, their fingers twined together. And for the first time in a long time, Beau felt at peace. He enjoyed these moments with Ethan. The times his husband would admit to his fears and concerns. It was rare for Ethan to do that, and Beau knew he didn't do it with anyone other than him and possibly Curtis.

"So what do we do now?" Ethan asked.

"We try again."

"And if that doesn't work?"

Beau turned and kissed the top of Ethan's head. "Have faith, baby."

"I'm tryin'."

"I know."

"You might have to keep remindin' me," Ethan whispered.

"I will." In fact, he would continue to remind them both, because in the end, this was what it was about.

His love for Ethan and Ethan's love for him.

As long as they had that, they could conquer anything.

ONCE THE CHAOS IN HIS HEAD AND heart settled somewhat, Ethan suggested they go back to work. Surprisingly, Beau hadn't argued. Perhaps it was because they both needed the distraction.

However, he was only willing to do so much work in a day. At five o'clock, Ethan encouraged Beau to call it a night. It hadn't taken a whole lot of persuasion, which meant Beau was as emotionally drained as he was.

"We headed home for dinner?" Beau asked when they climbed in Ethan's truck.

"I thought maybe we'd stop by and see Zoey," he suggested.

Beau's eyes widened and Ethan fought the urge to laugh. His husband obviously hadn't expected that from him.

"I just wanna check on her," he explained. "Despite my selfish responses to situations, I know it's not all about me."

"You're not selfish, E."

Yeah, that was debatable, but Ethan knew not to argue with Beau. In the end, he wouldn't win, so it was a waste of time and effort. Regardless of all his doubts, Ethan knew in his heart that Beau loved him. He knew deep down that they would spend the rest of their lives together. Unfortunately, the depression he battled wasn't always convinced of that. Which resulted in days like today. Thankfully, they were few and far between.

The drive to Kaleb and Zoey's didn't take long at all. Considering they were living in the house Zoey had grown up in, they were actually walking distance from Curtis and Lorrie's. It was nice to have them so close. While all of his brothers had started out living on the property after moving out of Mom and Pop's, a few had ventured farther into town.

Ethan parked in the driveway and climbed out. He met Beau at the front of the truck and they walked up to the door together.

"Uncle E! Uncle Beau!" Mason yelled when he spotted them through the screen door. "Momma! Uncle E and Uncle Beau are here!"

"Well, ask 'em to come in," Zoey said with a chuckle.

Mason shoved the screen door open so hard Beau had to shift to keep from being hit in the face.

Ethan stepped into the house as Zoey was coming out of the kitchen. She was wiping her hands on a towel, her smile sad.

"I didn't expect you," she said hesitantly.

"Just wanted to check on you. See how you're doin'."

Zoey stared back at him as though he had a third eyeball or maybe two noses. And fine, Ethan wasn't usually the type to check in like this. As he'd told Beau, his reactions were usually selfish in nature. He hated that he was that way, but even if he couldn't change, at least he could admit it.

"I'm good," she said, although Ethan wasn't sure he believed her.

Unable to resist, he walked right up to Zoey and hugged his sister-in-law. He wasn't much on physical affection, but he knew this was as hard for her as it was for them.

When he pulled back, Zoey was staring at him with tears in her eyes. "We'll try again."

"Damn right we will," he said with a grin.

Zoey wiped a stray tear, then motioned toward the kitchen. "Want somethin' to drink? Tea? Beer?"

"I'll take a beer," Beau said.

"Yeah," Ethan agreed. "Beer's good."

She pulled two bottles out of the refrigerator, removed the caps, and passed them over. "Kaleb should be here any minute. He called to say he was on his way."

Ethan nodded. "We didn't come by to see him."

Her eyes softened again. "I'm not sure if he told you, but I've already scheduled another appointment."

It was Ethan's turn to be surprised.

"We'll all go in on November seventh."

Ethan peered over at Beau, then back to Zoey. His throat was tight as he forced a response. "Thank you. For doin' this. I know it's not easy for you, either."

"I just wanna give you good news." As though she felt the conversation taking another emotional turn, Zoey smiled widely. "You boys hungry? I was just finishin' up dinner."

"If it's beanie weenies, we're in," Beau said, breaking through the rest of the tension.

"Sorry." Zoey giggled. "No beans this time. But we are havin' macaroni and weenies."

"What's up with your kids and weenies?" As soon as the words were out, Ethan realized how that sounded.

They were all laughing when the back screen door opened and Kaleb stepped inside. He surveyed the room, his gaze bouncing between them as he hesitantly smiled. "What'd I miss?"

"Just talkin' about weenies," Zoey told him.

Kaleb moved toward her. "Darlin', I'm not sure I'm comfortable with that. I mean, Ethan is my brother."

Zoey swatted him with the hand towel. "Hot dogs, silly."

"Oh." He scanned the stovetop. "No beans this time?"

"Nope. Mason insisted on macaroni."

Kaleb peered over his shoulder at Ethan. "I wouldn't mind you invitin' me to dinner sometime. I heard you have grown-up food. You know, like steak and baked potatoes."

"We do." Ethan nodded. "And next time I grill, I'll keep your request in mind."

"Uncle Beau!" Kellan came crashing into Beau's legs. "You're here! Wanna watch TV?"

Beau glanced up at Ethan as though seeking permission.

Ethan nodded toward the living room.

"Absolutely, kiddo. What're we watchin'?"

Kellan's voice trailed off as they moved farther away.

"Where's Barrett?" Kaleb asked.

"He's down for a nap." Zoey widened her eyes at Kaleb. "And yes, before you say anything, I know it's late. You didn't have to deal with his tantrum, though."

Kaleb leaned down and kissed her on the lips. "I didn't say anything."

"But you were thinkin' it."

The look on Kaleb's face said Zoey had pegged him correctly. "And Gabriel?"

"Sleepin', too. So be quiet when you go wake Barrett up."

"I'll try." Kaleb slapped Ethan on the shoulder as he headed out of the kitchen.

Ethan moved over to the counter and leaned back against it. "I know I sound like a broken record, but seriously. Thank you for doin' this."

Zoey turned to face him. "It's my pleasure, E. Really. And I know it's slow going, but I have a really good feeling about this." Her eyes slid toward the wall that separated the kitchen from the living room. "How's he doin'?"

Ethan smiled against the lip of his beer bottle. "Better than me."

She seemed shocked by that confession.

Not wanting to pour his heart out more than he already had that day, Ethan changed the subject. "Pop told us about the protection order."

Zoey's eyes hardened. "I didn't want to do it, E. I really didn't. But that woman is vile. And I refuse to be talked to like that. Not by anyone."

"You don't have to tell me." He knew firsthand how poisonous they were. "Just be sure to tell us if you have any problems."

She nodded. "I will. But Kaleb's gonna handle them."

Knowing Kaleb was more than capable of protecting those he loved, Ethan nodded. He glanced down at the pans on the stove. "So ... macaroni and cheese, huh?"

Zoey laughed. "Gourmet stuff right there."

Yeah. Gourmet wasn't quite the word he was thinking.

Chapter Ten

Friday, October 26, 2018
(Two days later)

IN AN EFFORT TO GET BACK TO some sense of normalcy during the chaos that had become their life, Beau opted for a date night.

Or rather, he *attempted* to have a date night.

He should've known Ethan would throw a wrench in his plans. The man had the uncanny ability to ensure their date nights ended up at home rather than out.

Not that Beau really minded. His idea of going out was to head to the diner for the special or to Moonshiners for a beer or two. However, in an attempt to be romantic, he had been known to make reservations at a nice steak house. Of course, Ethan always ensured those reservations were unnecessary.

Tonight was no exception.

"How long till you're ready?" Beau called out as he stepped into the master bathroom to brush his teeth.

When he glanced in the mirror to see Ethan, curious as to his response, Beau was shocked to find his sexy husband standing in the shower, water sluicing over every delicious inch of him as he stroked himself firmly. Even in the reflection Beau could see the intensity in Ethan's gaze. It wasn't difficult to figure out what was on his mind, either.

Beau finished brushing his teeth, rinsed, then put the toothbrush in the holder before turning around to face Ethan, leaning against the counter.

"What're you doin'?" Beau crossed his arms over his chest. "We're supposed to be sittin' down for dinner in forty-five minutes."

Ethan appeared to consider this, his face scrunching as though that was going to be a problem.

"We're not gonna be sittin' down to dinner, are we?"

Ethan shook his head.

"So, what are you gonna do about feedin' me?" Beau prompted.

Ethan crudely held his cock in Beau's direction, making him laugh.

"Oh, yeah? *That's* what I get for dinner?"

Ethan nodded, then crooked his finger, motioning for Beau to join him.

"I already had a shower."

"Take another," Ethan rasped, his voice thick with lust.

Beau would be lying if he said he preferred to go out rather than to indulge in one of Ethan's hot shower scenes. The man did like to play in the water, he'd give him that much.

Still stroking his cock firmly, Ethan nodded toward Beau. "Strip."

"You think I'm that easy?"

"I don't *think*. I *know*."

Beau chuckled, but he didn't move.

"If I have to get outta this shower, you're gonna pay with your mouth."

Beau laughed. "Is that right?"

Ethan nodded, then crooked his finger again.

Admittedly, his cock was already pressing insistently against his zipper, so resisting was merely part of the game.

"So, what's the point of date night?" Beau asked as he gave in, pulling his shirt out of his jeans and then slowly taking it off. "If you never make it past the shower?"

Ethan's smile was mischievous. "I thought this *was* date night?"

"In the shower?"

"Why not? Seems like the perfect place to be alone with you. No one's gonna bother us in here."

"You gonna cook for me after?"

"Whatever you'd like," Ethan promised.

Beau toed off his boots, then stripped off his jeans. A minute later, he was joining Ethan beneath the warm spray. Rather than go to his knees, though, Beau crowded Ethan up against the tiled wall. He held his mouth just out of reach.

"Tonight, I want your mouth on *me*," Beau whispered. "I wanna feel those lips wrapped around my cock."

"With pleasure," Ethan said, leaning forward until their lips touched.

Beau couldn't resist, cupping Ethan's face and kissing him. Sometimes when he kissed Ethan, it felt like the very first time. His insides coiled tightly, exactly as they had that first moment their tongues had dueled.

When Ethan moaned into his mouth, Beau reached between them and wrapped his fist around Ethan's cock, sliding it against his own. He loved teasing this man, loved the way Ethan reacted to it.

While he stroked them both at the same time, Beau trailed his mouth along Ethan's jaw. He went slowly, savoring his scent, his taste. Within minutes, he was intoxicated by him.

"Put your mouth on me, E."

Beau pulled back and stared at Ethan, loving the way he gave in to him. While Ethan was definitely the more dominant of them, Beau had his moments. And every time he decided to play the alpha card, Ethan submitted so easily.

Backing up a step, Beau gave Ethan room to lower himself to his knees. He placed one hand on the tiled wall, the other on his cock as he guided himself into Ethan's mouth.

"Love your mouth." Beau watched as his cock slid between Ethan's lips. He could feel the warm rasp of Ethan's tongue as he teased him. "This definitely beats eating in a restaurant."

Ethan's eyes lifted to his. The blue steel was molten.

"Suck me, E. Make me come down your throat."

Although he'd given the order, Ethan didn't rush and Beau didn't mind. He stood there, his knees weakening as Ethan drove him closer and closer to release. His hand remained on the tile, keeping him from falling over.

"God, E…" Beau closed his eyes as the familiar tingle started at the base of his spine. "I fuckin' love your mouth on me."

Beau drove his hips forward, sliding deeper into Ethan's throat with every pass. He was breathing hard, trying to hang on.

"I'm gonna come, E. Fuck … yes…" Beau groaned low in his throat as his release tore through him.

He opened his eyes to see Ethan licking his lips as he stroked Beau's softening dick, pushing to his feet.

"How did that rate for a date night?" Ethan asked, his lips brushing Beau's.

"Off the charts."

"Really? Because I'm not through with you."

"No?" Beau couldn't resist Ethan's kiss. He leaned in, sliding his tongue along Ethan's bottom lip, urging him to give in. It didn't take much before Ethan was kissing him roughly, shifting their places so Beau was up against the wall.

"Not by a long shot. After I dry you off, I'm gonna lay you out on the bed and lick you from head to toe. When I get my fill, I'm gonna slide inside you and fuck you until you beg me to come."

A shudder raced through Beau. "I'm all yours, E."

"Good answer."

ETHAN COULDN'T GET ENOUGH OF BEAU.

He'd spent the better part of the day eager to get home but not because he had any intention of going out. He knew Beau's date night proposals were for his benefit, but the truth was, Ethan didn't care to leave the house. Not when he had the opportunity to spend hours naked with Beau at his mercy. Or vice versa.

Pretty much for the past month, he'd been taking Beau every way he could, as many times a day as the man allowed. And yes, on occasion, Beau was known to say no. Granted, it was rare.

Ethan liked that Beau wasn't saying no tonight.

After shutting off the water, Ethan dried them both, then ushered Beau into the bedroom, where he followed through on his promise. He took his time licking and kissing every inch of Beau's big body until his husband was hard once more. He sucked and teased until the beautiful man was practically vibrating beneath him.

Beau was the only man Ethan had been with who succumbed in every way. He gave himself over to the moment, which, in turn, caused Ethan to do the same. When he was with Beau, he could block out everything else. Good, bad, ugly. Nothing intruded in his head when he had Beau like this.

Only once Beau was begging did Ethan give in, lubing his cock and sliding into the heaven of Beau's body. They were face-to-face—the way he preferred—as he pushed in deep, retreated slowly. With all the lights on, Ethan watched Beau. Memorizing every expression and moan, every sigh, every plea. All so he could repeat it again and again in the future, ensuring he gave Beau everything he needed.

Ethan leaned over Beau, planting his hands beside Beau's head as he stared down at him. "I love you," he said firmly as he continued to rock his hips forward and back.

"I love you, too."

While Ethan loved their erotic encounters, the time when the flames licked at them both until the heat became blistering, he loved these moments just as much. When he managed to take his time, to savor every second. It was rare, so he made it last as long as physically possible.

Granted, it wasn't easy for Ethan. His lust for Beau burned hot, his need for this man overwhelming. His intentions were always good. In the beginning. As the minutes dragged on, his pace quickened, his body humming as it reached the pinnacle.

Leaning down, he buried his face in Beau's neck, inhaling him, surrounding himself with the man who made him feel alive and solid despite how broken he knew he was. In these moments, there was no past, no future. No pain or heartache. Just pleasure and love. The only thing that mattered was now. Here. The two of them together, lost in each other.

Beau's hand curled around the back of Ethan's head and he fought to hold on as he continued to thrust again and again, his hips punching forward, his cock tunneling deeper.

"E ... fuck ... I love when you do that."

Knowing he did, Ethan continued, his only goal to please Beau, to make him come apart again.

Beau's other hand roamed over his back and Ethan sighed in ecstasy, loving the gentleness of his husband's touch.

He forced himself to remain in the moment, savoring it, wanting it to last forever but knowing it wouldn't. There would be more moments, and that was the only reason he allowed himself to inch closer to that pivotal point of ecstasy until he was hanging by the razor-sharp edge.

"Beau ... I'm close ... so *fucking* close."

Beau's arms tightened around him. "Come for me, E. Let go."

Wanting Beau to come with him, Ethan forced himself up onto his knees. He wrapped his fist around Beau's cock, mirroring the movement of his hips with his hand. He drove them right to the peak, watching Beau as he did.

Beau's eyes closed, his mouth opening as he shifted closer to release.

"Open your eyes," Ethan demanded. "I want you lookin' at me when you come."

Beau's eyes slowly opened, locking with his.

Ethan pumped his hips harder, faster. Beau took over stroking himself while Ethan focused on getting them there. He was past the point of turning back, so close he could feel the electricity of his release barreling down on him.

"Beau... Fuck, baby..." Ethan groaned. "Say my name."

"Ethan."

"Tell me you love me."

"I love you, E. With all my heart."

Ethan slammed his hips forward. "Fuck ... baby..."

Beau moaned loud and long, his cock pulsing as he came. Ethan followed him over, their gazes still ensnared.

Ethan remained just like that, unable to move, unable to look away. He felt his emotions churning inside him. A mixture of love and fear, happiness and anxiety. He never understood where the chaos came from, and he wished like hell he could fight it. However, it was during these moments, when he knew what a gift Beau really was, that his fears intensified. Fear of losing Beau, fear of not being enough for him.

As though he could read Ethan's mind, Beau reached up and pulled him down. Strong arms circled him, holding him tight. No words were necessary, because Ethan knew this man was strong enough to take care of him. He'd never felt safe before. Not until Beau.

"I've got you, E. Now and forever."

Ethan nodded, words not forming.

He simply held on.

Chapter Eleven

Thursday, November 8, 2018
(Two weeks later)

"HEY, E!" BEAU HOLLERED AS HE SET his cell phone down after checking the text message that had caused his phone to chime.

"S'up?" Ethan appeared from the other side of the warehouse, where he'd been working on one of the big machines Reese had asked them to look at that morning.

Beau started toward him. "Zoey's at home right now. Thought maybe we'd go see how she's doin'."

Ethan nodded, then grabbed a grease rag. "Can we grab lunch after?"

Beau nodded.

They had taken Zoey to the clinic yesterday to have the second procedure done, and ever since, Beau had been thinking about her. They had all been in good spirits, although the underlying anxiety was still there. This time, they were hoping for a pregnancy. In fact, they'd agreed to increase the number of embryos implanted to increase their chances.

The thought of having not one but two babies made him a little light-headed. However, it had nothing to do with fear or concern. More like anticipation. To think they could have two babies... It was more than Beau had ever hoped for.

Before they left the clinic, the doctor had suggested Zoey take it easy for a while. He'd gone so far as to order them all to treat her like a princess. So, they had. Last night, Beau and Ethan had babysat while Kaleb took Zoey out to dinner and a movie, wanting her to relax as much as possible.

Beau couldn't stop thinking about the fact she was doing this for them, about how amazingly generous she was. Zoey knew the risks, knew that there was a possibility of no pregnancy, but she was moving forward for them. These were emotional times for all of them and perhaps that was the reason he couldn't get Zoey off his mind.

It was highly possible she was now pregnant with their child. Or children. The thought made him smile. Since the first procedure hadn't taken, Beau was hoping this one would work. And he'd opted for the power of positive thinking. He figured it couldn't hurt.

Although he was keeping his thoughts in that little bubble with the smiley emoticon, he had a strange feeling. Something told him they needed to go check on her. They were planning to go over to Zoey's to watch the kids tonight simply so she could chill out at home. It was the least they could do, but something had him wanting to go see her now. Probably him being a little overprotective, but so what.

"I'll drive," Ethan announced as Beau grabbed his Stetson and set it on his head.

Ethan adjusted his ball cap as he grabbed the keys off the wall near the door. Beau pressed the button to lower the bay door, and a few minutes later, they were in the truck, pulling out of the Walker ranch. A minute more and they were pulling into Kaleb and Zoey's.

"Son of a bitch," Ethan growled when they turned into Zoey's driveway. "Call the sheriff, Beau."

Well, *that* certainly explained the weird feeling he'd had for the past few minutes.

Beau threw himself out of the truck and raced up to the front porch, where his mother was ranting and raving like a fucking lunatic.

"You're goin' to hell, woman!" Arlene shouted at the closed door. "You're doin' the devil's work."

"Arlene!" Beau stomped up the steps behind her. "What the fuck are you doin'? There are babies in that house!"

"I don't care. That woman's in there and she needs to hear this."

"No, she doesn't," he barked. "You need to go!"

"Yes, she does," a deep voice sounded from inside the house.

A moment later, Carl Stranford, Zoey's father, appeared with a fucking shotgun.

"Carl," Ethan warned. "She's leavin'. Put the gun down."

"You've got two minutes, woman," Carl snarled. "After that, I start shootin'."

Shit. Beau could tell Carl wasn't bluffing. The man was overprotective when it came to his daughter, even more so with his grandsons. And considering Zoey was home alone with the boys, it made sense that he was taking matters into his own hands.

"Hey, Kaleb," Ethan said into his phone. "We've got a situation at your house." There was a brief pause followed by, "Good. See you in a minute."

Beau reached for Arlene's arm, but she jerked out of his hold. "Don't touch me," she hissed. "You're goin' to hell, too. Every one of you."

"Well, you're goin' to jail," Ethan retorted, "if you don't get off the property."

Shit. Beau wasn't sure he'd ever seen Ethan as angry as he was in that moment.

"Arlene. Go," Beau commanded, pointing toward her car. "Now."

"Yeah," Ethan's voice sounded from behind him. "We've got a situation at the Stranford place. Need someone to escort Arlene Bennett off the property."

Fuck. Ethan was on the phone with the sheriff's department.

As much as he hated his mother in that moment, Beau did not want to see her go to jail. She was his mother. The mere thought didn't sit well with him. Then again, he also didn't want to see Carl fill her full of buckshot, either.

This time when he grabbed her arm, Beau didn't allow his mother to get away. He marched her down the steps, tugging on her when she attempted to pull away.

"Mom, go!" he shouted, trying to get through the crazy he could see brewing in her eyes. "The sheriff's on his way."

"I won't stand for this!" Arlene announced. "That woman will not bear your child. This isn't right. The devil's at work here."

Holy shit. Beau had never seen her so irate.

Carl stepped out onto the porch, the shotgun raised, aimed right at Beau's mother.

"Carl, put the gun down, now!" Ethan commanded. "My husband's standin' there, for fuck's sake."

"Dad!" Zoey shouted as she shot out through the screen door. "Give me that gun. You go inside right now and watch the boys."

Beau couldn't help but smile at the way Zoey took command of her father. Fortunately for all of them, Carl lowered the weapon and glared over at them. Zoey retrieved the rifle, then closed the front door with her father on the other side before setting the shotgun on the porch swing.

"Arlene, the cops are on the way," Beau told her again. "You've violated the protection order."

"I don't care," she said, although he heard a hint of trepidation in her tone. "I won't stand for this. I won't allow you and that … *demon* to bring a child into this world."

Beau released her and glared down at the woman who had birthed him.

"Go!" His voice was so hard it must've surprised Arlene, because her eyes shot to his face.

"Or what?"

"Or I'll make you," he snarled. "If you say one more word, I'll press charges myself."

Her eyes were wide and he could see the fear there. She knew he would do it.

"Fine," she snapped. "I'll go, but I'll be back."

"No you won't."

"Watch me."

Before she could get two feet away, the sheriff's car pulled down the driveway.

"I'm not goin' to jail," Arlene insisted. "And I'll be damned if I allow you to have a baby, Beau."

"Beau?" Ethan called from behind him.

He turned to look at his husband. He could see the banked fury in Ethan's gaze.

How the hell had his life gotten to this point? He'd never expected to be put in a position like this. To have to choose between the woman who had raised him and the man he loved more than life itself.

Not that there was even a question who he would choose. Ethan stood by him, supported him, *loved* him. Arlene had proven long ago that she couldn't care less what happened to him.

Beau turned back to Arlene as the sheriff was closing his car door.

No turning back now.

"What's the problem here?" Sheriff Endsley asked as he approached. His gaze swung up to the porch. "Carl? You better not be holdin' that shotgun."

Beau glanced up at the porch to see that Carl had opened the front door again and was peering out from behind the screen.

"He's not, Sheriff," Zoey assured him, pointing toward the porch swing. "It's right there. And no one's gonna touch it until I can unload it and lock it up."

Sheriff Endsley turned to Arlene. "Mrs. Bennett? Care to explain why you're back on this property when you've been told you can't be here?"

Arlene spun around to face the sheriff, her eyes hard. "I have a right to go anywhere I please."

"Actually, ma'am, you do not."

The sound of a truck in the distance had Beau looking up. Pulling down the driveway was Kaleb followed closely by Travis, with Gage riding shotgun, and Zane right behind them.

"I'm gonna have to take you down to the station, Mrs. Bennett."

"No you're not!" She backed up a couple of steps. "I'm not going anywhere with you."

Sheriff Endsley peered up at Beau. He wasn't sure what the man wanted him to do or say, so he gave a slight nod, letting the sheriff know he wouldn't be interfering.

"If you can come calmly, I won't handcuff you," Sheriff Endsley told Arlene.

She spun around to face Beau, her eyes wild. "Beau? You can't let them arrest me. You can't."

Actually, he could.

At this point, it was the *only* thing he could do.

ETHAN COULDN'T BELIEVE THE SHIT GOING DOWN right in front of him.

It was like one of those soap operas his mother used to watch back in the day. Only this was a redneck version, complete with the shotgun-toting old man and the belligerent old woman who swatted at the sheriff.

While Ethan was downright shocked by what was taking place, he had to admit, it was almost amusing.

Almost being the key word.

When the sheriff started moving toward his car, Ethan peered up at Zoey. While taking Arlene to jail would've solved this problem, it wouldn't help in the long run and Ethan knew Beau was looking to her for support. It was obvious Beau wasn't going to step in and change the direction this was headed. Ethan secretly hoped that someone would, because he couldn't stand the thought of Beau hurting.

Not that Ethan didn't think Arlene should go to jail. She deserved it for her actions, but it still made him hurt for Beau.

Ethan moved closer to his husband, touching Beau's arm, just to let him know he was there.

"Sheriff!" Zoey yelled from the front porch. She took a few steps out. "Can I talk to you for a minute?"

Sheriff Endsley glanced at Zoey, then to Arlene, then back to Zoey. He nodded but opened the back door of his car and helped Arlene inside.

As soon as she was sealed in the police cruiser, Ethan felt Beau stiffen.

Without thinking, Ethan took Beau's hand and linked their fingers together. Beau didn't take his eyes off his mother.

Kaleb joined Zoey and the sheriff on the porch while Zane, Travis, and Gage made their way over to where Ethan and Beau were standing near the driveway.

"Kaleb call you?" Ethan asked Travis.

His oldest brother shook his head. "No. I've got Reese keepin' an eye on her. He called to let me know she was headin' this way. How'd you know she was here?"

Ethan shook his head. "Didn't. Beau wanted to come by to check on Zoey."

Gage met Ethan's gaze, and Ethan wondered if he was thinking the same thing. That perhaps Beau'd had a premonition, something that alerted him that there was going to be a problem.

Not that Ethan believed in that weird shit, but the universe did work in mysterious ways, so he couldn't write it off completely.

They all glanced up at the porch to see Zoey talking to the sheriff while Kaleb stood beside her, his arm over her shoulder.

A minute later, the sheriff was approaching them.

"Zoey doesn't want to press charges," Sheriff Endsley informed them. "Does anyone have an objection to that?"

Beau's fingers tightened around Ethan's, but he didn't say a word.

Travis seemed to be studying Beau, waiting for a response. Ethan knew he didn't have one. Watching his mother go to jail—no matter how evil she was—would hurt him. And the last thing Ethan wanted was for his husband to suffer any more than he already was.

"No," Ethan said. "We don't have a problem with that."

"You know she's just gonna come back," the sheriff said as though it was obvious.

Beau turned then. "He's right. She's not gonna stop. She'll keep harassin' Zoey."

"But she won't hurt her." At least Ethan didn't think she would.

Beau looked at the floor. "I want to believe that, but…"

Ethan knew why he said that. When they'd arrived, Arlene had been out of control. Her anger was palpable and he honestly didn't know what Arlene was capable of.

"She needs to be arrested," Beau said, his voice strained. "It's the only way to get her to see that she can't do this."

"I agree," Travis said, his tone low. "However, maybe we don't have to go that far." His eyes cut to the sheriff's car. "I think she can be scared straight." He turned back to the sheriff. "Take her down to the station, but don't book her. We'll get her car back to her house. Her husband can pick her up."

"You okay with that?" Sheriff Endsley asked Beau directly.

He nodded.

While he wasn't sure there was any help for Arlene, Ethan agreed with Travis. Perhaps a trip down to the station would put enough fear in her that she would stop this bullshit.

"But if she comes back," Beau stated, his dark eyes meeting the sheriff's, "she needs to be arrested. No questions."

"Understood."

They stood there as the sheriff headed for his car. Ethan could see Arlene inside, her eyes narrowed, her hatred for him apparent. Honestly, Ethan couldn't give less of a shit whether she liked him or not, but he wouldn't stand for her hurting Beau.

"So what happened?" Gage asked.

Ethan relayed the details of showing up, finding Arlene on the porch. He explained how Carl came out wielding a shotgun and threatening to shoot.

"He's an ornery old bastard," Travis said with a grin.

"That he is," Gage agreed.

"I called Kaleb, but Zoey had already called him." Ethan glanced at Travis. "Then I called the sheriff's office."

Beau stood there motionless as the sheriff's car backed down the long driveway and onto the road. When the car was out of sight, Beau released Ethan's hand and headed for the porch.

Ethan followed, along with everyone else.

"I'm sorry about this, Zoey," Beau said as he climbed the steps.

"It's not your fault." Her eyes were full of sympathy. "I told the sheriff I didn't want to press charges."

"He's not," Travis told her. "Just takin' her down to the station. We're hopin' it'll scare her enough to keep her away from here."

"Well, I gotta head back to work," Zane said. "If anyone needs anything, just holler." He put his hand on Beau's shoulder. "That goes for you, too."

Beau nodded, remaining silent.

Not knowing what else to do, Ethan glanced at Beau, then over at Travis. He fucking hated this entire situation, but he wasn't sure how to go about rectifying it. Arlene had proven she was downright crazy. She was wound up tight over them having a baby and he feared something bad was going to happen unless someone stepped in to do something.

Unfortunately, he didn't know who and he didn't know what, but he hoped like hell someone could come up with a plan.

———————

WHEN CURTIS SAW TRAVIS'S TRUCK PULL UP in his driveway, he knew something was wrong simply by looking at him.

Curtis didn't even have to ask before his oldest son launched into an explanation of the events that took place at Kaleb's a short time ago, including how the sheriff had been called but no charges were being brought against Arlene despite the fact she had violated the protection order.

Perhaps that was a good thing, but Curtis had his doubts.

"Where's she now?" he asked Travis, getting to his feet and grabbing his wallet from the counter.

"At the station," Travis explained. "We were hopin' to scare her a little. Why?"

Curtis tucked his wallet into his back pocket and grabbed his hat. "I'm gonna go pay her a visit."

"I'll go with you."

Curtis shook his head. That was the last thing this situation needed. "No. I'm gonna have a civilized conversation with her. There's no need for extra intimidation."

Plus, what Curtis had to say to Arlene wasn't something that needed to be shared with anyone else. Not unless Arlene decided to ignore his ultimatum.

While he had more than enough ammunition to cut the woman off at the knees, Curtis had been damn patient up to this point. Unfortunately, Arlene was forcing his hand. It was time for the bullshit to stop.

"I'll just go in case you need me."

"I won't," Curtis assured him.

It appeared Travis didn't like his response, but he opted not to argue. "Fine. I'm headin' back to the resort, but if you need me, call."

Curtis nodded. He wouldn't need Travis. Not for this.

After telling Lorrie where he was going, Curtis got in his truck and headed into town. It didn't take long to get to the building the sheriff department used as their jail. It wasn't a big place, just two offices, a break room, and some storage space, along with three cells, which rarely had visitors.

Today, there was one.

"Curtis," Jeff Endsley greeted when Curtis stepped into the overly bright building. It was obvious the sheriff didn't approve of him being there based on the frown on his weathered face.

Curtis shook the man's hand, then nodded toward the row of cells at the back. "Good to see you, Jeff."

Jeff followed his line of sight. "I've already called Ben to come pick her up."

Hopefully the man wouldn't show up too quickly.

Curtis peered back at Jeff. "Before she leaves, I need a word with her."

"I'm not sure that's a good idea."

No, probably not, but Curtis was past the point of caring.

His tolerance for this bullshit had run its course. This woman was stirring up shit in their town and she was targeting his kids to do it. Unfortunately, the hate she spewed spread like cancer, viciously infecting those around her. Someone had to do something or he feared it would never stop.

If anyone should understand the hell this woman was putting his kids through, it should be Jeff. She was threatening the lives of every person in this town who loved someone others didn't believe they should. While same-sex relationships weren't frowned upon as much as they once had been, Curtis knew they had a long way to go until they were treated equally. Curtis also knew it required people to stand up to those who thought they could keep them repressed.

Considering Jeff had been in a relationship with Mack, the bartender/owner of Moonshiners, he would understand. While he didn't know the specifics, Curtis did know that their relationship had crashed and burned when Mack's son had arrived in town. He suspected that Mack was hiding who he was, and likely for exactly this reason. As far as Curtis was concerned, it was in Jeff's best interest that Curtis cut the head off the snake of this town's biggest opponent of gay marriage.

"I just have a few words to say to her."

Jeff stared at him for a moment, but finally nodded. "If she starts yellin', I'm gonna yank you outta there."

Curtis smiled. It wouldn't get to that point. He was sure of it.

The instant they started toward Arlene, her eyes widened but she remained quiet. Jeff opened the cell door, which hadn't been locked, then headed back to the front.

"Arlene," Curtis greeted as he leaned against the metal bars of the cell, just outside the door.

"I have nothing to say to you."

"Good," he told her. "I wasn't interested in hearin' it anyway."

The silence lingered for a few seconds before Arlene met his gaze again. "What do you want?"

Curtis eyed the woman for a moment. Her shoulders were tense, her hands clasped tightly in her lap. At one point in her life, Arlene had been a beautiful woman. Unfortunately for her, outside appearances didn't make a person attractive. The hate she bred in this community had long ago turned her into something that lacked any redeeming qualities whatsoever.

"I'm here to tell you to stay away from my family, Arlene. All of them. My sons, their spouses, my grandchildren. Every single one of them."

"You can't do that," she argued. "I have a right—"

"As a matter of fact, I can," he said firmly, cutting off her rant. "If you know anything about me, you know I'm not a tolerant man when it comes to threats against my family. I won't stand for it. I put up with shit from your husband a few years ago. If I recall correctly, he disowned your son. As far as I'm concerned, you have no rights where Beau's concerned anymore, either."

"I'm his mother."

"No, you're not. A mother doesn't turn on her son the way you did. A mother supports her children, protects them."

"You know nothing about me."

"On the contrary…"

Her eyes widened, and Curtis suspected Arlene knew where this conversation was headed.

"How can *you* stand for it, Mr. Walker? You seem like a God-fearing man."

Curtis pretended not to understand what she was referring to.

Of course, she continued. "Yet you allow these … abominations … to happen in your own family. Your children have been possessed by the devil and it doesn't seem to bother you."

"I'm not following."

Her dark eyebrow arched. "Your oldest boy is married to a man *and* a woman. That's not even legal."

"Yet they're quite content. I'm not sure how that's any concern of yours."

"And your other son has corrupted mine."

"Corrupted?" Curtis shifted, crossing one ankle over the other. "I recall your husband accusing my son of turnin' Beau gay. Is that what you mean by 'corrupted'?"

"Yes."

He kept his voice low, calm. "Love, Arlene, knows no gender. Of all people, I thought for sure you would understand that."

"*Me?*" Her face went stark white. "Wha—what are you talking about?"

"You forget that my family has been here for generations. And I know things … things most people have long ago forgotten."

For the first time, Arlene was speechless. It didn't surprise him.

"I'm not that much older than you are, Arlene." Curtis tapped his temple. "And my memory's still clear."

"I don't know what you're talkin' about." Her expression said otherwise.

"You might've married a man to hide who you are, but that doesn't erase the past. It doesn't change the fact that you were in a relationship with a woman before you turned your back on the very love you now detest."

Her eyes rounded and her jaw dropped open.

"As I said, love knows no gender. I'm not here to pass judgement on you. The path you chose is none of my business. However, my boys and their families *are* my business. Their happiness is my business. So, unless you'd prefer I share your secret with anyone who'll listen—and trust me, they'll listen—then I suggest you pull back on the high and mighty. If I were you, I'd be makin' peace with myself rather than tryin' to decide the fate of others."

She swallowed hard.

Curtis motioned toward the front door. "When I leave here, I've got two options. The first is to go home to my beautiful wife and spend time with her and my family. Or, before I do that, I can have a conversation with your husband. I heard he's on his way to get you now. Your choice."

"You wouldn't."

"Oh, I would and I will. It's up to you, Arlene. How do you think Ben will handle it when he learns the woman he married was at one point in love with another woman? A woman who, ironically, is my sister."

Arlene inhaled sharply.

Although his baby sister had married Hamilton Wilkes many years ago, Curtis knew the truth about Lisa. She'd been in love with Arlene back during a time when a love like that wasn't socially permitted. However, his sister had been strong. Lisa had wanted to fight for the love she had with Arlene. Unfortunately, Arlene had proven back then that she wasn't strong enough. Within two months of breaking Lisa's heart, Arlene had been engaged to Ben Bennett, a man who condemned anyone who wasn't like him. His evil ran deep. Not only was he a racist, a bigot, and a homophobe, but he was a sexist asshole. Ben believed everyone was beneath him, including his own wife.

"You wouldn't do that to your sister," Arlene argued, but the anger in her eyes had dimmed.

"Lisa's not ashamed of who she is," he clarified. "Her husband is well aware of the fact that at one point, she was in love with a woman. She loves him, there's no denying that. In fact, she loves him enough that she felt safe to share that with him."

Arlene obviously had no argument for that.

"It's your choice, Arlene. Do I go home? Or do I have a quick chat with your husband?"

The sadness he saw in Arlene's eyes… Curtis knew it wasn't because she'd lost this battle. It was because she'd lost everything, including the love of her life. A long time ago.

"You can go home, Mr. Walker," she said softly.

"I expect you to stay away from Beau, Ethan, Zoey, and everyone else in my family." He stood up straight. "Don't attempt to approach them. Not at their homes, not out in public. Don't even look at them at church."

She nodded, her gaze on her clasped hands.

Curtis pivoted to go but he paused, turning to face her once more. "Should you ever decide you want to be part of your grandchild's life, come talk to me first. Despite all the pain you've caused him, Beau has the ability to forgive." When she lifted her head to look at him, he held her stare. "The question is, can you forgive yourself first?"

Without looking back, Curtis headed for the door. His thoughts drifted to Lisa, to the pain he'd seen on his youngest sister's face all those years ago when the love of her life broke her heart.

Arlene Bennett had obviously fought to erase the love she'd once felt. And he suspected this was how she dealt with it. She had somehow convinced herself it was wrong.

But Curtis had seen it in her eyes. She was still affected. All these years later.

It saddened him to think that Arlene had suffered just as much.

However, he wasn't going to let her regrets cause any more pain to his family.

Not ever again.

Chapter Twelve

BEAU'S PHONE LIT UP WITH THE BABY alert text at seven thirty in the morning, just a few minutes after he and Ethan had arrived at the shop.

Their usual schedule of working half days on Saturday as a way to ensure they could keep up with the work had been switched up this weekend since yesterday had been Ethan's birthday. Because of that they had decided to skip church and come in this morning instead. They probably would've simply blown it off, but there were a few things they had to get knocked out. They'd missed quite a bit of work lately due to all the clinic visits, so they had to get caught up.

Looked as though they would simply have to double it up during the week to make up for it now.

The coffee had just started to brew when both of their phones lit up with a text message from Braydon. Jessie was in labor, already at the hospital, and the doctor expected it to be quick.

Quick was an understatement.

They'd locked everything back up after pouring two mugs of coffee and hit the road for the hospital. They arrived less than an hour after the text came through, but it appeared the baby had been in too much of a hurry. They were walking into the waiting room as Travis was stepping in from the labor and delivery hallway.

"Another boy," Travis announced. "According to his father, Waylon Matthew Walker has a head full of black hair."

As usual, everyone who was there congratulated everyone else. However, it appeared Beau and Ethan weren't the only two who'd been running behind. He didn't see Zane or V yet.

Exactly as he was thinking it, Zane appeared with V at his side. "Sorry. Had to ask Bristol to come by. Reid's got the sniffles, so we didn't want to bring him up here."

Made sense.

Beau surveyed the room, realizing Zoey and Kaleb hadn't made it, either. He shot a quick look to Ethan, wondering if he'd noticed it, too. Based on the frown on his face as he surveyed the room, taking in every person, Beau figured he did.

"Where's Zoey and Kaleb?" Ethan asked Travis when he sauntered over.

Travis peered around as though he hadn't realized they weren't there. And that said something about the craziness of the morning. If Travis didn't know what was going on, the planets were probably out of alignment.

Before words could come out of Travis's mouth, Curtis appeared, then nodded over Beau's shoulder. "Right behind you there."

Beau spun around to see Zoey walking in with Kaleb beside her. They were both grinning from ear to ear.

Without stopping to say anything to anyone else, she walked over and grabbed their hands. "Sorry I'm late, but I got a call from the doctor this morning."

On a Sunday? That seemed odd.

Beau held his breath, wanting to believe the huge grin on her face was a good sign. Why else would the doctor call on Sunday morning? Surely not to give bad news, right? She'd gone in for a blood test yesterday to see if the second transfer had worked since the first hadn't. For the past eleven days, Beau had counted down every minute, waiting for this moment.

"And?" Ethan asked, his patience clearly thin.

"You're pregnant," she proclaimed. Her smile damn near blinded Beau. "According to the doctor, he's estimating the due date for August fourteenth."

Without thinking, Beau pulled Zoey in for a hug. She giggled and hugged him back.

Holy fuck.

Holy … *fuck.*

They were pregnant.

Shit.

Don't hurt the woman, his conscience screamed.

He released Zoey as he fought to breathe. Beau's hands went numb, as did his feet. For a moment, he thought he would fall over, but Ethan grabbed his arm and pulled him close. Their eyes locked and a wealth of communication passed between them without a single word being said. Beau could see Ethan's excitement as well as his concern. Both of which he understood completely.

They were finally going to have a baby.

Ethan stepped closer and touched Beau's cheek. "We're pregnant, baby."

Yes, they were.

Hot damn.

"Well, then it's an even better day," Travis said. He peered over at Ethan as though asking a silent question.

Ethan laughed, a sound that shocked almost everyone around them. He nodded his head, then turned back to Beau.

"Y'all, we've got more good news," Travis said, loud enough for everyone in the room to hear. "Not only do we have a new Walker in the house, but we've got another one on the way. Ethan and Beau are pregnant."

"Ooh! That means we'll be pregnant together!"

All eyes shot over to Kylie, who had slapped her hand over her mouth, her eyes wide.

Travis and Gage slowly pivoted, a move that was quite comical, then stared down at her as though she'd spoken a foreign language.

"You're pregnant?" Travis asked, his voice rough.

She nodded, her eyes locked on both of her husbands.

"Holy—"

Gage slammed his hand over Travis's mouth before the curse came out.

"More babies!" Zane shouted.

You would've thought the Cowboys had just won the Super Bowl based on the shouting and celebration that ensued.

Beau didn't move. He stared back at Ethan, his heart in his throat.

The past month and a half had been both exciting and terrifying. And now...

"We're pregnant," Beau whispered, his eyes still locked on Ethan's face.

"Uncle Beau!"

Tearing his gaze away from Ethan, he peered down at Kate, standing beside him in her pretty dress, her big brown eyes peering up at him expectantly.

"What's up, kiddo?"

"Didn't you hear my daddy? The baby's *here*. That means we get to play a game, right? And go get donut holes?"

He laughed. "That's definitely what it means."

Beau turned back to Ethan, who was still smiling.

Ethan tilted his chin in Kate's direction. "Go on. We'll celebrate later. After the game."

With that, Beau herded the kids in a circle and explained the rules. For a brief moment, he envisioned the day his son or daughter would be part of that little circle, eager to head to the cafeteria to get donut holes. Or grapes, as the adults liked to refer to them.

As he was leading the kids out of the waiting room, Beau glanced over to see Ethan hugging Zoey. The smile on her face hadn't dimmed and his heart skipped a couple of beats. He still couldn't believe this was real. They were going to be fathers.

When Ethan pulled back, Beau waited until their eyes met and he mouthed that he loved him, earning the same in return.

"Come on, y'all," Beau said with a grin. "Let's go get some grapes."

"The *little* kids are here, Uncle Beau," Mason chastised. "We have to call them donut holes."

"Right. Donut holes."

Three hours later, Beau was still riding the high from the news that they were in fact pregnant. He'd done his best to focus on the kiddos, ensuring they had the best time he could offer, while he wanted nothing more than to go to the hardware store and buy paint.

Not that he could get paint. He didn't know what color to get yet.

"You want somethin' for lunch?" Ethan asked when they stepped into the house.

"Yes," Beau said instantly, closing the door and tossing his keys onto the side table.

Ethan continued walking into the kitchen, so Beau followed.

"I'm game for anything," Ethan said, heading for the sink to wash his hands.

Beau waited patiently until he was finished. When Ethan turned back around, drying his hands with a towel, Beau crowded him against the cabinet.

"What's on your mind?" Ethan asked with a grin.

"You."

"Me?" Ethan's dark eyebrows shot upward. "What about me?"

"I want you for lunch."

Ethan laughed. "I can hear your stomach, babe. You're starvin'."

"Maybe, but food can wait." Not wanting Ethan to come up with a dozen more excuses to give him a hard time, Beau took his hand and tugged.

"You sure you wanna do this?" Ethan asked, trailing behind him. "It's the middle of the day and all. I mean, I get that you can't keep your hands off me, but this is gettin' ridiculous."

Beau knew Ethan was just giving him shit. The man was horny ninety-nine percent of the time. Not once in all the time they'd been together had Ethan *ever* turned down sex.

And Beau was going to ensure today wasn't the first time, either.

OVERWHELMED.

That was how Ethan felt. Completely overwhelmed by everything, including the man who was kissing him like there was no tomorrow.

Yes, he'd given Beau shit about sex in the middle of the day, but it wasn't like he was going to argue for real. Hell, he'd take Beau any way he could get him at any time.

As they stepped farther into their bedroom, Ethan gripped Beau's head, letting the kiss consume him while Beau worked the button and zipper on Ethan's jeans. His stomach muscles tightened, heat flooding his body. He was on the verge of combusting when Beau gripped his cock, fisting it gently, stroking slowly.

Ah, Christ. This man knew exactly what Ethan needed and when he needed it.

It would've been easy for Ethan to let sex drown out the emotions he was consumed by. That was how he operated. Always had been. Except Beau didn't allow it. He always brought Ethan back to the moment.

With one hand still wrapped around Ethan's cock, Beau managed to force Ethan's jeans down his legs. However, when Beau started to go to his knees, Ethan stopped him.

"Naked," he insisted, releasing Beau's face so he could do the same.

149

Seconds later, they were both naked, their lips once again fused together. Ethan managed to ease Beau down onto the bed, crawling over him as he released Beau's lips.

"While I want you on your back, I'm not gonna pass up the opportunity to have my cock in your mouth," Ethan said, grinning.

Beau's eyes flashed with heat and a mischievous grin split his face. "You know how my mouth feels about that."

While Ethan crawled forward, Beau inched down until Ethan was practically straddling Beau's face. Without hesitation, that sweet mouth consumed his dick, causing Ethan to draw in a sharp breath.

Although fucking Beau's face until he came in a rush sounded so damn good right about then, Ethan managed to refrain. Instead, he rocked his hips forward and back, allowing the warm suction of Beau's mouth to steal what was left of his sanity.

Long minutes passed as Ethan allowed Beau to drive him closer to release. Before he got to the point of no return, he pulled free of Beau's mouth, then moved back over him, kissing him roughly.

"On your stomach," Ethan commanded. "Hands on the headboard. Ass in the air."

Beau gave him that million-megawatt smile before he nodded. While Beau got into position, Ethan bounced off the bed, grabbing the lube from the nightstand. He wasted no time getting into position behind Beau. Once he prepped his cock and Beau's ass, Ethan lined up and sank into the heaven of Beau's body.

"I'm gonna love you for hours," Ethan teased as he leaned over Beau, forcing the big man to flatten out on the bed.

"Bring it on." Beau moaned when Ethan retreated slowly, then pushed in deep.

He remained just like that, blanketing Beau's big body with his own as he rocked his hips, teasing them both.

"Do you know how much I love you?" Ethan whispered in Beau's ear.

"Yes."

"I don't think you do." He rocked in, pulled out. In again. "More than anything."

Beau released the headboard and Ethan took advantage, pressing his palms to the back of Beau's hands and twining their fingers, restraining Beau against the mattress.

"Anything in the world," Ethan added. "And I wanna spend the rest of my life loving you."

Damn. Beau felt so good beneath him, his body welcoming him inside. He could've stayed like that for the rest of his life.

"I love you, E," Beau said, his voice rumbling against Ethan's chest.

"I know," he assured Beau. "I know, baby."

Releasing Beau's hands, Ethan slid his arms beneath Beau's chest, curling his fingers over Beau's shoulders as he held on tightly. Pressing his lips to the back of Beau's neck, he kissed his skin, inhaling the musky scent of him. He would never get enough of this man.

Ethan got lost in the warmth of Beau's body, in the overwhelming emotion that always shocked him with its intensity. Sometimes it was hard to believe that he could love someone this much. To the point he could hardly breathe with it.

And while they weren't living an endless honeymoon—not almost five years into their marriage—it was still as perfect as it always had been. For them. Sure, they fought over who stole the covers, who snored louder, who left the toothpaste cap off the toothpaste—all Beau, for the record—but it was still perfect. No, they didn't make love and stare into each other's eyes for hours on end. But they loved each other. Passionately, endlessly. Always.

"E ... just like that ... oh, God ..."

Ethan continued to drive into Beau, keeping his movements slow and easy, relishing every sensation that coursed through him. He surpassed his own patience threshold, but just barely. He always had good intentions, but Beau tipped him over the edge so easily.

Unable to hold back, Ethan moaned softly as his orgasm neared. He was so close, but he didn't want the feeling to end.

"Beau..."

"Come for me, E." Beau's hand slid around and latched onto Ethan's thigh. "Let me feel you come for me."

Fuck.

"It's too good…" Ethan's cock swelled and jerked, pulsing with his release. Once he was spent, he immediately pulled out, then forced Beau over onto his back.

Beau instantly fisted his own cock and Ethan leaned down to take him in his mouth. Beau's other hand latched on to Ethan's hair, holding him in place as he rocked his hips upward.

"Coming, E … Fuck…"

Ethan drank him down, then collapsed on top of Beau. His husband's big, warm arms wrapped around him, and as usual, he felt safe, secure. Whole. There was no place quite like this. No one could calm the noise inside Ethan's head simply by being there the way Beau could.

"Now…" Beau said with a chuckle, "about the food you promised?"

Ethan laughed, lifting his head to look Beau in the eye. "*Now* you're hungry?"

Beau's grin was sheepish. "Always."

Ethan pretended to be put out. "Fine. But you get to clean the kitchen."

"Not a problem."

"You say that now. You might change your mind when I'm done. I'm feelin' a little … destructive."

WHILE ETHAN COOKED LUNCH, BEAU OPTED FOR a shower.

As he stood beneath the warm spray, he tried to clear his head, but it didn't work. His brain was overloaded with so many thoughts. Ethan. Their son or daughter. Maybe plural. What their life would be like when they brought their child home for the first time. All the things they'd celebrate together in the future. Birthdays, holidays. Christmas. Especially Christmas. Church. Sunday dinners. Family.

Beau couldn't seem to stop smiling. From the inside out.

It was easy to get carried away on those thoughts, but Beau knew he had to rein himself in a little. August fourteenth was a long time away. They had a ton to do before then, but he knew they couldn't rush out and do everything, either. Beau had read that there could be issues—God forbid—and he knew he had to be prepared in the event something bad happened.

Granted, he didn't want to dwell on the negative. He wanted to stay right where he was, walking on the cloud of euphoria from the good news and from the love he felt from Ethan.

Plus, he had some research to do. He wanted to know every single thing there was to know about their baby. What it looked like as it formed, how big it was, whether or not it could suck its thumb in the womb, what it could hear from its warm cocoon inside Zoey. He had so much more to learn.

Forcing himself to get out of the shower, Beau dried off and tugged on his jeans before joining Ethan in the kitchen.

"Somethin' came for you," Ethan said, nodding toward the front door.

"What is it?"

Ethan shrugged. "Don't know."

Hesitantly, Beau went to the front door. There on the table was a vase of flowers—a colorful fall arrangement that had him grinning even more. There was only one person in the world who knew Beau liked flowers. Beside the vase was a cardboard package about the size of a book.

After taking the card from the small plastic stick that held it, Beau unfolded the paper.

Before you, I didn't believe there was hope for me. With you, I'm learning that my life is worth living a hundred times over. Thank you for loving me and for sharing my dreams. Love, Ethan

Beau felt the emotion bubble up inside him, his chest constricting. Ethan pretended not to have a soft bone in his entire body, but Beau knew the truth. He picked up the cardboard box. Since the mail wasn't delivered on Sunday, he knew this hadn't come today. Which meant Ethan had been holding on to it. Beau ripped it open. Inside there were two books. One that detailed every step of the pregnancy, along with what appeared to be a journal for tracking the baby.

Carrying the books with him, Beau returned to the kitchen. "You didn't know what it was, huh?"

Ethan offered a one-shoulder shrug.

"Well, perhaps I'll have to get you a late birthday present," Beau told him.

"Nope. You already got me a new toaster." Ethan chuckled, not lifting his head from what he was doing. "Plus, you know there's only one thing I ever ask for for my birthday."

"Sex for a week?"

"Exactly." Those beautiful steel-blue eyes lifted. "All day long, every single day."

"I think I got a good start on today," Beau said, playing along.

"Yes, you did."

Beau moved toward the island. "I can't promise I won't get you a little something else just because I can."

"Well, sex is all I need." Ethan's eyes darted to him. "In fact, *you* are all I need."

"You're too good to me, E."

Ethan laughed. "It's the other way around. But I did make you lunch."

As usual, Beau's stomach rumbled in anticipation.

"So..." Ethan carried the plates to the table. "Think maybe you could talk me through what happens next? You know. With the baby growing and shit."

Beau laughed. Leave it to Ethan to be eloquent.

"I could probably be persuaded."

Heat flashed in Ethan's eyes causing Beau to grin.

Yeah. His husband was easy.

And it was one of the million reasons he loved him.

Chapter Thirteen

BEAU WASN'T SURE HE'D EVER BEEN HAPPIER to be home.

After spending the majority of the day at Curtis and Lorrie's, he was looking forward to a bit of silence. Like most Walker family functions, there had been so many people packed into one relatively small house.

Having grown up an only child, Beau sometimes wondered how the Walkers had survived all these years like that. So much chaos, so much noise. People talking over one another. Laughter interrupting a perfectly good television show. Hungry babies crying. *Tired* babies crying. Babies crying for no reason.

Yep. And he was looking forward to the day their child was in the thick of it all, enjoying time with family.

Granted, Beau had been around the Walkers most of his life, so he was used to it. Not exactly to the extreme it was these days, mind you. Back when he'd been a kid hanging out at the Walker house, there hadn't been nearly as many people under one roof. Add to that all the Christmas presents and the tree—something one wouldn't normally think about unless there were little ones looking to bring it down at every turn—and it had been a packed house.

"Is it just me, or are your brothers gettin' more daring with that gift exchange?" Beau shrugged out of his coat and laid it over the table by the door.

Once all the brothers had gotten married, they'd come up with a plan to do a secret Santa gift exchange. It started out relatively tame, but over the years, tame had turned into taboo.

"Have you *met* them?" Ethan countered, slipping his coat off, too. "They're competitive."

"I get that. But what's next? Sawyer's bound and determined to outshine Travis on those damn gag gifts. Pretty soon, we'll have to keep the babies out of the room."

As it was, Beau suspected Sawyer had gone on a shopping spree at the adult novelty store. And it seemed to him that the new goal was to see who could be embarrassed the most. He was pretty sure Gage won that honor this year. He'd turned ten shades of red when he opened that colorful jumbo penis lollipop. Thankfully, he'd managed to hide it before one of the kids could take notice.

Before Ethan could head for the stairs, Beau reached for his hand. "This way, husband of mine."

Ethan stopped and turned toward him. "Where're we goin'?"

He nodded toward the couch. "To sit."

Beau urged Ethan to get comfortable before heading over and hitting the switch to turn on the Christmas tree.

"How about a beer?" Beau offered.

"Sounds about perfect right now."

Beau slipped into the kitchen, grabbed two bottles from the refrigerator, popped the tops before joining his husband in the living room. When he stepped in front of the couch and passed over one of the beers, Ethan was pointing for Beau to sit in front of him. With a smile, he lowered himself to the cushion, settling between Ethan's spread legs.

"I'm gonna crush you if I lean back," Beau warned.

"Small price to pay." Rather than pull him back, his husband reached for the hem of his shirt and tugged it up.

"Is that a hint?"

"More like a command," Ethan said with a chuckle.

It took a little maneuvering and passing of his beer between hands, but Beau managed the feat of taking off his shirt. "If I have to be topless, so do you."

With a gleam in his eye, Ethan passed over his beer, then jerked his shirt off over his head and tossed it to the floor. The next thing Beau knew, he was leaning back against Ethan, skin to skin.

"What'd you think about Zoey's present?" Beau passed Ethan's beer back to him.

"The album she's keepin'?"

"Yeah."

"It's cool."

Beau tilted his head back so he could look at Ethan's face. "Cool?"

If he wasn't mistaken, Ethan blushed.

Not wanting to put him on the spot, Beau faced the Christmas tree once again. "I think it's cool that she's documenting that stuff. Since we can't experience it for ourselves, we get her firsthand account."

"It's more than I ever expected," Ethan said, his voice soft.

There was no doubt Zoey was going above and beyond to ensure they experienced her pregnancy in every way possible. She'd bought a pregnancy book—similar to the one Ethan had given him—and she was noting things for every week. Since she was only seven weeks along, not much had happened aside from some morning sickness, but Zoey said it wasn't too bad. Beau wasn't sure he believed her.

Ethan's hands slid over Beau's bare chest and he sighed, leaning into the man he loved. He really was crushing him, but since Ethan didn't seem to mind, Beau didn't move. He happened to enjoy times like this when Ethan would sit still, content to touch him so casually. These moments were rare, which made them all the more precious.

Not that he would tell Ethan that. He'd probably give him shit for even thinking something like that, but it didn't change the fact.

"Zoey said she's havin' some cravings?" Ethan asked, his hands still roaming over Beau's chest. "I thought I heard her mention it."

"Nothing major yet. Just chocolate. However, Jessie said that had nothin' to do with pregnancy."

"So, it's *not* a craving?"

Beau chuckled. "According to Kaleb, chocolate is far too normal to be one of her pregnancy cravings."

Beau had been at the center of the estrogen sandwich for a brief part of the afternoon. The girls had thought it amusing to talk endlessly about pregnancy. He wasn't sure if they were trying to make him feel included, but the only thing he'd felt was awkward. Baby or not, there was only so much a man needed to know about a uterus or the birth canal.

Nonetheless, he'd had a good time. For the most part. He could've done without the explanation of what an episiotomy was.

"Merry Christmas," Ethan whispered against his ear, his breath fanning his cheek. "I love you."

He would never tire of hearing Ethan say that. Never.

"I love you, too." Beau turned his head as Ethan reached around and cupped his face, their lips touching.

"I think it's time to take this upstairs," Ethan suggested.

"You won't get an argument from me." He said the words, but as soon as Ethan released him, Beau shifted so that he was taking Ethan down to the cushion, flat on his back. It only took a second to relocate both of their beers to the coffee table and then Beau settled over him.

"We're still on the couch," Ethan said with a smirk.

"Couldn't wait until we got upstairs." Beau's eyes locked on Ethan's lips.

Resting one knee between Ethan's thighs, Beau covered his body, then melded their lips together. He could kiss this man for hours. And since the house was quiet and there was no one wanting anything from them, maybe that was what he should do.

Of course, kissing Ethan always led to other things. While his intentions were generally honorable when they got started, Ethan had a way of pushing Beau to his breaking point. This time he did it by unbuttoning Beau's jeans and snaking his hand inside.

"Mmm," Ethan moaned, pulling back enough that their lips separated. "I wanna feel you in my mouth."

Fucking hell. Beau couldn't resist that if he'd wanted to. And he damn sure didn't want to.

He forced himself up off the couch and proceeded to shed his boots, jeans, and boxers. By the time he was naked, Ethan was sitting up, his hand circling the hard length of Beau's dick.

Their eyes locked as Ethan took him into his mouth. Warmth enveloped his cock as the rasp of Ethan's tongue sent a shiver down his spine.

"I've been thinkin' about that mouth all day," Beau admitted, sliding his hands over Ethan's head. He didn't hold him in place, simply touched him. "Thinking about your lips, your tongue … you swallowing me."

Ethan took more of him, his lips sliding down and up, his hands trailing up Beau's legs. The twinkling lights of the tree made Ethan's eyes gleam and Beau found himself transfixed by the sight.

Not wanting to end this encounter too soon, Beau cupped Ethan's head more firmly, halting his movements.

"What'd'ya say we move this upstairs?" he suggested.

"I thought you couldn't wait that long?"

"I can't, but if this is gonna escalate, which I hope like hell it does, we're gonna need lube."

Ethan's hand slipped between the couch cushion and…

Beau barked a laugh. "You keep lube in the cushions?"

"One can never be too prepared."

"You know when our kid gets bigger, you'll have to find a better hiding place."

Ethan grinned, then pushed to his feet and passed over the lube. Beau took one step back, allowing room for Ethan to remove his jeans.

"How do you want me?" Ethan asked.

Well, that was easy. Beau grinned. "Every fucking way I can have you."

ETHAN STARED OVER AT THE CHRISTMAS TREE as he spooned Beau from behind. They'd just christened their couch for the thousandth time, and now, as his breaths became more regular, he found himself settling into that comfort zone he'd been getting more familiar with lately.

Beau's hand shifted over Ethan's arm. "This time next year, our kid'll be roughly four months old."

"Yep." Ethan had thought about that a lot these past few weeks. With every passing day, some of his anxiety dissipated. He'd been reluctant to think about ever having kids, and then when they'd hit wall after wall, he'd almost lost all hope. Those doubts were easing and every time he thought about the day their son or daughter was born, Ethan found himself feeling the same sort of elation Beau was capable of making him feel.

Of course, he was still nervous. For many reasons. Some normal, such as worrying that their baby would be healthy. And whether or not it would make it to full term. Those were the most important at this point. Healthy and strong was the goal.

Then there were the other reasons. Those that the majority of people didn't have to worry about. How would their child be treated having two fathers? How would their child feel about it when they were old enough to understand? Would other people— kids and grown-ups alike—give them shit for it?

Ethan had lived with being bullied because he was gay. It wasn't something he could change about himself, so he'd dealt with it. But their child having two fathers … that was a decision he and Beau had made for their child. He couldn't help but be concerned that history would repeat itself.

He hated that his thoughts drifted to those dark places, so he tried to remain positive. There was no sense dwelling on what might never be an issue, so he pushed it back.

For now.

Beau turned his head, his cheek brushing Ethan's shoulder. "So, when do you think we should start gettin' the baby's room ready?"

"I was thinkin' we should wait until we know the sex," Ethan admitted, stroking his hand over Beau's chest. "When does that happen?"

"From what I read, they can pretty much determine the gender around eighteen to twenty weeks," Beau explained.

"Hmm. So that's what? Three months from now?"

"Yep. But Zoey's goin' in next week for her first ultrasound."

"Because they're concerned about multiples?" Ethan asked. He might not have asked a lot of questions during their meetings at the clinic, but Ethan had taken quite a few mental notes.

"Yeah."

Ethan wasn't sure what the actual odds were—or if they even mattered—but he was interested in finding out for sure.

"We're going, right?" Ethan asked.

"Definitely."

They lay there in the silence for a while. Ethan was starting to drift off when Beau shifted in his arms.

"E?"

"Yeah, baby?"

"Merry Christmas."

With his eyes closed, he smiled. "Merry Christmas."

"I really do think we're gonna have to go up to bed now."

"Yeah?"

"In case you didn't realize, this couch isn't big enough for both of us."

"It's workin' fine for me," Ethan said, tightening his hold on Beau.

"Yeah, well, that's because my feet are practically on the floor."

Chuckling, Ethan released Beau. "All right. But once we're up there, I'm gonna be wide awake again."

"Which means?" Beau shifted to sit then stood.

Ethan opened his eyes and smirked at the man he loved more than life. "Round two."

Beau laughed. "You're insatiable, Mr. Walker."

Ethan allowed Beau to help him up. "Yeah, but you love me, Mr. Walker."

"That I do."

As he followed Beau up the stairs, Ethan smiled. It had been a damn good Christmas.

And if he had his way, it wouldn't be over yet.

Chapter Fourteen

Thursday, January 3, 2019
(Nine days later)

BEAU DIDN'T PARTICULARLY CARE FOR DOCTORS' OFFICES. Certainly not the kind that catered to women. However, this was one of those times in a man's life when it was appropriate to follow a woman into an examination room.

Or so he'd been told just a few minutes ago by Zoey.

Thankfully, both Ethan and Kaleb were there with him, so he wasn't the only one feeling a tad uncomfortable. Granted, Kaleb looked right at home here. Since the doctor had delivered four of their children, it sort of made sense.

Beau took a seat in a vacant chair beside Ethan while Zoey sat with Kaleb. He peered around the room. There were a couple of ladies eyeing them curiously. Their attention seemed to bounce from Zoey to Kaleb, who was holding her hand, then over to Ethan and Beau before going back to Zoey.

It was hard not to watch them watching him. Beau wondered what they were thinking. Their curiosity was obvious, but it quickly started making Beau uncomfortable.

"She's having their babies," Kaleb stated, his voice firm.

Beau's head snapped over to glare at his brother-in-law.

"Sorry. I figured I'd put their minds at ease." He didn't look sorry at all.

Great.

Beau dared a glance at Ethan. He knew how much his husband hated being put on the spot like that. Not surprisingly, Ethan was studying a *National Geographic* magazine, pretending he didn't know the rest of them.

In an attempt to appear unfazed by Kaleb's outburst, Beau pulled out his phone and skimmed through his Instagram feed while they waited.

A solid ten minutes passed before a woman called out Zoey's name.

Beau looked up from his phone to see a smiling nurse staring back at them.

"Come on," Zoey urged with a grin.

"I'll wait here," Kaleb announced, leaning back, looking as calm and cool as ever as he played on his phone. "When he meets with you in his office, I'll join you."

Ethan pushed to his feet, adjusting his ball cap, while Beau followed Zoey.

Yeah, the awkwardness wasn't going away. Why was that?

The nurse motioned toward a scale once they'd passed through the door from the waiting room.

"How are you feeling?" the nurse asked Zoey, her smile blinding.

"Really good. A little heartburn, but it's not too bad."

Beau made a point not to look at the number when Zoey stepped on the scale, knowing that women did not like men to know how much they weighed.

After jotting down the information, the nurse led the way to an examination room.

"You ever been in one of these rooms?" Zoey asked.

Beau frowned. "Uh. No."

"I'm teasing, Beau."

He knew that. He did.

Glancing over at Ethan, Beau noticed he was smiling, most of his face shielded by the brim of his ball cap. But not that smirk. It was solid proof that he was amused at Beau's expense.

Zoey took a seat on the exam table, her feet resting on the step at the bottom, while the nurse took her blood pressure and pulse. When she was finished, the nurse told them the doctor would be in momentarily.

Beau's eyes were focused on the huge machine sitting on the far side of the room.

"So ... uh ... that doesn't hurt the baby, does it?"

Zoey glanced over at the machine. "No." She pointed to a small handheld piece. "He'll put some jelly stuff on my stomach, then use that to take a peek."

She must've noticed Beau's tension because she reached out and touched his hand.

"It's harmless, I promise. I had sonograms done with all my kids. We won't get to find out the sex today because it's too early, but we'll get to find out if you're having one baby or two."

He nodded, then stepped back and surveyed the room, cataloging all the various instruments. To be fair, it didn't appear much different than the exam rooms at his primary care doctor. There was a jar of cotton balls, another with tongue depressors, a bottle of rubbing alcohol. There was a sink and some cabinets and he couldn't help wondering if there were a bunch of weird girl-doctor tools hidden in them.

God, he hoped Zoey didn't have to change into one of those paper gown things. Beau wasn't sure he could stay in there if that happened. She was his sister-in-law, after all. Seeing her naked...

He did *not* want to see Zoey naked. He probably wouldn't be able to look at her at Sunday dinners if he did.

A few minutes later, a soft knock sounded before a man carrying a chart opened the door and stepped inside. He was wearing the familiar white coat a lot of doctors wore, but other than that, he did *not* look like a doctor. In fact, he looked more like a model.

Seriously. Mr. Tall, Dark, and Hot was Zoey's doctor? No wonder Zoey had made sure the clinic understood she would be seeing her OB-gyn instead of one they had on staff.

"How are you, Zoey?" he asked, his tone professional, his eyes sliding over them briefly before focusing on her.

"I'm wonderful," she said cheerfully. "I'd like you to meet the baby's dads. This is Beau and Ethan Walker. Ethan is my husband's brother. Guys, this is Dr. Tinder."

"It's a pleasure to meet you both," he said with a quick, firm handshake.

"Same," Ethan said, his voice quiet.

Beau couldn't find his voice. He was still feeling extremely weird standing here in this girl-doctor room with Zoey and Dr. Hot Stuff. It seemed a little ironic that his name was Tinder considering that was a hookup app.

Beau wasn't sure what he'd been thinking when he agreed to come to her appointments.

"Well, it looks like today's the day, gentlemen," Dr. Tinder said. "We're gonna get a peek at your little one."

"Might be plural," Zoey noted with a grin.

"Very true. And that's what we're here to find out."

"And if there is more than one baby, is that something you're equipped to handle?" Beau asked. The question had been plaguing him since his first meeting at the clinic. While Zoey wanted to see her doctor because she was comfortable with him, Beau wanted to ensure his baby would have the best care.

"Yes, Mr. Walker. I'm very familiar with multiples. Plus, I'm equipped to handle a high-risk pregnancy as well."

Dr. Tinder seemed quite confident. Beau liked that.

"This is an ultrasound machine," Dr. Tinder stated as he gestured toward the big machine in the corner.

"Is it gonna hurt her?" Beau asked, the words blurting out before he could stop them.

"Not at all," Dr. Tinder replied as though he'd heard that question a million times. "No harm to Zoey or your baby."

Beau breathed a little easier.

When Zoey started to lift her shirt, Beau spun around to face the wall.

"It's okay, Beau," Zoey said with a chuckle. "The only thing you'll see is my belly."

He made eye contact with Ethan, noticing his husband was most definitely amused.

God, this was embarrassing.

The spurting sound of a bottle had Beau turning back around. He watched as Dr. Tinder put some sort of thick jelly on Zoey's belly. While her stomach wasn't completely flat, it wasn't exactly big, either. More like a small, rounded hill. According to Zoey, they were either having two or they were having one really big baby because she was bigger than she'd been with any of her boys at this point.

"All right, gentlemen. You ready for this?"

Beau nodded although he wasn't sure that was the truth.

ETHAN HAD SIX SISTERS-IN-LAW, SO he'd heard more stories than he cared to hear regarding what took place in the OB-gyn's office over the years. He'd heard more than his fair share about forceps and speculums and all those weird tools that men had no business knowing about.

However, none of those stories had prepared him for this visit.

He had to wonder whether or not he would've been invited to the doctor's appointments if anyone else had been carrying their child. Oddly enough, Zoey had encouraged them to come. She had even attempted to get them to come to her first appointment with Dr. Tinder last month, but Ethan had kindly refused. A man could only endure so much and since she said it wouldn't be anything out of the ordinary, he figured he'd put off his induction into the OB-visit club as long as he could.

"I don't anticipate we'll see much today. I'm merely looking to see if there are multiples. I'm doing the transabdominal ultrasound first, hoping it'll give us a clear enough picture. If that doesn't work, I can always do a transvaginal."

Yeah, that did not sound like fun. Ethan had to assume that meant it went up inside Zoey.

God, he hoped this worked.

"How can you tell if there are multiples?" Beau asked.

Dr. Tinder picked up the wand from its holder and flipped on the small monitor on the machine. "Well, it's really noticeable when there are two gestational sacs."

Beau had briefly explained about gestational sacs, amniotic sacs, placentas, and a whole bunch of other shit that had made Ethan blush. He wasn't sure why that was, but it had. Hearing the doctor mention it wasn't any better.

"If you see more than one, will you be able to determine if they're identical or fraternal twins?" Zoey asked.

Good thing they were here because Ethan didn't have a clue what questions he should be asking, if any. And to be fair, he preferred to get his lessons from Beau. Less chance of him looking like a complete and total idiot.

Dr. Tinder continued to talk, but Ethan tuned him out the instant that wand landed on Zoey's belly and a god-awful noise came from the machine. It sounded like interference or static, and it changed as he moved the wand around.

Ethan's eyes darted between the monitor and Dr. Tinder, trying to figure out by the man's expression just what he was seeing. The wand moved around for what felt like forever and Ethan's anxiety ratcheted up a notch. It continued right up until Dr. Tinder's hand paused and a smile formed on his face.

"Those, gentleman, are two separate gestational sacs. You are definitely having twins."

Twins?

They were having twins?

Ethan's heartbeat sped up and his blood roared in his ears. He managed to tear his eyes away from the screen long enough to look over at Beau. When his husband turned to face him, Ethan's breath lodged in his throat.

"We're having twins," Beau whispered.

They were.

Not one but *two* babies. One was a blessing, but two … that was a miracle.

"Now for the heartbeats," Dr. Tinder said.

The noise returned as he moved the wand around, but then a moment later, there was a distinct *thump-thump* sound coming from the speakers.

Dr. Tinder continued to move the wand until there was another, fainter sound chiming in with the first.

"Two heartbeats," the doctor said with a smile.

Ethan's eyes shot over to Zoey and he noticed her smiling although there were tears flowing down her face.

Instantly, he moved over to her and took her hand while Beau shifted to stand behind him.

"Two babies, E," she whispered. "You and Beau are having two babies."

He couldn't form words, but he knew they weren't necessary.

That sound echoing in the room was all that was.

"All right," Dr. Tinder prompted as he cleaned off the wand and handed Zoey paper towels. "We've got a few things to talk about." Dr. Tinder looked at Beau. "And I'm sure you have tons of questions."

"I do," Beau confirmed.

"Once Zoey is ready, the three of you can meet me in my office so we can talk."

Ethan nodded, but he wasn't hearing most of what Dr. Tinder was saying.

Because they were having two babies.

Two!

Chapter Fifteen

Monday, February 4, 2019
(Five weeks later)

"SO, WHY DID DR. TINDER SAY HE wanted to see Zoey more frequently?" Ethan asked from his spot across the table.

Beau wiped his mouth with a paper napkin before setting it on his empty plate. "He said it's routine with multiples."

"So she's not high-risk?"

"Not yet. But the risks are higher for certain things. He just wants to keep a closer eye on her," Beau explained.

They'd taken Zoey to see Dr. Tinder last week and he'd changed a few things up on them. With Zoey being twelve weeks along with twins, he felt it was necessary to monitor her iron and glucose levels. He'd mentioned something about pre-eclampsia and though Beau didn't know what that was—yet—he got the impression Dr. Tinder was simply being proactive.

"Do you think he'll tell us if she is high-risk?"

"Of course." From what Beau could tell, there wasn't anything to worry about and he'd come to trust the doctor knew what he was doing.

That seemed to ease some of the tension in Ethan's shoulders.

For the past few weeks, they'd finally managed to settle into their routine again. Aside from the doctor's appointments and the chores they were doing for Zoey—going to the grocery store and helping out with the kids mostly—their lives were somewhat back to normal.

Beau would admit he liked routine. It worked well, especially for Ethan. When things were chaotic, Ethan tended to follow suit. So, he was doing his best to maintain some semblance of control when it came to the outside forces.

Beau stretched. He was tired and it was only Monday. He wasn't sure what that would say about the week, but he was hoping to go to bed early tonight.

"Dinner was great, E. Why don't you go take a shower and I'll clean up?"

"I think I'll do that," Ethan said as he pushed away from the table. "Then I'll get dessert ready while you shower."

"Dessert?" Beau locked his eyes on Ethan. This was the first he was hearing about it. "What's for dessert?"

Ethan grinned. "Me."

Damn. Beau liked the sound of that. "Well, then take your time in the shower. Maybe I'll join you when I'm thr—"

A loud knock on the front door halted him mid-sentence.

Beau shot Ethan a curious look, the kind that silently asked if he was expecting someone. Ethan shrugged before heading for the door.

Carrying their dirty dishes into the kitchen, Beau heard the deep rumble of voices when Ethan answered the door. He went back to the table to grab the rest, wanting the house to be somewhat in order if their guests were planning to stay.

He had just placed everything in the sink when Ethan called his name from behind him.

Beau didn't even have to turn around to know that something was wrong. His heart lodged in his throat, but he forced his feet to turn him around.

"Is it Zoey?" he blurted. He prayed nothing had happened to her or the babies. He wasn't sure he could handle that right now.

"Not Zoey. Let's go into the living room," Ethan said softly, motioning Beau toward him.

"Are the babies okay?"

"It's not about Zoey or the babies, Beau." Ethan gestured for him to go into the living room.

Beau shook his head. "No. Tell me what it is."

Ethan's eyes softened as he took a step closer. When he moved out of the doorway, Travis and Curtis appeared behind him.

He prayed it was a good sign that Kaleb wasn't there. Surely if there was something wrong with the babies or Zoey they wouldn't lie to him.

"Beau." Ethan's firm tone pulled Beau's attention back toward him. "Your father had another stroke." Ethan got close enough to take his hand.

Beau peered at Ethan, then over to Curtis. He wasn't sure why they'd made a house call to tell him that. It wasn't like he wanted to go visit the man in the hospital. Ben had very clearly stated that Beau was no longer his son.

"You could've just called."

Curtis didn't speak, but his expression said the news was worse than that.

Ethan squeezed his hand. "Beau, your father passed away an hour ago."

Oh.

Wow.

That was…

The next thing Beau knew, Ethan was tugging him into the living room and forcing him to sit on the couch. Good thing, too, because Beau was numb. From head to toe. But it wasn't necessarily a bad feeling. He just wasn't sure how to process the news.

Beau hadn't seen his father since last August, when he went to visit him in the hospital. He hadn't heard a word from either Ben or Arlene. No texts, no phone calls. Not even a Christmas card.

"How'd you find out?" Beau asked Curtis.

"Pastor Bob called," Curtis replied. "He thought you should know."

For a brief moment, he wondered if he would've heard the news otherwise. Would he have figured it out the next time he went to church and his father wasn't there? Or would he have heard it from someone else when he was in town? Would Arlene have ever called to tell him? Or did she truly not give a shit about him at all?

Curtis came to sit down beside him. "Lorrie insists on reaching out to Arlene. She knows your mother doesn't have any other family and not many friends."

Beau nodded, unsure what he was supposed to say to that, if anything. His first thought was not to console his mother. Perhaps that made him a horrible child, but he couldn't help it. Arlene had turned her back on him the same way Ben had. He figured if she needed him, she would have to be the one to reach out.

As he sat there, Beau was aware of the conversation taking place around him, but he wasn't listening. He was trying to determine how he felt about all of this. Part of him was glad because Ben Bennett was an angry, evil man. He took great pleasure in other people's pain and it was hard for Beau to feel any sympathy for him.

On the other hand, he hoped his father had gone peacefully. More importantly, he hoped Ben had made amends before he died. He wanted to believe his father would be forgiven for how downright mean he was to others, but he wasn't sure that was the case. And truthfully, he wasn't sure his father even deserved forgiveness.

He heard the front door open, then close. He was aware of Ethan moving around, then coming to sit beside him on the couch.

It wasn't until Ethan put his arms around him that Beau realized he was crying. Deep, broken sobs that tore him open. He hated his father… Or at least he wanted to hate him.

Unfortunately for Beau, he wasn't the sort who could draw on the negative, so as he sat there and bawled like a baby, he remembered all the good things about his father.

What little there were.

Friday, February 8, 2019
(Four days later)

ETHAN STOOD AT THE BACK OF THE church with Beau despite the fact there was plenty of seating.

Although Arlene hadn't invited them, they had come for Ben Bennett's service. Ethan got the feeling Beau had only come because Ethan had asked him to. Well, *ask* was putting it nicely. Beau had been adamant when he said he did not want to come, but Ethan insisted they pay their respects. It didn't matter how awful Ben was, the man was still Beau's father. While he understood Beau's reluctance to be here, it was evident Beau needed to get some closure where his father was concerned.

Ethan hadn't been exactly shocked to find only a few people sitting in the pews while Pastor Bob performed the service, but he was somewhat saddened. God forbid anything ever happen to Ethan's parents, but if it did, he knew the church would be busting at the seams.

He just didn't understand how one man could live in such a small town and not have people gathering around to say their goodbyes.

Of course, that was rhetorical, because Ethan knew Ben. He was the type who didn't help out when others needed it, nor did he allow his wife to do it. However, when it came to his own needs, he'd ensured people knew what his expectations were. Not many had liked the man, even if they had tolerated him.

"I don't wanna go up there," Beau whispered as Pastor Bob was drawing to a close.

Ethan squeezed his hand. "You don't have to, baby. Not if you really don't want to."

Beau turned to look at him and Ethan saw the uncertainty. Beau wasn't a hard man. He didn't have a lick of hate in his entire body, but he did have a keen self-preservation instinct. It probably resulted from a lifetime of dealing with his parents. Ben had always been hard on him, insisting Beau be better at everything.

Ethan remembered Beau playing football back in high school. He'd been a rising star and probably could've made it to the NFL if he'd wanted to. An accident his senior year had ended that, but it had been Ben who took the news the hardest.

It wasn't until after they'd married that Ethan learned that Beau had always hated playing football. He'd only done it to make his father happy.

"Will you go with me?" Beau whispered, the torment in his eyes evident.

Ethan swallowed hard, the emotion in Beau's voice tugging at his heart. "Of course I will. I'm here for you. Whatever you need."

Pastor Bob continued on about Ben being an upstanding citizen of the community. Ethan had to wonder if that was hard for him to say because it was difficult for Ethan to find any truth in the words whatsoever. Ben had kept himself in isolation. Arlene, too. The only time Arlene was part of anything was when it came to church, and even that was limited.

However, Ethan knew that this service was more for the family, to allow them to get closure, to say their goodbyes.

"We'll have the friends come forward first," Pastor Bob instructed after concluding his speech.

When Beau stepped forward, Ethan followed, his fingers securely linked with Beau's. While he was far more than a friend of Ben Bennett, he knew Beau was hoping to get out of here without having to face his mother. As it was, Arlene had sat in the front pew and sobbed during the entire service. Ethan figured hearing her heartache was hard enough for Beau.

When they approached the casket, Ethan kept his eyes forward. He stood beside Beau, determined to be his anchor in this storm. It wasn't exactly easy because he knew there were people watching them, but he didn't care. His loyalty was to his husband and he had no choice but to shrug off the thought of people judging them as they stood there.

"He looks peaceful," Beau said softly.

Ethan glanced down at Ben. He actually did look peaceful dressed in a suit and tie, his hands resting on his torso. It was almost possible to believe the man was sleeping.

A sob sounded from Beau and Ethan dropped Beau's hand and put his arm around him. He had known this wouldn't be easy. Seeing the man with his own two eyes was far more difficult than hearing the news from someone else.

More sobs tore from Beau and Ethan held him close. When Beau started to move away, Ethan ensured he couldn't get far as he guided him toward the back of the church.

As Ethan passed Arlene, their eyes met. Hers were red-rimmed, her expression tormented. But, perhaps for the very first time, she wasn't glaring at him or trying to kill him with her eyes.

In fact, he was almost certain there was a hint of longing there. A spark of hope.

With Ben gone, would it be possible for Beau and Arlene to make amends?

Unfortunately, only time would tell.

"Can we go home?" Beau asked in a hoarse whisper. "I just want to go home."

"Of course, baby."

Ethan took his husband home and he held him until the emotional tsunami crested. After that, he held him a little more.

Chapter Sixteen

Tuesday, March 26, 2019
(Seven weeks later)

DIDN'T MATTER HOW MANY TIMES HE DID it, sitting in the small waiting area with a handful of pregnant women around him made Beau feel extremely ... awkward. Yeah. That was probably the right word.

Ever since they'd come with Zoey to the first ultrasound appointment, Beau had come with her. Of course, he had remained stoically in the waiting room during parts of those visits mainly because she had sweetly given him a brief description of the events to come. Having been subjected to more than enough estrogen thanks to all his sisters-in-law, Beau saw no reason to invite more sessions with the chance of hearing about various female reproductive issues.

However, he had no problems driving her to the appointment or going in and talking to Dr. Tinder after he met with Zoey. As usual, they would go over the babies' development based on the information Beau was reading. Since the book Ethan had given him was for a single pregnancy, he found he had to do some additional research on twins. But Dr. Tinder had proven to be patient with Beau. He answered all his questions and tried to soothe his concerns.

And Beau felt better because of it.

For the past two weeks, Zoey had been feeling the twins move. The first time she felt it, she had called them and insisted they come over. Beau had locked down the shop and made a beeline to her house, worried something was wrong. When they arrived, Zoey had apologized profusely for making them worry, but made up for it when she let them feel their babies moving for the first time.

Beau might've shed a few tears that day. Okay, perhaps more than a few.

Today, Beau and Ethan wouldn't be keeping the waiting room chairs warm, though. No, even if this visit had some embarrassing female discussions, the positives far outweighed the negative by a million, so here they were.

Today Dr. Tinder was going to do another ultrasound, which would hopefully tell them the sex of their babies. There'd been no question in Beau's mind that he wanted to know. Ethan had agreed. Surprises weren't really their thing, plus, Beau was itching to get the room set up. He merely needed to know if it would be pink or blue, or both. In fact, he had every intention of stopping by the hardware store on the way home to buy paint.

"Zoey?" the nurse called from the doorway.

Beau was familiar with the process now, so he helped Zoey to her feet, then fell into step with her and Ethan.

His heart was beating faster than usual, his excitement palpable.

After Zoey stepped on the scale and the nurse jotted down the information, they were led to the examination room with the big machine in it.

Zoey's vitals were taken and then they were left alone.

"Are you nervous?" Zoey asked with a grin.

"Not at all," Beau lied.

She obviously saw through him because she chuckled, then peered around him to look at Ethan. "And you?"

"I'm cool."

Beau didn't believe that for a second, but he didn't say anything.

"So, are you hoping for boys or girls or one of each?"

"Healthy," Beau and Ethan said at the same time.

That was the one thing they agreed on. It didn't matter if they had two boys or two girls or one of each, as long as their babies were healthy.

Dr. Tinder stepped into the room a short time later, a smile on his face. He greeted them, then Zoey before setting his clipboard down on the counter.

"How're you feeling? How's the morning sickness?"

"It's not quite as bad as it was." Zoey's hand went to her belly in that protective manner Beau was familiar with. "They're moving a lot and it's hard to breathe sometimes. They're taking up so much room."

"Any contractions?"

Zoey shook her head. "No, but I'm having to stay off my feet more. My ankles are swelling."

Dr. Tinder nodded, keying in the information. Once he was finished, he put down his electronic tablet and rolled his stool over by the machine.

"I'm going to take some measurements today and hopefully we'll be able to determine the sex of both babies."

After squirting the jelly on Zoey's belly, Dr. Tinder grabbed that little handheld thing and used it to smear the jelly around.

"How's the heartburn?" he asked her conversationally.

"Better. But I knew it would be. I'm one of the lucky ones." Her eyes shot over to Beau and Ethan. "I thought it would last longer, but I'm happy to say that's one thing that's gone."

"Good." Dr. Tinder smiled as he glanced up at the screen on the machine. "Craving pickles and chocolate chip cookies again?"

Zoey laughed, her cheeks turning a pretty pink. "Not yet." She glanced at Beau. "When I was pregnant with Mason, I couldn't get enough of them. It was so weird."

Beau wondered if she ate them at the same time, but he didn't get the chance to voice the question before Dr. Tinder was speaking again.

"All right, gentlemen," the doctor said. "Are you ready to find out what you're having?"

"Yes!" Beau blurted, the word louder than he intended.

Thankfully, Ethan stepped up beside him and pressed his shoulder to Beau's.

"Well, before we do that, how about we listen to the heartbeats?" Dr. Tinder inquired, never looking away from what he was doing.

"That would be good," Zoey replied. "We love hearing their heartbeats."

Zoey smiled up at them. She had recorded on her phone the sound of the heartbeats for them at each of the visits. She had sent the audio files to them and Beau found himself listening all the time just because it made him feel closer to them. He couldn't help it, he was overly emotional these days.

Perhaps he was experiencing Zoey's pregnancy hormones empathetically.

Or maybe he was just weird.

None of that mattered when the sound echoed in the small room. A rough static noise followed by a distinct beat. First a solo one, then another joined in. His heart felt lighter, his chest bigger because of those steady *thump-thumps*.

Beau stared at Zoey's belly and he could feel her eyes on him.

And when Ethan took his hand, Beau's entire world focused on that moment in time, that sweet, perfect moment.

"THOSE ARE SOME REALLY STRONG HEARTBEATS. THE first and the second..." Dr. Tinder said aloud.

There was something in the doctor's tone that had Ethan looking up at him. The way he trailed off that sentence as though he was planning to fill it in with something else. Only he didn't, but there was a curious expression on his face.

Dr. Tinder moved the device around and only one heartbeat could be heard this time, but it wasn't as loud as it had been before.

"What's that?" Beau asked, his tone full of wonder. "A different angle?"

"More than likely." He smiled, but his eyebrows shot downward. "What do you say we take a look?" Dr. Tinder shifted the wand around and pressed a button on the machine, causing the monitor to light up. "Here we go."

When the doctor put the thing on Zoey's belly, the screen changed from black to a weirdly contorted image. Ethan had seen his fair share of images like that from his brothers in various stages of pregnancy. They were always showing off the pictures as though they were glamour shots of their babies. Ethan never understood it because most of the time he couldn't make out what they were anyway. Of course, he had a picture from their first ultrasound in his wallet, but the only thing he could really make out were two circles.

As he stared at the screen, Ethan was having the same problem now. No matter how hard he stared at it, he couldn't get a picture to form.

Based on the doctor's wide grin, he wasn't having the same problem. Dr. Tinder clicked a few things on the keyboard, a cursor moving across the screen.

"You can still tell there are two gestational sacs. And you see this?" Dr. Tinder pointed to a spot on the screen. "That's one baby's head." His finger moved lower. "And this is a leg. Come on little one, move just a bit to the left so we can take a closer look."

For several minutes, Dr. Tinder continued to shift the wand across Zoey's belly while clicking the keyboard and moving a small pointer on the screen into position.

The screen froze for a moment and Dr. Tinder lifted the wand.

"What's wrong?" Beau asked, his eyes shooting to the doctor's face.

"Nothing at all," he said, his voice sturdy, his smile genuine.

Ethan had been watching the doctor long enough he could tell he was holding something back.

"Can you tell if it's a boy or a girl?" Zoey asked.

"Yes." Dr. Tinder's eyes moved over to Ethan, then Beau. "You're having a … boy."

Ethan's heart thumped painfully hard against his sternum. They were having a boy? Holy shit. Beau turned his head, their eyes meeting, holding. The smile on his husband's face lit him up from within.

"And…?" Zoey prompted.

Dr. Tinder turned his attention back to the screen and put the wand on Zoey's belly again. He moved it around, punching buttons on the keyboard and mouse as he worked.

"And this little one here … it's a girl," he finally said, still smiling as he adjusted the wand and glanced back at the screen.

He hit a few buttons, clicked the mouse a few times. His attention remained on the screen as he moved the wand around for a while longer.

"Hold up," Dr. Tinder stated, leaning in closer to the screen. "I might've misspoken."

Misspoken? What the fuck? Ethan wanted to yell, but his heart was somewhere in his throat. They weren't having twins? They weren't having a boy and a girl? What? Why would he say that? Why would he get their hopes up and then yank it all away?

What kind of quack-fucking doctor was he?

"Is something wrong?" Zoey's voice was hesitant, her gaze surveying the screen.

"Not at all." Dr. Tinder shifted the wand up and down, pressing in a little more. "But it looks to me like…"

He trailed off again and Ethan was ready to grab him by the hair and shake him. Ethan glanced at Zoey, noticing the concern in her eyes.

"Dr. Tinder," she said quickly. "Please. They're hanging by a thread here."

The doctor seemed mesmerized by the screen, but when he turned away, his smile widened. "I … uh … well, you're definitely having a boy and a girl, but you're not having twins."

What the *fuck*? That didn't even make sense. How was it possible they were having a boy and a girl but not having twins?

"Oh, my God," Beau whispered gruffly, his hand tightening around Ethan's.

"What?" Ethan asked. "Why did you say that?" His head turned rapidly as he looked between Dr. Tinder and Beau.

"You're having triplets," Dr. Tinder announced.

Oh.

Well.

Um…

Yeah. A boy and a girl, but not twins because there were three. *That* kinda made more sense.

Okay. Now air seemed a bit scarce. Ethan's entire body went hot then cold.

"Grab him!" Zoey yelled.

Beau spun around, catching Ethan as his knees went weak beneath him.

"Triplets?" Ethan croaked.

"Yes, sir," Dr. Tinder said as he leaned in toward the monitor, his hand stilling on the wand. "There it is. You sneaky little boy." He smiled again. "Six legs, six arms, three heads, three rumps and"—he chuckled—"two penises."

"Two boys and a girl?" Zoey exclaimed.

"I can say with one hundred percent certainty that you're having triplets. That little guy did a very good job of hiding behind his brother. And with … hmm … I'd say ninety-nine percent certainty, there are two boys and one little girl in there."

Ethan glanced over at Beau, who was still holding him upright.

"But…" Beau swallowed hard, his eyes tearing up as a smile formed. "We're gonna need a bigger house."

The doctor laughed, as did Zoey.

"Yeah," Ethan said on a breathless whisper. "A bigger house."

"I've snapped some pictures," the doctor explained, passing over a strip of paper to Beau. "Plus, I've got the 3D recording that I'll have for you in a few days."

Dr. Tinder stood, grabbing a few paper towels and passing them over to Zoey.

"Because of this new development," Dr. Tinder told Zoey, "I'm going to need to see you more frequently. And I'd like for you three to take a tour of the hospital. It's not uncommon for triplets to be born early—even earlier than we'd like—and we need to be as prepared as possible."

Ethan knew it wasn't uncommon for twins to be born early. Beau had mentioned it, but Ethan hadn't actually thought it all the way through. So, it made perfect sense that triplets would.

One baby was a big deal. Three …

Well, he couldn't deny that he was terrified. How were they going to handle three babies at the same time? And if they came early? Would there be problems?

All the questions pinged around in his head, but he couldn't voice them. Not yet.

Dr. Tinder stood and patted Zoey's knee. "Why don't you clean up and the three of you can meet me in my office. It'll give you a few minutes to come up with the questions I know you'll have."

"Thank you, Dr. Tinder," Zoey said, wiping the jelly off her rounded stomach.

Ethan was still fixated on three babies…

There were only two of them. Beau was right, they needed a bigger house.

But he loved his house. He had envisioned raising their children right there.

What were they going to do?

Ethan's eyes lifted to Beau's.

As though he could read Ethan's mind, Beau smiled and said, "I think we need to call a contractor. We're gonna have to add on a couple more rooms."

Swallowing hard, Ethan nodded.

And that was when the tears tore loose.

Happy tears, of course. The kind that he couldn't hold back.

Chapter Seventeen

Tuesday, April 4, 2019
(Nine days later)

BEAU STOOD IN THE LIVING ROOM, WATCHING as men paraded through his now sparse house. Well, the downstairs was sparse. Their upstairs bedroom was still the same. The majority of their furniture was now stored in a POD sitting in the front yard. It was the only way to ensure nothing got damaged as the chaos that was now their life took root.

Things had been crazy from the instant they stepped out of the doctor's office after learning they weren't having two babies, they were having three.

Three.

In a mathematical equation, three wasn't that far off from two. However, when it came to the number of babies to care for, there was an astronomical difference between two and three. And based on all the information he'd gathered on the Internet, there was an art form to handling triplets. Beau had already subscribed to numerous blogs so he could get help in that regard from people who were managing to do it well.

Even thinking about it made Beau's heart swell. Both excitement and nerves battling for supremacy right there inside him. He still couldn't believe it.

Something crashed in the other room and Beau jumped, that giddy feeling gone, replaced by the irritation he'd been experiencing since yesterday, when the construction crew first showed up.

Because they needed a bigger house to accommodate three babies, they were now living in a construction zone. This was their new normal—albeit temporary—for the next six weeks provided everything went according to plan. Evidently, that was how long it took to turn one guest room and a half bath into three bedrooms and two and a half bathrooms. The half bath was for the guests who visited, and one for their daughter, since they figured she would eventually need her own space. It didn't seem at all fair to make her share with her brothers indefinitely. However, the boys would have to deal.

Two boys and a girl.

According to Dr. Tinder, the boys were identical and the girl was fraternal, obviously. The good doctor had gone into explaining how it all worked and attempted to ease their worries. Beau had admitted to reading horror stories online regarding all the problems that might occur. According to Dr. Tinder, not everything they read on the Internet was true.

Well, duh.

Beau had tried to keep up but made a mental note to use his good friend Google to help him understand more. However, he also agreed that he would let Dr. Tinder be the medical professional when it came to the important stuff.

What he had learned for certain was that Zoey would be going in to see Dr. Tinder more frequently now. With the babies at twenty-one weeks, he informed Zoey he would want to see her every two weeks going forward, more as time progressed. And they would still be doing more tests to determine iron-deficiency and glucose because nothing had changed on that front. Beau and Ethan had assured her they would be going to every appointment from here on out.

Another crash had Beau's teeth clamping together.

Yeah, the next six weeks were going to drive him out of his mind.

While he would've offered to do the construction himself—he figured it couldn't be too hard, right?—Ethan had convinced him to hire someone. Of course, Travis had recommended someone he knew and being that the general contractor owed Travis a favor, he'd taken the job and promised to make it quick and painless.

He'd already failed on the painless part.

The sound of footsteps on the stairs had Beau moving in that direction.

"What's up?" Ethan asked, his hair wet from his shower.

"They're gettin' started."

Ethan glanced toward the hallway where the demolition had already started. "You're gonna have to relax, babe. This is inevitable. Just remember, in the end, it'll be worth it."

It would, yes. However, it wasn't easy watching the house being destroyed in an effort to put it back together, only bigger. Beau had gotten comfortable in Ethan's house. It had never felt like it was only Ethan's. From the day he'd moved in, it had felt like their place and he wanted to protect that space.

"Let's go to work," Ethan said. "It'll get your mind off it for a bit. Plus, Kaden and Keegan promised to oversee everything."

Beau wondered if Ethan knew what that meant. Sure, he liked the twins, but even at thirty-five, they were rowdy as hell. They were going to entrust them with everything they owned? Seemed risky.

Ethan stopped in front of him and gave him the look that said, *Trust me, it'll all work out.*

"Yeah. Okay." He made sure Ethan heard the reluctance in his tone.

Beau knew there was nothing for him to do there anyway. They had agreed that the contractor would do everything from tearing it down to installing the new floors and texturing the walls. Beau was insistent that they paint the babies' rooms themselves.

And yes, the twins had promised to pitch in. In fact, the entire Walker clan had made that promise.

The day they'd learned they were having triplets, everyone had gathered at Lorrie and Curtis's to celebrate the news. And though everyone was excited for them, Beau had noticed the looks on their faces. They were trying to figure out how in the world they would've handled more than one baby at a time. According to Lorrie, taking care of Braydon and Brendon had been a challenge.

Beau could only imagine. Considering there were only two of them, they were going to be outnumbered when it came to babies. Granted, Beau doubted they were going to be on their own. Everyone pitched in whenever there was a birth in the family, so he figured they would have all the help they needed. Probably more than they even wanted.

In the meantime, Beau was worried about Zoey. He had overheard Ethan talking to Kaleb, discussing what was needed to take care of her. Carrying three babies was going to require her to stay off her feet and rest as much as possible. Which meant she would need help with the kids. Beau was more than willing to pitch in on that front. Whatever it took to ensure Zoey was pampered the way she deserved. Hell, Ethan even offered to come over and cook dinner every night. Beau wasn't sure he'd ever seen a smile on Kaleb's face quite that big. And yes, they had jumped on that offer.

Another crash caused Beau to spin on his feet and head to the door. Ethan was right behind him, chuckling.

"It's gonna be fine," Ethan reassured him for the hundredth time.

"Yep." Beau hopped in the driver's seat while Ethan climbed in the passenger side.

As he backed down the driveway, he did his best not to look at the house. Seeing it in shambles wasn't an easy thing for him to process. He figured Ethan would've been the one panicking as the outside walls were demolished so they could expand the house's footprint.

"It doesn't bother you?" Beau asked.

"What?"

"Seein' it like that?"

Ethan peered out the window at the house as Beau turned the truck toward the shop.

"No. The fact that we're stayin' here is what matters to me."

Beau had gotten that impression as soon as the doctor said *twins*. It was then that Beau realized more bedrooms would eventually be necessary, but they knew it would work as it was for the time being. Based on what Beau read, multiples often slept together for a bit after they were born because it soothed them. That was Beau's plan. To keep them together until they either needed more space or until their sleep patterns interfered with one another.

Of course, when Dr. Tinder announced they had a little boy hiding in there, informing them there was actually another baby squeezed inside Zoey's small belly, he'd wondered if it was even possible to stay in that house.

According to the general contractor, it was easily doable.

"I talked to Keegan this morning," Ethan said as Beau drove. "Told him that I need someone to give me an estimate on closing in our bedroom."

Considering the master bedroom was a loft, Beau knew it would be necessary to close it in. After all, parents did need a little privacy when the babies got bigger.

"Shouldn't take much."

"Nope."

"Are they really movin' here? The twins?" Beau asked, parking the truck in front of the shop.

"Yep. We're gonna need some help to keep up."

They definitely were going to need help. And he knew Ethan was referring to working at the shop.

Once he climbed out of the truck, Beau followed Ethan to the door.

"They have experience with large equipment?" Beau asked.

"No. But they're ASE certified. I figure between the four of us, we can make it work. Might have to give them the smaller jobs for a while."

They stepped inside the dimly lit warehouse building and Ethan flipped on all the lights.

"Plus," Ethan continued, "Zane said he'd help out however he needed to."

It was a big possibility they would have to take him up on that offer.

"Regardless," Ethan said as he opened the small office door, "it'll all work out the way it's supposed to."

Beau smiled.

As far as he was concerned, it already was.

THEY'D ONLY BEEN AT WORK FOR TWO hours when the first call came in. Ethan knew before he answered that he wasn't going to like whatever his cousin had to say.

"What's up?" he greeted, preparing himself for bad news.

"So ... uh ... there's been a slight problem," Keegan said, his tone oddly light-hearted as though a *slight problem* was no big deal.

"Do I need to come home?" Ethan glanced over to see Beau beneath one of the Walker Demolition trucks. They'd been dealing with a swarm of issues with their trucks recently and Ethan was about ready to tell Reese it was time to buy a new fleet. This was getting ridiculous.

"Naw." There was a smile in Keegan's voice. "Well, not unless you wanna see the scorch marks."

"*What?*" Ethan shouted.

"It's not bad."

"What's 'not bad'?"

"It won't delay the end date?"

"Are you assuming?"

Keegan chuckled. "No. Really. I just thought you should know in case ... well, the fire department's on the way."

"Seriously, Keeg?" Ethan was ready to hop in his truck and head to the house. The only thing stopping him was not wanting to get Beau in a panic.

"No."

"Fuck you." Ethan released the breath he'd been holding. "Are you fucking with me?"

"Actually, no. But it's fine. There really was a small fire, but it's out and there's no damage to the existing structure. And no fire department necessary. They're goin' strong once again."

Thank fuck. "Hey, Keeg?"

"Yeah?"

"Next time you call and fuck with me like that, I'm gonna kick your ass."

"Roger that." Keegan laughed. "Talk at ya later."

Ethan disconnected the call and tucked his phone in his pocket.

"Problem?" Beau asked.

For a brief moment, Ethan considered telling Beau what had happened. However, the last thing he wanted to do was add to Beau's stress. While Ethan was usually the one succumbing to the pressures of life, it appeared to be Beau's turn. Granted, his husband handled things far better than Ethan did, so even if he did relay the news, he knew it wouldn't become DEFCON 1.

"Nope. Keegan's fuckin' with me." It wasn't a lie exactly.

Beau headed for the water cooler and Ethan watched him. He hit the button and filled a paper cup before turning back to Ethan.

"So, I was wonderin' about somethin'." Beau took a sip from his cup.

"What's that?"

"You know when the twins come to work here?"

"Yeah?"

"That whole havin' sex in the office thing won't be all that easy."

Ethan grinned. Funny how Beau had been thinking about that. The instant he'd learned of the new additions to the payroll, that was oddly the first thought Ethan had had, too.

"I'm sure we'll make it work," Ethan told him.

Beau moved closer. "How?"

Ethan nodded toward the office. "There's a door. We'll just keep it closed."

"Hmm. Good idea." Beau stepped closer.

"And if we really want privacy, we'll just send 'em out to get lunch."

"So you've given this some thought?"

"A lot of thought." No sense denying it.

Beau's eyes flashed with heat. "You know, there's always another option."

Ethan cocked an eyebrow, encouraging Beau to continue.

"We could always fuck each other stupid until that time comes. Maybe we'll get it outta our system."

Ethan smirked. "And you think I haven't been tryin' that for the past five years?"

Beau laughed.

"I'll never get you outta my system," Ethan told him seriously. "Never."

Beau leaned in and kissed him. "Me, neither. But, it couldn't hurt to try, right?"

"Right now?"

Beau nodded.

"Right here?"

Another nod.

"No lube." Granted, it would only take him a second to get some.

Beau's eyes dropped to Ethan's mouth.

"Ah. You want me to suck you right here?"

Beau nodded.

Ethan glanced out the open bay door. "You gonna keep a lookout?"

"Of course."

Ethan turned back to Beau. "You're sayin' I can't distract you enough?"

"I didn't say that." Beau's eyes dropped to his mouth once more. "Put your mouth on me, E."

He didn't need to be told twice.

Ethan put his hand on Beau's chest and urged him backward until his back pressed up against the truck bed. Ethan allowed his lips to hover a fraction of an inch from Beau's. It was a tease that had Beau inhaling sharply. Ethan knew what his man enjoyed.

Rather than kiss him, Ethan lowered himself to his knees and went to work freeing Beau's cock. He was hard as steel and smooth as silk. Ethan took a moment to stroke him, staring up at his husband while he did.

"Be sure to keep an eye out," Ethan instructed.

Beau's nod was curt, anxious.

Leaning forward, Ethan took Beau in his mouth. His warm, salty taste teased Ethan's tongue. The man smelled like oil and musk, a scent that was unique to Beau. It turned Ethan on more than anything else. He loved the way Beau smelled.

He gave himself over to the man before him, allowing Beau to control his movements, how deep his cock went in Ethan's mouth, the pace. Every so often, Beau's gaze would stray out the door. Ethan seriously doubted anyone would be stopping by, but he knew the possibility made the encounter hotter.

Ethan remained on his knees, pleasuring Beau with his lips, tongue, and teeth until Beau's entire weight was held up by the truck at his back.

"E…"

Beau knocked Ethan's ball cap off his head and tangled his fingers in Ethan's hair. He wasn't easy about it, either, and the pain radiated down his spine, heating him from the inside. He fucking loved when Beau lost control.

"Take all of me," Beau commanded, still fisting Ethan's hair.

Ethan moved forward until the thick head of Beau's cock was in his throat.

"Swallow."

He did.

"Oh, fuck, E. Do it again."

He swallowed around the intrusion in his throat, breathing through his nose.

"Fucking hell," Beau said on a ragged breath. "I need to fuck your mouth."

Ethan arched an eyebrow, daring him to do it.

Beau didn't hesitate, grabbing Ethan's head with both hands as he began pumping his hips forward, driving his cock deep. Ethan took all of him, fighting his gag reflex as he worked to please Beau. He loved this man.

Beau growled long and low. "I can't… I'm… Fuck, E. I'm gonna come."

Ethan worked his throat around Beau's cock head, urging him to do just that. A few seconds later, Beau's hips stilled, his body jerking as he came roughly. Ethan swallowed him down, licking Beau's shaft a few times, teasing him because he fucking loved it.

Pushing to his feet, Ethan waited until Beau gathered his strength.

"I think you're right," Ethan whispered, leaning in and kissing Beau's lips.

"About?"

"Although it'll never work, I see no problem with us trying to fuck each other out of our system."

"No?"

Ethan shook his head, his eyes dropping to Beau's mouth.

Those sexy lips curved up and Ethan knew his husband knew exactly what was coming next.

"You want me on my knees?"

"Damn straight."

A few minutes later, Ethan was the one trying to keep his knees from giving out.

Chapter Eighteen

Saturday, May 18, 2019
(Six weeks later)

"YOU KNOW, THIS SEEMED LIKE A MUCH easier task when we were plannin' to paint only one room," Ethan announced when he stepped into the bedroom Beau was in the process of taping. This was one of the boys' rooms, although they weren't sure which one at this point.

Beau glanced over his shoulder at the sexy man surveying their progress.

"Agreed." They had finished painting two of the three bedrooms, but Beau was bound and determined to have all of them done by the end of the day.

They had chosen fairy-tale pink for their daughter's room, although it wasn't all that different than a lot of the light pink colors they'd seen. In fact, they had all started looking the same before Ethan finally made the decision for him. When Beau asked him why that color, Ethan said he liked that it was called fairy tale.

One boy's room had been painted the perfect blue-gray. It was almost the exact color of Ethan's steel-blue eyes. Beau had picked that one out for that specific reason. And this room was going to be air force blue. Or that was the name on the swatch, anyway. A deeper blue with less gray. Kind of like the sky on a cloudy day.

Now to get the last of the paint on the wall and they'd be done. At their current pace, it would be midnight before that happened, but hey, at least it would be finished.

"I was thinkin' I could cook dinner," Ethan said as he peered down at the baseboards that had yet to be taped.

Beau had asked the contractor not to put the baseboards on but to leave them once they were painted. However, his instructions had apparently been overlooked. And since the trim was already painted a bright, glossy white, Beau figured it was simply easier to tape them off rather than take them down and put them back up.

"Sounds like a plan," Beau told Ethan. "I should have it taped by then. We'll take a break, then finish it up."

Ethan nodded, but Beau could tell he wasn't looking forward to taking a break and then going at it again.

"Or," Beau said, "you can order pizza, schedule it for later, and we'll hopefully be finished by the time it gets here."

"Or I could do that," Ethan agreed, then turned and disappeared from the room.

Beau moved over to tape the last of the windows. As he'd done with the other rooms, he wondered if curtains would be nice in here. Something to match whatever motif they went with. He wasn't sure which one he would choose yet, but he had a few things selected and added to the online baby registry that Kylie had helped him set up.

He smiled as he stretched out the blue tape and sealed it along the window. He recalled picking out things for the babies with Ethan. They'd had a good time scanning through the lists of items, choosing what they felt would be perfect for their kids. Even thinking about it left a warm feeling inside Beau.

Who knew there were so many things for triplets? They'd found a stroller for three. It was a bit pricey and Beau wasn't sure they would really get any use out of it, but he'd added it to the list anyway. And though they were only at twenty-seven weeks, Beau was already counting down the minutes until he'd see his three little ones sitting in that stroller.

Ethan returned a few minutes later and Beau was finishing up the trim along the door.

"Which wall do I take?" Ethan asked, moving one of the paint pans.

"Whichever one you want."

"Hmm. How about we make this interesting?"

Beau stood, circling the roll of tape on his finger. "What'd you have in mind?"

"You take two walls and I take two walls. The one who finishes first…"

"Gets to tease and torment the other in any way they want," Beau finished for him.

Ethan seemed to consider that for a moment. "Deal."

Beau grinned. "But that means you have to paint the ceiling while I finish taping."

"Fine."

Fifteen minutes later, Ethan had a coat of paint on the ceiling and Beau had finished the last of the taping on the closet doors. The only thing left was to get the paint on the four walls and they were done.

"You take the one wall with the closet and the other door and that full wall," Ethan instructed. "I'll take the two with the windows."

Beau wasn't sure that was fair, but to be honest, he didn't care who won. It was a win-win situation regardless. Either he got to tease Ethan or Ethan got to tease him. No way to lose there.

"All right."

They didn't even say go before they were both grabbing rollers and slinging paint up on the wall. It took a good twenty minutes to each get one wall done, but they were neck and neck. Ethan had covered one wall with a window and had one left to go. Beau's last wall had the closet and the other door, which made it significantly easier.

Or so he thought.

"Hey!" Beau shouted when he turned to get more paint on his roller. "That's my paint pan."

"Not anymore," Ethan said. "Yours is empty."

All right. He wanted to play that way, did he?

Beau lost a good minute pouring more paint into the pan, but as soon as he had that done, he grabbed Ethan's roller from his hand and held it out of reach. He worked as much as he could with one hand above his head, the other dragging his roller down the wall.

When he went to get more paint, Ethan blocked his way.

Ethan motioned behind him. "You're gettin' paint on the baseboard."

He should've known it was a trap. When Beau turned to find the runaway paint, Ethan grabbed his roller out of his hand.

Since he still had the other roller, Beau worked as fast as he could despite the fact that Ethan made it more difficult by moving the pan every time Beau tried to get more paint. By the time they were finished, they'd worked ten times as hard as they would've if they hadn't put a wager on it.

Then again, they'd also gotten it done in half the time.

Ethan was on his back in the middle of the floor breathing hard and laughing. "I think it's safe to say I won."

Beau laughed. "Like hell. You missed a spot."

Ethan's eyes shot to the wall as he tried to find where he might've missed.

"I did not," he said, turning his head toward Beau's wall. "But you did."

He turned to look and…

"Son of a bitch." He *had* missed a spot. A rather big one, in fact.

Using what was left on his roller, he took care of it.

"Hold up." Ethan pushed to his feet. "Why do I get the feeling you did that on purpose?"

"Who me?" Beau gave his most innocent smile. "Why would I do that?"

Before Ethan could answer, the doorbell rang.

Beau held up one hand. "Hold that thought." He then turned and bolted from the room, racing to the front door. He heard Ethan right on his heels and he couldn't keep from laughing as he threw open the door.

The pizza guy stared at them as though they'd lost their minds. Beau figured they looked ridiculous. Ethan had paint on his face and in his hair, which meant Beau likely did, too. They were wearing shorts and T-shirts, no shoes, and what likely qualified as stupid grins.

Beau signed the credit card receipt while Ethan took the pizza boxes into the house. He added a hefty tip because he was in a damn good mood.

"Thanks," the guy said, smiling as he headed back to his car.

Beau shut the door, flipped the lock, and then headed into the kitchen. When he rounded the corner, his good mood...

Got a whole hell of a lot better.

ETHAN SET THE PIZZA BOXES ON THE counter and stripped off his clothes as fast as he could while Beau took care of the credit card receipt.

Sure, he was hungry, but he figured that could wait just a little longer. He had managed to get buck naked by the time Beau stepped into the room and his rushed actions were so worth it just to see that beaming grin on Beau's face.

"Now we're talkin'," Beau said with a chuckle. "Is this your idea of teasin' me?"

"Somethin' like that." Ethan hopped up on the counter, his naked ass on the granite. "Now come here."

Beau's eyes slid over him as he took a few steps toward him. Ethan pulled the pizza box closer. He flipped the lid open and grabbed a slice.

"Since your hands are otherwise occupied, I figured I'd help you out." Ethan held up the pepperoni and hamburger slice.

"And how are my hands occupied?" Beau's brown eyes flashed with heat.

Ethan loved when his husband looked at him like that. The same lust he'd seen all those years ago was still there and it drove him absolutely fucking crazy. The fact that they'd been married for more than five years and they still played games meant more to him than anything else. Before Beau, Ethan had never fantasized about getting married or spending eternity with one person, and now he couldn't imagine life without his husband.

"They're busy stroking my cock," Ethan told him.

Beau's eyes widened but his brain obviously registered what Ethan said because one big fist wrapped around Ethan's semi-hard dick. There was nothing semi about it a minute later as Beau stroked him leisurely.

"So if I keep doin' this..." Beau nodded toward his hand. "Then you'll feed me?"

"Yep." To prove it, Ethan lifted the pizza to Beau's mouth.

Admittedly, it wasn't easy to focus on ensuring Beau was eating because the man had nice hands even though they were rough and callused from working so hard. He knew just how to stroke him, just how much pressure to apply to make it unbelievably good.

"Just curious, but who's teasin' who here?" Beau asked after he chewed.

"It's a little give and take," Ethan said on a moan. "For now."

"And later?"

Ethan fed Beau more pizza. "Well, after we're done here, I figured we could both use a shower."

"I agree."

"Then I was thinkin' dessert might be in order."

"Does dessert involve chocolate sauce?"

Ethan grinned. "It just might."

"Mmm. I like the idea of that."

For the next few minutes, they feasted on pizza, although Ethan wasn't sure he tasted much of it. He was too focused on the pleasure humming in his veins. Beau never tried to push him over the edge, simply worked his dick with a firm grip.

"More?" Ethan offered after Beau had finished off his fourth piece.

"Good for now," he answered, his breaths a little heavier.

"Does this get you worked up?" Ethan reached for the bottle of water sitting on the counter.

"A little bit."

"What if I returned the favor?"

"In the shower?"

Ethan considered that for a moment. "I'm sure that can be arranged."

"Or…" Beau said, his eyes dropping to where his hand was still stroking Ethan.

"Or what, baby?" Ethan was all for suggestions.

"Or I could jack off and watch you do the same." Those dark eyes shot up to Ethan's face.

"I like that idea." Pushing Beau's hand away, Ethan wrapped a fist firmly around his steel-hard dick. "Strip first."

While he stroked himself, Beau removed his T-shirt and shorts. His cock was hard and huge, obviously inspired by the foreplay.

For the next few minutes, they simply stared at one another. It was so fucking hot to watch his husband pleasure himself. This wasn't the first time they'd done this and it damn sure wouldn't be the last.

"I want you to tell me when you're gonna come," Ethan told him. "Because I want you to come in my mouth."

Beau's eyes flashed with more heat. "Same for you."

Ethan only hoped he could hold off until Beau came. After all, he'd endured the pleasure of Beau's hand on him, so he was likely closer.

While Beau jacked himself off, Ethan openly ogled his movements. He wanted Beau to see how hot he made him, to ensure his husband knew just how much he wanted him.

"E…" Beau swallowed hard. "I'm close."

"Yeah?" Ethan hopped down off the counter and dropped to his knees.

He didn't offer up his mouth, simply allowed Beau to continue stroking himself, his big hand fisting tightly around his cock.

Ethan peered up to see Beau staring down at him. Heat wasn't the only thing he saw in Beau's gaze. There was something deeper, stronger, far more powerful than mere lust.

"Fuck…" Beau hissed. "I need your mouth, E. I'm gonna come."

Ethan noticed the way Beau's thigh muscles flexed as he stroked himself faster, tighter. When Beau aimed the head of his dick toward Ethan's mouth, he obliged him by opening wide. He didn't move, simply allowed Beau to do all the work until his husband was moaning, his cock jerking as he came in Ethan's mouth.

"Good?" Ethan asked as he stood.

Beau's hand shot behind his head, jerking Ethan close as their mouths crushed together. Ethan fell into him at the same time Beau gripped his cock, jerking roughly.

Unable to pull away, Ethan moaned a warning but Beau didn't release him. He nipped Beau's bottom lip as he came in Beau's hand.

"Now, I'm good," Beau whispered.

"Me, too." Damn good. "But we definitely need a shower."

Chapter Nineteen

Sunday, May 19, 2019
(The next morning)

"E." BEAU NUDGED ETHAN AS HE ROLLED over, pulling the blankets up to his neck. "We just got a text."

"Mmm." Ethan grunted, pulling the pillow over his head, effectively ignoring him.

"Kylie's in labor," Beau told him, shaking his shoulder. "We have to get up."

"Really?"

"Really." Beau closed his eyes, fighting the urge to drift off again.

"That means we have to go to the hospital," Ethan noted.

"That's what it means."

"Five more minutes?"

"No."

Forty-five minutes later, Beau bolted out of bed. He wasn't sure what woke him, but the second he came to, he realized they'd given in to that five extra minutes. Only five had turned into far too many and now they risked missing the birth of Travis's fifth child.

"Shit!" Beau grabbed the comforter and jerked it off the bed. "Get up, E. We're late."

Ethan's eyes opened slowly, squinting in the dimly lit room. The sun was starting to come up already.

"Late for what?"

Seriously? Beau glared at him. "Kylie's in labor, remember?"

"Oh, shit."

This time Ethan shot out of bed.

Ten minutes later, they were both dressed and in the truck. They hadn't had time to make coffee, which meant they would have to wait until either the baby was born or until they were told the labor was lasting longer than they thought.

That was if the baby wasn't born already.

God, he hoped that wasn't the case. They had yet to miss a single birth and the last thing Beau wanted was to fail them now.

"I texted Zane to see if she's had the baby yet," Ethan said as Beau put his foot to the floor.

"And?"

"He hasn't responded yet."

More than likely Zane was fucking with them. Likely punishing them for being late.

"Asshole's not answerin'," Ethan grumbled.

Of course not.

Thankfully, there were no additional Walkers born before they finally arrived at the hospital a solid thirty minutes later. As soon as they stepped into the waiting room, Zane's head lifted and a huge grin split his face.

"Nice to see you could make it."

Beau flipped him off by rubbing his finger along his nose. It was something he'd picked up from Ethan. It was effective and earned him a shit-eating grin from Zane.

"How's Travis?" Ethan asked his parents as they stopped directly in front of them.

Curtis chuckled. "He's Travis."

"Which means he's drivin' the nurses insane," Zane added.

"Along with Kylie and Gage," Sawyer said.

That didn't surprise Beau. It was interesting to watch Ethan's oldest brother. On any given day, Travis was the epitome of cool and collected. He never appeared ruffled. That wasn't the case when it came to his wife giving birth. And with every additional kid, he seemed to get a little unrulier.

"He's fine," Lorrie noted with a smile.

"How long?" Ethan peered over at the door that led to the rooms. "Did they say?"

Zoey appeared. "She was dilated to a four when they took her back."

Beau turned and hugged her close, automatically putting his hand on her belly. Since the first time he'd felt his kiddos kick, he hadn't been able to resist. In the beginning, he had asked, worried he would make Zoey crazy. She had simply told him they were his babies and he was welcome to let them know he was there any time he wanted.

"I want you to sit," Beau ordered softly.

Zoey was breathing hard, something she was prone to do because there were three babies inside her. Didn't help that they were likely big babies because Ethan and Beau were big men.

"Good idea," she said with a smile.

"Where's Kaleb?" Beau asked.

"He got a phone call." She motioned to the hallway. "Stepped out to take it."

Beau peered around, noticing Bristol was currently handling all four of Zoey's kids. Thank heavens for that woman. She always came through for them and these days, they all seemed to need her more than ever.

"Any pain?" he asked as he guided Zoey over to a chair.

"Nope. Just uncomfortable."

Beau figured she should probably be at home, but he knew that wasn't something he could insist she do. Being at the hospital for the arrival of a new baby was important to all of them. Luckily, there wouldn't be any more babies born until the triplets arrived.

And even if Zoey was having problems, Beau knew she would likely keep that information to herself. Zoey had learned not to share too many details after the first time she got a cold and let them know. Ethan had nearly come unglued. He had panicked until Kaleb had managed to calm him down. Thank heavens the woman hadn't gotten the flu. Ethan would've likely had a heart attack.

"Who's volunteering to go back and check in with them?" Ethan asked his parents when Beau came back over.

Everyone looked at everyone else and Beau laughed before he said, "I'll do it."

"You sure?" Sawyer asked dramatically. "We're talkin' about Travis here. He might scalp you and toss you to the wolves."

"He's not that bad," Beau countered.

Travis was a smooth operator. He simply was overprotective of his wife, husband, and kids. Beau understood it. He felt the same way about Ethan. And he would feel the same for their babies when they were born. Even now, before they were born, he felt extremely protective of them and Zoey.

"Well, it's your ass, not ours," Zane said.

"I'll go get an update," Beau told them before heading toward the hallway.

"Nice knowin' you," Zane called after him.

He'd been through this before so he knew everyone was being dramatic. Travis wasn't nearly as bad as they said he was. Granted, he wasn't calm by any means and it was a little disconcerting to see him with a less-than-cool composure, but Beau wasn't worried.

When he reached the nurses' station, he asked how they were doing. She said the doctor had not yet come back in but would be there any minute because it was baby time.

"Well, if that's the case, I won't bother them," Beau said. He knew when not to interrupt.

Just as he was turning to head back to the waiting room, the door to one of the rooms opened and Gage stepped out. His eyes widened when he saw Beau.

"Hey, man," he greeted.

Gage looked tired. Like maybe he'd been up all night long.

"Hey." Beau stepped closer. "How's it goin'?"

Gage's eyes darted back to the door. "Almost there."

"Kylie doin' all right?"

The man's face lit up with a smile. "She's actually doin' better than we are. Epidural and all."

Beau chuckled. "I figured after four, this would be a cakewalk."

"You'd think." He motioned toward the door. "Travis tends to … freak out a little."

Understatement of the century.

"Well, I'm just gonna hang here for a bit." Beau nudged his chin toward the nurses' station. "She said the doctor's on the way."

"That's the rumor. If he doesn't hurry up, I'm gonna have to sedate my husband."

Beau glanced over at the door to Kylie's room. He wondered how he would be during the delivery of his babies. He couldn't imagine it would be easy, but surely he'd maintain his cool.

Not that it mattered. He was ready for the day his babies were born. If he went a little crazy, then so be it.

Because becoming a father for the first time or the fifth … it had to be one of the most exhilarating things in the world.

"I'll let you know as soon as the baby's born." Gage grinned. "You look like you could use some coffee."

Yeah. Coffee would be good right about now.

Real good.

SITTING IN THE HOSPITAL MADE ETHAN ANTSY.

Not the way it made Travis, of course. Similar, perhaps, but not.

Ethan couldn't wait for the day his babies were born. Until the day they were sharing the news with his family, who would be sitting here just like this waiting for information.

Only twelve more weeks to go until they were full term.

That seemed like forever to him at this point. Every time Beau counted off another week on the pregnancy calendar he'd put up, Ethan felt fidgety. At first, the anxiety of becoming a father had kept him from getting too worked up. After all, he knew he had a lot to learn before the big day. But now that Beau and Zoey had been schooling him on all the things he needed to know—most of which he already knew because he was an uncle to eighteen kids—Ethan felt like he was ready.

He'd never been in the labor-and-delivery room, so that would be a new experience for him. His brothers had shared all their stories a million times over, so he felt as though he'd been right there with them, but he knew it wasn't the same.

"How're you holdin' up?" Braydon asked when he came to sit beside Ethan.

Ethan peered over at his brother. "Good. You?"

Braydon smiled, his eyes ringed with dark circles. He obviously wasn't getting much sleep these days.

"Fantastic."

"Really?" Ethan studied Braydon for a moment, wondering how that could possibly be. "Because you look like you haven't slept in a year."

"Well, that's because I have a two-year-old, a one-year-old, and a six-month-old. Sleep's a foreign thing at this point."

"How's Waylon doing?" Ethan had heard that Waylon didn't like to sleep when the rest of them did.

Braydon let out a rough sigh. "It's crazy. Rhett and Zach spoiled us. They slept through the night like clockwork. Waylon doesn't believe in that. He wants to play when it's time for everyone else to be asleep."

"Is that normal?"

Braydon chuckled. "When it comes to kids, I've learned nothin's normal. Each one is different. But if you compare Waylon to the other two, no. It's not normal."

Ethan wondered how his babies would be. Would they sleep through the night? Would one of them decide it was time to play when everyone else was in bed? Would he and Beau have to alternate schedules to keep up with them?

According to what Beau had told him, they had to get the triplets on a schedule right away. Beau had been reading blog post after blog post, trying to get the best practices of parents with multiples. Ethan had vowed he would do whatever Beau thought was best. He figured they had to have some paternal instinct that would kick in at some point, but until they knew for sure, studying others was evidently Beau's method.

Oddly enough, even that thought made him smile.

Sure, he liked his sleep and he knew there would be an adjustment period, but he was okay with that because he would be taking care of their children.

"It's just a good thing Jess stays home," Braydon noted. "She's the best wife a man could ask for."

"How's that?"

"Well, for one, she's Jessie. That makes her the best."

Ethan rolled his eyes.

Braydon chuckled. "She makes sure I get to sleep for eight hours during the week. On the weekends, we trade off. I take the midnight feedings and the playtime with Waylon. But during the week, she goes to bed earlier than me, and once I get Zach down, I hit the sack. She handles the overnight rotations so I can get up for work."

Hmm. Ethan wondered if Beau would want to do that. Stay at home with the kids while Ethan went to work. It would be an adjustment, he was sure, but Ethan could see Beau doing it.

As far as stay-at-home moms, most of his sisters-in-law had opted to keep working.

Zoey had been working part-time—although right now she wasn't working at all—because, according to her, having four kids was far too much work to balance out with a full-time job. However, she said she needed to work to keep her sanity. Because Kaleb co-managed the resort, he had quite a bit of flexibility to help her out when needed.

Kennedy was a veterinarian and she'd gone back to work as soon as she could after the kids were born. Matthew and Brody were both enrolled at Bristol's daycare and Kennedy traded off with Sawyer on certain days when it came to taking care of them. They'd announced that, after Brody was born, they were not planning to have any more babies. Two was enough for them, or so they said.

The same went for Brendon and Cheyenne. They said they were quite content with two. Cheyenne's schedule was a little different because she was a world-famous country star. Brendon and their boys—Remy and Thad—now traveled with her when she was on the road.

Vanessa had also opted to stay at home. Since she and Zane were expecting their fourth—their last according to V—in December, she had her hands full. Since Zane was responsible for one of the clubs within the resort, he had some flexibility to help out as well. According to V, it was good that Reid was almost four because he helped out with his brothers, too. And V's way of maintaining her sanity was sending the kids to Bristol's daycare one day a week.

Of course, Kylie hadn't given up working because she loved what she did. Restoring historical homes was her passion, but since she worked for herself, she had some control over her schedule. Ethan thought she was Superwoman at times because she balanced a full-time job, two husbands, and four kids—soon to be five—as though it was nothing.

Ethan peered over at Braydon. "And she likes it? Staying at home with the kids?"

Braydon smiled over at his wife. "She says it's the hardest job she's ever done, but also the most rewarding. And I believe her, too. On both counts."

Hmm. Maybe Beau really would want to stay home with the kids. He'd be the best one out there, that was for sure. And with Keegan and Kaden working at the shop, Ethan would be able to manage the workload without him.

Not that he would enjoy it as much. He loved working alongside Beau. It made getting up to go to work every day worth it.

However, he also knew it wasn't about him. It was about Beau. And their babies.

Ethan would have to add that to the list of things they needed to figure out in the next couple of months. Along with what brand of car seats they were supposed to buy, what types of bottles and nipples were best for their kids, and of course, whether or not they should buy a bigger car before or after the kids were born.

So many things.

That twelve weeks they had left—although Dr. Tinder said to expect sooner than that—wasn't looking like such a long time after all.

Chapter Twenty

Saturday, June 15, 2019
(Four weeks later)

BEAU WAS CONTENT TO SIT ON THE couch beside Zoey, who was currently reclined, her feet propped on an ottoman, while everyone sat around them.

Every so often, she would grab his hand and place it on her belly so he could feel his little ones shifting around. At thirty-one weeks, they weren't moving as much as they had, but they were certainly active. According to Zoey, there weren't many kicks, merely lumps shifting around—probably elbows and knees as they tried to get comfortable.

Zoey said the babies were keeping her up at night with their antics. Because of that, Beau had started going over to her house first thing in the morning to get the kids their breakfast. With Kaden and Keegan helping out at the shop, it was working out well. Kaleb would wake the kids up, and Beau fed them breakfast at Zoey's, then took the kids to the daycare. Kaleb was the one who picked them up, then Beau and Ethan would meet them back at Zoey's so Ethan could handle dinner. At this point, it was Beau's goal to keep Zoey as relaxed as possible and off her feet as much as he could.

Needless to say, they'd enjoyed every step of Zoey's pregnancy because she had made sure they did. Despite the fact it was obviously getting harder on her body to have three babies inside her, Zoey always managed to smile. She was including them in everything. Beau and Ethan took her to every doctor's appointment. At first it had been about listening to the babies' heartbeats and seeing their images on the ultrasound, but as the weeks progressed, it became more about their concern for Zoey.

Because none of Ethan's brothers had twins or triplets, this was a first for everyone. And thankfully, there was always someone willing to help out. Beau didn't hesitate to call someone when necessary, either.

One of the funniest parts, though, was the way Zoey had started texting them whenever she had a craving. For the past two months, Kaleb had ensured they knew just how amused he was that they had insisted on being allowed to get her the weird things she wanted. They'd followed through every time. From the first time when she wanted sweet pickles, then when she wanted vanilla ice cream to go with her sweet pickles.

At Zoey's insistence, Beau had tried it. And for the record, that was just … no.

She'd craved a ton of things, too. Chips and salsa was a big one for her, although it gave her heartburn. Along with Double Stuf Oreos, Goldfish crackers, peanut butter and mango jam, just to name a few. All of which also gave her heartburn.

Of course, her biggest request was for a Slurpee. At least two per week. Couldn't be just a regular Icee, either. Had to be a Coca-Cola/cherry Slurpee from 7-Eleven. While the nearest one was twenty minutes outside of Coyote Ridge, it didn't bother Beau one bit to make the trek.

"All right, all you co-ed baby shower attendees," Zane said when he walked into the living room. "I've been told the games are now concluded and it's time to move on to the gifts."

Finally.

The baby shower had been going for roughly two hours. And when he said everyone was there, this time Beau was serious. All of Ethan's brothers along with their significant others and the kiddos. Plus Bristol, who was helping out with all those kiddos. Plenty of Ethan's cousins had showed up, too, including Kaden, Keegan, CJ, Jaxson, Jared, who had brought his wife and their kids, and Hope's sisters, Grace, Trinity, Mercy, and Faith. Even some of Ethan's aunts and uncles had made an appearance.

Needless to say, the house was bursting at the seams. Thankfully it was nice out because seating areas had been needed out on the back deck. Except now everyone was gathering around so Beau and Ethan could open the many gifts that had been brought.

Beau glanced over at Ethan and his husband discreetly shook his head. Evidently, he did not want to be the one to open the gifts. Which meant Beau would do the honor.

He knew Ethan wasn't trying to sit this one out, but admittedly, Ethan had been rather emotional when it came to the pregnancy. Beau found it endearing. And though he attempted to keep his husband's spirits up, Beau could feel his tension. He was wound up again, probably running a million worst-case scenarios through his head ever since Dr. Tinder had sat them down and explained his concerns with the triplets. Well, not with them specifically, but with their delivery and the timing. Dr. Tinder did not expect the babies to go full-term, so he said it was imperative that they be prepared for a premature delivery that could happen at any time on any day at this point.

Because of this, Beau had done a ton of research, looking into the issues and concerns with delivering multiples. They had even gone to the hospital to look at the NICU because there was a very good chance their babies would be there. Beau prayed that wasn't the case, but he was taking the doctor's concerns at face value.

"You're up, big guy," Zane said, motioning toward Beau.

For the next half hour, presents were shoved in front of him one after the other. He opened everything with a smile, sometimes a few tears forming, but he fought them back. They got all the necessities: car seats, bouncers, sheets, diapers, baby bath, powder, nail clippers, small plastic bathtubs, blankets, socks, various outfits, some hair bows. Everything came in threes. Well, except for the bows.

Then there were the more creative things that were specifically for triplets. The stroller Beau had put on the registry had come from Travis and family. A very cool table/high chair contraption that was designed specifically for triplets had come from Sawyer. And a portable crib with two bassinets for when more seating was necessary had been a gift from Jared.

"You've got a few more," Zane said with a wide grin.

Beau knew his best friend was attempting to embarrass him. Considering it didn't take much, he waited patiently for it to happen. Expecting every gift to be something that would make him blush.

He slowly opened the next gift, watching as Zane continued to smile widely.

"A breast pump," Beau said, hoping his cheeks weren't as red as they felt. "Nice."

"It'll take a little work," Zane said, nodding toward Beau's chest. "Your boobs aren't all that big."

Travis made a noise that sounded like a missile soaring through the air, then crashing and burning.

Everyone laughed because, yes, the joke had failed.

Zoey had agreed to bottle her breast milk for as long as it was possible. According to her, her milk had dried up early with all of her kids, but she promised she would do everything she could. She also assured them the triplets would transition to formula just fine.

And it was during those times, when Zoey was helping them to learn what they would need to know, that Beau felt a sense of trepidation creeping past all the elation clouding his mind.

No doubt about it, he was scared shitless. Having a baby was a big deal. Having three seemed damn near impossible. He worried endlessly, fearful that he wouldn't know what to do when the time came.

Ethan continued to assure him he would be the best dad ever and not to fret.

If only it were that easy.

ETHAN SAT ON ONE OF THE MANY hard chairs that had been set up around his parents' living room, elbows on his knees as he watched Beau open all the gifts in front of all the people. And there were a ton. Both gifts and people.

When he initially heard there was going to be a baby shower, Ethan had tried to get out of it. He did not like events that were centered on him. He preferred to be anywhere else than in a room full of people trying to make him feel like a king for the day. It was the reason he hadn't had a birthday party since he was old enough to refuse to go.

Obviously, he'd lost the battle with the baby shower. Beau and Zoey had insisted that they have one and that he attend, so here he was.

Not that Ethan wasn't grateful. To see all these people gathered there for them filled him with an emotion he could hardly contain. Throughout the pregnancy, his parents, all of his brothers, as well as their significant others had been more than helpful in every way. They were always there to help Zoey with the kids, the grocery shopping, and other mundane tasks, trying to ensure she was pampered the way Beau and Ethan wanted.

And while he loved his family for their generosity, he still did not like sitting in a room with so many eyes looking his way.

Thankfully, almost everyone was focused on Beau and not him. It was hard enough to be here while everyone was chatting him up, asking about the babies, eager to find out how excited he was. He'd probably answered the same questions at least a dozen times.

"Are you anxious about having three babies?" He had lied and said no. Of course he was fucking anxious. Hell, he was surprised he hadn't pulled all his hair out at this point.

"Have you picked out names yet?" He had lied and said no. Technically, they had some names they were seriously considering, but Ethan didn't want to share them with anyone yet.

"Are you curious what all those gifts are?" He had said no and it had been the truth. As far as Ethan was concerned, the gifts were for Beau. Ethan would take all his cues on being a father from the man he loved, which meant the man he loved deserved to get all the attention in the interim. It was no secret that the attention made Ethan uncomfortable. Always had, always would.

Granted, he knew he would have to overcome, because once the babies were born, people would be all over them, wanting to help out however they could. And Ethan would welcome the assistance, he couldn't deny that. However, the more people who came around, the more anxious he became.

"Time for cake!" Travis announced when Beau had opened the last of the gifts.

"Can I get you somethin'?" Ethan offered Zoey, who was still sitting on the couch beside Beau.

"Cake would be amazing," she said with a brilliant smile.

"Be right back."

Ethan slipped through the crowd toward the dining room, where his mother had the cake set up.

"Uncle E?"

He peered down to see Kate standing there, waiting patiently—as patiently as a four-year-old could—for cake.

"What's up, shorty?" he asked, squatting down beside her.

"My momma said you're having *three* babies." She held up three fingers.

He grinned. "I am."

"Do I get to play with the babies?"

"Well, of course you do."

She smiled sweetly. "Good. 'Cause I wanna play with them."

Before he could respond, Kate threw her arms around his neck and hugged him tightly. "I love you, Uncle E."

"I love you, too, kiddo."

Kate pulled back and he passed her a paper plate with a piece of cake on it. When she turned and raced away, Ethan watched until she disappeared into the other room. He couldn't help but laugh. Admittedly, all these kids had changed him. He had never imagined himself having a boatload of nieces and nephews, much less kids of his own.

Sure, he was scared. More so that he wouldn't be a good dad or that he would be easily overwhelmed and let Beau down in a big way, but he was still looking forward to the opportunity.

"The pregnant woman's gonna want her cake."

Ethan pushed to his full height, smiling at his father, who was in the process of moving plates around so they would fit on the table. "That's why I'm here, Pop."

"You doin' all right, boy?"

"I am."

"Good." With that, Curtis walked out of the room.

Some people might've thought his father was a bit standoffish when it came to him, but Ethan knew better. Curtis was the sort of man who understood people. He knew what they needed and what they didn't. He didn't hesitate to add his two cents or to get his kids to talk when he felt it was necessary, but he also knew that a few words went a long way, too.

Ethan wanted to be the type of dad his father was. Strong, resilient. A man whose children didn't fear him but they had a wealth of respect for him. Curtis was their rock. All of them. Not once in his life had his father ever let him down.

He prayed he could be that man for his children and for Beau, too.

After grabbing a plate with a piece of cake on it, Ethan snatched a plastic fork and a bottle of water, then headed back to the living room. He passed everything over to Zoey and smiled.

"Thank you," he told her just as she was saying the same thing.

Zoey frowned. "What're you thankin' me for? You got the cake."

"Yeah, but you gave us babies."

Tears formed in Zoey's eyes even as she smiled. Ethan had to look away to keep from tearing up himself. These days, he was overly emotional. To the point it irritated him, but he was learning to deal with it.

"Well, this is the last hurdle before the big day," Zoey told them as she wiped her eyes. "For me, once the baby shower was over, it seemed like there was only enough time to get the rooms set up and ready for the day the little ones came home."

Ethan glanced over at Beau. The babies' rooms were painted and the furniture assembled, but they'd been told not to buy all the necessities because of the baby shower. If he knew Beau, everything would be washed and ready by the end of the weekend. Without Beau, Ethan wouldn't have known that anything needed to be washed in the first place. It was new, right?

Six more weeks until the babies were full-term. Probably only four more at the most before they arrived. Both felt like an eternity, but it seemed like no time at all considering they'd come this far.

Ethan was ready.

Scared, yes. A little anxious.

But ready, nonetheless.

Chapter Twenty-One

Tuesday, July 2, 2019
(Ten days later)

"It's just another routine appointment," Zoey assured them as they took their seats in Dr. Tinder's waiting room. "We're at thirty-three weeks, so they're just going to increase from here on out, but make sure you ask any questions you have."

"And you're positive Dr. Tinder's got the neonatologists who'll need to be there?"

Beau had read that there were specialists who would be in the delivery room. Doctors and nurses who were familiar with births of multiples and knew what to do if an issue arose.

God forbid.

"He does," Zoey said firmly, her tone obviously an attempt to assure him. "I specifically asked him that in the beginning because they say there's a big possibility of multiples with in vitro. And there's a high risk of preterm labor with multiples. I promise, between the two of us, we've asked all the important questions."

Beau nodded. He knew all that and he'd been asking more and more questions the further along they got.

"We should ask about vaginal delivery versus C-section," Zoey noted.

The thought of Zoey having to undergo a C-section bothered Beau. He knew she hadn't signed up for that in the beginning, but from what he was learning, a C-section was the route usually taken for triplets. Best case, it was a high possibility they would have to resort to a Cesarean delivery if there were problems during labor.

However, he had also read that the doctor could still plan a vaginal delivery if several factors were met.

Those were all questions he had to ask the doctor today.

Beau wanted more than anything to witness the birth of his children, which meant, at the very least, seeing her private parts, and at the very most, seeing her cut open. A chill ran down his spine. The thought made his stomach churn. He wasn't very good with blood.

"We'll be seeing him weekly until the babies are born," Zoey continued as she eased down into one of the cushioned chairs with Ethan helping her.

"Which may be sooner than you think," Ethan mumbled under his breath.

Beau was just about to ask him what that meant when the nurse called Zoey back.

"Well, that was a waste of effort." Zoey chuckled as she tried to get back to her feet.

Once again, they helped her to stand, then followed her back while the nurse weighed her, then led her to a room.

"I'm betting those are some big babies," the nurse said with a smile as she pulled the blood pressure cuff off the wall.

Zoey was holding her stomach, her face pinched in a grimace.

"Are you in pain?" the woman asked as she pumped the cuff around Zoey's arm.

"No." Her voice was slightly strained. "I've been havin' some Braxton Hicks' contractions lately."

The nurse's eyes narrowed as she set the cuff on the wall and walked over to the electronic tablet where she logged the information.

"How long have you had them?"

"Just since last night, I guess."

"Hmm."

Beau stood up straight, his gaze darting between Zoey and the nurse. "What does that mean?"

The nurse turned to face him. She obviously misunderstood, because she launched into an explanation of what Braxton Hicks were.

"No," he said, forcing a smile. "I know that. Why'd you say hmm?"

She shook her head, and the smile on her face seemed forced. "No reason. Dr. Tinder will be right in."

Beau glanced over at Ethan, who was holding up the wall as he always did.

When she slipped out, Beau turned to Zoey. "Can I get you anything?"

"No. I'm good." She was taking deep breaths. "It's just a little hard to breathe, but it's only because they're so big. I think they're taking up more space than I have."

Once more, Beau glanced at Ethan. He was studying Zoey from beneath the brim of his ball cap.

A soft knock sounded on the door and Dr. Tinder appeared.

"Good morning," he greeted with a smile, his eyes locking on Zoey instantly.

"I think she's in labor," Ethan said suddenly.

Beau inhaled sharply as did Zoey. Dr. Tinder didn't seem shocked by the revelation.

Rather than argue that this was natural, Dr. Tinder said, "That's a big possibility."

The doctor laid Zoey's chart on the counter. "Your blood pressure's up this morning." He touched her belly. "How bad are the contractions?"

"Not bad," she said, her tone reassuring. "I'm pretty sure it's Braxton Hicks."

He didn't confirm or deny that, and Beau held his breath, waiting.

Dr. Tinder looked between Beau and Ethan. "Gentlemen, I'm going to check her cervix right quick."

Beau knew what that meant, so he turned toward the door, Ethan hot on his heels. Rather than go back to the waiting room, they stood in the narrow hallway just outside the door. He could hear the deep cadence of Dr. Tinder's voice, but he couldn't make out what he was saying.

"What makes you think she's in labor?" Beau whispered to Ethan.

He shrugged. "Just a hunch."

"But she's not quite thirty-four weeks."

Full-term was forty weeks. And yes, Dr. Tinder had told them that there was a high probability that she would have the babies early since there were three of them, but Beau hadn't prepared himself for it. Not completely.

"It's gonna be all right," Ethan whispered, stepping up to him. "Have a little faith, remember?"

Beau stared into Ethan's eyes and nodded. "I'll try."

They were still standing like that when the doctor stepped out of the room.

"Is she okay?" Beau blurted.

Dr. Tinder smiled and nodded, his demeanor calm and cool. "She's perfectly fine. She's also in labor." His smile widened. "It's time to go to the hospital, gentlemen. You're going to be fathers in the very near future."

Hospital.

Babies.

Fathers.

Holy shit.

Beau was feeling a little light-headed. Okay, a lot. More than a lot, actually.

He leaned against the wall as Dr. Tinder walked away, giving his nurse orders. From the way he sounded, he wasn't nearly as calm and cool as he pretended. Something about neonatologists, pediatricians and nurses, and prepping for a Cesarean just in case.

"I'll call Kaleb," Ethan announced, pulling his phone from his pocket.

Beau heard him on the phone but the roaring in his head was loud. His heart thumped painfully against his chest. When the door to Zoey's room opened, his head snapped over.

"What are you doin'?" he asked.

Zoey smiled up at him. "I'm going to the hospital?"

"Shouldn't you be sittin' down or somethin'?"

She laughed, then took his hand in hers. "It's good for me to walk right now. I'm not dilated much, so we've got time. But..." She glanced over at Ethan, who was still on the phone. "It really is a good idea for us to get checked in at the hospital."

Beau nodded, but he couldn't move.

"It's going to be fine," Zoey assured him. "I promise."

God, he hoped she could keep that promise.

"Kaleb's sending out the alert," Ethan told them when he stepped back over. "He's already on his way."

"Well, if we don't start walking," Zoey said with a chuckle, "it's a good possibility he'll beat us."

Swallowing hard, Beau pushed off the wall. "We're gonna be dads," he whispered, not speaking to anyone in particular.

"You are." Zoey let out a small grunt. "So what do you say we do this, huh?"

Yeah. Okay.

After all, it appeared his babies were ready to make an appearance.

ETHAN HAD NEVER BEEN ON THIS SIDE of the labor-and-delivery doors.

Not before a baby was born, anyway. He'd visited his sisters-in-law *after* they'd given birth, but that was way different than this.

For one, there was a nurse moving about, checking Zoey repeatedly, while three more were getting things set up for the babies. According to Dr. Tinder, they would have a packed house for this delivery. Apparently, premature births of multiples required a multitude of medical professionals. Pediatricians and nurses ... a dedicated team for each baby, along with the doctors for Zoey and the anesthesiologist in the event they did have to undergo a Cesarean delivery. There was also a neonatologist on call, ready and waiting. He'd come in and introduced himself to Ethan and Beau when Zoey was first admitted. From what Dr. Dillard told them, he'd been in constant communication with Dr. Tinder throughout Zoey's pregnancy, so he was up to speed and ready to treat the babies should they need him.

Ethan liked knowing they were taking precautions, ready for anything that might happen.

There were also several machines, and Zoey was hooked up to all of them. They were monitoring her blood pressure constantly, as well as the fetal heart rates of all three babies.

Just thinking about how quickly this had escalated made Ethan's head spin.

While Dr. Tinder said there were several factors that supported a vaginal delivery for Zoey—they were past thirty-two weeks, the presenting baby was the biggest, all of the babies were presenting head first, and Zoey was in very good health—he also said that he had to be prepared just in case.

Zoey had assured them she knew a C-section was a possibility, and if it was required, she was ready.

According to Dr. Tinder's last visit a short time ago, when he did a check of Zoey's cervix, it would likely be a little while longer, but his staff would be keeping a very close eye on Zoey and the babies in the meantime. They had already given Zoey an epidural to help with the pain from the contractions, but it hadn't started working yet.

Never were the four of them the only ones in the room at this point. There was always at least one nurse, which made Ethan a bit nervous. Not because they weren't alone but because he'd seen the increased stress level of everyone. Which meant this birth was not going to be simple by any means.

Beau was sitting in one of the large reclining chairs on the far side of the room, doing his best to stay out of the way. They'd moved in an extra one for Ethan so they would be able to sit and hold the babies once they were born, *if* they could hold the babies when they were born. While Ethan didn't care much for the things Dr. Tinder was saying, he respected the man's candor. According to the doctor, with the babies being seven weeks early, they would likely be moved immediately to the NICU before they were able to hold them.

Ethan prayed that wasn't the case. He wanted his children to be strong enough when they came into the world to not need immediate medical attention. He knew that likely wouldn't happen, but he was still praying and trying to remain calm in the face of all this chaos.

And that was the reason Ethan had insisted Beau remain in that chair, because his husband was close to having a panic attack. It would've been funny if Ethan wasn't worried Beau would actually pass out. Having the big guy hit the floor would not be fun for anyone.

"Have you come up with names yet? I mean, final names?" Zoey asked, her face flush, sweat slicking her hair back. The contractions weren't fun, from what he could tell. And while Kaleb had been feeding her ice chips up until he offered to go find more, it was apparent she was extremely uncomfortable.

"We have," Ethan confirmed, glancing over at Beau as he nodded.

Zoey's attention turned to Beau.

"John Michael, Aiden Curtis, and Kiera Renee."

Zoey's head snapped over to Ethan, then back to Beau. "Really? You're giving your daughter my middle name?"

They both nodded. It was the least they could do. In fact, they'd considering naming their daughter Zoey but figured it was hard enough to keep up with all the people. It would've added too much confusion during family get-togethers.

Tears formed in Zoey's eyes.

There was a knock on the door and Kaleb peeked inside. "Everything cool?"

Ethan turned to face him. "Still hangin' in."

Beau

Kaleb stepped into the room, his eyes on Zoey. The guy had only been gone for roughly five minutes, but apparently he knew things could change quickly back here.

"How're you feelin', baby?"

Zoey smiled. "Better. The epidural's startin' to work."

Although Kaleb had offered to remain outside if they didn't want him there during the birth, Ethan had never even thought that an option. Zoey needed her husband, and Ethan knew Kaleb would've gone crazy not being with her. Especially if she had to undergo surgery to remove those babies.

"You're still lookin' a little pale there, Beau," Kaleb said with a chuckle.

"Yep." That was all he could muster, his eyes locked with Ethan's.

Today had already been an emotional day. For whatever reason, Ethan had thought the birth would be a quick thing. The sort of rapid delivery that wouldn't give him too much time to think. Not that he was complaining. He didn't want his babies to be born before they were ready, and although he'd told Beau to have faith, he was terrified it was too early.

But he was trying to put on a brave front for both Beau and Zoey. The last thing they needed was for him to unravel. While most people had the ability to fall apart in a way that didn't threaten to take a room out in one shot, Ethan wasn't one of those people. He figured there were as many family members out there worrying about him as there were worrying about Zoey and the babies.

And he fucking loved every one of them for it. However, he was going to be strong for Beau and Zoey. Today was about bringing the babies into the world. Tomorrow he could have a breakdown.

Or maybe he wouldn't. Perhaps this was the start of a new sort of chaos for him.

He could only hope.

An hour and fifteen minutes later, Ethan was rethinking the whole falling-apart thing.

Dr. Tinder's *little while longer* had turned into just under sixty minutes when he came in, ready to deliver. Based on his assessment, he said that waiting would only cause the babies and Zoey distress. While he was still moving forward with the vaginal delivery, Ethan could tell the doctor was concerned.

At Dr. Tinder's insistence, Zoey was pushing while the doctor sat between her legs, a sheet draped to somewhat cover her. Not that Ethan gave two shits about seeing her girly parts. His babies were coming, and to be fair, he couldn't think about anything more than that.

There were so many people stuffed into that one room. And while the room was large—it was a surgical delivery suite—it still felt like a shoe box with so many people. As promised, there was one pediatrician and one nurse for every baby and they were prepared to do everything necessary once the baby was in their care. Then there was a doctor assisting Dr. Tinder and a nurse assigned to solely monitor Zoey.

The only thing Ethan was trying to do was stay out of the way. As it was, he'd taken up a spot beside Beau, who was standing on the right side of Zoey while Kaleb remained on her left.

"I need you to push, Zoey."

She bore down, grunting as Kaleb stood by her head, holding one hand while Beau held the other. She had warned them ahead of time that it was possible she would break some bones. While they had laughed at that, Ethan had to wonder how true that might be. From what he could tell, this damn sure wasn't easy for her. In fact, it made him appreciate her even more. She'd been through this four times, yet she had offered to have their babies. The woman deserved sainthood.

"Good, Zoey. One more time," Dr. Tinder urged, his tone slightly clipped.

She cried out, her face turning red even as the doctor smiled.

"There we go. Baby A is a boy," he announced, his words even, voice calm. The man was a professional in every sense of the word.

Due to the risks, the option to cut the umbilical cords had been eliminated. Ethan completely understood because the most important thing was the babies and Zoey. He trusted that the doctors and nurses knew far more than he did, anyway, so he preferred to leave all that stuff up to them.

One nurse was standing there, taking the baby when Dr. Tinder passed him over. A loud cry sounded and Ethan's heart started beating again. He glanced over at Beau, who wasn't trying to hide the tears streaming down his face. The nurse and the doctor got to work in the far corner of the room while Dr. Tinder kept going as though he hadn't just brought a human being into the world.

"All right, you know the drill, Zoey," Dr. Tinder said. "We've got two more to go and we can't wait. You ready?"

"Mmm-hmm," she groaned.

"Let's do this then."

A short time later, Dr. Tinder announced they had another boy. When Baby B—as they were referring to him—came out, Dr. Tinder's eyes widened and his easiness shifted into something else. Something that had Ethan's heart stopping.

"Cord was around his neck," he said, passing over the baby after clipping the cord.

Although the doctor didn't follow that information with an instruction, it was obvious the nurse knew what to do, because she nodded, her movements quick and steady.

Chaos the likes of which Ethan had never seen ensued as a doctor rushed over to the nurse, taking the baby from her immediately. There were now several medical personnel blocking his view of the babies, but Ethan could tell they were working furiously to … do whatever it was they were doing. In that moment, he appreciated the medical staff more than he ever had. They handled life-and-death situations for a living. Ethan knew for a fact he would never be capable of that. They were true angels.

"Baby number three, let's go," Dr. Tinder said gruffly, his complete focus on Zoey.

Ethan had no idea how much time had really passed since it all started. It felt like an eternity. He wasn't sure his heart could take much more. Then, once again, the doctor was instructing Zoey to push, informing her it was almost over.

Things escalated at that point. Dr. Tinder no longer appeared cool and calm. The other doctors and nurses were working furiously on the other side of the room. The seconds felt like days as Ethan stood there beside Beau, his heart lodged in his throat.

Then suddenly, Dr. Tinder announced that Baby C was a girl. And when their daughter let out a shocked scream, Ethan stumbled backward. Beau grabbed on to him, holding him close. Tears flowed unbidden and Ethan didn't give a shit.

The nurses and doctors didn't stop what they were doing. It was obvious there was a problem, but no one was telling them anything.

"Congratulations," Dr. Tinder said when he finally got up from whatever he'd been doing to Zoey. While the word was meant to be positive, it was obvious Dr. Tinder was worried.

One of the other doctors came over. "We're gonna have to move them," he said. "Right now."

Ethan was sure that the lump in his throat was his heart.

They weren't going to get to hold their babies and Ethan felt as though his chest had cracked wide open, his heart broken and bleeding.

"What's wrong?" Beau croaked. "What's going on?"

As the medical team rushed the babies out, another nurse came over. "We're taking them to the NICU. Dr. Dillard is already there waiting for them."

Ethan wrapped his arm around Beau when his husband nearly collapsed. He watched as they wheeled his babies out of the room, the chance to see them stripped away in an instant.

It hurt to breathe because seeing them, holding them, knowing they were all right was what he wanted more than anything in the fucking world.

Chapter Twenty-Two

BEAU HELD ON TO ETHAN, WISHING THE pain in his chest would subside. He hadn't even had a chance to *see* his babies before they were whisked out of room. In fact, the only way he would even know them was from the hospital bracelets that they'd all been tagged with.

A nurse had come over with identification bracelets. They'd been informed they would all three be tagged—Zoey, Ethan, and Beau—before anyone left the delivery room. That process didn't take long and another nurse had verified the information on every bracelet before slipping back over to the babies.

But still, Beau hadn't been allowed to see them.

The tension in the room had been palpable ever since Aiden was born. The casualness the medical staff had attempted to display had done nothing to ease Beau's nerves, either.

"Is everything all right?" Beau asked the nurse who'd been trying to explain what the next steps were.

God, he'd already had a mild heart attack earlier—not literally, of course—when Aiden hadn't started to breathe on his own. And yes, he knew that was what had happened. While Dr. Tinder hadn't announced it, Beau had heard the pediatrician say.

"Right now, all three babies are being attended to."

"Is Aiden breathing?" he asked, tired of beating around the bush.

Ethan gasped beside him

"He is," she said, her eyes locked on his. "But remember, the babies are premature, Mr. Walker. We're not prepared to give them the care they need here in this room. The NICU is set up to handle their needs, as are the doctors with them."

"How long will they be there?" he asked, his voice pitched higher than usual.

"We don't know at this time."

"Can we go see them?" Ethan asked.

"Yes, of course. I can't promise you'll be able to go right in, but you are more than welcome to go down to the NICU. They're expecting you. Once all three are stabilized, you'll be able to hold them. A nurse will let you know when you can go in and visit."

Visit? That meant they were staying there? Beau swayed slightly. The room felt like it was closing in on him. He knew it had been a possibility, but he honestly hadn't prepared for it.

"It'll be all right," Kaleb said, attempting to reassure them when everyone cleared out of the room. "I'm not leaving Zoey's side, but you should go down there."

Beau spun around to face Ethan. He knew how he looked. Panicked, shocked. Fucking terrified.

Ethan pulled him into his arms again and held him. "It'll be okay. Trust them to take care of the babies, Beau. They know what they're doing."

Of course they did, but that didn't help to settle Beau's fears. Tears pooled in his eyes and he couldn't fight them. He'd never felt more helpless than he did right then.

"I wanna go with them," he whispered to Ethan. "Please, E."

Ethan pulled back and nodded. "Okay. Let's go see what we can do."

Beau turned to look at Zoey. She smiled, although Beau knew it was only for his benefit. She'd been crying right along with him. "We're good here." She squeezed Kaleb's hand. "Please ... as soon as you know something..."

She didn't have to finish that sentence. "I will let you know. I promise."

Beau followed Ethan out of the delivery room. One of the nurses gave them directions on how to get to the NICU.

Ethan held his hand and led the way down the hallway, then out into the waiting room, where the entire family was still waiting. Beau glanced at the worried faces and his chest constricted.

Everyone was on their feet and it was obvious they'd already heard. Curtis was holding Lorrie close, his arm over her shoulders. He could tell she'd been crying and it nearly had him sobbing like a baby once more.

Thankfully, Ethan explained what was going on, informing everyone that Zoey was fine and that Kaleb was staying with her. Although Travis had announced the births, no one realized exactly how bad things were until Ethan relayed the details.

"They'll be fine," Kennedy assured them, coming to stand beside Beau. She put her hand on his forearm. "Remy was in the NICU for two days. He had some issues breathing on his own. They took good care of him."

Beau nodded and swallowed. Remy hadn't been seven weeks early.

There was a tug on his shirt and Beau glanced down to see Kate and Mason staring up at him. He forced a smile.

Kate's tone was hesitant when she asked, "Do we get donut holes, Uncle Beau?"

His heart constricted.

"Of course you do," Zane announced. "But I'm in charge of the game this time. Coolio?"

The kids all turned to Zane and Beau met his best friend's gaze.

"It'll be all right, man," Zane said, squeezing Beau's arm. "And we're all here for you. Let me know."

Beau nodded. It was all he could do.

A short time later, Beau was standing outside the NICU with Ethan, Lorrie, and Curtis, watching through a window as three nurses tended to their sons and daughter. Everything seemed relatively normal. There was no running, no shouting, no orders of any sort being barked.

However, there were a lot of machines.

As they stood there, Dr. Dillard checked over the babies, then looked up when a nurse motioned toward them. A minute later, he stepped out into the hall.

"Ethan. Beau." He shook their hands. "First, I want to tell you that they are all doing relatively well right now. While I'm keeping a close eye on Aiden, there is no need to panic."

Relatively? Beau did not like the sound of that.

As for not panicking... Yeah, right. It was far too late for that.

Dr. Dillard peered down at the electronic tablet he was holding. "Aiden is having a hard time breathing on his own," he explained. "Kiera and John are both doing very well, considering. I'm monitoring John's iron levels. He's jaundiced, but I expect that to rectify itself naturally. If it becomes necessary, I'll address it. But I am keeping them together. I've learned that with multiples, they tend to thrive when they're together."

"What do you mean? Aiden's lungs aren't working?" Ethan asked, his tone calmer than Beau expected.

"Being that he's premature, it's not surprising. His lungs simply haven't developed fully at this point. Truth is, I'm surprised the other two aren't having the same issue. I'm having him hooked up to a C-pap machine to help him along. But I assure you, I'll keep an eye on him."

"How long will they be here?" Beau asked.

The doctor met his gaze. "At this time, I can't estimate that. Thirty-three weeks for triplets is quite the feat, but it's still early. I'll continue to assess them. I won't release them until I'm positive they're healthy enough to go home."

"But—"

Ethan squeezed Beau's arm, cutting him off.

"When can we see them?"

Dr. Dillard smiled for the first time. "Give us a few more minutes and we'll get them prepped for you to come in."

"Thank you," Ethan told the doctor.

"I'll have an update for you in a bit. And feel free to ask the nurses any questions that you have. Our staff is very well trained. If there's anything they can't answer, they'll pass it along to me and I'll get you the information you need."

Ethan nodded, then pulled Beau away from the window when the doctor slipped back inside.

Beau stared at him. He couldn't hide the terror building inside him. Ethan must've felt it because he wrapped his arms around him and held him close. He trusted the medical team, but he hated this feeling of helplessness. Beau wanted to hold their babies.

"Aiden's strong," Ethan whispered. "All three of them are. We just have to be patient. We knew they were gonna come early. Let the doctors and nurses do their jobs."

"What if…?" Beau sobbed.

Ethan pulled back and cupped his face, his eyes narrowed. "Do not think like that, baby. Not at all. Before you know it, we'll be at home. With all three of them. Understood?"

Beau nodded, although he didn't feel it. He was scared, which he knew was normal, but he didn't like the feeling one bit.

"But we can't rush this. They can't go home until they're ready."

Again, he nodded. He understood everything Ethan was saying. He even understood everything the doctor had said. Didn't mean he could simply shut down his fear.

As they stood there, Beau's emotions rioting, Curtis and Lorrie moved closer. To his surprise, Lorrie was smiling, although there was a hint of sadness in it. She quickly reached up and pulled him down for a hug. He went willingly, wrapping his arms around the woman who'd been a mother to him all these years.

"Congratulations," she said softly. When she pulled back, her light blue eyes met his. "While this is hard, it's imperative you stay strong. Those babies need their fathers. It'll take some time, but before you know it, you'll be bringing those sweet ones home."

"Does it get easier?" he asked, searching her eyes for a confirmation that this fear would go away and it'd be smooth sailing at some point.

Lorrie shook her head, but her smile became brighter. "No." Her gaze cut to Ethan momentarily, then back to him. "Not even when they're grown. But you learn to breathe through it. Kids are more resilient than you give them credit for. And believe it or not, they are fighting as much for you as they are for themselves."

He swallowed the lump that formed in his throat. Beau wasn't sure why he always tended to tear up when he talked to Curtis and Lorrie, but it never seemed to fail. They made him emotional. Or *more* emotional, as was the case now.

"We were gonna go down to the cafeteria before everyone starts to head out," Curtis explained after hugging Beau and offering his congratulations. "Do you boys need anything?"

Beau shook his head. He did not want to leave the babies. Not right now.

Curtis gave a curt nod. "All right. If you do, don't be scared to speak up."

"Can you tell everyone they should go home?" Ethan stated. "As soon as we have updates, we'll let them know."

"I've already told them. But if I had to guess, you'll find someone sitting in the waiting room from time to time."

That didn't surprise Beau. Not one bit. It was times like this when family was everything. No matter how tough things were, it was good to know there were people who had their backs.

"I'm gonna call up to Zoey," Ethan said. "Let her know what's going on."

Beau nodded, turning back to face the window so he could see his children.

Not for the first time, Beau wished his mother…

He shook his head and swallowed the emotion in his throat. No. He wouldn't go there. He hadn't talked to Arlene. Not even after his father's funeral. He had hoped that without Ben, she would seek him out.

Since that hadn't happened yet, Beau wasn't sure it ever would.

Thursday, July 4, 2019
(two days later)

TWO DAYS IN THE HOSPITAL WAS AN interminably long time to Ethan. Probably for most people, and Ethan wasn't even a patient. He wondered if that made it feel longer. Maybe if he was lying in a hospital bed eating green Jell-O and watching *The Price is Right*, the time would pass faster.

No. Probably not.

But here he was, and while this wasn't the most ideal place to be, he couldn't deny that sitting here in this rocking chair while Kiera slept peacefully on his bare chest was one of the greatest feelings in the world. Beau was beside him, in the same position, but with Aiden and John on his chest.

While Aiden was still hooked to the machine that was helping him breathe, the doctor did allow them to hold him for short periods of time. They took advantage of that opportunity every chance they could.

Ethan peered over at Beau and the boys. They looked so peaceful. He often wondered if this was what it would be like when they were home. Would there be bonding moments like this one where the five of them could relax and not worry about everything going on around them? He hoped so.

Of course, he wouldn't miss the timed visits. While they were allowed in frequently throughout the day, there were occasions when they had to stay out. Those were the worst, but they were learning to deal. Ethan knew this was only temporary, and the truth was, watching their babies get stronger by the minute made it all worth it.

Didn't even matter that the country was celebrating Independence Day while they were inside the walls of the hospital. Didn't matter that most of his nieces and nephews were likely out watching a fireworks show. There would be plenty of those in the future for them.

Sadly, according to Dr. Dillard, these past two days were just the beginning. The doctor was fairly certain Kiera, John, and Aiden would be in the NICU for seven to ten more days, perhaps two more weeks. All three babies had weighed in at a little over five pounds—which, according to Dr. Dillard was a miraculous feat but not surprising considering Ethan's and Beau's size—however, all three were losing some weight already. The doctor said that wasn't unusual.

And despite the current situation, Ethan was managing to keep his head up. With every passing minute, Beau was calming down as well. That first day had been the worst. For everyone.

Thankfully, Zoey hadn't had any complications after the delivery. They had kept a close eye on her but had deemed her to be in good health. While she'd been a patient, and even after her release a few hours ago, she had come down to visit the babies as often as she could. However, with Kaleb's help, they had convinced her that going home to recuperate was the best thing for her. She had agreed, albeit reluctantly.

Unfortunately, Zoey had a difficult time with her milk. Ethan had figured out right quick that it caused her significant stress and while he certainly appreciated her trying, he assured her they were comfortable with their babies being on formula. Of course, she had argued and tried again and again to produce enough milk to bottle, but it didn't work and Ethan didn't want her to worry. She needed to heal, too, and the stress she was putting on herself wasn't helping.

Ethan and Beau had promised her that once they came home, she would be able to spend plenty of time with the triplets because there was no doubt they would need help and he knew the babies would miss her.

Although not all the family members were permitted in the NICU, Ethan's mother had come on more than one occasion. She would sit and rock whichever baby needed to be held. It was clear they were bonding with their grandmother nicely.

Ethan was doing quite a bit of bonding himself. He spent every single minute they allowed him to in the NICU with his babies and Beau. Oddly enough, when he held them, it soothed something deep inside. They brought about a sense of calm he hadn't expected. The only other person who managed to do that for him was Beau. He knew it meant that these four were his heart and soul. And he couldn't wait until the day he could take them all home.

However, he wasn't rushing things. He had a good feeling that Aiden would let them know when the right time was. Until then, he was going to keep praying.

After the evening shift change, Ethan held Beau's hand and led him out to the NICU waiting room to find Travis and Gage talking softly.

"How're they?" Travis asked as he pushed to his feet, his eyes scanning over them, probably looking for signs of stress.

Ethan could've told him that things were better now.

"Doin' well, considering," he said truthfully. "Kiera's eating more, so they're happy with that."

There was relief on their faces. It seemed every time he gave some news, it eased a little of the anxiety the family was still feeling.

"How's everyone else?" Beau asked, still holding Ethan's hand. "Zoey?"

"Good. We checked in on her earlier. She's resting at home with Kaleb. Kylie's got Jessie, Cheyenne, and V over at our house to help with the little ones, while Braydon, Zane, and Brendon took the bigger ones to a fireworks show."

Ethan nodded. Sounded as though they had it all taken care of.

"So, why are y'all here?" he asked his brother.

"We thought maybe you two would want to head home. Shower. Maybe grab a bite to eat and get a few hours' sleep," Travis suggested. "We can stay here for a few hours. Keep an eye on things."

Ethan glanced over at Beau. While he didn't necessarily want to leave the hospital, a shower and some food that didn't come from the cafeteria sounded just about perfect. While they'd been given a hospital room for the past two days, it wasn't the same as home.

Beau looked his way and nodded.

"We'll take you up on that offer. I'll let the nurse know you're out here."

"We'll probably be right here when you get back," Travis said. "If not, we'll let the nurse know that we're leaving and to call you if needed."

Ethan knew the nurses had everything under control and that they would call if something came up. He had to force himself not to worry about it because they did need a few minutes to breathe outside of these walls.

After telling one of the NICU nurses that they were leaving for a few hours, Ethan took Beau's hand and led him out into the darkened parking lot. They were silent on the drive back to Coyote Ridge, even after they stopped and grabbed burgers.

When they got home, those burgers were scarfed down, and shortly thereafter, they fell into bed. Ethan set his phone alarm for three hours. He figured that was more than enough time for a decent nap.

Ethan was awakened by the bed shifting. He opened his eyes, glanced at the clock. They still had another thirty minutes before the alarm went off. He turned his attention to Beau, who was staring up at the ceiling.

He curled up next to him, resting his head on his husband's shoulder.

"What're you thinkin' about?"

"The babies," he said softly. "I hate leavin' them there."

"They've got plenty of people keepin' them company."

"I know."

"So why aren't you asleep?"

Beau shrugged, the movement shifting Ethan's head.

"Well, if you're ready to go back, I just need to take a shower," he told Beau.

Beau's head turned.

"Join me?"

Rather than get up, Beau shifted, turning to face him as his big hand curled around Ethan's cheek.

That familiar sense of comfort enveloped him as he gave himself over to Beau's kiss. This was something he'd missed these past few days. They hadn't had any alone time, and although he knew there would be plenty in the future, Ethan needed this. He needed to feel close to Beau.

It was a security he would never be able to let go of. His husband settled him, made him feel whole.

"I love you," Beau whispered when their lips separated.

"I love you, too."

When Beau shifted so that he was covering Ethan's body more fully, Ethan rolled with him, circling his arms around Beau's neck. He lost himself again, holding on tightly as their tongues worked in tandem, searching, seeking, soothing.

A few minutes passed before Beau broke away, reaching his long arm over to the nightstand and retrieving the lube from the drawer.

Ethan could've told him there was a bottle tucked by the headboard—never hurt to be prepared—but he didn't. He waited patiently, running his arms over Beau's arms, his chest, his thighs while Beau prepared them both. And when Beau shifted over him, pushing deep inside, Ethan closed his eyes, relishing the warmth of the man who owned him, heart, body, and soul.

Beau took his time, making love to him in a way only Beau could. Those extra minutes ticked by as they loved one another, moaning, groaning as they both neared a cataclysmic release. It was these moments, the slow, easy times, when Ethan came the hardest. His entire body engaged as well as every emotion that churned inside him.

"E…" Beau pushed up on his hands and stared down at him. "I want you to come with me."

Stroking his cock slowly, Ethan nodded, keeping his eyes locked with Beau's.

A few minutes later, Beau followed him right over the edge.

Chapter Twenty-Three

"IT WAS A GREAT SERVICE," CURTIS TOLD Pastor Bob as everyone was leaving the sanctuary now that the morning service was over.

"How're the babies? And Ethan and Beau?" Pastor Bob asked as he stepped out of the way for others to move toward the door.

"They're hanging in. According to the doctor, they'll be there for a while longer," Curtis told him. "Beau and Ethan said to thank you for coming by. It means everything."

"Anything I can do." Pastor Bob smiled. "And I'll stop by again midweek to check in."

"Thank you for that," Lorrie said, smiling.

"Well, I won't keep you." Pastor Bob touched Curtis's shoulder before motioning toward someone who appeared to be waiting. "Let me know if you need anything from me."

Curtis stepped back out of the way with Lorrie right beside him. She peered up at him and he got the feeling she was trying to tell him something with her eyes.

"What's wrong?" he asked, leaning closer to her.

"I think someone wants to talk to you."

Curtis turned his head in the direction Lorrie was looking to see Arlene standing by one of the pews.

"I'll meet you out front. I want to go talk to someone," Lorrie told him.

Curtis nodded, then watched her walk away before he pivoted and headed toward Arlene. He took stock of her body language as he attempted to predict how this conversation would go down. She didn't appear confrontational, but Curtis knew better than to assume anything.

"How are they?" Arlene asked, her eyes lacking the anger he'd seen there previously. "Beau? Ethan? The babies?"

Being that they were in a small town, it wasn't surprising that Arlene had heard about the triplets and the issues they were having after birth. It was slightly surprising that she was mentioning it at all considering no one had heard from her since Ben's funeral. While they saw her in church every Sunday, she didn't stick around after and she never talked to anyone other than Pastor Bob.

"The babies are doing better," he told her, not sure what information she was really looking for.

While Arlene had graciously accepted help from the church's women's group when Ben passed, it had been five months since, and to be honest, he'd been hoping she would've come around sooner. He knew deep down that, despite the things she'd said and done, Beau still loved his mother.

But it was never too late as far as Curtis was concerned. And from what he could tell, she had genuine concern for her son and her grandbabies.

"I know it's a hard time for them right now," Arlene said softly. "But I was wondering if maybe…" She clutched her purse strap tightly. "Maybe Beau would be open to seeing me. I … would really like to apologize." Her eyes never wavered. "And it doesn't have to be right now. I know he's dealing with a lot, I just…"

Curtis could feel the tension coming off her. She was terrified that Beau would reject her. While it would've been easy to say she deserved it, Curtis wasn't that sort of man.

"Let me talk to him. I'm headin' to the hospital when we leave here."

Arlene's eyes glistened with unshed tears. "Tell him that I only want to apologize. I don't expect acceptance, and I certainly don't expect him to let me back into his life. But ... I need to tell him I'm sorry."

She did. Curtis agreed.

"You also need to tell him your reasons for the things you've done," he said simply, keeping his eyes locked with hers.

"About Lisa?"

"Yes."

"You didn't tell him?"

Curtis shook his head. "It's not my place. That's your story to tell, but I think he deserves to hear it. He needs to understand where some of your anger came from."

Arlene nodded. "I've been going to counseling. Since Ben died..." Her gaze dropped to the floor. "Just let Beau know I'd like to speak to him if he'll allow it."

"I will." Curtis stood tall. "And I'll let you know what he says."

"Thank you."

Arlene held on to her purse strap as she hurried out the door. Curtis watched after her. He didn't feel any malice coming from the woman and he was generally a good judge of people.

As for whether or not Beau would agree to meet with her, that was completely out of his control. Arlene had a lot to atone for, and while Curtis knew his son-in-law was capable of forgiveness, Beau had a lot on his plate at the moment.

But he would relay the information.

They would have to take it from there.

BEAU GRINNED WHEN AIDEN SMILED. IN FACT, a chuckle bubbled up, perhaps the first in quite some time. He couldn't help it—the little boy looked so perfect when he smiled.

"Hey, Beau," Ethan said, drawing his attention over to where Ethan was standing near Kiera's and John's bassinets.

"What's up?" he asked, not looking away from Aiden.

"My mom and dad are here."

He glanced over at Ethan. Based on the way he said that, Ethan wasn't simply announcing their presence.

"My dad would like to speak to you."

"About?"

Ethan shrugged.

Beau glanced down at Aiden. "All right, little guy. I'm gonna go talk to your grandpa for a bit. But you keep smiling 'cause I'll be right back."

It only took a moment for him to get Aiden settled. When he started for the door, Ethan didn't follow.

"Are you coming?"

"No. He wants to talk to you by yourself."

Beau frowned. That was unusual. Had he done something wrong? Surely not, considering he'd spent every possible moment here in the hospital since the triplets were born. The only time he left was to shower at home, have a real meal, and to get a few hours of sleep.

"Could you send my mom in?" Ethan asked.

"Sure." Beau studied Ethan's face for a moment, but his husband's expression was blank. He was learning nothing from him right now.

Figuring he had to face the music no matter what, Beau stepped out into the hall to find Lorrie and Curtis standing there.

"Ethan would like you to join him," he told Lorrie.

A beaming smile spread across her face. "It would be my pleasure."

Curtis waited until the door closed behind Lorrie, then turned to face him. "Let's take a walk, boy."

"Uh ... okay." He fell into step with Curtis. "Did I do something wrong?"

Curtis's smirk said he was amused by Beau's concern. "Not at all."

He breathed a sigh of relief and was surprised by how loud it was.

"How was church?" Beau asked, simply to make conversation as the moved slowly down the wide hallway of the hospital.

"Good." Curtis stopped and turned toward him. "I talked to your mother today."

Well, the man certainly wasn't one to mince words.

Beau's head snapped over as he took in Curtis. His words made sense, even as they didn't.

"Is she okay?" he asked, trying to keep his initial response to himself.

"She seems to be."

He couldn't hold back any longer. "Did she say something? Did she confront Zoey?" He hated that his first thought was that Arlene had caused problems for Zoey.

Curtis put his hand on Beau's shoulder. "No. She did not. She came to me and me only. She asked how you and Ethan are doing and she wanted to see how the babies are doing."

His heart did a weird thump mixed with his regular heartbeat and it felt a lot like hope.

"Arlene said she wants to apologize," Curtis explained. "She said she doesn't expect anything from you, but she wants to clear the air. I told her I would pass along the information."

Beau glanced down the hallway, back toward the NICU. He wasn't sure he had time to deal with Arlene right now. He certainly didn't if this was some sort of trick. The last thing he wanted was for her to cause harm to his family.

"That day she was taken down to the jail..." Curtis said, pulling Beau's attention back to him, "I went and had a talk with her. I told her if she ever wanted to have anything to do with you or your family to come to me first. I think this is her doing that. She respected my wishes and she stayed away."

"Did she seem angry?"

Curtis shook his head. "No. Remorseful, maybe."

"And you trust her? You think she's sincere?"

"I do."

"So she knows about the kids?" Beau glanced down the hallway again.

"She does. It's all over town, of course. And there was a prayer at church today. If I had to guess, she's genuinely concerned about all of you."

"But can she accept that I'm gay? That I will never leave Ethan? Because no matter what, she can't be a part of my life if she can't accept that. And I won't let her near my children, either."

245

Curtis met his gaze and held it. "That's something you have to discuss with her. I think the two of you need to sit down and talk this out."

Beau knew he was right. There was no way they could resolve the problem if they didn't talk. And while he was terrified she would try to hurt Ethan, he wanted to give her the benefit of the doubt. She was his mother, and although he disliked a lot of things about her, he still loved her.

"Can I think about it?" Beau asked Curtis.

"Of course," Curtis replied with a chuckle. "I'm gonna text her and let her know I talked to you. I told her I would. Everything else is up to you."

Beau really would have to give this some thought. Plus he wanted to get Ethan's feelings on it. No way would he make a decision without talking to his husband. It was no longer just about the two of them. Every decision they made affected their children and he refused to make the wrong one.

"Now, what'd'ya say we grab some coffee?" Curtis suggested. "Give those two a few minutes together and then we'll go back."

"I could go for some coffee."

When they turned to head toward the cafeteria, Curtis squeezed Beau's shoulder. He didn't have to say a word and Beau knew the man supported him. No matter what his decision was on this matter, Curtis would stand behind him one hundred percent.

Because that was what family did.

Friday, July 12, 2019
(Five days later)

ETHAN SMILED AT BEAU. "DON'T BE NERVOUS."

"How can I *not* be?" Beau shook his head. "I feel like this is the first time I'm meeting her and she's my mother."

When Pop had taken Beau aside for a conversation, Ethan hadn't known what it was about. While he'd tried to convince his mother to share the details, the stubborn woman told him she knew nothing and was only there to see her grandbabies.

Ethan knew she was lying, but he hadn't pressed her.

It wasn't until later that evening when he and Beau were sharing dinner at a restaurant around the corner from the hospital that Beau broke down and revealed everything.

Evidently, Arlene wanted to make amends.

At first, Ethan had been angry, but he'd managed to mask it as best he could. The last thing he would do was stand between Beau and his mother. However, he instantly went into protective mode. That woman had the ability to hurt Beau in so many ways and Ethan would be damned if he allowed it to happen. Not again.

However, Beau seemed genuinely interested in talking to her, so here they were. They had agreed to meet Arlene in the hospital cafeteria in the middle of the lunch rush. According to Beau, this was the best way to keep things civil. With so many people around, there was less chance for things to go bad.

Ethan wanted to tell him that was bullshit. Arlene had never had any qualms about going off in public, but he didn't say that. He was going to remain positive because even Pop believed Arlene was sincere.

"Oh, crap. She's here," Beau said in a harsh whisper. "What do I do?"

Ethan stood up and motioned Arlene over. It would've taken some time for her to weave through the throng to find them, so he figured he could help things along.

Arlene approached slowly. He noticed her eyes were calm, and there was even a small smile on her face.

"Thank you for meeting with me," she said softly when she glanced down at Beau.

Ethan waited until she took a seat. "I'll just go for a walk," he told them. "Give the two of you some time alone."

"No," Arlene said, looking up at him. "Please. I want to talk to you, too."

Trying to hide his surprise, Ethan nodded, then took a seat beside Beau at the four-person table. Arlene set her purse in the chair beside her.

"Would you like something to drink?" Ethan offered when neither of them started to talk.

She tore her gaze away from Beau long enough to look his way. "No, I'm good. But thank you."

Okay, then.

Ethan sat there, feeling the tension coming off Beau. He knew the man was conflicted about this, but Ethan was proud of him for dealing with it rather than putting it off. That was something Ethan would do. Take the emotions and shove them down deep until they festered and became something vile. Beau wasn't built that way, which was one of the many reasons Ethan loved him.

"What did you want to talk about?" Beau prompted after a few painfully long moments of silence.

"First, I want to apologize," she said softly, her eyes bouncing to those who were closest before coming to rest on Beau once more. "To both of you. For my behavior these past few years."

Years?

Wow. She was going to go back. That was interesting. Ethan expected her to apologize for what she'd done to Zoey, but he hadn't expected her to make amends for anything prior.

"And I wanted to say I was sorry for the way I treated you when you came home to tell me you were gay…"

Wow. She was going waaaay back.

Now it was Ethan's turn to look around, wondering if anyone was paying attention to their conversation. No one appeared interested, but it still left him feeling awkward. He didn't care much for sharing personal information in public places.

"I should've stood up for you that day. I should've told you how proud I was that you had the strength to come out."

Ethan's gaze locked on Arlene's face as she spoke directly to her son. There was something in her tone, something that sounded painful.

"You couldn't," Beau said, as though he understood her reasoning.

"No," Arlene said, adamantly shaking her head. "That's not true. I'm my own person." Her eyes shot over to Ethan. "I pay for my own sins."

That was what he'd told her in the hospital months ago.

"But Dad…"

She held Beau's gaze. "I should've stood up for you because you're my son. Instead, I let my own insecurities, my own regrets get in my way."

Wait. What?

"Regrets?" Beau asked.

Yeah. What he said. Ethan was suddenly curious as to what the story was here.

Arlene took a deep breath. "Although I loved your father, Ben was not the love of my life. I walked away from my first true love. I wasn't strong enough to see it through and I've been punishing myself for it since. I regret that I didn't stand up for myself back then."

"Who was he?" Beau asked, his voice full of curiosity. "Your first true love?"

"She," Arlene clarified.

Ethan wouldn't have been more shocked if Arlene had started dancing the Macarena and claiming she was Elvis's secret bride.

She was gay?

Seriously?

"I was in love with a woman." Arlene's eyes took on a dreamy look, as though she was reliving the past. "Head over heels. But back then, it wasn't okay to be open about that sort of thing."

Ethan knew it still wasn't for a lot of people, but he kept his mouth shut.

"Rather than fighting for that love, I panicked. I shut her completely out of my life and forced myself to move on. To do what was expected of me. To ignore my heart." Arlene took a deep breath and her eyes cleared somewhat. "The next thing I knew, I was married to your father and pregnant with you."

"I didn't know," Beau whispered.

"You couldn't. No one knew. Not even your father." She dropped her gaze to the table. "Especially not your father."

Because Ben Bennett never would've touched her if he'd known she had been in love with a woman.

Arlene cleared her throat. "I don't regret marrying Ben, because without him, I wouldn't have you, Beau."

Beau sat up straight. "You have a funny way of showing it."

Ethan reached beneath the table and took Beau's hand. He wanted to ensure he knew Ethan was there to support him in whatever way he needed him. He couldn't blame Beau for being defensive. And he wouldn't even blame Beau if it took some time for this relationship to rebuild, if there was even the possibility for that. That was completely up to Beau.

"I know it'll take time to prove to you how sorry I am." Arlene's eyes filled with tears, but she fought them back. "And I don't blame you if you want nothing to do with me. I'm not here expecting anything."

For whatever reason, Ethan sensed her honesty. He didn't know Arlene, had never spent any time with her, but the woman before them was laid bare. She was nothing like the evil he'd encountered in the past.

Her gaze swung over to him. "And I owe you an apology, too, Ethan. I said some horrible things to you and I've *done* some horrible things. I never should've interfered with your attempt to have a baby."

"You're right. You shouldn't have." No way could he not let her know that. She had caused Beau tremendous pain with that stunt and it would take a long, *long* time for Ethan to ever forgive her for that.

"I am undergoing counseling to deal with … many things. And like I said, I don't expect your forgiveness, but I want you to know my apology is sincere."

"Thank you," Ethan stated.

Beau squeezed his fingers under the table.

Arlene pushed her chair back. "Thank you again for meeting with me, Beau. I'm not sure you could ever forgive me or even if you should, but it's important you know I am truly sorry and I love you with all my heart."

When she got to her feet, Beau got to his. Ethan released his hand and watched as Beau reached out and pulled his mother in for a hug. Emotion clogged Ethan's throat as he watched them. It was so clear they needed each other, and he hoped, with time, they could establish the sort of relationship they should've had from the beginning.

"I need some time to think, Mom," Beau whispered when he pulled back and stared down at her. "But I'll call you."

She nodded, her smile sad. "I look forward to it. And if I can do anything for you, just let me know." Her eyes shot to Ethan's face. "Goodbye, Ethan."

Ethan remained seated as Arlene walked away. Beau joined him when his mother was out of sight.

"She's gay," Beau said, as though that was the only part of the entire conversation she'd heard. "I just can't imagine. She's spent most of her life married to a man, repressing who she really was."

"Even if they accept it, it's not always easy for people to admit," Ethan told him.

And Ethan knew that better than anyone. He'd remained in the closet for most of his life despite the fact that he accepted he was gay. It was easier to keep it hidden than to risk what others would think or say or do. Thirty-plus years ago, back before Arlene married Ben, would've been a different time altogether. Two women in a small town would've been crucified, so he got it.

As for how she treated her child, her own flesh and blood—that wasn't something she could blame on being gay. She'd fucked that up all on her own. Ben Bennett might've been an asshole, a racist, and a bigot, but Arlene had married him. She had known going in what she was doing.

Unfortunately, Ethan got the feeling Arlene had lost herself before that happened. And she'd spent the past thirty-plus years paying for it.

Chapter Twenty-Four

Thursday, July 18, 2019
(Six days later)

A LOT HAD HAPPENED IN THE FIRST sixteen days of their babies' lives. So much that Beau spent endless hours thinking about it all. The whirlwind of activity that had changed his life in amazing ways.

Between dealing with the heartache of having his children in the hospital and then talking to his mother for the first time in … forever … it was all starting to wear on him. Which was likely why, when Dr. Dillard announced the news that the triplets were ready to go home, Beau broke down.

Granted, it was because he was elated, not upset.

He had hated every second of being away from Kiera, John, and Aiden. He'd spent damn near every minute he could in the NICU, trying to stay close so they knew he was there. Ethan was right alongside him and they'd somehow managed to bond with their babies even when Beau had thought it impossible.

From the moment they came into the world, Beau had felt a tightness in his chest and that constriction was easing for the first time today.

Not that he expected that feeling to go away simply because they were on their way home, either. However, he felt a little more in control even if they'd been warned that the fun was only beginning. They were about to get a real taste of what it meant to take care of triplets.

If their inability to have an appropriate vehicle was anything to go by, they weren't doing so hot.

Thankfully, Travis had brought Kylie's Tahoe to the hospital along with all three car seats. Since neither of their trucks was big enough to hold all five of them, it was a damn good thing. But Beau already had plans to shop for an SUV in the very near future. It was one of the many things still left on their to-do list, but luckily, they'd been prepared for the triplets' early arrival, so the house was ready and waiting.

Once they situated all the babies in the Tahoe, Travis took Ethan's truck back while Beau rode in the back with their sons and daughter.

Three babies.

They had three babies.

Beau was on top of the world every time he looked at them. They were the most precious things he'd ever seen and he found he could stare at them for hours, especially when they slept so peacefully.

Which was what he did. Lucky for them, they were snoozing so they didn't notice. He figured one day Ethan would tell them how Beau had hovered over them endlessly. It would turn into a joke and they would all think Beau was weird. He wanted to be weird like that. He wanted his kids to laugh at him because he was overprotective.

"So, what are they gonna call us?" Ethan asked from the front seat.

"What do you mean?"

Ethan briefly peered at him in the rearview mirror. "Well, it'll get confusing if they call us both Dad, right?"

"Well, Kate calls Travis Dad and Gage Daddy."

"True." Ethan chuckled. "But I was thinking they could call you Pa."

"Pa? Seriously?" Beau laughed. "Do I look like a Pa?"

Ethan glanced back quickly one more time. "Actually, yeah."

"Whatever." Beau grinned, glancing down at the babies. If they wanted to call him Pa, they could call him Pa.

The rest of the car ride was silent, which was a relief. Beau had feared the babies would wake up hungry before they ever made it home. Fortunately, that didn't happen and they didn't wake up even after he and Ethan situated them each into their cribs, which had all been moved into Aiden's room. Beau had read that allowing them to sleep in the same room was good. As for whether it would work for them, he figured it wouldn't take long to find out.

For a solid thirty minutes, Beau stood in the doorway, peering in on them, ensuring they were all right. He figured this was only the beginning. He spent every second thinking about them, so it made sense that he was going to hover.

"You're gonna have to give them some space, big guy," Ethan said with a chuckle when he joined him in the hallway. "I've got your lunch ready. Come eat, then you can shower. When you're done, it'll be time to wake them up to eat."

Beau smiled sheepishly. "Am I bein' ridiculous?"

Ethan laughed. "No. Of course not. You're bein' a protective father."

Beau paused when he stepped into the kitchen. "Is this real? Or am I gonna wake up from a dream and find out we never left the hospital?"

He really didn't want this to be a dream.

Ethan walked back over. This time he put his arms around him. "It's real. They're healthy and they're home. Safe and sound."

Relief flooded him and he leaned in and kissed Ethan. "Thank you."

Ethan took a step back, his eyebrows shooting downward. "For what?"

"For taking care of me this whole time."

"I'm not sure I took care of you."

"You did." In fact, Beau wasn't sure what he would've done without Ethan's support. The man had handled everything for the past couple of weeks. Including getting constant updates from the doctors and ensuring they spent every possible minute with the triplets that they could.

It was usually the other way around. Beau running point while Ethan allowed Beau to take care of him. In this case, Ethan had been his anchor in the storm.

"We have to get them on a schedule," Ethan said when he pulled away. "I was reading that it's best to wake them all up at the same time to eat."

Beau chuckled. "You're doing research?"

Ethan looked at him, a blush climbing up his neck. "Maybe." Ethan motioned toward the table and the sandwiches waiting for him.

"But you're right, we will have to wake them every three hours." They hadn't slept much since the babies were born, and he knew it was going to catch up to them quickly. But the schedule they'd been on in the hospital would not work at home, so it would be an adjustment for a bit.

"My mom wants to come over and help out," Ethan said, joining him at the table. "I'm actually surprised she's not here now."

"Me, too." Honestly, Beau had expected Lorrie to be waiting in the living room when they got home.

"I'm sure she'll be here shortly."

Beau knew they could use all the help they could get. In fact, he was even thinking about inviting his mother over for a visit. She hadn't met the triplets yet, and for some reason, he wanted her to. Although it would take a while for Beau to forgive her for the hell she'd put him through, he fully intended to do so. Since their brief visit at the hospital cafeteria, Beau had texted back and forth with her a few times when she would message to ask about the babies. It was obvious she wanted to be a part of their lives and he was hoping that could happen.

Only time would tell.

"Kaden and Keegan are handlin' the shop," Ethan continued. "I told 'em to call me if they have any issues, but Zane promised to keep an eye on them."

Beau didn't even want to think about going back to work yet. He knew they wouldn't. Probably not for a couple of weeks at least. At that point, they would likely have to alternate until the babies were big enough to go to the daycare center, where Bristol could keep an eye on them.

The thought of being away from them had his chest constricting again.

"Eat," Ethan demanded. "Then I want you to shower. Zoey and Kaleb are on the way over in a little while. They wanted to help us get settled in. And Reese wants to stop by. He's got a present for us."

"A present?" Beau was curious.

Ethan smiled. "Eat. Then shower."

Since he wanted to be there when the babies woke up, Beau did as Ethan instructed. He scarfed down both sandwiches before marching upstairs for a shower. He was finished in record time, back downstairs before anyone had arrived.

Beau found Ethan standing in the doorway to Aiden's room.

"Are they awake?" Beau whispered.

Ethan shook his head. "Nope. Just movin' around a little."

Beau tugged on Ethan's arm, turning him around to face him. Pressing him up against the wall in the hallway, Beau leaned in and kissed him. He couldn't resist for whatever reason. Not that he ever needed a reason to kiss this man, but sometimes, the urge was impossible to ignore.

"You smell good," Ethan whispered as Beau's mouth trailed down Ethan's neck.

Their impromptu make-out session lasted a good five minutes before Aiden decided it was time to get up.

When Beau pulled back, he met Ethan's gaze. He was flushed, his eyes filled with heat.

"You're gonna make up for that later," Ethan stated.

"Oh, I will. I promise." Beau kissed him quickly. "Now why don't you go take a shower and I'll tend to Aiden. Hopefully you'll be back before Kiera or John decides it's time to eat, too."

Ethan nodded, adjusted himself, then headed back to the living room.

Beau was still smiling as he moved into Aiden's bedroom.

"Hey, little man," he whispered, leaning over the crib to see Aiden had opened his eyes. "How about we sneak outta here before you wake your brother and sister?"

ETHAN SHOWERED AND DRESSED AS QUICKLY AS he could, returning downstairs to find Beau in the kitchen, Aiden in his arms. Ethan's mother and Zoey were there, preparing three bottles.

"How's he doin'?" Ethan asked, leaning in and gently kissing the top of Aiden's head.

"Better now that he's dry," Beau said with a beaming grin. "But he's hungry."

Ethan glanced at the clock on the microwave. It was time for all three of them to eat.

"I should go wake—" A cry sounded from the monitor on the kitchen island. Ethan listened closely, wondering if he could guess who that was. "That's my cue," he said before making a beeline for Aiden's room.

He slowed his pace as he walked into the room, still listening to the sound. He peered into Kiera's crib first because that was his guess on who the cry belonged to.

The scrunched up face proved that he was right. His beautiful baby girl was lying there, her eyes squeezed shut as she screamed for her dinner. At least he assumed that was her dinner cry. Maybe it was her wet-diaper cry.

"Hey, pretty girl," he whispered as he placed his hand softly on her chest, trying to soothe her.

It seemed to work because her scream turned into a sob. Not wanting to wake John before he had a free hand, Ethan lifted Kiera up and cradled her to his chest, cupping the back of her head for support. Her sobs lessened as she relaxed in his hold.

Honestly, that was probably the best feeling in the entire world. To know that he could ease her tears. Rather than move to change her quickly, he paced the room, back and forth, doing that whole knee-bend bouncy thing he'd seen some of his brothers do.

It worked.

Her sobs stopped completely.

All right. It was time for Dad duties. The mental list formed in his head as though it had been there all along. He knew she was probably wet, which meant a diaper change was in order.

"Give me just a sec, baby girl."

With one hand securely holding her against his chest, Ethan grabbed a diaper and wipes, then set them on the changing table.

"All right. Time for the kid." Ethan leaned down and laid her on the padded table. "You ready to do this, kiddo? Dry butt, then you get food."

Ethan had perfected the art of the diaper change in the hospital. Or so he thought, anyway. It took him a little longer than he remembered, but that was because he continued to watch Kiera's little face, the way her eyes followed him as he moved. He doubted she could really see him or that she would recognize him by sight, but he knew she recognized his voice, maybe even his touch.

She was the most beautiful little girl in the whole world. Her eyes weren't quite as dark as Aiden's and John's and Ethan suspected hers would be the only ones who remained blue, while the boys' turned brown. Which meant the Walkers were capable of producing girls. For a while, he'd wondered whether or not it was possible.

Not that any of that mattered. As far as Ethan was concerned, all three belonged to him and Beau in every way.

"Good to go?" he asked when he tugged Kiera's T-shirt down over her belly.

A minute later, he was wandering into the living room. Lorrie was sitting on the couch with Aiden in her arms, Kaleb reclining beside her, flipping through the channels on the television, and Beau was in the kitchen with Zoey.

Ethan didn't even make it to the kitchen before John was crying, his little voice blasting through the monitor.

"I've got him," Beau announced as he streamed past. "Kiera's bottle's ready. Zoey's got it."

"Awesome."

A second later, Beau's voice sounded over the monitor as he talked to John. Ethan hadn't considered that the entire house could hear him when he'd been talking to Kiera. Surprisingly, it didn't embarrass him like he'd thought it would.

"Here you are," Zoey said, passing over Kiera's bottle, then smiling at the little girl in Ethan's arms. "She's so sweet."

"That she is," Ethan agreed.

"For now," Kaleb said, joining them in the kitchen. "Wait until she's keepin' you up all night. You'll be thinkin' of a different adjective at that point."

Zoey swatted Kaleb. "Hush it."

Kaleb chuckled. "But she is beautiful. You and Beau do good work."

Ethan laughed. "Thanks."

He couldn't help but smile as his family moved about his house, helping to get them settled. He'd never been big on having get-togethers at his place, but he got the sneaking suspicion this was something that would go on for a while. And he wasn't upset about it, either.

But this was how it was supposed to be.

Truthfully, Ethan had never felt as whole as he did then. With Beau, Kiera, John, and Aiden. All home. Healthy and safe.

When he married Beau, Ethan had felt a sense of belonging and purpose. And now that he was a father, he felt the same, but in a different way.

It was a feeling he never wanted to lose.

One he knew he would fight to the ends of the earth to keep.

Chapter Twenty-Five

Saturday, August 10, 2019
(Three weeks later)

"IT'S TIME YOU PAY UP," ETHAN ANNOUNCED when he walked into the kitchen.

Beau had been standing there, watching the baby monitors. They were a gift from Reese. Three high-def cameras had been installed in the nursery to watch over their babies while they slept. Beau had researched baby monitors until his head spun, and never had he seen anything like these. Then again, they were from Reese's brother, Z , who worked at one of the country's most prestigious security firms. They had all sorts of high-tech gear, so this was probably nothing.

"Pay up?" Beau asked, pretending not to know what Ethan was referring to.

Ethan's gaze narrowed. "Yes. So, I suggest you get your sexy ass up the stairs and get naked. Right now."

Bossy Ethan was so fucking sexy.

Beau peered at the screen again. For whatever reasons, it had been easy to get all three of them on the same schedule. He wasn't sure if it was luck or merely the calm before the storm, but they'd had a relatively peaceful first month at home.

He spun around to face Ethan. "And then what? *After* I get naked?"

Ethan glared at him but there was a crease in his cheek because the man was trying to hide his smile.

Beau stood, as though he was going to head for the stairs, but he paused to hear Ethan's answer.

Ethan laughed. "Just get your ass upstairs."

With a smile firmly in place, Beau headed up the stairs. He was curious as to what his husband had in mind. For the past month, ever since they'd brought the triplets home from the hospital, they had spent every waking moment with the babies. And when they weren't awake, he and Ethan slept. Only, for now they weren't sleeping in the same bed. They had set up an air mattress in the nursery and they were alternating nights sleeping in there. And that meant they weren't getting a whole lot of cuddle time together. In fact, their alone time had dwindled down to almost nothing.

Before he could even take his shirt off, Ethan joined him, pressing up against Beau's back. Ethan's arms snaked around him, pulling him backward.

"I need you naked," Ethan whispered against his ear. "Right now."

"That's what I was tryin' to do," he said with a chuckle.

"Not fast enough."

Those warm arms slipped beneath Beau's T-shirt, then hurriedly shoved the cotton up his torso. Beau helped by pulling it over his head and tossing it to the floor.

He spun around and grabbed Ethan, jerking him close and crushing their lips together. Lust fueled the urgency he felt thrumming in his veins.

"Eager?" Ethan chuckled as he guided Beau toward the bed.

"Yes." When his ass hit the mattress, he leaned back at the same time Ethan reached for the button on Beau's jeans.

Within seconds, he was naked, staring up at Ethan. The man practically ripped his own clothes off before launching himself on top of Beau.

The heated kisses ensued as Beau ran his hands over every inch of Ethan that he could reach.

"Fucking hell," Ethan breathed out roughly. "Touch me, Beau."

Knowing what Ethan needed, Beau slipped his hand between their bodies and fisted Ethan's cock. He loved the way Ethan groaned as his fingers tightly curled around the thick shaft.

"Eager?" Beau asked, throwing Ethan's taunt back at him.

"Fuck, yes. I just want your hands on me. Every-fucking-where."

In a fumble of hands and mouths, they rolled around on the bed for long minutes, trying to get closer, but never getting right where they needed to be.

Finally, Ethan pulled away. He snatched the lube from the nightstand and tossed it to him.

Beau stared back, curious as to what his plan was.

"I'm gonna ride you," Ethan said, his eyes locked on Beau's cock.

The damn thing throbbed at the thought of watching Ethan sink down on him.

Without hesitating any longer, Beau slicked his cock while Ethan watched, his eyes wild, his breaths raspy. He was seriously worked up and that only fueled Beau's lust more. He loved seeing Ethan like this, so close to the edge he could barely hold back.

"Hop on up here, cowboy," Beau urged with a chuckle. "Sit on my dick."

Ethan crawled up onto the bed, tossing Beau a T-shirt to wipe his hands with. He laughed because it was his own T-shirt, but it didn't matter. There were more.

Air shot from his lungs in a rush as Ethan wasted absolutely no time, guiding himself down on Beau's cock. Heat consumed him, running the entire length of his body as he watched the man he loved take his own pleasure from him.

Beau put his hands behind his head and stared up at Ethan, admiring the long, lean lines, the way his muscles bunched and flexed as he lifted and lowered on Beau's cock.

"You're fucking perfect," Beau whispered, meeting Ethan's eyes. "So fucking perfect."

He hoped Ethan knew he meant that in every way. Not just physically.

Ethan planted his hands firmly on Beau's chest as he continued to work himself up and down Beau's shaft. The pleasure was blinding, stealing the air from his lungs and sanity from his mind. He lost himself to Ethan until he couldn't hold back.

Reaching for Ethan's hips, he held him still, kept him hovering just above him as Beau began thrusting upward, driving into Ethan from below.

"Oh, fuck, yes," Ethan cried out, his eyes closing. "Fuck me, baby."

The angle didn't allow him to do everything he wanted, but he continued for several long minutes, driving them both closer to the blessed edge of release. When he knew Ethan was close, Beau pulled Ethan down to him, then flipped them over. He drove his cock deep into Ethan, this time from above him.

"Christ, you feel good," Beau growled. "Fucking amazing."

It was wild, passionate, and so fucking good Beau found himself hovering on the edge before he was ready. He couldn't hold back, though. Ethan did it for him in ways he could never explain.

"Coming, E…" Beau stilled, his cock lodged to the hilt inside Ethan as he watched the man stroke himself to completion.

When Ethan came, a shudder raced through him, prolonging that exquisite, almost painful pleasure that assaulted him.

Beau fell down onto Ethan, pressing his face into his neck. "So, are we even now?"

Ethan chuckled. "Not by a long shot. You'll owe me for the rest of your life, baby."

And he would gladly pay up. In all the ways that mattered.

ETHAN COULD HARDLY BREATHE.

He had no idea what had happened there, but holy shit. It had damn near blown his mind. Granted, part of his efforts to inhale were thwarted because his gigantic husband was crushing him into the mattress.

"Am I suffocating you yet?" Beau asked, laughing as he rolled off.

"I didn't need air, anyway."

Beau flipped onto his back and Ethan remained right where he was, his chest expanding rapidly as he came down from that incredible orgasm.

"Okay, so maybe this whole not having time for sex thing isn't as bad as I thought it was," Ethan told him. "I mean, if we can go a couple of days and do that…"

Beau chuckled. "A couple of days? *Really?*" Beau's head turned toward him. "Babe, we haven't had sex in almost two weeks."

Ethan bolted upright. "What? What about…?"

The shower? No.

The couch? No.

The kitchen table? No.

Shit.

Beau laughed. "I know it's gonna be hard since you're insatiable, but we'll have to sneak that in when we can."

Yeah, fine. He got it. It wasn't like they'd spent the past five years fucking like rabbits anyway. Of course, the attraction hadn't abated even a little, but life had a way of imposing.

But two weeks? That was ridiculous. No man should go two weeks without sex.

Then again, he was still breathing, so it obviously wouldn't kill him.

Maybe.

"I'm gonna shower," he told Beau as he pushed to his feet. "Then maybe some lunch."

Beau's stomach growled and Ethan laughed. It never failed, but the big guy was always hungry.

After he took his turn in the bathroom, Ethan got dressed and headed downstairs while Beau took a shower. As he stood there in the kitchen, prepping lunch for the two of them, he stared around the house.

For whatever reason, he thought it would be different. More so than this. Sure, there were a variety of new things in the house that had never been there before the babies. Car seats in the living room floor, blankets and burp rag on every surface, bottles and nipples lined up on the counter, baby wipes and diapers stashed every-damn-where because they'd learned that making it to the changing table wasn't always the most convenient thing.

But other than that, everything seemed so … normal.

Of course, things would change once he went back to work in two days. While his mother had offered to keep the triplets so they could both go back to work, Ethan knew it wasn't possible. Maybe once a week or so. And she would have to have help. Three babies at one time was more than any one person could handle.

Granted, that wasn't his real reason for turning down her offer. He had a plan. The one he'd been meaning to discuss with Beau but had been holding off since they'd spent the past month settling in with the kids. Ethan had enjoyed being home with them, but he knew he had to get back to work.

A few minutes later, Beau came sauntering into the kitchen, his hair wet from his shower. Ethan grabbed two plates from the cabinet, then turned and set them on the island, his eyes shifting to Beau's face.

"What's on your mind?" Beau asked, obviously in tune with Ethan's thoughts.

"Lunch is ready."

"Good. 'Cause my stomach's ready for lunch."

They opted to stand in the kitchen and prep the hot dogs Ethan had thrown together. Not his favorite thing in the world to eat, but he knew Beau liked them. They were quick and easy, and these days, quick and easy was often their only option.

"I was thinkin'," he told Beau as he loaded his dog down with catsup and mustard after turning the baby monitor so they could both see the three separate pictures on one screen. From where he stood, all three of the kiddos were still snoozing.

"About?"

"Goin' back to work."

Beau frowned and Ethan realized how that had come out.

"No. I mean, no, I'm not *ready* to go back," he clarified. "But it is time. We've been away for a long time, and although Kaden and Keegan are managing the place relatively well, there's some stuff that's not gettin' done." He set the mustard bottle on the counter and met Beau's eyes. "But that's not my point at all."

Beau stared at him, his heart in his eyes. It was obvious Beau wasn't ready to go back to work.

"So, I was thinkin'…" he said again. "Maybe you'd like to be a stay-at-home dad."

Ethan half expected Beau to be upset at him for making the suggestion, but the look in his eyes certainly wasn't anger.

"Really?" Beau stood up straighter.

"Yes. Now that we've got Kaden and Keegan here full time, I thought maybe I could keep them at the shop. It'll take two of them to keep up with one of you, but I think it'll work."

Beau didn't say anything and he still didn't say anything and Ethan was starting to worry that he'd said the wrong thing when, finally, Beau nodded.

"I would love that," he said softly. "At least until they're in school. At that point, I'd want to work."

"Well, no one will ever replace you at Walker Demolition," Ethan told him. "Your job's there no matter what."

"Are you sure about this?"

Ethan noticed Beau had pushed his plate away, his hot dogs uneaten. Considering the man lived to eat, that likely meant his thoughts were overloading his circuits, confusing his brain.

"Yes," Ethan told him.

He was more than sure. And not simply because he wanted the best care for their kids but also because he knew it would make Beau happy.

"That would be amazing."

Ethan grinned. "I really like the idea of having a housewife."

Beau barked a laugh. "If you expect me to cook…"

"Not a chance. I trust you anywhere except for the kitchen."

Beau got to his feet and moved closer. Ethan stared back at him, wondering what he was going to do or say. When he leaned in and kissed him, that warm sense of security came over him again.

"Well, then that's settled. We can talk to Bristol. Let her know that the babies will only be coming on a part-time basis."

"Part-time?" Beau asked, stepping back and staring at him.

"Yeah." Ethan smirked. "You know, for the days that I need you to come to the shop and take a look at somethin' in my office."

Beau's grin lit up his entire face, making Ethan chuckle.

"Ah. *Those* days. I'm sure somethin' can be arranged."

Ethan was pretty sure this was what his new normal felt like. And while he was still scared shitless, he was content.

And so fucking in love with his family he could hardly stand it.

Chapter Twenty-Six

"I'M OFF," ETHAN CALLED OUT AS BEAU was coming into the kitchen.

Beau went to the sink and rinsed Aiden's bottle out before setting it in the dish drainer. He would have to do the dishes shortly, but he figured saying goodbye to his man was more important right now.

"Have a good day at work, dear." Beau leaned around Ethan and kissed his cheek.

"What's on your agenda for the day?" Ethan asked as he grabbed a thermos and filled it with coffee.

According to Ethan, he'd had to start bringing his own coffee because Kaden and Keegan had a penchant for draining the pot at work. Rather than continue to refill it, Ethan had resorted to bringing his own so they were forced to do so.

"My mom's comin' over," Beau said quickly, preparing himself for Ethan's response.

Ethan turned slowly, his eyes locking with Beau's. "That's great, baby."

"Really?" Beau wouldn't necessarily say it was great.

"Yes. I know you've been talkin' to her and I saw the way she was with them at church. I think this is a good thing."

"I asked your mom and dad to come over, too," Beau admitted.

"Are you worried?"

"No." It was the truth. He was beginning to trust Arlene. It had been almost two months since she had apologized and they were making great strides. Although he hadn't been alone with her, Beau wanted to work toward it.

"Well, you know I'm five minutes away if you need me." Ethan capped his thermos and set it on the counter before walking over to Beau. "And I'll be home for lunch."

Beau grinned. He liked the fact that Ethan now came home for lunch every day. While he didn't miss going to work because he got to spend the days with the triplets, he did miss spending time with Ethan. Their lives had changed drastically since the babies were born, but not in a bad way. It was simply different and they were adjusting nicely.

"Call me if you need me." Ethan kissed him quickly, then grabbed his thermos.

"Will do."

As though she heard her daddy leaving, Kiera let out a cry that had Beau grinning. Time for him to get to work, too.

**

Almost two hours later, all three of the babies had been fed and were sitting in their car seats on the floor in the front of the couch. Beau had learned that was the easiest way to keep them in the same room with him and still allow him to move around and get things done.

While the television tried to portray having a baby as this perfect, fairy-tale setup, it hadn't taken long for them to realize they really didn't need a bunch of fancy shit. In fact, the changing tables were used more for holding clothes than changing diapers. And the fancy diaper bucket thing ... yeah, that shit was for the birds.

There was a knock on the door and Beau turned his head as though he could see who it was.

Not that he didn't know. It was nine thirty on the dot. The exact time his mother had agreed to come over.

"Here goes nothin', kids," he told his little ones as he moved to the door.

Beau took a deep breath and pulled it open.

Arlene was standing there, her eyes wide, a smile on her face, and a huge basket hanging on her arm.

Beau glanced down at it.

"I brought something for the babies," she said hesitantly. "I hope it's okay."

His throat clogged up as he took it all in. Arlene had handmade a basket with baby blankets and other baby items—rattles, teething rings, etc.—decorating it. Everything was in pink and blue.

Beau took it from her when she passed it over. "It's perfect, Mom. Come on in. We're just hangin' out in the living room."

Her eyes shot to his face and her smile widened. That was the first time he'd called her mom in quite some time.

"Wow," she said as she glanced around. "You have a beautiful house, Beau."

"Thanks. That's all Ethan's doing. This was his place before we got married. I didn't have to change much because I like it just the way it is."

"It suits you," she said kindly. "Both of you."

"Come in." He motioned her father into the room. "The babies are awake right now."

Beau glanced back at the door, wondering if Lorrie and Curtis were going to make it. He'd told them nine thirty, and they'd never been late to anything, so he was starting to wonder.

"Oh, my," Arlene said in a rushed breath. "I still can't get over how beautiful they are."

"Thank you." He urged her toward the couch. "Have a seat and you can hold them."

Her head snapped around, her eyes widening. "Really?"

"Yes. Really."

While his mother got seated, Beau set the basket on the coffee table, which had been moved to the far side of the room to make space for the car seats.

"Who do you wanna hold first?" he asked.

"Oh, I definitely can't pick. I want to hold them all."

"Okay." He chuckled. "One at a time, then. We'll go left to right."

Beau reached down and lifted Jack up, cradling his head before settling him into his mother's arms.

"This is John Michael," he told her. "But for some reason, he's adopted the name Jack."

Arlene stared down at him. "He looks just like you did, Beau. When you were a baby."

"Really?" That was surprising.

Beau didn't have any pictures of himself as a baby, and he'd been wondering. Kiera looked so much like Ethan it was uncanny. Granted, she was much prettier, but still. A lot of Ethan's family had mentioned that the boys looked like Beau, but he didn't really see it.

Arlene looked up. "I have an album at home. Maybe the next time I come over, I can bring it."

Beau squatted down in front of her. "I'd like that, Mom. I'd like that a lot."

When tears dripped down Arlene's cheeks, Beau knew this was a different woman from the one who had raised him with Ben Bennett. He got the feeling under all that obedience and anger was the heart of a woman who had simply wanted to love and be loved, but life hadn't turned out how she'd planned.

Now he and his mother had a chance to start over, and his kids would have two grandmothers to spoil them rotten.

Because Beau got the feeling that was exactly what was going to happen.

"So, tell me about them," Arlene said as she stared down at Jack. "Are they sleeping through the night?" She looked up at him. "You were the best baby. And I'm not saying that because I'm biased, either. From the day you came home from the hospital, you slept through the night. One feeding before you went down around ten, and you weren't back up until five o'clock. Every morning. Just like clockwork."

"They've got a routine. Not quite that nice," he teased, "but I can't complain."

"And staying at home? Do you like it?"

"Wouldn't want it any other way." For the first week Ethan went back to work, Beau had felt guilty. He hated not going with him to help out, but at the same time, he loved being home with their kids.

As time progressed, and he established a routine, he felt better about it. Ethan didn't seem to mind, either. In fact, Beau figured Ethan was content knowing the four of them were together, waiting for him to return.

"Well, you have to make sure you get out of the house a little, too. Being a stay-at-home parent is hard work. Probably harder than most day jobs."

It had its moments, there was no doubt about that.

"And if you ever need anything, you can always call me. I'm not far and I'll be more than happy to come over. I talked to Lorrie the other day." Arlene smiled. "She showed me a bunch of pictures."

Beau knew that Arlene and Lorrie had started talking more at church. He suspected Lorrie was slowly bringing Arlene into the fold, similar to the way Beau was. While everyone was still reluctant, Arlene was proving she genuinely wanted to be a part of their lives.

His phone buzzed on the table and Beau picked it up.

Speaking of Lorrie... Well, more like Lorrie's husband.

Curtis: Holler if you need us. We thought this would be a good time for you to spend with your mom. We're here at the house, though, if anything comes up.

Yeah. He should've known.

Then again, he suspected his husband might've had a hand in giving Curtis that excuse. Ethan probably called them as soon as he left the house this morning, telling them to hold off.

It proved how much Ethan had come to trust Arlene in the past couple of months and that was saying something.

He shot Curtis a quick text back: *Cheesy excuse, Pop, but I'll accept it.*

Another text came through. This one a laughing emoticon with tears streaming down its face.

It made Beau smile.

"You look good with that smile on your face," Arlene said.

Beau peered up at her. "Yeah?"

"Yeah."

Well, that was a good thing because he sure had it a lot these days. And he really hoped it didn't go away.

Tuesday, December 10, 2019
(Three months later)

"TELL ME YOU DON'T LIKE WORKIN' WITH US," Keegan teased when Ethan came out of the office shortly after he'd returned to work after lunch.

"I don't like workin' with y'all," he said, deadpan.

"Oh, shut up. You do, too."

"You told me to say it."

"Do you do everything you're told to do?" Keegan retorted.

"Are you supposed to be workin'?"

"I *am* workin'."

"Yeah, well, if that's the case, I pay you too damn much," Ethan said, turning away from his cousin.

For the past three months, he'd been working alongside Keegan and Kaden, and to be honest, it wasn't all that bad. While they annoyed the shit out of him from time to time, they were hard workers. However, he certainly liked to give them shit, too. Truth was, the three of them worked well together. The twins were fast learners and they weren't afraid to get into the thick of things. In fact, Kaden was looking to get certified in heavy equipment, which would certainly help Ethan out tremendously.

"Well, that tells me you're not up for talkin' about a raise." Keegan grinned.

Before Ethan could respond, his cell phone buzzed. Keegan's followed right after.

Keegan barked a laugh. "Well, well, well. It looks like your little brother is about to have another baby."

Ethan checked his text message and sure enough, there it was.

Zane: Better hurry. The best of the best is about to be born.

"I'm pretty sure he said that about all his kids," Kaden said when he wandered in, looking down at his phone.

Ethan was positive he had. "And he believes it, too."

"All right, so who's on kid duty? And who's headin' to the hospital?" Kaden asked Ethan directly.

"Y'all head on up to the hospital. See if you can help out with the kiddos there. I'll call my mother-in-law, see if she'll come watch the triplets while Beau and I head up there for a bit."

"Sure thing." Kaden saluted him. "But if Arlene needs help, we're happy to head over there."

"I'll let her know," Ethan said as he pulled up Beau's number to call him. "Hey, babe. You get the text?"

"Yep. I already called my mom. She's on her way now."

"Perfect. I'll be there in a few minutes."

Ethan grabbed his keys and locked down the shop. It would take a good forty-five minutes to get to the hospital and he worried they would be late. Knowing Zane, he had texted everyone at the last minute. They'd already been told that this was going to be Zane and V's last baby. And that made today a much bigger occasion than usual.

If all of his brothers held true to their word and there were no unexpected pregnancies in the future, Curtis and Lorrie would officially have tallied twenty-three grandbabies. Twenty boys and three girls.

Needless to say, they were going to need to start renting a banquet hall just to handle the Sunday dinners and birthday parties. His parents' house was so full Ethan sometimes wondered if the walls were groaning when they were all there.

Ethan hopped in his truck and turned it toward home.

He would have just a few minutes to greet Aiden, Kiera, and Jack, before they had to head out. Despite Ethan's initial objection, John Michael had been officially nicknamed Jack. He wasn't sure where it had come from, but it had definitely stuck.

Just thinking about them made him grin.

He missed his babies. They were growing so quickly, developing their own personalities. When they were two months old, Beau had decided it was time to move them to their own rooms. That had taken a little time to adjust to, but it was working. And though Ethan didn't mind sleeping on the air mattress from time to time, he definitely liked that he and Beau were back to sharing a bed most nights.

It was absolutely amazing the changes that could take place in the first five months of their lives. And not only with the kids' development.

The about-face they'd experienced with Arlene was one for the record books. Ethan was pretty sure Beau had never been closer to his mother than he was now. They talked all the time and Arlene came over to visit whenever they allowed her to. Which was usually several times a week. Many of those times were when Ethan's mother was there. And surprisingly enough, Arlene and Lorrie had become rather chummy.

For the first three months the triplets had been home, they'd been surrounded by family. While Ethan and Beau kept them at home more often than not to ensure they got stronger and healthier before they subjected them to all the germs, the family had consistently dropped in to check up on them.

Now that they'd gotten bigger, stronger, healthier, they were venturing out more and having fewer guests at the house. Since Ethan was still keen on his private time with his family, he was okay with that. A night in with the kids was what he looked forward to all week.

Granted, he knew Beau needed to get out of the house from time to time, which was where the grandparents came in. Arlene and Lorrie were always over on a Friday or Saturday evening so Ethan could take Beau out on a real date night. His preference was still their shower time, but since Beau was cooped up in the house with three babies all day, he figured it was only fair. His husband's job as a stay-at-home dad was one Ethan wouldn't tackle if someone begged him. Only the strongest of mind and body were cut out to be stay-at-home parents, and honestly, Ethan had a new respect for them.

Back in October, Ethan had sent Beau and Zoey to the spa for a weekend just to give them a little time to themselves. He had subjected himself to having Kaden and Keegan over to help with the kids, which was proof in itself how much he loved his husband and the woman who had given them the greatest gifts of all. There was no doubt they'd become much closer to Zoey in the past year and Ethan wanted to ensure they didn't lose that. She had given them three miracles, something he often wondered if they would've ever had without her. She was always telling them it was no big deal, but … yeah, it was a big fucking deal. She'd made them fathers and they owed her their gratitude for life. The spa was the least he could do.

Ethan pulled up to the house, and turned off the truck. Before he could make it inside, Beau stepped out onto the porch.

"What's wrong?" Ethan asked, curious as to why Beau looked ready to pull his hair out.

"I need a break."

Ethan laughed. That wasn't the first time Beau had said that. "We're gonna go to the hospital. You get to take the big kids for donut holes."

Beau nodded. "Okay. Yeah. That's good."

"Somethin' wrong?"

Beau peered back into the house. "Not unless you consider Aiden squealing at the top of his lungs wrong."

Ethan started for the door, concerned. "Is he hurt?"

"No. I didn't say *screaming*. I said *squealing*. I have no idea why he started doin' it, either, but I'm pretty sure he thinks it's funny."

A high-pitched squeal came from inside and Ethan laughed because, yeah, Aiden sounded as though he was definitely enjoying himself.

"Well, when your mom gets here, we'll run up to the hospital. By the time we get there, the baby'll likely be born, so we can get the kids their donut holes and then I'll take you to dinner."

Beau nodded. "Yes. Please. I just hope my mom doesn't go out of her mind."

"I'm sure she can handle it." Ethan moved closer to Beau, lowering his voice. "And if you're really nice, maybe I'll give you a massage tonight."

Beau's eyes heated instantly. "Really?"

"Yep." Ethan leaned in and kissed him quickly. "A naked massage at that."

Beau smirked. "Well, I'm sure that'll make it all better."

Yes, Ethan thought so, too.

Chapter Twenty-Seven

Wednesday, December 25, 2019
(Two weeks later)

BEAU WOKE UP EARLY ON CHRISTMAS MORNING.

His internal alarm was set to waking up for the babies, but this morning, he woke up for another reason.

Glancing at the clock, he did the math in his head. If the triplets' schedule remained true, they had about an hour of free time before the kids were up for the morning.

While it would've been polite to let Ethan sleep, Beau couldn't help himself. He wanted his husband to be awake.

Technically, he wanted his husband, period. Which meant Ethan had to be awake. Otherwise … that would just be weird. And gross.

"E…" Beau whispered, curling his arm over Ethan's chest.

"Hmm?"

Beau slid his hand beneath the blanket, his fingers trailing over Ethan's stomach before searching lower until he found what he was looking for. When he wrapped his fingers around Ethan's cock, he earned a moan in response.

"Merry Christmas, baby," he whispered as Ethan shifted his hips toward Beau's hand.

"Merry Christmas," Ethan rasped, his words slurred by sleep. "Is this my present?"

"Not quite."

Ethan's hand slipped down between Beau's thighs. "So, there's more?"

"There's definitely more."

"I like more."

Beau's eyes closed as they remained like that, stroking one another leisurely beneath the blanket. Beau would've been fine doing that for hours, but he knew they had limited time.

Leaning in, Beau pressed his lips to Ethan's neck, kissing his way up to Ethan's ear. "I want to feel you inside me."

Ethan groaned, his hips jerking again. "I fucking love when you say that."

Beau reached between the mattress and the headboard and retrieved the bottle of lubricant Ethan kept tucked there. He quickly tossed the blanket down to their feet and resumed the hand job, only this time he added lube.

"Fuck." Ethan shifted, his eyes opening as he stared over at Beau. "Don't stop doing that and hand me the lube."

He passed over the bottle but maintained his leisurely pace as he watched Ethan.

"Now, flip onto your other side and prop your leg up. But I want your hand back on my dick."

Beau did as instructed, which wasn't all that easy for him, but he knew what Ethan was aiming for and he damn sure wasn't going to pass up the opportunity. Once he was facing away from Ethan, he put his hand behind his back and sought Ethan's cock. When he wrapped his fingers around the steely length, Ethan pushed his thick fingers inside Beau's ass. He paused his hand on Ethan's cock as the sensations assaulted him.

"Don't stop," Ethan growled. "If you do, I do."

Beau had to focus to keep moving his arm behind his back, stroking Ethan while his husband finger-fucked his ass. The man knew exactly where that spot was that made Beau's eyes cross.

"Is this what you wanted?" Ethan whispered as he propped himself up on his other arm behind Beau.

"Not exactly, but it works."

"Then tell me what you wanted."

Beau moaned softly when Ethan massaged his prostate. "You to… God, that feels good. I want you to fuck me, E."

Ethan's fingers fucked into him deeper, harder, faster. "Like that?"

"No… Oh, fuck." Beau's cock was rock-hard and the sensations were driving him quickly to the point of no return. "Fuck me, E. Put your cock inside me. Please."

"I do love when you beg." Ethan's fingers retreated.

The next thing Beau knew, he was on his back with Ethan kneeling between his legs. As though their bodies knew exactly how this dance worked, Beau's knees came up as Ethan pressed his cock against Beau's asshole.

Their eyes locked as Ethan pushed inside him.

Beau succumbed to the pleasure, his eyes closing as Ethan began to move. Ethan rocked forward, pushing in as deep as possible before retreating while Beau let the sensations assault him.

"Faster," he pleaded.

As good as it felt, he needed to be fucked. Hard.

"Open your eyes," Ethan demanded.

He did.

"Now tell me again."

"Fuck me, E. Fuck me hard."

Ethan slammed into him. The pain quickly morphed into pleasure until ecstasy was flooding his veins. Ethan fucked him roughly, slamming forward, driving into him harder, faster. He didn't slow down. The rough grind of their breathing combined with their grunts and groans filled the air.

"Beau … baby …" Ethan didn't stop fucking him. His hips drove forward and back. "You feel so good. You're gonna make me come if I keep this up."

"Yes," Beau urged. "Come for me, E. God, yes."

Beau pulled Ethan down, crushing their mouths together as his orgasm tore through him. He wasn't touching his cock and the damn thing detonated at the same time Ethan growled low in his throat. They came in a rush, wrapped tightly together, and it was so fucking amazing Beau wasn't sure he was going to be able to walk.

By the time their breaths returned to a steady pace, they were still lying there, covered in sweat. Ethan's body was on top of Beau, pushing him into the mattress, but Beau hadn't let go, so he had to accept some blame for that.

"Think we have time for a shower?" Ethan mumbled against his neck. "Before it's time for breakfast?"

Beau forced his eyes open and peered over at the clock. "Think we can do it in fifteen minutes?"

"Eh. Probably. Twenty, tops."

Beau chuckled. He got the feeling that Ethan was going to make up for lost time.

From the sound of it, the shower was going to be round two.

Definitely a merry, merry Christmas.

BY THE TIME ETHAN PULLED UP TO his parents' house at six o'clock, it looked like half the town was there. Cars and trucks were everywhere, haphazardly parked on the driveway, some on the side yard, some farther down, lining the road that led back to their house. The vehicles belonged to every Walker in probably a two-hundred-mile radius.

Okay, maybe not that far, but there were a lot of damn vehicles. That was all he was trying to say.

And it looked as though they were the last to arrive.

He hadn't intended for that to happen, but Ethan might've gotten carried away with presents this year, and because Aiden, Kiera, and Jack weren't quite six months old, it had taken some time to open them all. More accurately, it had taken some time to keep the babies from eating all the wrapping paper. Everything was going into their mouths these days it seemed.

They climbed out of the Yukon, then got to work unlatching car seats. They'd learned that it was much harder to carry them in the car seats than simply to put them in their arms and tote them into the house. They would be out by the time they got in there, so it didn't really matter.

They hadn't made it two feet from the truck when Arlene and Lorrie came out, their arms open and ready for a kid. Beau passed off Aiden to Arlene and Ethan handed Jack to Lorrie while Beau kept a firm hold on Kiera.

"Merry Christmas," Arlene said, a huge smile on her face as she glanced to every person.

"Merry Christmas, Mom." Beau reached the door first and pulled open the screen to allow Lorrie and Arlene in first.

Ethan followed, the diaper bag hanging from his shoulder. They'd packed light for the trip, but with three kids, that wasn't saying much.

"It's about time y'all got here," Zane said, although his voice was lower than usual because he was holding his two-week-old son, Dustin, close to his chest.

"Sorry. It took some time to get ready," Ethan lied. He figured it wouldn't do any good to tell them he'd gotten caught up in the moment, watching his kids and his husband sharing their first Christmas together.

"Well, I'm starvin'," Travis said when he joined them in the kitchen. Rather than go for the food, Travis held out his arms for Kiera. "Come here, cutie."

Kiera grinned up at her uncle.

"Let's go see what presents you've got under the tree."

"Seriously?" Zane grumbled. "We're not gonna eat?"

"Oh, hush, boy," Curtis admonished. "I saw you steal three rolls already."

Zane peered over at Ethan and winked. "But I'm a growin' boy."

"Boy, maybe," Beau teased. "But I think you're past the growin' stage." Beau paused and let his eyes drop lower. "Unless that's a gut I see on you."

Zane glared at Beau and sucked in his stomach although there was no gut there.

Ethan couldn't help but laugh.

While everyone cooed over the babies, Ethan wound his way through the house, greeting his brothers and cousins, their husbands, wives, and offspring. When he came to Zoey, he hugged her close. It seemed she liked that he did that, and though Ethan wasn't much of a hugger, he would forever make an exception for her.

"So, how was it?" she asked. "First Christmas?"

He couldn't hide his stupid grin. "Fantastic."

Her eyes softened. "I'm glad."

Beau made his way over, hugging Zoey and answering the same question with a smile.

"Just wait," Zoey said. "It gets better. There's their first Valentine's, their first Easter, and of course, their first birthday."

Ethan was looking forward to every single one of those.

Jessie appeared, holding a two-and-a-half-year-old Gabriel on her hip. "You forgot one."

All eyes moved to her.

"We did?" Zoey asked.

Curious, Ethan cocked an eyebrow. "What's that?"

"The first day of school," she said with a loud sigh.

Zoey laughed loudly. "Oh, God, yes."

"Really?" Ethan wasn't sure he understood.

"Yes, definitely," Beau chimed in. "*That's* going to be a day to celebrate."

Ethan was obviously out of the loop on that one and he figured that out because Zoey, Jessie, and Beau were all three staring back at him with weird looks on their faces.

"What? What'd I miss?"

"He wouldn't know," Beau said, nudging Zoey with an elbow as he reached over and mussed Gabriel's hair. "*He* gets to go to work every day."

"Ha ha ha. Funny," Ethan said when it finally sank in.

While this bunch of comedians were only half-joking, Ethan knew they would all celebrate every minute of every day up until that point.

And if he had to guess, there would be tears shed when the last of these kiddos started kindergarten.

Granted, there would probably be a few drinks shared, too.

But still.

"All right! Who's ready for gifts?" Sawyer asked, that shit-eating grin on his face.

Travis was the first to grumble and then everyone else chimed in.

"What? Y'all worried I picked the best gifts this year?"

Yes. That was *exactly* what they were worried about.

Epilogue

First day of kindergarten
(Five years later)

"ARE YOU SURE YOU'RE READY FOR THIS?" Ethan asked as they stood in the living room waiting for Kiera and Aiden to join them so they could head out.

Beau peered over at his husband.

"No," he admitted truthfully, although he realized as soon as he said it that Ethan's question hadn't been directed at him.

Ethan laughed. "I was talking to Jack."

"Right." Beau grinned as he peered down at his son.

All three kids were dressed, fed, and ready for school, eager and excited to finally get to be big kids like their cousins. Beau was pretty sure they'd been counting down the days.

For the past few weeks, they'd been overloaded with stories passed on from almost every single cousin about what they should expect on their first day of kindergarten. Since the triplets, Maddox, and Dustin were the last of the Walker kids to start school, the bigger ones apparently found it amusing to relay their horror stories to the younger ones.

Beau and Ethan had attempted to assure the triplets that it would be fun and not to worry about what Kate or Mason had told them. Being the oldest, Kate and Mason had become the idols for all the younger ones. And Beau was pretty sure that was a huge honor for Kate. Somewhere along the way, she'd picked up Travis's aptitude for being the one in charge. Not that he was surprised. Like father like daughter.

As for Beau, he hadn't been counting down the days and he wouldn't exactly say he was excited. Sure, he was looking forward to some peace and quiet. While he had loved every single second of taking care of the triplets up to this point, he could admit that the stay-at-home-dad thing was far harder than he'd initially anticipated. But he had powered through and his babies were now five years old and ready for big school, as they referred to it.

Kiera appeared. She was wearing a different bow in her hair than the one she'd had on earlier. Beau smiled to himself. Their girl was as independent as they came. She looked so much like Ethan. From her blue-gray eyes to her long dark hair and the stubborn chin. There was no way to deny who her father was.

Aiden strolled into the room with his eyes on his shoes.

As for that little one and his identical twin, they were the spitting image of Beau. All three were off the charts on the growth curve, Aiden and Jack both already taller than their sister. Aiden and Jack had dark brown eyes and Beau's nose. He often found himself going through the photo albums his mother had, comparing his picture to theirs. Definitely his boys.

"Well, we don't wanna be late," Ethan told them, motioning toward the door.

"Aiden? Where's your backpack?" Beau asked.

Aiden turned to look up at Beau, offering a shrug.

"You have to take your backpack. It has your supplies."

"I don't *need* supplies, Pa," he argued, his tone matter-of-fact. "Kate said the teacher's gonna take it away. I don't wanna give the teacher my backpack."

Beau squatted down in front of Aiden. "She'll give it back, I promise. You'll get to bring it home every day."

"How do you know? You're not in kindergarten." His eyes locked on Beau's face.

"Nope, I'm not. But I was at one time."

"A long time ago," Ethan chimed in from his spot near the door.

Beau fought the urge to smile. He'd get Ethan back for that in a bit.

"Did you have the same teacher I have?" Aiden asked, those brown eyes hopeful.

"Probably not."

Although, he wasn't certain of that. Beau had gone to the same elementary school they were going to, so he figured it was possible. He didn't recognize the teacher's name, but he wasn't sure he could even *remember* his kindergarten teacher if he wanted to. Perhaps he should ask his mother. She would probably know.

Granted, any teacher who'd been there when he'd gone to school there would now be…

Okay, fine, it had been a long time ago.

"Go get your backpack," Beau urged Aiden as he stood. "We'll talk to the teacher when we get to your classroom. I'll make sure she knows you don't want her to keep your backpack."

"Okay." Aiden strolled toward his bedroom, his head hanging down.

A few minutes later, they were all piled in the Yukon, heading toward the elementary school.

Jack and Kiera were bickering over who got to sit in the middle seat on the way home that afternoon. It was one of their longest-running arguments. So much so, they'd had to develop a schedule so each kid got the appropriate amount of time riding in the middle seats versus the back.

For some strange reason, their argument caused a million memories to flood his mind.

The first day Jack took a step. He'd walked right into Aiden, knocking him flat on his butt. Aiden, of course, had cried and Beau was pretty sure Jack had smiled.

And their first birthday party. God, that had been a crazy day. More so because Travis had thought it was a good idea to bring a pony to the party. All the kids wanted to ride. Of course, Kiera had screamed her head off as soon as Beau perched her in the saddle. It had taken nearly two hours to calm her down. Since that day, she hadn't wanted anything to do with barn animals.

He couldn't forget the Easter egg hunt when they were three. For some unknown reason, Aiden had decided to crawl up underneath the deck at Curtis's and take a nap. Beau and Ethan had nearly come out of their skin for the fifteen minutes it took roughly twenty adults and twenty-three always helpful children to find him. They'd kept a tight leash on Aiden after that.

Beau found himself smiling as he pulled into the elementary school's parking lot.

"You lookin' forward to havin' the day off?" Ethan asked, his voice lowered so the kids couldn't hear him.

"Off?" Beau grinned. "I'm not takin' the day off. I'm comin' to work."

"Really?" Ethan sounded surprised but not disappointed.

While Beau enjoyed the hell out of being home with the kids, he had to admit, he'd been looking forward to going back to work. He was fairly certain he needed it for his sanity at this point.

Granted, he wasn't sure how long it would last. If he got involved in all the school functions, plus whatever sports his kiddos wanted to play, he doubted he would have much time for a job. But for now, he was going to get back in the swing of things and see where it went from there.

"Yep," Beau answered. "And I even called Kaden and Keegan and told 'em to take the morning off."

Ethan's smirk was devilish when he said, "Well, aren't you the take-charge kinda guy today?"

Oh, he was that. And when they got to the shop, Beau was going to show his husband just how take-charge he could be.

AS THEY WERE WALKING OUT TO THE SUV after the kids had finally settled into their classroom, Ethan watched Beau closely. Although his husband was putting on a strong front, he could see the tension in his eyes. Being away from the kids all day wasn't going to be easy for the big guy.

"You sure you're gonna be okay?" Ethan teased.

"Perfectly fine."

"I'm pretty sure those were tears I saw when you gave Kiera a hug," Ethan noted.

"No tears."

Whatever. Those had definitely been tears.

However, Beau wasn't the only one who had teared up. Although he hadn't thought it possible, Ethan had gotten rather emotional sending his babies—although they weren't babies anymore—off to kindergarten.

And to think, he'd been preparing for this day. In fact, he'd prepared for every single big event since his babies' first Christmas. Although Beau was definitely the researcher in the family, Ethan had found he enjoyed knowing what was going on. It would've been easy to sit back and let Beau handle all the legwork, but he had wanted to be an active parent.

Truthfully, Ethan had felt better since he became an active participant, as well. Although his depression would never go away completely, he had learned to anticipate it better. He could generally sense it coming on, and in turn, he was able to cope. Sure, there were those times it hit him when he didn't expect it, but with Beau's help, he had learned to work through it. There was no doubt about it, his husband and his kids made him a stronger man.

So, sure, Ethan might've been a little emotional because his babies were growing up far too quickly. Of course, he did a better job of hiding it, but he wasn't about to tell Beau that.

"Be careful," Beau said. "I'll show you tears."

"Is that a threat or a promise?"

Ethan turned the Yukon in the direction of the shop. Ever since Beau had told him he was coming to work today, Ethan had been slightly more chipper.

Not that he didn't like Kaden and Keegan. They'd come a long damn way in the past five years. They'd matured, but he knew that was through no fault of their own. It tended to happen when a man—or men in their case—settled down.

But Ethan was looking forward to having Beau at the shop. It had been quite some time since they'd worked alongside one another.

Not that there would be much working going on. Not this morning, anyway.

"Definitely a threat," Beau said, a mischievous gleam in his eyes.

Oh, boy.

They were going on eleven years of marriage at this point and Ethan was happy to say the flame hadn't burned out. In fact, he was fairly certain it was burning hotter and brighter than ever.

"I like threats," Ethan said, keeping his eyes on the road. He could feel Beau staring at him and he fought the urge to smile. "I like them a lot."

"Well, get ready, baby, because it's been a long damn time since I've had you bent over that desk. I've gotta make up for it."

Ethan cut his gaze over to Beau. "Who said I was gonna be bent over the desk?"

Beau's brown eyes flickered with heat. "Are you sayin' I will be?"

"That's what I'm sayin'."

There was no doubt Beau liked the idea of that.

Truth was, before the day was over, Ethan was pretty sure they'd both have their turn.

If he was lucky, maybe more than once.

And to think, with the kids in school, they could even make it a routine.

Yeah. That sounded like a good plan for the future.

A damn good plan.

ACKNOWLEDGMENTS

From the day I finished writing Ethan, I have thought about him and Beau. Every single day. I've always known that there was more in store for them. And I have to say, it was all of my wonderful readers who convinced me that I should continue their story. Your love for the Walker brothers awes me. I will be forever grateful to every single one of you.

Of course, I have to thank my wonderfully patient husband who puts up with me every single day. If it wasn't for him and his belief that I could (and can) do this, I wouldn't be writing this today. He has been my backbone, my rock, the very reason I continue to believe in myself. I love you for that, babe.

Chancy Powley – Your uncanny ability to research everything and anything is what made this book what it is. I could've never done it without your input.

Denise Sprung - Thank you for agreeing to read Beau. Your input was invaluable. So many changes were made to incorporate the storyline you felt was necessary. I definitely think Beau and Ethan have had their true happy ever after.

Amber Willis - You, my friend, always make me smile with your feedback. I'm honored that you took the time to read and provide your input.

Allison Holzapfel – As always, I look forward to the input you provide. And I'm so glad you love these men as much as I do.

Thank you to my proofreaders. Jenna Underwood, Annette Elens, Theresa Martin, and Sara Gross. Not only do you catch my blunders, you are my friends and it is an honor to call you that.

I also have to thank my street team – Naughty (and nice) Girls – Your unwavering support is something I will never take for granted. So, thank you Traci Hyland, Maureen Ames, Erin Lewis, Jackie Wright, Chris Geier, Kara Hildebrand, Shannon Thompson, Tracy Barbour, and Toni Thompson.

I can't forget my copyeditor, Amy at Blue Otter Editing. Thank goodness I've got you to catch all my punctuation, grammar, and tense errors.

Nicole Nation 2.0 for the constant support and love. You've been there for me from almost the beginning. This group of ladies has kept me going for so long, I'm not sure I'd know what to do without them.

And, of course, YOU, the reader. Your emails, messages, posts, comments, tweets… they mean more to me than you can imagine. I thrive on hearing from you, knowing that my characters and my stories have touched you in some way keeps me going. I've been known to shed a tear or two when reading an email because you simply bring so much joy to my life with your support. I thank you for that.

About Nicole Edwards

New York Times and *USA Today* bestselling author Nicole Edwards lives in the suburbs of Austin, Texas with her husband and their youngest of three children. The two older ones have flown the coup, while the youngest is in high school. When Nicole is not writing about sexy alpha males and sassy, independent women, she can often be found with a book in hand or attempting to keep the dogs happy. You can find her hanging out on social media and interacting with her readers - even when she's supposed to be writing.

Want to know what's coming next? Or how about see some fun stuff related to Nicole's books? You can find these, as well as tons of other stuff on Nicole's website. You can also find A Day in the Life blog posts, which are short stories about your favorite characters, as well as exclusive contests by joining Nicole Nation on Nicole's website. To join, simply click **Log In | Register** in the menu.

If you're interested in keeping up to date on any new releases and preorders, you can sign up for Nicole's notification newsletter. This only goes out when she's got important information to share.

Want a simple, fast way to get updates on new releases? Sign up for text messaging. If you are in the U.S. simply text NICOLE to 64600 or sign up on her website. She promises not to spam your phone. This is just her way of letting you know what's happening because Nicole knows you're busy, but if you're anything like her, you always have your phone on you.

Connect with Nicole

Website: NicoleEdwardsAuthor.com

Facebook: /Author.Nicole.Edwards

Instagram: NicoleEdwardsAuthor

Twitter: @NicoleEAuthor

DEAD HEAT RANCH
Boots Optional
Betting on Grace
Overnight Love

DEVIL'S BEND
Chasing Dreams
Vanishing Dreams

MISPLACED HALOS
Protected in Darkness
Salvation in Darkness
Bound in Darkness

OFFICE INTRIGUE
Office Intrigue
Intrigued Out of the Office
Their Rebellious Submissive
Their Famous Dominant
Their Ruthless Sadist
Their Naughty Student
Their Fairy Princess

PIER 70
Reckless
Fearless
Speechless
Harmless
Clueless

SNIPER 1 SECURITY
Wait for Morning
Never Say Never
Tomorrow's Too Late

SOUTHERN BOY MAFIA/DEVIL'S PLAYGROUND
Beautifully Brutal
Without Regret
Beautifully Loyal
Without Restraint

STANDALONE NOVELS
Unhinged Trilogy
A Million Tiny Pieces
Inked on Paper
Bad Reputation
Bad Business

NAUGHTY HOLIDAY EDITIONS
2015
2016